Praise for
Queen of Exiles

"A sweeping look at the political, social, and romantic intrigue surrounding Haiti's first and only queen. Riley's depiction is richly imagined and wholly original."

—Fiona Davis, *New York Times* bestselling author
of *The Magnolia Palace*

"From the very first page, I was drawn into the Kingdom of Hayti and into the life of Marie-Louise Christophe. This book is majestic—from the characters that were so well written it seemed as if 1 could feel each one's heartbeat, to the travel between the decades where I felt the joy of her triumphs as the queen, to the pain of her exile. *Queen of Exiles* is one novel that you will never want to put down. It should be required reading."

—Victoria Christopher Murray, *New York Times* bestselling author
of *The Personal Librarian*

"You may not know Marie-Louise Christophe, but once you have met her, you won't forget her. Vanessa Riley's historical novel feels timely and relevant, commemorating a time when Black women were queens."

—Jodi Picoult, #1 *New York Times* bestselling author

"A gripping tale of triumph and tragedy. . . . The immensely talented Vanessa Riley traces the little-known yet crucially important life of this real-life nineteenth-century woman, immersing readers in Queen Louise's inspiring history. A tour de force!"

—Marie Benedict, *New York Times* bestselling author
of *The Mitford Affair*

Queen of Exiles

A NOVEL

VANESSA RILEY

WILLIAM MORROW
An Imprint of HarperCollins*Publishers*

HarperCollins books may be purchased for educational, business, or sales promotional use. For information, please email the Special Markets Department at SPsales@harpercollins.com.

A hardcover edition of this book was published in 2023 by William Morrow.

FIRST WILLIAM MORROW PAPERBACK EDITION PUBLISHED 2024.

Illustrations by Ekalerina_Vakulko, MaryMo, Avatem/Shutterstock, Inc.

Library of Congress Cataloging-in-Publication Data

Names: Riley, Vanessa, author.
Title: Queen of exiles: a novel / Vanessa Riley.
Description: First William Morrow hardcover. First edition. | New York, NY: William Morrow, [2023] | Includes bibliographical references. | Summary: "Acclaimed historical novelist Vanessa Riley is back with another novel based on the life of an extraordinary Black woman from history: Haiti's Queen Marie-Louise Coidavid, who escaped a coup in Haiti to set up her own royal court in Italy during the Regency era, where she became a popular member of royal European society" —Provided by publisher.
Identifiers: LCCN 2022051079 | ISBN 9780063270992 (print) | ISBN 9780063271012 (ebook) | ISBN 9780063271005 (paperback)
Classification: LCC PS3618.I533 Q84 2023 | DDC 813/.6—dc23
LC record available at https://lccn.loc.gov/2022051079

ISBN 978-0-06-327100-5

24 25 26 27 28 LBC 5 4 3 2 1

For every queen standing with a king, binding wounds.

For every mother fighting for her children and her children's children.

For every woman choosing self over duty.

For every Haitian—we lift and believe.

Cast of Characters

COURT OF EMPEROR JACQUES I	ALTERNATE NAMES AND TITLES
Dessalines	Jean-Jacques Dessalines Emperor Jacques I Jacques I
Marie-Claire Bonheur Dessalines	Empress of Hayti Madame Dessalines Marie-Claire Bonheur

ROYAL COURT OF HENRY I	ALTERNATE NAMES AND TITLES
Henry Christophe	President Christophe King Henry I
Marie-Louise Christophe	Madame Christophe Madame President Queen Louise HM Marie-Louise Henry Marie-Louise Coidavid-Melgrin
François-Ferdinand Henry Christophe	firstborn son of the Christophes François-Ferdinand
Améthyste Christophe	second child, first daughter of the Christophes HRH Princess Françoise-Améthyste Christophe Madame Première
Athénaïre Christophe	third child, second daughter of the Christophes HRH Princess Anne-Athénaïre Christophe

ROYAL COURT OF HENRY I	ALTERNATE NAMES AND TITLES
Victor	fourth child, second son of the Christophes
	Jacques-Victor Christophe
	HRH Prince Jacques-Victor Henry, Prince Royal of Hayti
Armande-Eugène	son of Henry Christophe
	HSH Monseigneur Prince Armande-Eugène (Christophe)
	Duke (Duc) du Môle
Noël Coidavid	brother of Marie-Louise
	HRH Monseigneur Prince Noël (Coidavid)
	Duke (Duc) du Port-de-Paix
Prince Jean	nephew of Henry
	Jean-Bernadine Sprew
	Admiral HRH Monseigneur le Prince Jean
	Duke (Duc) du Port-Margat
Brelle	Archbishop Jean-Baptiste-Joseph Brelle
Souliman	servant to Queen Louise
Zephyrine	maid to Queen Louise

NOBLES AND PEERS IN THE KINGDOM OF HAYTI	ALTERNATE NAMES AND TITLES
General Paul Romain	HSH Monseigneur Paul (Romain)
	Prince du Limbé
Dieudonné Romain	Dame d'Atour
	lady-in-waiting to Queen Louise
	Princess of Limbe
	Madame Dieudonné Romain
Julien Prévost	Count (Compte) Limonade
	secretary of state and minister of foreign affairs

NOBLES AND PEERS IN THE KINGDOM OF HAYTI	ALTERNATE NAMES AND TITLES
Noël Joachim	Duke (Duc) du Port-Margat
Jean-Pierre Richard	Duke (Duc) de la Marmelade governor of Cap-Henry
Marie-Augustine Eléonore Chancy	Toussaint's niece HRH Dame Marie-Augustine Eléonore Chancy Madame la Princesse Jean Princess Jean Dame d'Honneur to Queen Marie-Louise, widow of Lieutenant-General His Grace Monseigneur André (Vernet) Princess of Gonaïves
Cécile Fatiman	Madame Pierrot Countess (Countesse) de Valière Duchess (Duchesse) de Valière
Louis Michel Pierrot	brother-in-law to Marie-Louise Christophe General Louis Michel Pierrot Jean-Louis Michel Pierrot Baron de Louis Pierrot Count (Comte) de Valière Duke (Duc) de Valière
Vastey	Pompée Valentin Vastey Baron de Vastey secretary to King Henry
Dupuy	Baron Alexis de Dupuy friend and adviser to King Henry
Stewart	Duncan Stewart friend and physician to King Henry
Prince Saunders	American adviser to King Henry

OFFICIALS OF THE REPUBLIC	ALTERNATE NAMES AND TITLES
Pétion	President Alexandre Sabès Pétion General Pétion
Boyer	President Jean-Pierre Boyer

EUROPEAN ARISTOCRATIC AND ROYAL CIRCLES	ALTERNATE NAMES AND TITLES
Prince Regent	George IV, regent during the late reign of King George III
Popham	Sir Home Riggs Popham, Commander, British Royal Navy
Archbishop of Canterbury	Charles Manners-Sutton
Pope	Pope Leo XII
Louis Bonaparte	brother of Napoleon Bonaparte Count Saint-Leu ex-king of Holland
Jérôme-Napoléon Bonaparte	youngest brother of Napoleon Bonaparte ex-king of Westphalia Prince de Montfort
Chateaubriand	Viscount Chateaubriand French ambassador to Prussia
Count M	Comte de Maltverne
Prince Pückler	Prince Hermann Ludwig Heinrich von Pückler-Muskau
Lady Robert	wealthy socialite
Mrs. Camac	wealthy socialite
Dieterich Ernestus	Major Ernestus Colonel Ernestus

ABOLITIONIST CIRCLES	ALTERNATE NAMES AND TITLES
Monsieur Wilberforce	William Wilberforce
Madame Wilberforce	wife of William Wilberforce
Clarkson	Thomas Clarkson, adviser to King Henry
Madame Clarkson	Catherine Clarkson, wife of Thomas Clarkson
Marianne Thornton	Mrs. Smyth friend of the princesses
Patti Thornton	friend of the princesses Sister of Marianne Thornton
Mary Inglis	friend of the princesses

OTHER NOTABLES	ALTERNATE NAMES AND TITLES
Geneviève Coidavid	Aunt Geneviève
Monsieur Michelson	David Michelson, reporter for the *Globe*

The newspaper clippings presented are authentic and taken from European and West Indian papers circulating during the life and times of Madame Marie-Louise Christophe.

Public Ledger and *Daily Advertiser* (London), Tuesday, November 20, 1821

It is rumoured that Madame Christophe, the Queen of Hayti, while resident at one of the hotels in town, lost jewellery in the amount of £1500.

1821 London. England

Dumping the contents of my last trunk onto the floor, I wanted to shriek. I checked again and again, ripping at petticoats, throwing gowns into the air in my suite at the Osborne Hotel.

Nothing.

"Madame, it's not here. Madame—"

Shaking my head, I blocked Zephyrine's reasonable words. My jewels had to be here.

A bag with emeralds, diamonds, and rubies, along with a cluster of gold coins, items I'd risked my life smuggling out of Hayti, needed to be wrested from its hiding place. The insurance of being able to pay our way in this strange new land couldn't vanish.

"I'll . . . I'll search again," I said in a voice breaking with tears. Turning to my weathered portmanteau, something I'd gotten from my sister during my captivity, I hunted and hoped.

More tossed silks, flopping to the ground like ghosts.

More bruising of my knuckles, slapping along the bottom of an empty trunk.

More punishing fear, rocking and shredding my insides.

My maid grabbed my wrists and pulled me to the burgundy tapestry, the covering used to warm the cold floor. "It's stolen, ma reine."

Wet streaks drizzled down Zephyrine's brown cheeks to the front of her white bib apron. Prim and pressed and resolute in her service to me, my friend awaited orders from her sovereign.

"I'm not that anymore. I'm no longer queen." Flat and pulsing, wanting to grab onto something real, I stilled my hands. "I'm just Madame Christophe. Nothing more."

My fingers sank deeper into the softness of the woven silk, the colorful Indian rug. I could picture the care and labor it had cost to produce this treasure upon a loom, but I had to clutch, to claw at something, something I could fight.

"It's not here." Zephyrine sniffled, then gulped a breath. "We've checked and checked. The necklaces, the bracelets, and the pins are gone."

She was right. We had nothing.

Nothing to sell to pay for food or these fancy lodgings.

No rings.

No pearls.

Not even my favorite emerald pieces.

The yellow satin bag with all the valuables that the man I loved, my king, had given me had disappeared.

Turning from her, I wanted to pretend nothing had happened, but I'd lived through so many things I wanted to wish away.

Couldn't this merely be another nightmare, oui?

Exile to Europe was to be salvation, renewal. I wanted to pray, but God wouldn't hear an angry woman.

My life, my fairy-tale life of being picked from obscurity to reign over a nation, all had been torn away. The evidence of that other life, my jewels—some thief had stolen.

But we had lived it . . . we'd been wealthy and happy and royal.

"Madame, how will we survive? To be robbed of your treasures means ruin. At Lambert House, fruit grew on trees. A beggar can eat in the jungle."

"Back to Hayti? Barely existing, surrounded by armed guards, hoping their fickle leader won't execute what remains of the people I love? Non!"

I covered my mouth, wanting to erase my words from the air.

No one needed to know how helpless I felt in my beloved Hayti. Ever since I left my parents' care, I'd stood on my own, grown up fast, outlived rebellions, and kept my babies safe in the wilderness. A robbery couldn't be the thing that destroyed me.

Fury roiled in my gut. The dread, the fear I'd kept to myself, exploded, quaking my insides, flooding my face like a turbulent river. I dug into a pile of clothes, strangling a shift like it was the robber or the man who ended my kingdom.

"Madame," my maid said. "You've shown the pieces to Monsieur Wilberforce. He was to help you sell some to get money. He'll visit tomorrow. Wouldn't he know what to do?"

The creamy hem of a discarded dress became a handkerchief. Taking my time, I dabbed at my face, letting the soft lace soothe my skin. "I don't know." I mumbled more scared words and swallowed tears. "I just don't know."

Zephyrine pulled me to her shoulder. "How could this happen? Have we not been careful?"

I hadn't been showy, but I'd worn my bracelet over my mourning drape. The gold had surely caught a criminal's eyes.

Reclaiming my posture, the etiquette Lord Limonade, the Haytian court's protocol master, had ingrained, I sat up straight and fingered the scuffed lock on my trunk. "It's been gouged. Someone came into our rooms, pried this open, and stole my valuables."

This crime was blatant, occurring during the day, perhaps when we'd gone downstairs to sup. Did *he* think we'd not notice? Or did *she* assume no one would help the poor exile, the foreigner?

"We'll not let them win, Zephyrine. Monsieur Wilberforce will help."

"The hotel maids." She wiped at her eyes. "Perhaps they saw something."

Only the Osborne staff had access to enter.

Zephyrine began picking up the clutter I'd created. "At least a Blanc saw the diamonds and emeralds in your possession. He'll be believed. Otherwise, no one here would think a Black could have such finery."

Her words kicked me in the gut.

Bang, I sank again to the floor. My stomach pushed flat. Air gushed out of my mouth. I wept, wept as hard as when the kingdom fell.

Unprotected, my girls, my household, and I were in a place of danger where skin color was more important than truth. The safe Black world we'd built was gone.

A WEEK HAD DRAGGED BY SINCE THE THEFT OF MY PROPERTY. THE manager of the Osborne Hotel seemed apologetic, and in his blue eyes, I saw embarrassment. Dignitaries stayed at this place. He begged Wilberforce to give him a chance to make inquiries.

Leaning by a window looking out at the Thames, I noted the fog had lifted. In Milot, that meant sunshine. Here, it held no meaning. The temperature might barely rise. The humidity and heat of my lush home would be another lost memory.

Chastising myself for my complaints, I reached for my wrist, the empty spot where my emerald should be sitting. I was lucky to be here, lucky to be alive, lucky to have brought with me my daughters and my loyal attendants, Zephyrine and Souliman.

How would I lead them when our escape to London had gone so wrong?

Going to their bedroom door, I peeked at the girls sleeping together on a single mattress. Snuggled in warm bedclothes, piled under blankets in a world that for the moment wasn't moving, wasn't rocking or shifting like international alliances, I merely watched them breathe. I'd checked on them several times throughout the night, as if goblins might steal them, too.

There should be more beds, holding more of my family. If the kingdom had to end, we all should be exiled from Hayti.

Leaving the suite like a silent mouse, I crept down the stairs. Souliman waited at the bottom—no flintlock rifle but a cane in his hands. His scowl menaced.

The large bags under his eyes declared he hadn't slept, either. I dared not look in a mirror. The papers once called me Henry's old Black wife. I'd surely aged thirty years since the kingdom fell.

"Souliman, are you well?"

"Peu importe. Non. Don't matter. I failed." He beat at his chest. "I let them thieve you."

He talked fast, using bits of Kreyòl and French. Again, he pounded his white shirt. "I should've been with the trunks. Pa ta dwe janm! Should've never taken my eyes off your treasures."

No one could watch everything forever. Couldn't even stare at a son wishing for his safety or comfort him when darkness came. I took a handkerchief from my pocket and gave it to Souliman. He was twenty-eight, an age my Victor would never see. "You had to eat. Seeing to maids is not one of your duties."

"It is now." He wiped at his nose, which had just made a trumpet noise. "Madame Christophe, forgive me. Pardonne-moi."

Placing a palm to the shoulder of the jacket a naval officer had given him to wear, I caught his eyes. "Souliman, this is not your fault. I forgot that we cannot let our guard down. Just because we don't see bayonets doesn't mean the enemy is at rest."

"I will find this thief, madame. I'll hang them upside down. They will be—"

"Non. We don't rule here and have no authority. We're barely making our way. Promise me, Souliman. I can't fret about you and the girls and a hundred other things."

Leaning on his cane, one he'd carved and notched with lost faces, he bowed to me. "As you wish, ma reine."

Unlike with Zephyrine, I didn't have the strength to admonish him. The new president of Hayti wasn't around to hear and issue new orders to kill my surviving family or me.

"We're little more than refugees. The archbishop has money that my husband sent for me. When we gain access, we'll no longer be destitute."

His hands dropped to his sides, strong rock-hurling arms. "Madame, I believe no Blanc priest here any more than I believed Brelle in Cap-Henry. I'm prepared to fight. I won't let my queen be in rags."

My sister, dear Cécile, once said there was honesty in poverty. Non. The truth—poverty made one naked, vulnerable, and dependent. It would leave the royal Christophes easy prey to be shunned.

We had no shield.

I had to become one. "I've led us here. I'll protect you, all of us."

"I will get strong. My lameness won't prevent it. I promise." He grumbled more, mouthing sentiments like my husband, my chivalrous Henry, about keeping women safe, then retook his seat. Souliman's unsmiling countenance looked frightful, as if he were readying to attack a new band of robbers.

They wouldn't appear yet.

Hayti's new president and my jewel thief might be in league, working to torment me, but they'd need time to strike again.

Somehow, I had to prepare. I had to be that woman, that mother in the wilderness protecting my children from war. I'd done it—survived pregnant with Victor in caves and kept the girls alive while their father fought the French.

If I had to outwit, outthink, even deceive, I'd do what I had to in order to protect my girls and keep safe all the ones entrusted to me. I went for a walk under thick afternoon clouds praying the archbishop of Canterbury wasn't my next villain.

MY RESTLESS SPIRIT HAD ME WALKING TO THE NEIGHBORHOOD outside the Osborne Hotel. I expected Monsieur Wilberforce any minute. As an adviser to Henry, he'd taken the fall of the kingdom hard. During our reign, the man had been faithful sending teachers and doctors and scientists to Hayti. These laborers were all a part of Henry's vision of making our people the smartest and healthiest in the world.

A church tower somewhere close chimed. Anglican ones more than Catholic, I welcomed the toll and headed back to the Osborne.

The red brick of the hotel was smooth, not like Haytian rubble brick. When the clouds lifted, London revealed towers, taller and closer together than in Le Cap before the wars. Henry had just started his plan to rebuild the capital. I wondered if it would've looked like this, stiff and foreboding. Or would it have been more like Sans-Souci, with space and curves?

I stuck my hands in the empty pockets of the coat Madame Clarkson gave me. I had brought with me a few dresses but nothing like this indigo-colored greatcoat. It was thoughtful, but I hated that I'd become a royal beggar.

At least this woman was genuine, giving to me in true Christian love. Wondered if the maids who'd smiled in my face and stole my jewels had any. I was very sure the thief was one of the staff.

A carriage stopped in front of me. It was a gig, the type where the driver is the sole passenger. Monsieur William Wilberforce descended. Tall, lank, with a slightly bent posture, he rushed toward me. "Madame Christophe, walking alone?"

"It clears my head." I offered the assessing blue eyes the best smile I could. "I'm glad to meet you away from the family."

He held out his arm to me.

Staring at the smooth ebony wool of his coat sleeve, I hesitated. "Are you sure you want my hand? The scandal mongers will accuse you of being entangled with the Blacks again."

"They already do when I'm not walking with a queen." His thin red cheeks glowed. "It's the cartoonists who do the worst. They reduce everything to tittle-tattle and scandal. With you, the honorable Queen Marie-Louise, in my company, my reputation can only improve."

A good-humored charmer, this dear man. I claimed his arm and we proceeded down the street. I observed more tall houses, more smooth bricks, more crowding.

"Are you here to tell me to return to Hayti? Should I leave before thieves steal my dresses?"

"No. The manager dismissed the maids assigned to your rooms."

Justice for us . . . in exile? "Truly? I'm astonished."

"When I reminded him of the king's interest in your safety and welfare, the manager promised to redouble his efforts in finding the criminals."

King George IV, the former regent, during his father's madness, allowed his Captain Nicholson to bring my family across the sea to safety. The boat, the *Missionary*, bounced with every wave. I remembered looking out my cabin window at Port-au-Prince harbor disappearing. Fool that I was, I thought I had said goodbye to trouble.

"Madame Christophe, you stopped walking. Are you tired?"

"Non. Just thinking. The work my husband did to normalize relations with Britain seemed to have some impact. Thank His Majesty for me."

"My prime minister will, and perhaps you can help me think of ways to begin talks with the new government. They seemed very dismissive when I offered to help."

"Don't think those men wish to hear from me, monsieur."

"They should listen for the good of the nation. You're logical, madame. I wish there were more like you in Hayti. It seems those with level heads have been imprisoned or executed."

He said the last bit so softly that I might've missed it because of the hullabaloo of the city—the passing carriages, the dockworkers heading to the Thames.

A Black face was one in the crowd. Arms swinging, he trudged forward, heading toward the water.

"Ma'am? You've stopped walking again."

"Just looking at the diversity of this city. All types of workers."

Wilberforce nodded. "I think your nation would've become this—"

"If Henry hadn't died."

The cold air of the Thames surrounded me, separating us, as if my king stood between me and Wilberforce. This was the first time on this soil I'd said it aloud, said Henry was gone.

"What am I to expect of my circumstances? Without my jewels, I need the archbishop to return the money that my husband gave him. It was for me."

"I've spoken with the manager of the Osborne," Wilberforce said. "You'll remain here, comfortable and cared for, until all matters with the archdiocese are settled."

That wasn't an answer. "And my funds?"

"It's not that simple, madame." The gentleman urged me to walk with him again. When I did, he said, "A record must be established. We have to make sure the dispensing of funds can't be challenged by others."

By *others*, he meant my enemies in Hayti. They didn't want a woman's blood on their hands, so they had allowed me to leave, but the upstart government wasn't done tormenting me. "Must be a great sum for there to be worries?"

"Nine thousand pounds."

That was a lot of money, but not the amount I thought Henry had set aside.

"You're frowning, Madame Christophe. You expected more?"

Pacing a little ahead of Wilberforce, I looked out at the busy shipyard. "My king made a great deal of money facilitating trade for the kingdom. There should be more, but perhaps his fortune has been commandeered like the spoils of Sans-Souci."

"King Henry was very wealthy. Our papers talked often of things he purchased for the kingdom."

His mouth twitched. I saw the same foul judgment that I initially had for Henry's dealings, but after what my husband's vision of setting Hayti above all nations cost him, I knew every gourde was earned. "How long before things are resolved?"

"That I don't know. And there may be more money in our banks to which you're entitled."

Entitled was the devil's word, meaning different things to different people. To me, my family was entitled to live in freedom without duress or sneers or thieves. I doubted many others saw it the same.

"Well, let's hope after you and the priests are finished, there is enough for dresses and coats. I hear your winters are horrid."

He sighed but kept us heading down the street. "I can't imagine what you've been through."

Turning from his soft, sad eyes, I watched barges unload barrels containing either cane or rum. "The world still needs its sweets and its liquor, no matter where it comes from or from whose hands, free or enslaved. But for a moment, it was shipped by a free nation, a powerful Black nation. Monsieur, that shouldn't be forgotten."

"It won't be, but it will be upon you and your children to take up King Henry's mantle."

This sweet man was a fool if he thought for one moment I'd risk more Christophe blood. The world was on its own to figure out how to end enslavement. "Non. No more demands upon me or my living children."

A man shouted, and I trembled.

Wilberforce steadied my hand. "It's a worker on one of the docks."

"Yelling can be as disconcerting as silence. There needs to be some sort of noise to let you know life is still happening." I stood up straight and filled my lungs. "I want silence, slowness, some sense of lasting peace."

"I'm sorry, Madame Christophe. Give me more time. Things will be better."

Offering him what smile I could, we headed back to the Osborne. Though I didn't want to fight, I knew I had to be ready for one. As long as we lived, whether in exile or in power, those who sought to destroy us wouldn't stop until they succeeded. I vowed in my heart to figure out how to be the dignified widow of a king and protect the loved ones who lived.

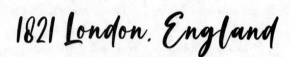

2

1821 London, England

At my breakfast table, I sat across from my younger daughter, Athénaïre, as she sipped her tea. Her oval face bore a drooping Cupid's bow, a small flattening frown. Her smile had become a memory, something she hadn't shown since the kingdom ended.

I wished I knew how to help her heal, but I didn't know how to fix myself. Wasn't I a shell, hard and fragile on the outside, trying not to crack with the next crashing wave?

How did one learn to become stiff, even unfeeling? It would be a year in a few days since the kingdom fell. I'd begun crying again for Hayti and Henry and all the sons lost. I wasn't numb, though I wished to be.

My mourning drape, freshly laundered jet bombazine, still felt warm from Zephyrine's pressing iron. The chill outside had become more prevalent, hindering my morning walks. Soon, the white ice Monsieur and Madame Clarkson told us about would come. In Hayti, I'd heard that snow, a yellowish ash mix, fell in the mountains, but I hadn't seen it.

The religious fellow, Clarkson, was another of Henry's advocates in England and in discussions with Russia and France on the kingdom's behalf. Passionate about abolition, the man, this contemporary of Wilberforce, seemed caring, wanting to help. His quiet wife seemed to study us, my daughters and me, comparing our grace and station with the caricatures churned out by newsmen. She had invited us to stay with them in Suffolk for the winter.

Wasn't sure whether I wanted to spend the cold season as an exhibition for country farmers or stay in London, in our colorless royal limbo.

"Maman," Athénaïre said, putting her smooth hand over my ashy wrist. "Something upset you again? Another death? Is that what the Clarksons disclosed as I visited with Miss Thornton?"

The couple had brought a young lady, a neighbor from a nearby farm, to our visit. Polite, pale from hiding from the sun, Marianne Thornton accompanied my daughters downstairs to the galleries in the hotel.

"Non. They talked of ways to help. Nothing grim."

Her lips wrinkled into a dot. She wanted more. At twenty-one, she deserved the full truth. "There's been no update on the funds of ours that the archbishop of Canterbury has in his possession. With no jewels to sell, I won't be able to pay for these rooms. It's nonsensical to expect King George to keep intervening in our circumstances when his priest and his rules are keeping us from receiving our due."

"Your brow furrowed. You do that when you're fretting about something." Athénaïre looked down at her stationery. "Merci bien for sharing your thoughts."

My girl. Why did she demur after being bold? "Oui. Now share yours. How did you find Mademoiselle Thornton?"

Golden eyes beaming a little, she raised her countenance. "I like her. She's very polite. Her gossip is good."

Normally, I'd chastise my daughter for delighting in such tattle, but this was Athénaïre, my dramatic girl, who'd been too silent since leaving house arrest in Cap-Henry.

"She said she liked meeting a true princess." Her lashes lowered. "Miss Thornton was afraid I'd be another pretender like the Caraboo woman."

Caraboo? I'd read about the actress who'd convinced all she was a princess from a foreign land. Made up her own language and took advantage of people's kindness until she was exposed. People from her Devonshire village came forward and identified her as a cobbler's daughter.

My girls hadn't been born yet when I served Blanc women who stayed at my father's hotel. They never had to bow and smile at them through slights. This Thornton person and Mrs. Clarkson were the first Blanc ladies they'd spent time with who weren't employed by the king.

Moving closer, I stroked a curl that fell to her forehead. She'd straightened it as the American governess had shown her. "Are you sure Mademoiselle Thornton was being kind? I find that some women can be duplicitous, smiling in your face while they openly scheme."

"Non. She was kind."

Kind?

What about deferential or impressed? Were those feelings reserved for other nobles?

"Maman, you are not pleased?"

My hand tightened about the handle of my bone-china teacup. I closed my eyes and counted. The memories I wanted to be numb to, their pain returned. Henry's court had been filled with men and women plotting for their own interests. Ladies . . . friends I trusted broke my heart. "Bringing up a fake princess to a true one might be the mademoiselle's way of challenging your station. Never forget who you are."

"Non, Maman. Marianne is genuine. I like her. She's funny. She doesn't act like some we've met. I'm glad the snickering maids are gone."

With no jewels or large sums of money, we were paupers. I hadn't expected a Blanc woman of means to be any different than the terminated maids, who loathed serving Black royals.

"This is good to hear, Athénaïre."

She stirred her tea, adding a little more milk. "Marianne mentioned that the Clarksons want us to stay the winter with them. I hope you accept. The Thorntons live nearby. I'd like to see more of her. I want some society if I can ask for such."

My girls were young ladies. I should treat them as proud women, not hide them away. "Mrs. Clarkson did offer. It would be good for you and Améthyste to meet more people. I'll consider it."

She squinted at me, then returned once more to her stationery. "If things don't change in Hayti, this will be our new home. It could be good if we find our footing."

With a nod, I agreed. I had to accept Britain as our new world. But what did that mean for us, displaced royals?

I sipped my tea, letting it warm my tongue and throat. And I prayed my daughter would grow bolder and that her golden eyes would never see the hate her sheltered, privileged life had kept away.

THE LOWER LEVEL NEAR THE HOTEL'S MAIN RECEPTION HAD DEEP indigo carpets with woven designs of orange and red. It wasn't an orchard or a forest, but it was the best I could manage to keep my nervous pacing secret while London's weather turned cold and bone-chillingly wet.

Sighing, wanting sun, I stopped and gaped at the paintings on the wall.

Big bold images of people surrounded me. I supposed that meant I wasn't walking alone.

"Miss?"

Startled, my hand flew to the shiny onyx buttons on my gown. With a quick spin that made my long skirt flutter, I found that an older gentleman with sparse white hair had entered the room. "Wait, miss?"

He waved his cane, something drab and smooth, different from Souliman's. "I said you there." He glared at me as if I had defied him. "Excuse me, ma'am. I need more hot water."

"Dommage qu'il y ait pénurie, Monsieur."

"So you don't speak English."

"I do." I replied with proud tones, the ones I'd mastered for the kingdom's grand fetes. "But I don't know where your water is. You might try asking a servant."

My glance met him dead in his eyes, then I turned and left. I was Madame Christophe, the only representative of Black royalty this man had ever seen. I didn't fetch water for anyone but my family.

Halfway down the hall, I heard a squeak. Then a cough.

Barging inside the parlor, I found Améthyste sitting on a bench. Her slim figure was trimmed in solemn black, and she had donned a matching turban to cover her thick braids. I hadn't thought she'd venture from the safety of our rooms.

I guess Athénaïre wasn't the only one who wanted to explore, but did Améthyste have the physical strength to do so?

"What are you doing here without an attendant? Do you want someone to think you're a maid, too? Or worse?"

"What's worse than a maid in London? They have no enslaved, Maman. And if we are unable to secure funding or recover your jewels, we'll have to seek a profession. To work as a maid is honorable labor."

Her logic, as always, was flawless, and unlike her brother, she didn't appear frightened by honest work. Victor. I missed him. I felt my son's pride when I'd balked at the presumptuous old man. My sweet boy wouldn't fetch water, either.

"You're right, Améthyste. I did a good job cleaning for my father at the Hôtel de la Couronne. And your père was once a waiter, a good one. He collected a lot of tips serving wealthy patrons. He was so handsome. When I met him, Henry commanded the room and took abuse from no one. Once he—"

I stopped before I uttered the devilish things my love did to a customer's soup because the Blanc had insulted me. My daughter needed to remember the stately king, not the willful man who chose revenge when it came to protecting me. "Well, he was passionate at everything he did."

"He was a bricklayer, too. Père often did shifts at the great Citadel until the fortress was complete." My daughter pulled her shawl, a white creamy thing with fringes on the ends, closer to her throat. Good Haytian cotton. "I'm not afraid of hard work."

I clasped the empty spot on my wrist, twisting that invisible bracelet. I wasn't ready to face what our life would be without means . . . without him.

I'd focused so much on getting us to safety, I forgot to plan how to live, truly live on these shores. Any meaningful experience required taking risks, and letting my girls—my only living children, the only existing pieces of Henry and our life together—be brave and take chances, too.

How did one do that when almost everything had been lost?

How, when I was tired of losing?

With strength I didn't know she had, Améthyste rose and towed me toward the larger-than-life mural. "Come, Maman. Look at this art."

Unlike the paintings in the other room, these canvases stretched the length of the wall.

"I'm amazed, Maman. It's titled *Orpheus Instructing a Savage People in Theology and the Arts of Social Life.*" She started laughing. "Instructing savages. Don't you get it?"

The canvas was dark and foreboding. It felt like a nightmare. Stark enough to be one of mine. "Dearest, can't you enjoy a different style of painting? Fruit, perhaps? A nice still life?"

"You seriously don't see it?"

I shrugged and felt a little like my Victor when he couldn't readily grasp a concept. My chest ripped open again. He should be here looking at art with his sister. He should've lived. A boy barely sixteen should've been spared the alleged sins of his father.

"Maman, a whole painting of alleged savages and not one is African. Not one made to look Black or Brown. The savages are them. The Romans, the Europeans, the French or British." She smiled more broadly. "Not us."

Squinting at the creams and grays of the characters, I began to understand.

"Art is what the creator intends it to be," she said. "I like them being cast in suspicion."

"Why, Améthyste?"

"Because the papers haven't been kind to Hayti or Père. The British struggle to abolish enslavement. I've seen all kinds of hateful images of free Blacks." She gestured toward the art again. "This is the first thing I've seen where we're not the joke, nor the subject of cruelty, nor made to look like killers. They are the savages, the Blancs. Not us."

"The Blancs are savage, Améthyste?"

"Oui. I imagine that some are paying for their thefts. Others for killings."

Well, that could be true.

Henry had fought a war because of Blanc sins and the quest for freedom, but I knew Black and Brown could be as cruel as the French. I couldn't enjoy this painting.

"Maman, let me show you my favorite."

She led me to the other side of the room to another haunting image. "This one. It is the same artist, James Barry. He calls it *Elysium, or The State of Final Retribution*. I call it *The Last Judgment*."

When she pronounced that word, *judgment*, the sconce light seemed to brighten and center upon me. I saw confusion, lots of different people, and then a hole, a depiction of hell.

"It's powerful, Maman. And everyone is there, from rulers like Peter the Great to scientists like Descartes, even us."

My heart beat faster. The pounding in my veins made me weak. "What?"

Améthyste pointed out faces and objects like lyres and palm trees. "Those women with the head wraps, they are from the Caribbean. See, all are included."

"So we all will be judged. But I see no heaven. How is that supposed to be good?"

Beaming, she tilted her head. The light fell to her smile. "Makes me feel we all have a place, a role. Despite how it all ended, Père tried to create a perfect place for everyone."

Perfect? We were far from that, but I couldn't focus on our missteps, Henry's and mine, not with Améthyste radiating as if she'd been touched by invisible sunshine. "You have a painter's soul."

"Maman, you made the right decision to bring us to these shores. Don't doubt that."

I wanted her words to be true. In poverty there might be honesty, but no protection. In Barry's painting, the West Indian women were away from everyone but angels. I wanted my family safe, not isolated and lonely, looking to heaven for comfort.

Fingers rubbing that empty place on my arm, I packed away my fears and dwelled on now. This daughter had found her smile. She'd opened her heart to something new.

"Would you like to paint, Améthyste? I recall some of your sketches. They were very fine."

"Oui," she said, this young woman whom I was grateful to see reach twenty-three years. "I've wanted to draw and paint for a long time. Père's doctors convinced him the fumes would be bad for me, but Madame la Comtesse d'Ouanaminthe thought I showed great progress before I was forced to stop."

Coddling her because of her health, we had forced Améthyste to make this sacrifice. I was guilty again.

The governesses Dupuy brought from America were meant to educate the girls to be as sophisticated and as polished as King George III's daughters, Princesses Augusta and Elizabeth.

When poor Princess Charlotte died so young, it greatly disturbed Henry. He mourned for the prince regent's lost daughter. Then he commanded Améthyste not to put herself at risk. Can't remember if I agreed with the caution or merely allowed Henry to win the argument, but I surrendered, and my daughter lost her art.

A warm hand drew me back from yesterday, from my tangle of regrets. "Maman, are you saying I should paint again? You went silent for a moment."

"Will it tire you? Will it . . ."

She danced off to another canvas, holding her hands high, as though she could measure happiness. "I can do this. I can do it with your blessing."

"Oui. It sounds as if it will make you happy."

"It does. It's something I can do and be good at, and even represent Père and the kingdom he tried to build."

"What of the future? Art should be about that, not just the past."

Another look at her sweet countenance: the tension in her eyes, the darkening circles weren't from illness but fretting. "I don't want anyone to forget Père. Aunt Geneviève writes that the Citadel is abandoned. That the people call Père 'L'homme.'"

Didn't know what to react to first—the Citadel deserted or the sister I couldn't trust writing my daughter?

"What does Geneviève want?"

"She says she'll beg the government in Hayti for our safe return. That Lambert is safe. We still have a home."

It would be naïve, foolhardy, or even hubristic of my sister to think she'd have influence over the butchers who slew my family.

"Maman? You're shaking."

She wrapped her arms about me. I felt her calming passion, but Améthyste was a little too warm. "You have a fever. You should be in bed."

"No. Let me hold you. I don't get to be of use. My lungs seem to prefer me small and wasting away. While I have strength, I'll give it to you."

The fuss I'd started to work up died, and I allowed her to feel powerful and support me.

"We're safe from violence, Maman. The archbishop here isn't like ours. Canterbury will return the money Père gave him. We'll be able to continue here and see the wonders that my father esteemed."

Henry had craved British approval.

He wanted all the European powers to respect him. He'd made strides. The tsar and other leaders stayed France's hand. With Henry gone and the Citadel shuttered, how would evil be stopped?

"Everything will be all right, Maman. Père's looking down on us, granting us favor."

I embraced my feverish Améthyste, holding her tighter, keeping my lips closed, not whispering, *I disagree.*

No favor from my king.

No grace at all for me.

Forever, I'd be tormented, savaged by questions or disagreements or circumstances that I didn't fight. I yielded. I gave in. I should've risked more before all actions became risky. Shoving my memories, my guilt aside, burying them deeper in my mind, I existed in the moment with my daughter. Later, I'd figure out how to forgive myself for the omissions and sins that led to the kingdom's rise and ruin.

In the morning, my maid brings me the papers.
I find great humor in the lies printed as truth.
—MADAME CHRISTOPHE, 1847

National Protector. Saturday, April 24, 1847

HAYTI. The new president opened the session of the Chamber of Representatives on the 11th ult., with the following speech: "Gentlemen,—It is a matter of congratulation to me, that so soon after my election to the presidency of Hayti, I find myself in the bosom of the legislative body. I owe this gratifying circumstance entirely to my illustrious predecessor, who has lent stability to the affairs of our country."

3

1847 Florence, Italy

Shivers sweep my arms, so odd for a warm afternoon steeped in Tuscan sunshine. In Florence, late-spring days are special treats filled with movement—walking the cobbled rues, crossing the immovable stone bridges—and gazing at the shimmering waters of the Arno.

My footfalls slow.

I stumble.

The notion of being watched covers me. The embrace feels tired and old, yet intimate like a lover, like the tangle of the thin shawl about my shoulders.

The airy creamy thing with worn fringes is good Haytian cotton. I've kept it, or it's kept me, all these years, along with my memories and regrets stitched in the seams.

I push away from the past and steady my gait along the solid cobbles. In all my travels, Florence's steely-blue stones are my favorite. The smooth surfaces make me think they're a path to a river or that beneath each rock hides treasure.

Zephyrine, my lady's maid, my right-hand *Dupuy*, walks at my side. The wrinkles on her golden-brown face match the ones on my darker skin. I lean into her and grab her arm. "My dear friend, I think I'll treat you to your favorite pleasure."

Her face brightens as she licks her lips. "The soup? The one with the toasted bread?"

"Yes, ribollita, with lots of vegetables and broth. The taste is delicious, but I think you merely enjoy sopping up the goodness."

"Madame, it's a hearty treat. Which trattoria . . . did we choose?"

Figuring out the direction I should go has been the challenge of my life. The times when I blindly followed love, closed my eyes to truth, or let my passions lead me mix up my guilt with the good.

When last rites are offered and my final requiem is sung, I hope to be judged fairly for what I've done. That Saints Michael and John, angels of war and loyalty, will be more generous than my conscience.

The mild breeze brings the savory smell of roasting tomatoes. Since we left the palace in Milot and traveled across the sea, it took coming to Italy to taste the same beefy ripeness.

Unlike grapes, tomatoes—or pomodoros as the locals call them—are best at the start of the season. Beginnings are always better than endings.

"And a little vino, madame?"

"Oui," I say to the happy woman. Grapes are the exception. The first fruits picked for wine are the tartest. The ones left, the last harvested, are the sweetest. Life should be juicy, sweet until the end, like jet Sangiovese grapes.

"Madame, I can taste the lush ribollita. Let's go down Via Ricasoli. The best café is there, but so are many other places to dine."

Like the numerous bridges, places to eat and drink abound in Florence. We head down the rue letting our noses, proudly lifted, guide the way.

People come and go all around us.

Some lugging bundles. Others haggling.

None stare at us.

Busyness has consumed them, and our skin is just another monument in this city of monuments—preserved and still standing.

Yet I'll always search, hunting for a gaze that lingers too long. Habit or a nightmare or love—I suppose I'm always looking.

As in Le Cap, a cart seller passes me, but her hot buns, the ciriolas, draw Zephyrine away. Alone, the ease with which I hide my memories is harder to maintain. For a moment, a mere few seconds, I surrender. I let my mind remember the stately city of old, Le Cap before the rebellions, Le Cap before the ashes, Le Cap before the wars.

I wonder what has become of its cobbles.

Then I catch myself.

I'd promised my heart to never, ever dwell on the past.

An old woman stops in front of me. Her gape isn't at my ruched ribbon bonnet or the braided silver chignon my maid took the time to do.

Perhaps the emerald necklace dangling about my dark throat, with flesh colored by *Eurafrican blood*, as mine has been described, holds her attention. An admirer once admitted my skin held its own draw, as forceful and compelling as the glimmer of gems.

The questions in this stranger's eyes are never uttered. She twists her yellow umbrella and steps away with a smile. "The Black Russian princesses. I got to see one."

Joyous, she hurries off.

It's been years since I've been called that. Abram Gannibal, the Black King of Russia, as he was whimsically known, was an enslaved man whose brilliance was recognized by Tsar Peter the Great. Gannibal was freed and made a royal godson, and through his family, the legend of Black Russian princes and princesses was born.

With a hand to my hip, I sigh, thinking of my princesses, their love of lore and our endless adventures across Europe. It's been a life.

A whiff of crusty goodness proceeds Zephyrine's return with a full basket. Her glance is swift, gaping from my slippers to my hat. "Madame, are you well? Is your leg paining you?"

Her tone is filled with worry, but a little exertion never hurt. It makes me better.

"Nonsense," I say. "I'm leaning like a scale, weighing the direction we should travel. Which trattoria will gain my gourdes. I mean fiorino, these heavy Italian coins."

My weathered fingers sink toward the rosary in my pocket, but they stop before it, at the usual spot, the area on my wrist where a bracelet would reside. Fear of losing my favorites makes me lock away what I treasure.

Maybe that's why it hurts to think of the past.

"The one with the red sign, Zephyrine. It's far, but we've eaten there before. Delicious soup."

We start moving, and my pinkie has made it to the beads. The smooth surfaces, the knotted silken thread supporting jade spheres, remind me of the comforts the last twenty-six years in exile have afforded. The Holy Father set my feet upon these shores to heal, to nurture, to build . . . to lose and let go, saying, *vas en paix*.

"Your Highness."

Expecting the old woman with the parasol, I'm surprised to see a young Colored man, a well-to-do-looking homme de couleur, bowing before me, here on this public street.

Panic fevers my brow. Fear of a scene brings my insides to a rapid boil. Coloreds and Blacks are the same. None should bow; I motion for him to rise and go. "Leave me."

"I know it to be you, Queen Marie-Louise Christophe. I knew it when I saw you at a distance."

That's the intrusion I felt.

Again, a man with dark eyes has come to make trouble. I'm in no mood to haggle with another fortune hunter or to be solicited for a misguided cause. "That woman doesn't exist anymore. The continued chaos in Hayti, with new leader after leader, makes everyone long for the stability of the past."

My voice diminishes. I'd replied to his English with the same and given myself away.

"It is you. And I remember the kingdom, the Kingdom of Hayti, the nation formed by Henry Christophe."

The scar on his temple reminds me of someone, but my being good at placing faces and not recalling this squared jaw brings new worries.

"Madame Christophe, exiled Queen Marie-Louise Coidavid-Melgrin Christophe, wife of the august sovereign. There's no denying it."

I step around him, but he persists, following and repeating the name of the forgotten queen.

"I was in Cap-Henry, Queen Marie-Louise. My family saw you at the prince royal's fete. You were a lovely hostess. The perfect wife, I think that's how the speech maker said it."

The king's ministers, Limonade, Vastey, and Dupuy, were long winded and boastful in their toasts at celebrations. This fellow, who seemed to be in his thirties, would've been very young, younger than my son, Victor.

Images of my boys, both boys, and the happy years fill my head. If I close my eyes, I see one waving, boarding a boat, the other straddling a step on the grand stone balcony of the palace.

Non. No to the memories.

Like a flooding Rivière Mapou, they rush at me. I hear the music of harps, children reciting prayers in English and French.

Then bitterness intrudes. The sorrow at what Hayti could've been sours my soul.

Non. Not again.

I have peace, and the sadness takes too long to escape.

Eyes wide open, I pass the bothersome young man and lead Zephyrine. "If we can't make the red one, I'll choose a closer trattoria."

"Madame Christophe? Please, ma'am. Wait." The fellow hasn't given up. "This is of the greatest importance."

"Chasseur de fortune!" My handmaiden swats at him. Her retort in our native French makes me chuckle and remember that some fortune hunters are quite the charming rogues.

"A spy for Boyer. Espionner, madame! Espionner!"

My skin burns at the mention of that horrible fool, but he doesn't lead Hayti anymore. Riché . . . no, Faustin Soulouque does. It's easy to make mistakes about who rules now. Men of little vision, lusting for power, come and go quickly.

Waving impatient hands, the young man says, "I'm no fortune hunter. I'm not from the gov'ment. I know you've been hounded."

Until this moment, his English has been impeccable and proper—something I've heard in fine drawing rooms among men sent by foreign crowns or genteel women dancing in ballrooms of affluent resorts.

But this accent or phrasing sounds different, coarse . . . common . . . familiar.

He adjusts the midnight-colored stock about his shirt collar. "I need to speak with you about the king."

"Tu ne me connais ni moi, ni le roi." It's a little late to pretend I don't know, ne connais pas l'anglais, but this stranger has never met me or His Majesty. I move away, clutching those beads in my pocket as if they hold the magic. If they did, I'd wish all my troubles to disappear.

Yet my sœur taught me not to ask for magic you don't understand or to remove hills when you don't see the next mountain.

"Queen Marie-Louise," the fellow says, begging. "I know how you've been harassed, but please hear me."

Persistence is an endearing quality in sisters, not in men pursuing me . . . unless I want to be caught.

"Madame, what do we do? The young man insists upon making trouble."

"I guess no one outruns the past." Stomping a loose cobble, I stop, my slippers kicking up dust, no treasure. "Tell me your business at once."

The fellow paces in front of me with cherry-red cheeks on his light face. "With what's happening in Hayti now, I've been given an article to review for my paper, the *Globe*. What I've read is not the man I remember. People need to hear King Henry's vision, to think again of his great plans. As it's currently written, the newspaper will frame the good king as a despot. His name will be besmirched worse than how they tarnished Dessalines."

Poor Dessalines. "Emperor Jacques I was a great man. He did the impossible. He and his generals liberated Hayti from monsters who still wish to suck the country dry."

"Your husband was the emperor's second-in-command. Henry Christophe, the first king of Hayti, would never submit to pay tithes to France as if to the pope."

"No. I don't think he'd do that." I begin walking again. I see a closer trattoria, one with a blue and gold sign. Not the best, but I'll settle for it to lose trouble.

My insides turn; nausea shadows my steps. Settling—isn't that a different form of hell?

"Ma'am, the papers, the king and his advisers used them to get his message to the world. Perhaps this *Globe* can be made to help."

My old friend nods toward the reporter. Zephyrine hates all the false reports about Henry and my family. How can we trust those who print falsehoods?

"Let's go." My head is up like the day I was crowned. "There, to the left," I say to her. My words are a command.

At my side, he persists. "Madame, only you can speak to the king's goals, his mission." Again, this reporter's words are crisp, perfect English, seductive. "It's a chance to correct the record and resurrect the king's wondrous legacy. People need to know what he did. What you did, too."

Legacy was the one thing Henry loved more than his family or me.

"The serene look on your face, Your Majesty, tells me you're considering. Come have a coffee with me. I can explain more."

"And there, you'll mention the terms of your extortion. Do you know how many have come at me and my daughters?"

"No bribes, ma'am, just coffee and a chat. When this article is published, I can remind the world of Hayti's glory. The nation was on the verge of becoming a world power. The country's treasury was full. King Christophe made Dessalines's economy thrive. The world needs to know, and only his wife, the last queen of Hayti, can do it."

It is a huge thing for any man to attempt to make a name for himself, but to correct slights from years long past is a miracle. I pause, force the Latin, the Italian, the Kreyòl, the French away from my tongue to make my English words clear. "The Hayti you remember is gone. There's no new story. Now be gone, Monsieur—"

"Michelson. David Michelson."

The name and the dark eyes mean nothing. One ambitious man or English paper is as ruinous as the next. Spending years in exile with reporters targeting my every step has taught me this. "Non, monsieur. A good newspaperman will have multiple sources to write the story he wants."

"I have a few, but I'm not going to risk my reputa'ion without you, the woman who saw it all." He raises his glasses and swipes at the lenses with a cloth. The accent he tries to suppress sounds nasal. Is he mimicking the British upper class?

"Queen Marie-Louise, I'm not going to risk my repu . . . reputation and fight for the truth without cooperation from you. Please, madame, just a coffee."

The price of my peace is worth more than a caffè with milk. It's never easy for a woman to trust or for a man to value what's precious to her. "All my memories are mine. They belong to no one else. Definitely not the *Globe*."

Zephyrine tries to shoo him away. She whips her basket like a weapon. "Combien de façons la reine a-t-elle de te dire non?"

She asks him again, *"How many ways does the queen have to say no to you?"*

The frown her face radiates says she wishes to curse him in Kreyòl or the bits of Italian she's learned, but she'll only speak French in public. Deference to my husband's command of royal behavior continues after all these years.

"I just want to invite the queen to a conversation," Monsieur Michelson says. "If the vile things are true, then there's no need to talk. I'm heading to the café at the end of Via Ricasoli. I'll be there for the next hour."

Well, that means none of the best ribollita today. My maid and I will settle for less. I refuse to follow.

Michelson offers me his card. "If you forgo coffee and decide to meet later, I'm staying at the Grand Hotel. Help me help you and Hayti."

He bows again and walks away.

Zephyrine gawks at me. Perhaps after all these years, she's succeeded at reading my mind. "Madame, you'll do as this stranger wants?"

"Oui, but not today. We'll send for him. He'll come to me. Zephyrine, we have an appointment for tomatoes."

She folds her arms; her full lips part showing a bit of a devilish smile, one long missed. "Someone who visited the kingdom in its prime? He must've been very young, or he's aged well."

The lure, the need to understand exactly what's at stake draws. I've always loved the chase. To learn the nature of Monsieur Michelson's true gambit intrigues.

"There are questions to be discovered and answered." From 1811 to 1820, a mere nine years, Hayti did something special, as special as the English Regency. Perhaps the world should know. Mayhap the newspaper, this medium that has been used against me and my family, can be made to set things right.

"Zephyrine, we'll settle with decent soup or whatever we can order at the closer restaurant, not the one Monsieur Michelson's going to.

Then I'll invite him to tea at our residence. There I can have more control over the conversation. It will be done in private."

"Very good, ma'am." She hooks her arm in mine, and we walk toward the trattoria, the one with a blue and gold sign. I hope what we find is delicious.

As intrigued as I am about the pushy Monsieur Michelson, I won't be pressured to say anything, and I'll warn my solicitors of the gentleman if a new scheme to defraud me is afoot. No strongman, no prince, no do-gooder, no priest, no person other than me will ever decide my fate.

Nonetheless, I've lived long enough to know negotiations have to be endured. If Michelson is sincere and chooses to write of the Kingdom of Hayti's accomplishments and to make clear my husband's vision, I'll sit for a lengthy interview and steer the reporter to subjects I want to discuss.

It's been a long time since I bartered for anything. My pulse races. Anticipation can be intoxicating. I trust my skills are as sharp as ever, and that I alone wield control, the power to price pieces of my soul.

A REGENCY

Star (London), Thursday, February 7, 1811

The Prince of Wales upon swearing in as Regent spoke to the following effect: "MY LORDS.—I understand, that by the Act passed by the Parliament appointing me Regent of the United Kingdom, in the name and on behalf of his Majesty. I am now ready to take these oaths, and to make the declaration prescribed."

A REBELLION

London Chronicle, Wednesday, March 27, 1811

Henry Christophe, President and Commander in Chief of the Land and Sea Forces of the State of Hayti. Having employed all means of reconciliation in my power to put an end to the calamities of the rebellion which has so long afflicted the South and West of the State; I declare in a state of blockade all the ports which are yet in the possession of the rebels and against which I am about to march my land forces.

4

1811 Milot, Hayti

A walk always settled my soul.

This one, in the low mountains to the north of Milot, was majestic, framed with bois chênes sporting long emerald leaves and tiny pink buds. January, the middle of the dry season, was beautiful. Hayti at its best.

Tilting my bonnet to shade my eyes, I noted coconut palms looming, edging a cleared path in thick forest. "It's wider than I remember."

"Louise, can you wait?"

"Oui, of course, Geneviève. It's not much farther to the plateau. Don't fret. Souliman has gone ahead. That young man never tires. He's fit, full of energy, and will drive us back in my dray when we are ready."

She waved her hands, panting and nodding. "We should've stayed with him and not gone on another of your treks."

My baby sister should have been used to my becoming lost in my thoughts and hiking every hill. With my children safe at our older sister's house, I relished this treat.

"Isn't there a stream somewhere nearby?" Geneviève fanned her sweating face. "We could dip in it like we used to and cool down."

Rivière Mapou ran close to where we grew up. Nothing was better than cooling off in swirling waters when everything was hot and steamy in Le Cap. "There's one nearby, somewhere. But I think we shouldn't stray. Henry will come soon."

Covered in muslin and long sleeves, as befitted the wife of a president, I wasn't sure it best to strip to bare skin and risk being discovered by one of his generals.

Henry wouldn't be amused unless he found me alone. Then we'd argue, forgive one another, and be free of the tensions besetting us.

"Louise?"

"Trois Rivières. That's what it's called, but I don't remember which way it cuts. When we reach the plateau, we may be able to find it, but you'll swim alone."

"Of course, Madame President," she said with a laugh. "But I mourn, remembering when you were more fun, willing to take risks."

Laughing, she bent over and then lay on the ground. "I think I'll rest."

Stretching in the grass in the shade of a coconut palm, my sister at twenty-three had no cares, no lasting sorrows.

I did.

Memories. Bad memories.

Images of war painted my closed lids.

Heartache and death stayed in my chest.

It wasn't that long ago that the battles of the revolution ripped Saint-Domingue apart. My dreams often returned me to the woods where my family hid, when I hoped brave Henry would come to our rescue.

"The past is always with us, Geneviève." My words sounded soft, mimicking her carefree tone, but last night I heard my husband talking about full-scale war with France, of all the nations siding with his enemies, coming to seize our free Haytian world.

My sister sat up. "Well, let's look to the future and see what your husband is building." She locked arms with me and we managed a slower advance. At our sides lay more felled trees, stacks of chênes, dwarf palms, and bayawonn trees.

Another house for Henry.

Another thing to stoke jealous hearts.

Jacques I, the late emperor, our General Dessalines, had allowed his officers to acquire land and habitations as a reward for their loyalty. Though Henry and others were grateful, the emperor never understood the envy this created, and he never saw how the nation he unified remained divided by color. Black and Brown didn't want to coexist. Brown wanted Black power to diminish. Brown generals lusted for Black ones to die. They murdered Jacques I.

"What are you thinking, sœur? Your face is wrinkling. Louise?"

"Pétion. Alexandre Pétion wants my husband to lose power."

Still moving and leading me, her eyes bloomed, wide as the flat clouds drifting overhead. "Why isn't Pétion content ruling the south of Hayti? Must he be jealous that his share of the country isn't as prosperous as the north?"

"I'm tired of war, Geneviève. Henry would be dead if he hadn't outmaneuvered Pétion. They've battled for five years to claim Hayti's soul."

"Stop thinking of the enemy. Your husband will come, see you sad, and become cross."

"He should be here now. Has some new chaos made him forget he asked us to join him here?" Henry should be here preening, preparing to show my sister and me the latest changes to . . . Sans-Souci.

My mouth fell open.

A large building sat where nothing had been. This thing was almost done—brick walls, a level courtyard. "He's had this land for years and done not one thing. I heard him talking about it again in December."

"Oh, my goodness." Geneviève gaped. "So much work! You think he intends to move in soon?"

I shrugged. I didn't know what Henry's plans were anymore. At one time I knew his thoughts. As of late, only his adviser Alexis Dupuy and his doctor, Duncan Stewart, did. After all Hayti had been through, all that Henry had survived, it meant something that his best advocates were a mulatto man and a Scottish physician. Henry was complex, a warrior, and now the president of northern Hayti.

As if the sight of stately limestone columns had cast a spell upon her, my bone-tired sister bounded with new energy, leaping and looking here and there at the construction. "It's going to be as big as a palace. Does your husband require a ballroom to house all of Hayti, all at once?"

That would probably be part of Henry's plans. He didn't shy away from extravagance. "If there was a way, he'd have it built unless someone, some wife with a level head, explained the folly of such cost."

"Sis, you're frowning. Are you not happy with this?"

"It's Henry's Sans-Souci, Geneviève. The place where he can be free of cares. That's what the name he chose is supposed to mean. But the man's not carefree."

She clasped my elbow, spinning me. "Are things well between you? The demands on politicians are bad. The demands on their wives must be terrible. All with Pétion looming—the pressures must be horrid."

They were.

Henry suffered in silence, except for nightmares. I watched his agony and wasn't allowed to help. I didn't know what to do. "Sometimes, I wish we could travel. He's from Saint Kitts, fought in the Americas for their revolution, and even traveled to Grenada. I've never left this island."

The wind stirred a little. The scent of the sawed pine added a lemony, citrusy air to the sandalwood smell of the bayawonn piles. "It's natural, this fragrance of progress, yet very unnatural."

"You're looking for problems. Don't do that. Revel in what you have—a man who loves you and will build you castles." Geneviève dashed to Henry's walls, but I set my gaze to the mountains.

Looking up at the sleek white clouds that floated overhead like a shelf housing treasures, I missed the old days when it felt as if my husband and I were in the same place, with our fingers touching the same treasures on the bookcase. I used to read to him the translated Italian fairy tales like "Ancilotto, King of Provino" and "Biancabella and the Snake" in the loft of my father's mews. Those innocent days were the best.

Didn't need a castle, just the old comfort of knowing Henry's mind.

Souliman, my footman, stretched his thick arms as he held my mule's reins. He'd unhitched it from my dray and allowed the poor beast to graze in the emerald grasses edging the property. He whipped his straw hat to me. That was his signal that all was well.

The young man, the age of Henry's nineteen-year-old son, Armande, seemed at ease in his flowing white shirt and black breeches. I knew he watched the area for unwanted visitors. Though wives and families of politicians weren't typically targets of ambush, there was no rule that said we'd be spared. An angry mob or furious avenger might want to burnish their credentials assassinating someone they assumed to be aligned with the wrong side.

With dark hair tied up in a red and blue scarf, looking festive though sweating, Geneviève grabbed my hand. Her wet palm felt squishy in mine. "This must be Christophe's presidential palace, like the governor's building back in Le Cap. I've never been more jealous."

"What are you talking about?"

"Pure jealousy," she said in a half-serious tone, then she chuckled. Geneviève was the youngest in the Coidavid-Melgrin family. Stately and poised, but also assertive and ambitious—these words fit her like her beautiful maple-brown skin. If she could marry someone as driven as Henry, she would. If she could push a man to claim the limelight, she'd do that, too. Geneviève wanted accolades and comfort now, not merely enjoying mine or our sister's.

"I'm only slightly kidding," she added. "You don't understand because you're old. Thirty-three and settled." She stopped and pumped each fist to the sky. "Cécile is very old, settled and a national hero. I'll always feel as if I'm in your shadows."

Our half sister was seven years my senior and could run faster than Geneviève and my children. Cécile was fleeter and braver than most women. She was revered by all. In her teens, she had helped start the rebellions that led to our independence.

I admired her. She'd reached that rare position of being comfortable in her sandals and her golden skin.

That type of serenity was something to envy.

No longer swishing her hips, Geneviève moved about the perimeter in her mango and green skirt. "This is fantastic, Louise. When the gardeners finish, you'll have the perfect grounds. I'm sure you can go for your treasured walks—"

The sharp buzz call of an oriole interrupted her words, but Geneviève was right. I'd love to stroll in this peace every day as I once did on Rue Dauphine. That was my and Henry's first house as a married couple. I'll never forget the views of the sea from my window or the squawks of gulls that accompanied my morning prayer.

We no longer had Rue Dauphine. Henry and Dessalines and Toussaint, even horrible Pétion, had had a part to play in freeing our world.

Under order to burn the capital before the French landed, Henry set a torch to our home.

If I closed my eyes, I'd see the inferno, the fire licking the curtains that dressed the shutters like a chemise. The tart smell of the whale oil my husband doused on our furnishings stung my nostrils. Not even the crib that had held our baby was spared.

But that was the kind of man I'd married, one who believed sacrifice began at home.

"It's strategic, too, Louise."

Geneviève's voice snapped me from my reverie.

"Enemies," she said, "can only approach one way. The mountains all around us are too steep."

"That's something." After all the tragedies Henry and I had lived through, something strategic sounded good. "You don't suppose there will be guards and a gate? I remember Dessalines's house in the Artibonite, Habitation Frère, had those."

"Whatever it takes to keep his family safe, Henry Christophe will do it, Louise."

We kept walking, careful not to fall into the steep ravine, until we came upon piles of cobbles. The type used in the old roads about my father's inn.

"Remember Henry stumbling into the Hôtel de la Couronne on rocks like these. Then he snapped to attention and immediately began sweeping."

"So handsome. If he needed a second wife—"

I glared at her and she burst with laughter. "Kidding, sœur. But oh, how he stood out. Six inches to a foot taller than most men. As I remember it now, I do appreciate that image of Henry with cuffs rolled up, exposing muscular forearms carrying dishes . . . you're lucky, Louise."

My raised brow lowered and accounted her zeal as a general appreciation for beautiful or powerful men. And from the beginning, Henry was strong and dignified, well above the station of a waiter. Tall and assured, the new indentured servant had stolen my heart.

"Oh, the parties the president and his wife could have here." My sister's joyous tones reminded me of how lucky we were and of the expectations of my duties as Madame President, the helpmate of the leader.

Geneviève tugged on the light sleeve of my gown. "Now you've gone silent. Is my outright jealousy too much?"

"Hmm . . . It wouldn't be you if you weren't lusting for something that wasn't yours."

With a saucy turn and a hand on her hip, she frowned at me. "Can I help living in a world where my sisters and brother have everything? Or that my family has been selected by God to lead?"

As the bishop would say, to whom much is given, much will be required. It was best she didn't have to endure the sacrifices I had to gain these earthly rewards. Only a few women, like Madame Dessalines and Madame Louverture, knew the full truth. Both were widows with children lost to the cause of freedom. Though Henry still lived, our firstborn son, François-Ferdinand, had died because of France.

"You're quiet again. I didn't mean to upset you."

"No. I was thinking of the children. With Henry's other building project, the Citadel La Ferrière, four miles away, I wonder if he's there. As involved as he is in that design, the man could lose track of time. He's usually early or not coming, nothing in between."

"Well, he didn't pass us coming up here, despite my pokey pace." Geneviève gave my shoulder a playful tap. "That's a joke, sis. I know you have a lot on your mind. So does Christophe. The sooner he finishes the Citadel, the less he will fear France attacking."

Evil France. Killer of innocence.

Geneviève embraced me. "I'm not sure where you are. But you're safe. The children are safe. Henry Christophe is safe."

The dread that France wasn't done, that they'd return and kill us all, wrapped about my neck like a strangling rope. "France is out there. That's what Henry says."

"The Citadel, our president's fierce fortress, will have thousands of cannons. It will keep the enemy away." Patting my back, she offered strength. "No more war with foreigners, Louise. When this chaos in the south is squashed, there'll be no opportunity for it." Her face shone. The hope in her eyes bolstered me.

I wanted no more battles. Yet the man responsible for keeping our current peace hadn't arrived. Punctual Henry wasn't coming.

My resolve returned, and I kissed her cheek, then wrested free, and pointed to the mountain peaks. "My husband dreams like you, wanting to be at the top. Sans-Souci nestled here must be what he wants now."

"Well, all this construction says soon. Maybe by the wet season, you and the president will awaken in these hills. Know that you and Henry deserve all of this. He bested all enemies, foreign and, hopefully soon, domestic."

Was that it?

Was he in the midst of troubles from Port-au-Prince?

Was treacherous Pétion wreaking havoc again? Were Henry and his faithful advisers ambushed?

With her fingers, Geneviève lifted the edges of my mouth to force a smile. "The president of Hayti is probably delayed by suppliers, maybe buying marble to finish this house."

Marble? How was he paying for all of this? Where did the president of a divided nation find support for this opulence?

I stooped and picked up a heavy rock. "When this is cradled with lime mortar and even molasses, it makes an impregnable wall. It's fitting that sugar in all its forms serves as the basis for building. It's restarted our economy."

Dropping the cobble, I listened to it smack into others on the pile. "And why France still wants to conquer us."

Geneviève, the sprite, swirled around me. She twirled to the ravine and back. Her festive tunic caught air like a sailboat's mast. "Come along, dancer, let's see what the inside of the place looks like. Let's explore like we did along Rivière Mapou. You were brave and without a care. Remember jumping in the water without looking."

"That was foolhardy. I was lucky there were no crocodiles."

"Louise, you did have words with a flamingo once. I think he flew away when you finished."

Laughing, my silly sister and I walked to the house.

"Beautiful," she said with pouty lips, then looked away to the arches being erected. "There should be balls here. When other nations recognize Hayti as independent, then ambassadors and ambassadors' wives will come and dine here."

"Can I count upon you to help? I'll need your help."

"Oui." My sister pranced up unfinished steps that formed one half of a pair of staircases that met at a balcony. "Christophe has great ambitions, and the size of this place must match them. It will be my pleasure to support you, to help you make your mark on Hayti."

"Don't lean too far. There's no rail. If you fall, you could hurt yourself."

Pounding of hooves.

My heart shook, then settled into an easier rhythm. Then stuttered again—only one lone set of hoofbeats.

Geneviève and I ran into Sans-Souci's field.

Souliman had pulled out a flintlock rifle from the dray. The bayonet attached gleamed. He waved us to stop. "Kache, madame, mademoiselle!" he said in Kreyòl, yelling at us to hide.

When the rider made it up to the plateau, Souliman doffed his hat and gave a yell. "Misye Noël Coidavid Boy mwen te ka touye ou."

"You wouldn't kill me," my brother, Noël, said. "You're afraid of my sœurs."

My footman lowered his weapon and whipped at his chest. "Sa a se vre, Coidavid."

Souliman was a dear, but he didn't fear me or Geneviève, just Henry's seldom-displayed hot temper. He spoke French in front of my husband, but alone with just me, it was Kreyòl, the tongue of independence.

"Sorry, Souliman. Ladies!" Noël rushed over, then cantered his horse around us. "I bring salutations from the president."

I watched him jump down from his silver mare. "Where is he, Noël? Henry was supposed to meet us."

"Unfortunately, President Christophe has been delayed. This morning he sent me to inform you, but I had to make a stop or two."

My handsome brother was twenty-seven and enjoyed courting women as much as he loved being a trusted aide of Henry.

"This morning, Noël?" I said to the cheeky fellow.

"Oh, my." Geneviève feigned shock with her hand dramatically sailing to her brow. "To not give Louise an urgent message from Henry Christophe?" She offered him a mischievous smirk, as she had when we were younger and she'd discovered a secret. "I should tell. He'll reward me."

Smile falling and eyes widening, Noël said, "Would a bolt of lace change your mind? I know where to get my hands on some fancy bits that could make a formal dress special."

"Oui," she said. "But why would I need something formal?"

Now his lips perched into a big grin. His face brightened, and all his boyish charms reappeared—nothing of the man who'd been to war since he was eighteen.

"I'm not at liberty to say." Noël draped me in a hug, then scooped up our sister, too. "Now, let's get you back to Cap-Henry."

"It's Le Cap—Cap-Français."

"For now. But it will be changed to commemorate all President Henry Christophe has done."

Souliman put his weapon to his side and saluted. "Nou pare pou ale? I mean, Nous sommes prêts à partir?"

"Oui. They are ready to go. Good. Keep practicing that French, sir. It's the official language." Noël bit his lip as if he'd said too much. "S'il te plaît, Souliman, get the ladies back to town at once."

"Wait, Noël. When will Henry be home?"

He looked at me, his deep brown eyes turning soft. "Sœur, he has many tasks to complete, plenty of obligations. Be prepared for him to sacrifice more. It's for Hayti, for all of us."

With a nod, I took my seat, then slumped against the cushions. Our family had already given too much. I wasn't sure if I'd survive the next demand.

5

1811 Milot. Hayti

Two months of broken promises had me both stewing and driving to Sans-Souci again. My daughters and I were to await Henry there. My dray, under Souliman's hand, rose toward the plateau. The north winds stirred, blowing away the fog.

A busy work site came into view.

The house . . . this palatial structure was almost finished, now fully painted and bearing a bright gingerbread-tiled roof.

As he helped Améthyste, my eldest, and Athénaïre down, Souliman's eyes beamed. He was proud of his employer's accomplishment.

I was mortified.

Henry hadn't listened to my concerns. His generals, the naysayers in the south, even the common folk here in the north had to be uncomfortable with this extravagance. All the battles and deaths our people had suffered couldn't be seen as lining my family's pockets.

"Maman," Athénaïre said, "we will go exploring inside. Père said there was a surprise for us."

Soft, encouraging words wouldn't form, so I nodded and stared at the expensive sparkling glass in the window frames, double the number I'd seen before.

"Fitting fè pwodiktif tè a nan esklav." Souliman fanned with his wide-brimmed hat. "Pisan itil."

Oui, it was useful to make the former slave ground where this building stood into something good. "More French, Souliman. My husband will be here soon."

"Oui, madame," he said, then grumbled Kreyòl under his breath.

Had Henry found an Old Frenchmen's purse?

Surely, he'd taken workers from the Citadel to finish construction.

I felt sick. My fingers sweated and I stared at my palm as if I were Lady Macbeth. Were the complaints of Henry stealing from the public's coffers true?

"Madame, President Christophe plans to take residence soon, oui?"

"He has plans, Souliman. I'm sure of it." Moving from my footman, I kept going until I stood among busy workers and endless piles of rubble.

The filled ravine made the plateau longer. I suppose the earth had to obey my husband, too. Henry wasn't building a house but a castle.

Squinting, this big thing could be a sketch from a picture book, probably what he'd imagined from the old fairy tales. "Can't be upset over what I'd caused."

Yet I was.

This was another thing that Henry wanted without taking the time to explain why or ask my opinion. Flustered, I blamed myself. I'd read him lore and legends. Why wouldn't they stir an ambitious man's lusts?

I told my daughters not to grow upset over things they couldn't change. One couldn't undo stone walls, but I could stop deferring to a president and speak my mind to a husband.

Today, Henry would listen to me roar. No longer would I make excuses about how busy he was or allow his dreams to diminish mine. We were husband and wife. I was a helpmate, not a maid to keep his house or mistress to warm his bed.

Fuming, I found my way to the north side and slunk into a courtyard. A fountain bubbled, allowing crystal water to rise and fall into the basin. Beautiful, even solemn, I listened to it and watched circles form.

Wrought-iron rails dressed the double staircases leading into the house. Moving closer, I touched the curl of the metal at the bottom. It was stiff, anchored well, almost posing in the quiet to be painted. My demanding father, the late Monsieur Melgrin, would be impressed by such handiwork.

This grandeur, the rich architecture—Pétion and his ilk would use this against Henry.

How could this opulence be legal? How could it be right?

Wandering around Sans-Souci like an aimless shepherd, staring at podiums that would hold statues and planters that would house flowers—everything done without my consultation—I felt abandoned.

How could Henry claim to love me and do all of this without my knowledge or consent?

My being Lady Macbeth ended today. I'd tell Henry he was wrong, that he had to slow down. He couldn't have everything.

As if the rebellion in my head had summoned troops, Améthyste and Athénaïre marched out of Sans-Souci onto the curved stairs.

They were up high, as my sister had been, and they waved as if they were on parade. As different as dawn and midnight, each girl chose a separate staircase to descend. Chin lifted, thirteen-year-old Améthyste started first. With slow and steady steps, taking long, breathy pauses, she descended.

Elegant but impatient, Athénaïre came down faster, as if gliding on a rainbow. The eleven-year-old beat her sister to the courtyard. "The inside is fantastic, Maman."

Then she bowed, allowing her long sunny-yellow dress to spread out over the newly laid tiles of the courtyard. "Fitting for a president and his family."

Améthyste nodded. "It truly is magnificent. Père has outdone himself. It's ready to move in."

Watching their big, joyful eyes—Améthyste's indigo irises and Athénaïre's golden ones—made my heart happy. My lovely daughters had spent the first years of their lives in dirt, hiding in ravines and caves.

"Maman," Athénaïre said, grinning, "you think next week is too soon to leave Le Cap for this?"

Her smile, gleeful and daring with a big Cupid's bow lifted, was even more like her father's than our youngest, Victor's.

"You haven't said anything, Maman. You haven't ventured inside." Améthyste came to me at the edge of the courtyard.

"Maman?" Now Athénaïre's voice held concern.

Hiding my anger, I offered what truth I could. "I'm overwhelmed by what your père has done. Sans-Souci is too much."

"But our rooms are finished, Maman. Père has surprised us. There's bedding and furnishings." The way Améthyste sneezed, I suspected he'd imported feather beds.

He'd done all this for them, his beautiful girls who deserved the world.

My rebellion was losing.

How could I be mad at a man providing for his family, gifting treasures to these special young ladies? Again hoping that this was legal, not grift, I forced my mouth to stop frowning. "I suppose Victor's room is done as well."

"Looks like two boys' rooms are painted blue. Equally as fine, Maman."

One would be Victor's, the other for Henry's son Armande, born before we met. Armande was a good young man.

Sighing at the inevitable, Henry and his wishes winning, I said, "I suppose your père intends our moving in before the mortar dries."

Améthyste frowned. "He's working hard to make us feel at home here. Père once managed these lands. They mean a great deal to him." Her small tone became sharp, rightfully accusatory. "You know he has so much on his mind. All of Hayti is depending upon him."

She coughed, and I heard the rattle in her lungs, one she'd hidden from me this morning so I wouldn't leave her in Le Cap with her brother. The construction dust couldn't be good.

I rubbed her back to help soothe her. "Pretending, hiding, never acknowledging pain are traits too common among us."

"I don't want to miss a moment, Maman. I've missed too many already."

But what if her time was short and could shrivel to nothing from smoke or soot or silt, anything that smothers the lungs? "Améthyste, you shouldn't be here if you're feeling poorly."

"Missing life because of the limitations of my body or your fears is not living." Her mumble was as good as a slap. The rebuke was true. I coddled her because she was sickly. I coddled Victor because he was my only surviving son. I'd coddle Athénaïre if she'd let me.

That one was too quick.

I folded Améthyste into my arms, then reached for Athénaïre's neck, embracing my loves. "You girls have to tell me the truth. And I'll do better at letting my pretty parrots fly."

When I released them, Améthyste stayed close, but her sister wandered beyond the courtyard to the edge of the plateau.

Again, my eldest lifted her chin. "The truth is we want to move here as soon as possible. It's closer to Père's Citadel. We'll see him more often. I hate not seeing him."

The girls loved Henry.

Unlike my own father, my husband allowed his daughters to do as much as his sons. He didn't limit anyone's abilities. My père was afraid that Geneviève and I would become free-spirited like our half sister, my mère's first daughter. Cécile was sired by a Blanc massa's rape when my mother was enslaved in America.

My père was wrong. The fearless fervor entwined in Cécile's spirit was never bad.

"Once this place is finished and dusted from top to bottom, Améthyste, we shall all come to Sans-Souci. It's obvious that's what Henry wants."

My eldest shrieked with delight and danced about me. Her tan muslin gown, with silk ribbons at her bosom, floated. She turned faster and faster until she bent over heaving.

Instead of cautioning her to take care, I waited for her to settle. I let her enjoy her moment, but then her tawny complexion darkened. Not enough air went into her lungs.

Silently, I took her in my arms and held her against my chest. Her heart pounded beneath my ribs. The flesh at Améthyste's throat felt clammy. Then she stilled. Her small body found my heart and mirrored its rhythm.

"I'm better. I should be more mindful," she said. The admonishment in her low tone was enough. My voice needn't add further condemnation.

Nonetheless, I prayed thanks to Mother Mary for sparing my child again, for allowing her to breathe.

"Père thinks I can overcome this."

Miracles still happened. Wanting to hold her tighter, to never let go, I flung my arms away and allowed her to stand on her own. If lives could be made better by perseverance and willing obstacles into submission, Améthyste would be healed and our world would be saved.

Nonetheless, pretending hadn't made the bad flee.

Positive thoughts and affirmations hadn't banished weakness.

Prayer? The power of it? Maybe the saints heard the sorrows of a mother's cry and kept us from greater disasters.

Waving, Athénaïre motioned to join her at the edge of the plateau. "Look, there's a stream below and soapberry trees. Women will gather here and wash clothes. Maybe the military uniforms Père ordered will be cleaned down there."

The girls seemed privy to more of their father's plans than I.

Cupping her hand to her brow, Athénaïre stared into the sun. "We're up so high. You think if I shout, the workers at the Citadel will hear?"

"We shouldn't try. No need to interrupt the men. Your père—"

"Both sexes, Maman. Men and women are participating in the defense of this land. That's how our war for independence from France was won."

Améthyste's voice boomed. It echoed and probably could be heard at the top of Bonnet à l'Evêque, the mountain that housed the Citadel three thousand feet in the sky. From there, Henry's telescope could see here, Milot, to Le Cap, the bays, and probably Pétion's advance.

"The Citadel and this house will be grand," Athénaïre said. "Everyone will fear us."

Améthyste left me and stood next to her sister. Straight backs, holding hands—these were the proud daughters of Henry Christophe.

My rebellion reduced to a trickle, not enough force for steam.

Athénaïre tugged on my lacy sleeve, something imported from Philadelphia, I think. "Maman, isn't it peaceful up here? Can't you see us being up here forever?"

"Forever is a long time."

And sometimes, it wasn't long enough. It wouldn't be forever, my husband said. I believed him when he sent our firstborn, François-Ferdinand Christophe, to France for an "invaluable education."

It hadn't come to pass.

Not forever became infinity. France starved our son to punish Henry for rebelling against its tyranny.

It haunts me how my boy spent the last of his eleven years—hungry and weak, crying out for us. One misguided decision cost my son's life.

An echo reached my ear.

Out of habit, out of fear, I yanked the girls close, hiding them within my arms. Horses with riders in uniforms charged in our direction.

The workers dropped their tools and ran.

"Maman, what is it?"

I couldn't answer Athénaïre. I was too busy watching Henry and his advisers arrive. I needed strength to challenge my husband, to make him rethink whatever new dream he had in his head that could get us killed. I wasn't prepared to lose him or another child because Henry didn't understand how much hate there was in the world for our blood.

6

1811 Sans-Souci, Hayti

After sending the girls away with hugs and pats on the head, Henry dismissed the laborers and came toward me. His golden-brown eyes glanced at me as if he hadn't seen me in years.

Married almost eighteen years, four children, hundreds of war battles, and two violent revolutions between us, and it warmed my fretting heart that I still had his love.

But I wanted his respect more.

Having married him so young, I was convinced that if I didn't speak up now he'd still see me as a lovestruck girl. Not a proud partner or equal, just another medal for his chest.

"Louise, aren't you impressed with Sans-Souci?"

He knew me well enough to know I fancied architecture and art.

Still halfway to me, handsome Henry seemed larger than life in his military uniform of black knee breeches and heavy jet boots.

"Frowning, my love? Before you say anything, may I state how lovely you look in this sunshine. And are those rosebuds embroidered on your gown? You know how I love those."

The charmer, with a way with words. Oui, I knew he adored me, always praising and lifting me onto pedestals, but even an object of worship needed more than viewing. It must be polished and held with care. I wanted something more in our marriage than pretty words. I needed his thoughts and to be his confidante again, to be like we were when he was a mere waiter and I was a hotelier's daughter.

A few feet from me, Henry dipped his wide-brimmed hat, which bore the shape of a crescent moon. "Madame Christophe, Marie-Louise Christophe, you have my ear. Tell me your heart."

"How can we afford this, Henry? We have a fine house in Le Cap, Lambert. It has an orchard. It's enough."

"Louise, I decided to rush the construction here in Milot. Do you like the petite maison?"

Petite maison, as if this were some meager house. It was a castle, a sprawling palace. "It's very fine, Henry, but this must've cost a fortune, one we do not have. Why did you do this?"

"The builders weren't moving fast enough. I took some laborers from the Citadel and ordered the work to be done at Sans-Souci day and night. Half of the house is done. Enough for us to move in."

"And the imported furnishings the girls are talking about? We can't afford those, either."

"We can. I've done very well. The north of Hayti is prospering. Thus, I prosper."

"We aren't the people's taskmaster. This is our house. You're the president, not a Grand Blanc using the people. I don't want the citizens thinking you've robbed their inheritance."

His expression blanked. "You believe this? You think so little of me?"

"Never." I rushed to his side. "But there are whispers among the women gathering water and at the washing streams. I know you to be good. But the same forces that struck down the emperor will strike at you."

His face clouded. He hated gossip, hated the notion of others condemning him. "Despite what you heard, I'm not stealing from the people, Marie-Louise."

He used my full name when his temper rose, but he had to hear me. "Pétion is smearing you and your administration. He'll turn the people against your presidency. The man who killed the emperor will win the whole country."

"I'll make it known about the finances. I will codify into law how the treasury is split. My gourde system of exchange is working well. All are benefiting. I can afford taking on projects that benefit the nation."

"But a castle for us? Our home in Le Cap is warm and filled with life. This half-done thing must cost millions. What type of split—"

"The people pay a portion of their earnings from their farming in gourdes of sugar. This pays for the upkeep of the country and the military. Then I commission ships to send the sugar to America and Europe. I earn my share, because it's my merchants doing the trading. I ensure their protection and property. I'm entitled to my wages."

The thunder in his voice raced my pulse. He was innocent of the charges.

I put my hand to my bosom. My hearted pounded. I'd begun to convict him. All of this building was too fast. "Henry, I believe you, but your enemies will use Sans-Souci as a cudgel to strike at you. They're inciting the poor, those who won't understand trading and commissions."

"And wives, too. Those who should know better." He trudged away from me, his boots pounding the loose dirt.

I followed him to the edge of the plateau, right where the girls and I had been. "Henry, forgive me. And you . . . we've given to Hayti more than most. We don't need Sans-Souci now. Send the workers back to the Citadel. In another year—"

"Lambert's not enough for me. It will never be good enough for my queen."

Drawn to him, I stood at his back. "I'm glad you love me. I see you, Henry Christophe. I know your restless moments." If I mentioned his nightmares, the proud man would stop talking. I needed him to unburden himself. "Something's troubling you. Been troubling you many nights. Tell me what's happened."

He whipped around and held me close. "You would be out here walking the grounds rather than enjoying the wing of Sans-Souci I've finished. It's for you, our family. I know the sacrifices you've made. My being made a leader has cost so much."

His golden-brown eyes became distant. François-Ferdinand's name was on his tongue, as heavily as it was on mine.

My feet lifting from the ground, he turned us to face the stone palace. "Sans-Souci is about pleasure. I want you . . . here. In something I've fashioned. Not Lambert, a house that former slavers built."

Most of the fine estates were just that, previously owned by habitation owners, French massas, the Grand Blancs.

"Louise, I want nothing of theirs. They should rot in hell."

I stroked his strong back and made him set me down. "I feel the same, but I have patience. I can wait a year or two. That will give you more time to design this mansion to your exacting specifications."

"No more waiting. This will be made ready for my queen by week's end."

He leaned down, capturing me with his eyes. "Sans-Souci is for *my queen*."

This time, I realized his term of endearment was more a statement of fact. "Henry, tell me every detail."

Rearing back, he folded his arms. "The northern territory will become the Kingdom of Hayti. I will be its first sovereign. Sans-Souci is my palace. The only thing I need to know is if my wife will remain my wife and be crowned at my side."

His words, his threat, his command was a whisper, but it ripped at my soul.

"No, Henry. This will cost you your life. It may cost our children theirs."

He swatted his hat against his breeches. "This is our destiny."

I clutched his hand as if I could pull him back from a cliff, one he seemed determined to jump from. "Our eldest son, our firstborn, died because of risks like this. Jacques I was slaughtered. No. We can't do this."

"Marie-Louise, I need for you to listen."

"Non. You need to answer my questions. Is this why you don't sleep anymore? Why you walk the floors at night? The burden of deciding to be a king, a bigger target, is too much?"

Henry pulled away, then clapped for Souliman, who came running. "Get madame's dray ready. I'll show her the plan for the garden."

Eyes switching between us, Souliman nodded and slipped away.

When we were alone again, Henry took off his jacket and spread it under the shade of a tree. "Sit. It's been a long day."

"Is that a command, mon roi?"

"Non, ma reine." Blinking and smiling in the sunshine, he picked up a blade of grass. "It's a request from the king."

I sat beside him. "I'm waiting for you to tell me how you came to the decision."

He put his hands to my shoulders. "You're upset. This was not the way I wanted to tell you."

"Non? Wait another year, then say something? How about reasoning with me, Henry, like you used to when you valued my judgment. Am I the last to hear your plans?"

The Cupid's bow on those strong lips lifted. His smirk confirmed that I was; even Noël knew. "My frère hinted at this. When did I lose your trust?"

"You've lost nothing. You're the most noble of women. This place is for my patient dove, and it will have all the paths to walk everywhere your feet can tread in the safety of fences and guards."

"That's how we must live? We must fear the people you want to rule?"

"Enemies and friends look the same. Dessalines discovered this too late. Half the country is lost. France will use the division as our weakness."

"Our weakness comes from failing the people. And surely, I must have failed you for you to be so secretive."

"Don't the views here inspire you? Living here will be amazing."

"Exercise and being in nature comfort me, Henry. You've always known that. But I don't walk all the time. While you have clandestine activities and occupy yourself with secret decisions, I've kept busy making sure the children are doing their lessons and trying not to fear that their father will never come home."

"You're mad, becoming hysterical, and you wonder why I've not shared my thoughts."

How dare he!

I bounced up before I said something I'd regret. "I should get Améthyste and Athénaïre and return to Lambert. They've loved exploring your latest extravagances."

"And what of Victor, does he not love it? Is he here?"

"He's still studying, working with the tutor in Le Cap."

"You have our hardheaded son studying? Must've been a taxing day." The grimace overtaking Henry's face stung my chest. I wished he and Victor could see how similar they were. Their headstrong natures were the cause of the animosity between them.

"The boy can be a handful," he said.

"Store up your patience. I promised Victor that if he improves, you'd take him riding."

"A bribe to get our son to do what he must? That boy must take things more seriously." Henry's lips flattened, radiating scorn. "How will the prince lead someday if he's lazy?"

"Victor is not lazy, he's just young. I'm surprised that Armande is not your successor. You dote on him well enough, more than our only living boy."

Henry stood. "Armande is very capable, but only a legitimate son born of my queen can rule." He claimed my hand and held it to his soft lips. "Only a son of our marriage can be my successor. I'm proud of the man Victor will become. Prince Victor is my legacy."

To hear him say this about our baby would make any mother's heart swell, but the heir was to have been François-Ferdinand, our first. He would've been old enough to handle the pressure of Henry's demands. "Give this one time to grow up. He'll be rooted in the same ambition that makes you take risks. But Jacques-Victor Henry Christophe may not want a career in the military or politics. He may have a mind for business like his grandpère."

"I'll make him ready to lead. I wish he was more like Athénaïre. She's smart and brave."

"She might help him. Women were instrumental in Hayti's victory. Cécile started the fervor for war in the fields of Bois Caïman. She rallied the people with Dutty Boukman. If not for her, for that team, this country might still be divided between enslaved and free."

Tentatively, with the lightest touch, I eased a palm atop his shoulder. "Both our girls have taken to books. But our son hasn't found his calling. Maybe he needs ambitious advisers like your Dupuy and Dr. Stewart to tell him what to think."

Henry stiffened. "I'm led by no one. I have advisers for what's necessary, papers and such. I'm no one's fool."

He was embarrassed that he could read very little French and could write only a few words. None of that mattered when he commanded armies and the respect of the people. Henry was brave and talented.

I took his bicorne and dusted the dirt that matted in the felt at the brim. "It's not terrible, Henry, to depend upon others—secretaries and statesmen, and your sanctimonious wife. That's what Dupuy says about me."

"He talks too loudly." Before reclaiming his hat, he kicked a rock, shooting it into the section of uncut timbers. "I'm fortunate to have people I trust. A lazy son won't be as lucky. He'll be exploited if he doesn't ground himself in knowledge. Victor must see this."

"And you, Henry, need to recognize hero worship for what it is, the desire of a son to find approval from his father in all the ways that matter. Don't be hard on him. And don't push him to dreams that aren't his."

Neither agreeing or disagreeing, he took my arm in his and strolled with me away from my approaching dray toward the forest.

It was odd to call for something, then change his mind. Perhaps I could make him shift course. Hayti didn't need a king.

We walked together in silence until we left the cut grasses of the lawn and were knee deep in the brush.

"Here, Marie-Louise, we'll plant more pepper trees. I believe I proposed to you under—"

"Henry Christophe, I recall it to be a pepper cinnamon tree, and you always call me Marie-Louise when there's bad news."

"Not always bad."

"Always bad, and something happens that harms us. To go to war for years. To burn Le Cap to the ground so the expeditionary forces have nothing. You followed Toussaint's command and set fire to our house by the sea."

"It was Dessalines's order on behalf of Toussaint. But none of this matters. I lead by example. My son will learn by my sacrifice. And now, I must be king."

"Pétion will say it was your intention all along. He'll gain by blam-

ing you for what he did to Dessalines. Then he will plot your assassination, too."

"The swine of the south are already plotting my demise." Henry
ground his teeth. "He and all of his brown followers, all the murderers
of our late emperor, can come at me, and I'll cut them to pieces."

Pulling away from the growling anger of his words, I sighed.
"You're the strongman I married. My Henry also loves peace and
has patience."

"I was only patient in winning you. My heart had no other choice."
He reclaimed my fingers. His gaze seemed to peer through me as if I
were one of the glass windows he'd installed. "To think that our mulatto brothers are behind so much treachery makes my blood boil. I'm
not Dessalines. I'll see it coming. They'll never surprise me."

Planting myself in front of him, like a proud pepper cinnamon tree,
I put my hands to his chest. "I don't want to talk of your enemies. I
want to know why you? Why must you be king? Haven't you given
enough?"

"Because a king will rally the world against France."

Backing away as if he were on fire, I cupped my hands to my face
and tried to stretch my vision to see the impossible, French ships flooding our sea. "When do they come, Henry? Is the Citadel ready to fire
upon them? And what general will they send now that Napoleon is
gone?"

"What?"

"The French, Henry. Who will they send to try to defeat our forces?
You've always said they would return. When do they land? When's the
attack?"

He took me in his embrace as if to comfort me. His arms were everything. Too brave. Too bold. Too consuming. Too perfect for me and
my wilting resistance.

"Lovely little Louise, the French for now stay away. Pétion is too
busy running his country's treasury into the ground. While he tries to
destroy the late emperor's legacy, I build."

"Why make this a kingdom, not a republic, like France after their
revolution?"

"Their government fell to Napoleon. He may rise again. Hayti can't afford more instability. We must lead and command the world's attention. We are going to be crowned the king and queen of Hayti. Le roi and la reine."

"But we had an emperor—"

"Dessalines didn't understand the ambitions of those around him. He believed the lies. My eyes are wide open. I undertake this to reestablish a royal legacy. We need a history to rival Europe. The Blancs only understand titles and power."

"And wealth? That's why you need large commissions."

He put his hat to his head, pushing it forward as if it was a crown. "A king can't be a pauper. No one wants to befriend the poor."

"The presidency is a good form of governing, like the Americans. It will put no demands on Victor."

"Well, Adams's son is already eyeing the position. He's steadily climbing in politics. I'm sure his whole family knows the pressures of leading."

"Then you can remain as president. You can slowly introduce Victor to politics."

"The world doesn't recognize me as the leader of Hayti. The office of president is meaningless. Black and Brown war while the Blancs refuse to choose a side. They won't formally recognize either Pétion or Hayti as a nation."

"And you think these people will suddenly give you honor and choose you because of a noble title? With the Dahomet blood infused in the colony, we all have royal beginnings. We don't need to follow a path that will get you killed."

"Marie-Louise, I think I know best. I've made a decision. I'll be crowned and gain credibility in the eyes of the world."

"Look at my eyes. Don't you see there's credibility and acceptance and love? You shouldn't care what the world thinks."

He put his hand to my cheek. "You'll never understand. That's why you don't need to fret over these things. I've decided. We will be crowned. Sans-Souci will be our palace."

His hand fell to his side, tugging the dark-blue jacket that wrapped about him. "I need you to honor this decision. You're either for me or against me."

"I love you, Henry, but why must you look at everything as a battle? And why can't you see the dangers this path will bring to us, to our children?""

"Louise." He knelt as he had in my father's lobby. After taking away my serving tray, he had proposed. Now, his lips pursed with the same tension. "Will you be my queen? I need you."

"In sickness and health, I'll support you, Henry, even when I think you're wrong."

"Père!" The girls stood at the top of the stone stairs again, which overlooked this lawn and the future gardens and the safety that Henry promised. "Père, come up and see everything. And guess which rooms me and Améthyste chose."

Athénaïre laughed so hard, her voice bellowing with joy, I didn't know what to say.

Then the only words that Henry would hear rose in my throat. "Go on to your princesses. Show them more of the palace you've built."

With his devastating smile, he stood. "You'll see. This is the best course of action."

Henry proceeded to his girls in the courtyard.

I remained near the planned garden trying to absorb my fear and anger over this decision. We would be crowned. The northern district of Hayti would become a kingdom. As Henry welcomed his reign, I'd again be the one left to figure out how to keep the family whole and safe and sane.

THE KINGDOMS

Britain

Salisbury and Winchester Journal, Monday, June 3, 1811

Yesterday the Prince Regent held a Levee at Carleton House, which was so numerously attended as to exceed even the first Levee after his appointment. The Earl of Shrewsbury and the Earl of Fingal presented the Address of the Roman Catholics of Ireland to the Prince Regent, on his entering on the Regency.

Hayti

General Evening Post, Thursday, June 13, 1811

Christophe assembled a Council of State in March last, by which he was declared King of Hayti, and the Sovereignty made hereditary in his family. He imitates Bonaparte very closely in the creation of Nobility; but he has not yet ventured to dismiss his old black wife, in order to get a young Arch-Duchess.

7

1811 Palace of Sans-Souci, Milot, Hayti

In the bedchamber of the king in the palace of Sans-Souci, Geneviève helped me sort my gowns to find the right one for a coronation. Which would be the best to make me appear pleased and in agreement with this wrong action?

I'd been silent. To speak out would bring dishonor. That would hurt Henry, but how could I celebrate this?

"What about this one?" My sister lifted another one. "The white gown will go well with the red velvet mantle."

Velvet in the middle of hot tropical weather. How appropriate and European. I put another false smile to my lips but shook my head.

Sitting at a silver-inlaid vanity sculpted of fine mahogany wood, I looked about the room. This grand bedchamber was as large as it was ornate. Imported lamps from Italy sat on fine bedside tables. A mattress of horsehair and wool and linen bedding from Hamburg had arrived last week.

Then there were the jewels from London.

I had stopped asking how much Henry and his generals earned ruling the north. Now it was quite obvious. Each shipment of sugarcane, and now coffee, meant thousands of gourdes for Henry and his nobles.

His secretary, Julien Prévost, became the new Count of Limonade. His stalwart general Paul Romain donned the title Prince du Limbé. Noël Joachim was the Duc de Fort-Royal, and Jean-Philippe Daux, the new Duke de l'Artibonite. There were more, many with multiple titles, all bowing with gratitude to Henry . . . bowing to the money.

What of the people without military rank, the ones not sporting fancy titles of duke, count, or baron? Though a king might be able to keep them safe, how did that put food on their table?

Geneviève held up another gown. "You've rejected them all. Let's start again. The gold one? The embroidery is lovely." She laid that one down, then lifted another. "The silver, Louise?"

"Perhaps the king should come and pick it. He's made all the decisions thus far. Do you know he's named my court? All the wives of the military officials. I know some of them, but—"

"But they are not me or Cécile." Geneviève's smile slipped. Though Henry had elevated our brother, Noël, to be a prince and given him the title Duke du Port-de-Paix, he did nothing for my sisters.

"Sorry." It was all I could say. If Henry and I had sorted things out, I might've been able to advocate at least for Geneviève. I knew Cécile wanted no part of this.

"It's not your fault entirely, Louise. He must think I'm too young and Cécile, too Cécile. Roman Catholicism is the official religion of the kingdom. He's left no room for Vodou or African Vodun."

My face dropped to the vanity's surface; the cold lacquer felt good. Perhaps it'd soften the lines that a good cry could bring. "No one is happy with me. The girls are elated, but they think I'm being mean to their père or stopping their fun. No one sees the dangers."

Stooping beside me, Geneviève offered a sly smile. "Perhaps you do not see the opportunity."

"What are you talking about?"

"The queen has a role to play in the kingdom. You get to design it to please you."

"No, I get to design it how Henry sees it."

She lifted the necklace Henry had left for me on his empty pillow. "This looks like a good design."

It was a long gold chain on which hung the perfect emerald.

"He's been doing this the past week, leaving gifts. Silver pins, pearls, brooches."

With one hand on her hip, Geneviève swung the necklace. "This is obviously his way of saying sorry. What do you expect a king to do?

He's a proud man. He has everyone expecting a coronation. It's too late to change his mind."

My fist pounded the vanity. The echo deafened. I sat up and rubbed my ringing pinkie. "I know."

"He can't be seen as weak. As much as he loves you, he'll not call this off and say he made a mistake because his wife said so."

She again knelt in front of me. "Are you mad at the decision or that he came to it without consulting you?"

I went to the window and looked out to the terrace and the big copper tub where we bathed. Beyond this were my gardens, and those darn pepper cinnamon trees.

Geneviève looped the necklace about my throat. The chain felt cold and slippery against my skin. "Louise, you need to end this argument you're having with the king. It's not gone unnoticed. There are plenty of other women who'd wish to be his queen."

"As long as you have no designs, I think my marriage is safe."

"Of course not, silly. And this isn't about me." Her words came out fast and sounded a little guilty. "There's talk, Louise. Your defiance weakens him. And everyone knows it."

To hurt Henry wasn't what I wanted. "I guess setting up a European court means we get all of their intrigue, too. Rich people earn extravagant gossip." I pressed my brow against hers. "Thank you."

"Today's a big day." Geneviève kissed my cheek, then moved backward as if to bow before flopping onto my mattress. She pushed lace and silk and muslin out of the way. "This might not have been your plan, but this is the path that God and Hayti have set you upon. Accept His will."

I supposed that was better than thinking Henry was power hungry.

"This is very fine, sister," Geneviève rubbed her hand along the soft bedding. "Something the king imported from Hamburg?"

With a nod, I conceded that it was another of his expensive gifts and the most comfortable thing I'd ever slept upon. I'd tell Henry this, if he'd come to me. He slept in another chamber and kept his distance except for these offerings he had servants bring. The ceremony might be the first time since he told me of his plans that we spent more than ten minutes together.

Geneviève bounced up again. "You must wear the white with the gold threads, to go with the necklace. It's exquisite."

She waddled to me in her full-length court dress, kicking out the train of raw silk she'd wrinkled.

The joy in her face transcended time. We were little, in our rooms at our father's inn, the Hôtel de la Couronne, playing dress up in my mother's trunk.

Fanciful, fluffy, full of ruffles—this was the garb Célestine Coidavid had worn upon being freed in Saint-Domingue.

In America, Célestine's massa forced her to *entertain* a prince who'd come to help fight in the Revolutionary War. "Geneviève, you know our sister may be the only one of true royal blood."

"Ha! Yes, a Corsican prince raped Maman. No one knows who the fiend truly was. Maman might have spun tales to gloss over the abuses she suffered as chattel. Don't bring up the Vodou priestess. Henry tolerates Cécile Fatiman for you."

"The king's going to elevate her husband and make him a count, the Comte de Valière . . ."

General Louis Michel Pierrot, Cécile's husband, was also a mambo like my sister, but he'd publicly cast off Vodou. Outwardly, he was now a good Catholic and faithful ally to Henry.

It took at least a minute before Geneviève spoke. Then she said, "So Cécile wins again. She's going to be a countess, even though she wants none of this."

"Sœur—"

Geneviève winced. "It's not Henry's mind you're hoping to sway. It's hers. Are you waiting for her to show? Do you need her approval for this coronation?"

Shouldn't I desire having my older sister's blessing on something this important? And if Cécile could see good in this, there had to be a lot of good. She was a hard judge of things but also fair minded.

"Cécile keeps in tune to the will of the people—the ones working at the Citadel and the fields, those toiling in the cities and beyond. She would tell me what everyone truly thought of the kingdom and how to use my position to do good."

Geneviève's mouth shriveled to a dot, as if she were sucking on a lemon.

Then I decided to admit the rest. "I still want her approval. Why break old habits now?"

My younger sister offered a tight smile. "She'll be here, Louise. Or shall I call you, for a final time, Madame President, wife of the president and generalissimo of the country? Soon to be Queen Christophe."

I hadn't the heart to correct her on what my title would be. The new Lord Limonade had gone over and over the exact titles of me and the children. If European monarchs were to come to our shores, I'd be ready, along with Madame Première, who was Princess Améthyste, Princess Athénaïre, and the prince royal, Prince Victor.

"What does it feel like, Louise, to be moments away from being crowned a queen?" Her tone was jovial, with a pinch of our youthful competitiveness. I knew she wanted what I had—a husband and children and now the power she believed came with my title.

"I know this all seems fantastic, to go from dutiful daughter to soldier's wife, to general's wife, to queen, but remember I sheltered in caves as my husband tried to help wrest our land from France. It's not been easy. It's been very hard."

"Père and I fled the blockades, migrating to different parts of Hayti until the battles ended. That was hard, too. Everyone was in motion. You're just the luckiest. Your gambit has paid off. These are the things dreams are made of."

"Or nightmares. When Toussaint led, he and his family became targets. The French killed him. They tortured his wife and children."

"He trusted the French. Christophe doesn't."

Not anymore, not since they let François-Ferdinand die. "Like Pétion's ilk going after Dessalines's sons, they'll hunt Victor and Armande—"

"Nothing's going to happen. Christophe is smart. Everyone fears him. He doesn't show weakness or deference to anyone but you, sœur."

I went out onto the terrace, where the aroma of the lemon and guava trees blended with the sweetness of the English tea roses. Henry had made it all happen, my wishes to go slow be damned. High on our mountain, he believed we could see forever, but the clouds in the sky showed me I couldn't. "There's something telling about the weather. It's gloomy. An omen, perhaps?"

"It won't rain today. But where's your hopefulness. What is it, Louise? You're always sunny."

"I saw the empress last week in Le Cap."

"You mean the former empress, Madame Dessalines." Geneviève tugged me back to the vanity. Tearing off my pink robe, she brought the white gown and pulled it over my chemise. "How was she? What did she say?"

"She's well but refused to come live with us. Hayti's chief widow would rather live in poverty than be here in comfort and safety."

"There's safety living with the people." My half sister, Cécile Fatiman Pierrot, stood in the doorway. She wasn't dressed in a fine gown but in the everyday clothes of commoners: a madras skirt and white tunic. Did that mean she wasn't coming to the coronation ceremony, even though her husband had to take part?

"I suppose I don't have to ask if you approve."

"My opinion doesn't matter much. But the people's should," she continued. "They love Madame Dessalines. They'll protect her and her young children." Her tone was ominous.

"You always have something to hate," Geneviève said. Her tone was tart, not even hiding her animosity to our sister.

Cécile, some claimed, was the prettiest of Célestine Coidavid's girls, but she defied any claim to European beauty. She didn't give a whit about her golden skin and green eyes, the features that made many mulatto women believe they were better than others. Not our eldest sister. Cécile, hero of the revolution, believed in equality. The people revered her for her actions, not her face. She didn't have a vain bone in her body.

And my sister, my hero, stood before me judging me.

My breath stabbed. My chest ached. I was before her in jewels and fine silk that she probably assumed came from the people's backs. "Condemn me, Cécile."

"I have no condemnation for you. Just know, the people rallied around Madame Dessalines, but they may not do that for you. Strongmen fall. Being the king's bride doesn't offer lasting protection. Many don't like Christophe, Louise. There have been rumors that he, too, was behind Jean-Jacques Dessalines's assassination, that he schemed to take the throne for himself all along."

"Not true." I shook my head hard, forcing the beginning of a headache. "He respected the emperor. He had complaints about his administration, but he'd never be party to that murder. That was Pétion and his butchers in the south."

Geneviève pushed the soft royal mantle over my shoulders. The bloodred velvet was edged in gold ribbon, with rubies sewn at the collar. "Our *old* sister is being difficult and tragic. She's missing all the fun. It's her fault I'm not elevated like our brother."

I held my breath.

Yet there was no cannon blast from Cécile, no grapeshot sprayed on the butter-yellow walls of the room. Instead, she moved closer; her bare feet slapping the shiny wood floor. "What have you done but cling to Louise's robes, Geneviève?"

"I support her and the king; you don't. And you come here dressed like an urchin when you're the wife of a count."

"I don't like showy, Geneviève. Never did. And you make poverty sound dangerous. It's not. It's honest. The elegance you crave hides lies."

I glared at Geneviève, hoping she'd quiet. Each of us had led very different lives. We had all triumphed merely by surviving the wars.

Cécile folded her arms. "Crowning men leads to spite and hate. Kings crave jewels and spectacle more than honesty. Louise, can you stop Christophe? Turn him from this course before he loses more of the people's favor?"

"Which people?" Geneviève rolled her neck and shook a finger at our sister. "Mulattoes like you who think they are more righteous than the rest? Or the good salt of the earth, the Blacks building the Citadel, rallying to show the world we'll not be conquered again?"

One. Two. Three.

Hovering like a cloud, Cécile drew near with her arms outstretched.

Any moment, she'd slap Geneviève with the force of a thunderbolt. "While you were cowering under your bed sucking your thumb, Brown and Black joined together to fight the enemy. The late emperor wouldn't want people working to death building castles that only the Blancs admire. Jacques I didn't live for Blanc admiration, and he didn't want Hayti split into two countries, either."

I raised my hands and my voice. "It's my husband's coronation. Mine, too. Like my vows said before God, I'll be at his side. Stop this fighting. Maman wouldn't want us like this. We're sisters."

Rubbing the acacia-beaded necklace our mother had given Cécile before she left home, my sister moved to the window. "Don't forget the people, Louise. Freedom means they are free to dissent." Standing in front of the glass with sun rays falling at her shoulders, Cécile shook her head. "I know this is not your doing. A good Catholic wife will always honor her husband. I understand."

"I must support my husband. He says this is for the people, for every Haytian who loves freedom and respects humble beginnings. Henry says all will benefit under his rule. I must believe him."

Cécile moved forward and clasped the emerald draped at my throat. "Hard to stay humble with gold flowing about your neck."

After a kiss to each cheek, Cécile went to the door. "You're a good wife, Louise, but you're your own woman. Let the people see the sister I love. Temper the excesses, and be a good queen to them. I wish you and the kingdom well."

I took a step, but the mantle tangled in the vanity's chair and stopped me. "You'll not join us today? The festivities—"

"From a distance, not participating and condoning . . . I've seen all that I wish. You look beautiful, Louise. Maman would be proud. You're loyal to Christophe, but remember those who fought for freedom didn't do it for approval of the kingdoms across the sea. They'll not serve another master."

Cécile never minced words.

I kicked at the chair to free the mantle, but she'd left.

Geneviève smoothed my train, then stood at my side, pointing me to the mirror. "Don't be bothered, my queen."

Our joined reflections looked out of the glass. She looked happy, happier than me. "Thank you for your unwavering support."

"I'm so proud of you and Christophe." She bit her lip and I realized she had something else on her mind.

My brow furrowed of its own volition. I needed her to confess. Left to simmer, Geneviève would boil over into trouble. I held her hands. "Say it."

"I want a title. I want to be nobility. The king has even elevated our brother. Why not me? I'm punished for being unwed, with no husband of my own."

I put my hands to her face. "Our Coidavid family has been advanced enough. You are twenty-three. There's still time. Let's build Hayti and prove the kingdom right before we ask for more."

"That's easy for you to say. You always get whatever you want, even the riches you don't."

"Geneviève, the kingdom needs to last more than a year. Cécile's not wrong about the opposition to Henry. If we fail, possessing a title could be the same as a death sentence."

My sister embraced me. The pounding in her chest conveyed both love and fury. I doubted she fully understood. But she helped settle my mind. I knew what I needed to do: prove myself as queen. Then I could ask for more.

Pulling back, I put on my best smile. "Go see how the girls are progressing."

She offered a small bow. "Oui, ma reine." Still frowning, Geneviève slipped out the door.

I needed to talk to Henry. On the day of his biggest triumph, we were at odds. Why did it seem his coronation was torturing him as much as me?

The knock at the door, solid and heavy, told me I'd soon hear directly from the king.

8

1811 Palace of Sans-Souci, Milot, Hayti

Still wearing the warm velvet mantle about my shoulders, I steadied myself against the bedpost. "Come in, Your Majesty."

With a red box in his hand, Henry opened the heavy door carved of fine mahogany from our forests, not imported from Europe like so many of the palace's furnishings. He wore a blue sash with a star across his white waistcoat and jacket. I was sure I'd seen something similar in newsprint or magazine plates from England of their now mad king.

My husband stopped as he crossed the threshold. I felt his glance, inspecting me from the bit of ankle exposed by the lace hem of my gown to my high chignon of braids, then he settled on my throat, where the emerald sparkled.

Heated from his stare as much as these robes, I pulled the ribbon in my braid. "I can put my hair down if you like. I won't try to straighten my curls, as Lord Limonade wanted. He—"

"No. Don't move," Henry said. "Let me look at you another moment." He lifted the box. "This crown will look beautiful on you."

His gaze made my pulse pound. "Henry, you've seen me before. Does hot velvet make a difference?"

"You don't know how lovely you are, Louise. That was one of the first things I noticed. So unassuming and composed."

"I'm hardly composed. This is a big thing we're doing."

He'd seen me a thousand times but still had a way to make it feel as if he'd just happened upon me for the first time. "Look at you. The woman I love. The woman who will be queen."

Time and children and war had tested my figure. I was self-conscious. My hands fidgeted on the mantle's ribbons. "Henry, where were you last night? You've stayed away from our bed."

He cast his robes to the mattress but held on to the box. "I couldn't sleep. I know you don't approve of this."

"I've been mad at you before. You didn't have to go. Convince me of this."

Turning the box in his hands, Henry came to me. "The kingdoms of this world will see Hayti rise. They will acknowledge us—our court, our art, our bravery, our advancements. From the ravages of the cane fields and battlefields, they'll see a people with power, noble and desiring the same things that they want. Then they'll let us be at peace. As the nations did during the revolution, they will come to our defense against France."

Stilling the gift, clasping the big red bow, I nodded. "I hear your heart, Henry, but this is a lot of change. It requires us to place a great deal of faith in others beyond our shores."

"I have faith in you, Louise. I can do anything if you believe. You have all of me. Always have, but some days it feels as if I'm not enough."

"You're the tallest. The strongest . . ."

"The weakest when I think you disapprove."

"Henry."

"I'll not lie. I've lusted for power. I bear the dreams of an unconquerable people. I think Hayti can be that. But I'm nothing without your support."

"You know I'll support you, even when I think you're wrong. You listen to your men, but when do you listen to me? Can you even hear my voice when I disagree?"

He put the box on the near table, looking down at me over his high-bridged nose. "I hear you, but sometimes the other voices are louder. Hayti and the past—they're always calling." His hands draped around my neck. His fingers traced curls loosed from my chignon. "Tell me that this is what you want."

"If I didn't want us to be crowned, would you stop this?"

"No. I'd work harder to make you understand."

I stepped away and returned to the window. "At least you're honest."

"You know the good we can do. You've pushed our children to read, to have an education. What if you advocate for all children, but as their queen? What if all the kingdom's sons and daughters knew English and French, not just Kreyòl?"

Henry rarely spoke anything but the most regal French. Kreyòl unified all the people, but the newspapers and books in Hayti, anything from the outside world, came in the old languages.

His fingers glided upon my tense shoulders, and I rested against his wide chest as he spoke. "How can you do this? How can I love you so much that I forget myself?"

"Henry."

"I live in agony of disappointing you. I fear for my children, for all Hayti's children, if I cannot get the world to recognize us as a sovereign nation."

His thumbs pressed my temples, massaging away the pain. "Louise, I need your support. I need you."

He spun me to him and his lips fell upon mine.

My world of doubts stilled. It was me and Henry against the stars, the skies, all the heavenly firmament.

But this was love and passion, not respect.

I grasped his shoulders to steady myself. It took everything to step away. "If this is our course, Henry, I must define my role as queen. Do I get to use my imagination and strength to create something meaningful?"

For the first time since entering our chambers, his gaze turned away. Had he not thought I might have ideas or an opinion on our reign?

"What are you asking, Louise?"

"You loved me when I was young, just fourteen. My father kept us apart until I turned fifteen. I'm not that girl anymore. I have ideas. I want to help you shape this nation."

"Marie-Louise, I should ask Dupuy. Lately, his opinion—"

"Listen." Now I put my hands on him, reaching up to smooth his round cheeks. "My role as queen must matter. It must be something of substance."

"You'll do that, Louise. I'm confident that with my advisers—"

"You're the king. Don't they listen to you? Henry, I'm not asking for the impossible. I'm asking for a say in my role as queen. I'll implement plans to bring honor to you and this country."

He snatched me up, his hands working the buttons and sleeves of my gown, kissing me, wishing for me to submit.

Resolute, I moved away. "The ceremony. It'll begin soon."

With a nod, he rubbed at his face. "Sorry. But you have the power to reduce me to nothing but desire."

"I want you, Henry, but I want your trust more. Trust me to define the duties of the queen. I want to design a role for future queens."

He seemed confused by my words, but I refused to relent or release him to Dupuy and Stewart or his generals-turned-nobles who'd find fault in a woman having opinions. "Henry, make your first act as sovereign to free me to support your legacy, to raise up women and men who can best anyone in their intellect and knowledge of the world."

A timid knock to my door. "King Henry, Madame Christophe. It's time."

That was Limonade, another man who encouraged the inequity of women's status. He only cared about adhering to European etiquette.

"A moment, my lord," I answered. With my palms to my husband's sides, I stood before him. "I need an answer from the king."

Without saying a word, he retreated and retrieved the box. Slow, careful fingers undid the bow. He lifted the lid and removed a jeweled crown, encrusted with emeralds, like something from a fairy tale.

This beautiful thing had been purchased by steep commissions. How many books could they have bought for teachers? Or soup for those who still hungered?

"I had this made especially for you. Emeralds make your dark eyes sparkle." He set it on my head and then hooked diamond-and-emerald drop earrings to my lobes. They jingled as I peered at the mirror.

From his pocket came a gold bracelet. It was big on my wrist, and the heavy emerald made it turn and point to the floor. I rolled it back, smoothing my finger along its fine engraving. "It's too much, Henry. I understand how you make money, but I don't think the people will."

"The people will see we are as fine as any British or French royal family. Their queens possess gems. Their children, too. I had tiaras made for the girls and a crown for Victor. We all will remember this day. The Christophe family will be revered like the house of Tudor, Stuart, Romanov, or Bourbon."

He went behind me. Caressing me by the shoulders, Henry positioned us in the mirror. As if we'd been painted in a gilded frame, the glass made us look regal. "Queen Marie-Louise is ready to be crowned."

"I suppose Cécile is right."

"What is the mulatto mamba right about? What?" The anger in his tone concerning my sister or what she represented—Colored and not Catholic—wasn't hidden. "Tell me."

"That this is about excess and the Christophes more than it is about the concerns of the people."

"Louise."

"I'm an ornament. Perhaps you should elevate all the Coidavid women, so we can all shine for you and the kingdom."

"Cécile Fatiman has been elevated enough being married to a count. Louis Michel Pierrot is one of my trusted allies, even if his judgment sometimes is lax."

"Then what's Geneviève's crime? You've not elevated her, and she's devoted to me."

The Cupid's bow of his lips deflated. "The king doesn't want to."

"Suppose that's my answer."

He picked up his velvet mantle and spread it over his big shoulders. "No more dawdling. Ready, my dear?"

I was ready, ready to do something more than be a faithful wife. Henry had forced me upon the world stage. We should both get what we wanted.

9

1811 Palace of Sans-Souci, Milot, Hayti

In silence we walked down the steps at the front of the house, and Henry led me to a large carriage accented with gold leaf. It was stunning.

"You like it, Louise? I had it designed for you."

It shimmered in the sunlight. "I saw fancy carriages at my father's hotel, but I've never seen anything like this. Your commissions must be thousands."

Chuckling, Henry's lips parted. "With the lust for Haytian cane and coffee increasing, I'm destined to be one of the richest kings in the world."

He laughed, but I grew more fretful. What would stop one of his newly made princes from wanting the wealth of a newly created king?

A man wearing a blue uniform with a scarlet hat came toward us and ushered us to the carriage door. "May I help you, my lady?"

"No." Henry waved the fellow away, then put his big hands about my waist and lifted me inside. He took care to make sure the velvet mantle laid about my feet. Then Henry joined me inside.

He rapped on the roof. The monstrous carriage drawn by eight gray horses began moving down Sans-Souci's hill toward Le Cap.

Soldiers marched alongside. Their uniforms looked new, as did their long guns.

Dupuy and Limonade, on horses, trotted ahead. I saw their grins. They'd masterminded this day as much as my husband had.

Sitting across from me, Henry stared at me and then out the window at Sans-Souci.

"You've not made Améthyste walk, have you?" I said. "I don't want to risk her health."

"Our daughters are in a second carriage. Victor in a third. We're all being crowned today."

I glanced at the crowds walking along. "It's too far for everyone to go to Le Cap."

"It . . ." Henry's gaze turned to the side. I spied his other son, now called Prince Armande-Eugène. He favored our boy who died in France.

I wished for the one who was not there, François-Ferdinand, our lost son. I longed for Henry to look at our Victor with the same love. Clasping fingers to his, I whispered. "Let's start anew. Completely new. And let Victor show you he can make you proud."

The softness in Henry's eyes faded. "He will be heir to all I . . . all we do. Louise, he has to be more."

"He's seven. He needs guidance. He can do better."

"He must do better." Henry wrenched at the ties around his neck, knocking the scarlet mantle from one shoulder. I leaned into him, fixing it. "What we build will make everything different for the kingdom."

The carriage turned from the cobble road to a field where a brilliant white tent the size of Place d'Armes had been erected.

The carriage stopped.

The world slowed as Henry waited for the door to open. He leapt out, then stuck his hand back inside. "Now, my queen. It is time."

I hesitated. This was my last opportunity to gain a yes without conditions. "Do I have the king's permission to design my role as queen?"

Dupuy waved at us to come, but I didn't budge.

"Henry?"

"You're embarrassing me."

"No. I'm being difficult. There's a difference. Tell them the heat with this velvet robe has made me succumb. I've swooned. Send your doctor and anyone else whose permission the king needs to act."

"Fine. You win. You can define your duties, but don't embarrass—"

"Non, Your Majesty. Never." I descended, holding tight to the arm he extended. We walked to the tent.

Henry's face was blank. Then his gaze was on me, and I beamed at him, offering a bright smile.

For a moment, he sent a small one back, then he turned forward.

Under the canopy sat an ornate throne. This one was bigger and more finely polished than the one used for Dessalines's coronation as emperor.

Our nobles, the counts and dukes and barons of the land, surrounded us dressed in finery—silks and braiding, tailored sleeves with epaulettes.

The princesses and other titled women looked like the fashion plates in English newspapers, with fine long gowns of silk that banded under the bosom and dropped to the ankles. The dresses hovered over delicate slippers, not bare feet.

My husband took my jeweled crown and placed it on a pillow for Comte de Limonade to carry. With Henry keeping his upon his head, I realized this ceremony I'd threatened not to come to was for me, to offer his queen and the children a memory of the day we came to lead Hayti.

Victor descended his carriage dressed like Henry in a smooth blue jacket, but with white breeches. My prayer was for our son to be given the time to come into his own and redeem himself in his father's eyes.

The archbishop, Jean-Baptiste-Joseph Brelle, stood before us to the right of the throne. Dressed in a perfectly cinched alb, he held a Bible in his hands.

Perspiration danced along my brow, but the priest appeared unbothered, not the least bit damp in his robes. He spoke to Henry in fine Latin, telling him to come forward and kneel.

My husband took a few steps forward, then waited. He wanted me at his side.

In a blink, time slowed. I caught the gazes of those I most loved—Améthyste and Athénaïre, Victor, then my younger sister. Geneviève was in the front of the crowd. She'd changed into a beautiful pink gown with printed green palms along the hem, no train.

Off in the distance, Cécile stood on the hill. With her hand toward her neck, I imagined she clutched Maman's necklace, the one she kept when she'd left home, the one she said was the luck of the Coidavids. Long life and luck.

I felt Cécile whispering that now.

My brother grinned, looking good in garnet red. My daughters were in a gauzy white material. Their shiny tiaras made them angels.

Henry's palm glided over mine, rolling the bracelet he'd slipped on my arm. With the jewel upright, pointed to the sun, glowing, he led me forward. "It's time, Marie-Louise. People are waiting."

Music—French horns and a harp—played a triumphant march.

"Hail! Hail! Hail!" the crowd around us cheered.

My attention returned to my husband's gaze burning upon me.

We sank to our knees and recited the archbishop's vow to protect the Kingdom of Hayti.

In my head, I beseeched the saints to guide us.

In my heart, I prayed for strength. I had a new nation and a king I couldn't disappoint.

EXILE

Oxford University and *City Herald*, Saturday, October 20, 1821

The late Queen of Hayti (Madame Christophe), and her daughters, now on visit to Mr. Clarkson, at his seat, Playford Hall, Suffolk.

10

1821 Suffolk, England

The large window of Playford Hall's drawing room drew my attention. Ice dripped and formed what they called icicles. Suspended glistening from the low part of the roof, they looked like daggers.

"Are you warm enough, Madame Christophe?" Madame Clarkson asked as she refreshed my tea.

Glad that I'd accepted her offer to spend the winter here, I tugged the soft wool blanket about me and nodded. Then my eyes went back to the ice weapons and to the frozen moat surrounding Playford, offering protection.

"It's as white as you said. Not a bit of yellow in it, the snow."

"Yes, Madame Christophe." She sat in her chair.

Everything along the drive north of London, particularly once we passed Ipswich, was dusted in white. Here everything was covered, with only the tops of fenceposts sticking up.

London made me aware of how different we were. The Clarksons' generosity made us feel normal. My servants were treated like theirs. Old Souliman enjoyed staying in the attic. He liked looking down on the world.

"Koi fish are lurking under the ice." The bubbly Catherine Clarkson could talk on small things such as gardening and floral arrangements as well as the larger things like politics. "You'll see them in the spring."

That was Britain's dry season. It sounded like a long way off and that we'd have to be under this woman's roof until then.

A few years older than me, madame was full of energy, without a single graying hair in her dark locks.

Her husband, Thomas Clarkson, on the other hand, was fully gray—that prettiest kind of silver. It fit his gentle spirit.

He doted upon his wife, both her spirit and her mind. I thought it a rare gift for a man to respect a woman's intellect. Before power and crowns interfered, Henry and I had had that type of love.

In the quiet of my nights, I saw things more clearly. When we were young he'd given me his heart. It was honest and pure. I remembered his head on my lap, my fingers splaying into his fine tight curls as I read aloud "Ancilotto, King of Provino." Henry joked I'd always be the bird from that story, which spoke the truth, whispering it into his ear, keeping him from evil.

I'd failed. I was filled with shame and sorrow.

"Madame Christophe, do you wish to walk in the snow? The storm has slowed."

Blinking away tears, I cleared my throat. "Non. I do admire things… like the park. It's probably very lush when it's warm. It will get warm again?"

Her brow furrowed, then she laughed. "It will. And it is lovely. Playford Hall is my pride and joy. My husband has given it to me to run. He's so busy with his writings. He's always working for change."

She smiled as he came into the room, and I saw what her words didn't have to say. They shared a great love, one suited to their personalities, one that would endure. As Geneviève would say, something to envy.

Over the years, my husband had paid six thousand pounds to Clarkson to compensate him for his representation of Hayti to Britain and France. On our behalf, he traveled and spoke with ambassadors, urging France to recognize the kingdom. The bastard slavers wouldn't, not without reparations.

The French wanted my country to pay indemnification to each habitation owner for their lost property. Why should the winning nation pay the loser spoils? Where was the compensation for the enslaved for being stolen and forced to work in violent conditions?

As Clarkson negotiated with Paris, Henry gained allies in Russia via direct correspondence. He'd started to succeed. If our kingdom had survived, I was sure Hayti would be recognized without paying France more treasure.

Clarkson and Wilberforce made sure to publicize their paternalistic oversight of Hayti. Their allies in papers called them Henry's fathers, saying that they were shepherding the kingdom. The news columns printed inches and inches lauding these two men as having built our nation on their own, conveniently leaving out the Black people who had fought and bled for freedom.

I should be more charitable.

Their kindness to our family had been wonderful. Yet I doubted that Clarkson and Wilberforce saw Henry's genius, that the king had used them to gain legitimacy. My husband wanted their Blanc sovereign to recognize our Black Hayti. I wished it had happened. Now I doubted it ever would.

I looked away from the Clarksons, huddled together discussing some letter, and again glanced at Améthyste in the corner silently sketching.

Her cough had improved, and unlike the rest in my party, she refused to stay in her room. She drew by the fire, and her charcoal sketches captured the oddest interactions.

"How's the fight in Parliament, Monsieur Clarkson?" she asked.

"Two steps forward with a transport bill, three steps back with an appeal or a delay or a loophole." He sighed his obvious frustrations. "Wilberforce can tell you more of their gamesmanship. He's expected tonight. That's if this storm hasn't made him change his plans."

I'd have crossed my fingers if Améthyste and Madame Clarkson hadn't been looking. I needed an answer about our finances.

"Once things are settled, have you given thought to where you will live, Madame Christophe?"

Conveniently, I had the tea to my lips, so I offered a small shake of my head. The amount of money would decide everything. Castles and palaces were the things of fairy tales, not the reality of budgets and potential dowries. The girls were old enough. If we had been in Hayti, one or both would have been engaged by now to a highly respected officer or some peer of the realm.

"This is a good place," Madame Clarkson said. "I originally met Thomas through friends when he stayed in the Lake District to improve his health."

"He moved for his health? Near water?"

"Yes," she said. "It can be very beneficial. The air is the freshest there."

This was a new consideration. Anything to improve Améthyste's health had to be at the top of my mind. "I miss being near the water. But here it's quiet and feels relaxing."

"Moving for love is also a consideration. Madame, you're barely forty and so lovely."

Forty-three. I shrugged and sipped my tea. My heart had had the love of a king. No man could ever match Henry.

Dramatic as ever, Athénaïre swayed into the room with a newspaper wedged under her arm. She tossed her hand to her forehead. The action made the hem of her indigo dress flap against the beige wall.

"What's wrong, dear?" Madame Clarkson asked, her smile blooming. She was prepared to be entertained.

My youngest girl would never disappoint.

"The prince regent . . . I mean King George IV has attended a large ball in Dublin. That's in Ireland. Not in London."

"He's had one, well, several in London." Madame Clarkson took the paper from her. "The event was held at the Rotunda, and his subjects made everything joyous. A blue velvet canopy over the throne. Festoons of flowers in every window about the room."

She put a finger to her pink lips. "They even used artificial flowers made of silk for more adornment."

"That's George IV, always extravagant." Madame Clarkson offered a chuckle." Did they run out of chalk for the floors? He doesn't dance unless everything is properly marked."

Athénaïre looked genuinely disturbed.

"What is it, dearest?"

"Maman, his wife just died in August. A few months ago. He's dancing and carrying on. Why isn't he in mourning?"

Madame Clarkson looked at me, and I looked at her for an explanation. In Hayti, we mourned a long time to show our respect. I thought the British did, too.

She folded up the paper and returned it to my daughter. "Unfortunately, the king didn't love his wife. He tried to divorce her unsuccessfully last year. They'd been estranged for a long time."

Silence descended.

I saw Athénaïre wrestling with the revelation that marriages sometimes didn't work. At twenty-one, she was more than ready to want the happiness love could bring, but she must know a wedding didn't fix everything. Sometimes, no matter the best intentions, people hurt people. If she'd paid attention to me and Henry, she'd know that.

Améthyste looked up from her sketchbook. "Focus on the number of guests. Twenty? A hundred?"

"Hundreds. All wishing to pay respect to the new king during his stay." Madame Clarkson counted on her fingers. "Thousands may come out during his visit. Ireland is a special place."

"Thousands would be like one of our fetes. Remember, Maman," Améthyste said, "how everything smelled so fresh, like the flowers of your garden."

"Oui. Our king liked a big party. He was happy to oblige as many as possible."

The light in Madame Clarkson's blue eyes brightened. "That's a large party."

Her lingering gaze on my face told me she understood better what we'd lost. "Madame Christophe, I'm sorry, truly sorry."

"No use dwelling on the past. Tell me of the improvements you'll do to the garden in the warm season, this summer."

She came to my side and began talking about her tenant farmers, and I kept my fixed smile in place.

There was a fine line between acknowledging what we'd had and accepting pity. I wasn't ready to accept that we'd never see such splendor again.

11

1821 Suffolk. England

The snow finally stopped and began to melt. All the ice daggers fell from the shutters. But through the window, the world was still painted white.

I lusted for a quiet walk outdoors, but it was too cold. Couldn't get sick again, not when Wilberforce had sent word that he'd arrive today.

The Clarksons continued to be excellent hosts, but the newspaper mentioned we were in Suffolk. More reporters looking for the tragic Madame Christophe would begin showing up here as they had to the Osborne Hotel.

Next, the fortune hunters would arrive. Someone claiming to be a surviving relative to confuse us or gain a share in our imagined wealth.

A rider galloped up the way. The fellow was young, making his horse sprint. It wasn't Wilberforce.

Sitting close to the window, I couldn't finish my sweet biscuit.

My nerves were raw. Perhaps it had been a mistake to leave London without my legal affairs concluded.

The laughter of my girls allowed me to breathe and not second guess myself. I calmed, my rapid pulse slowing. My daughters were happier here than they had been in the hotel. Neighbors of our host, Madame Alexander and Madame Shaw, visited often. We read the Bible. At first, I thought they were missionaries trying to proselytize the natives.

That was unfair.

They'd heard we were Catholic. In some quarters of England that was nearly as bad as being a savage. The women were gentle dears. We got along better when they realized my saints were theirs, too.

The girls made fast friends with young ladies their age—Marianne and Patti Thornton and Mary Inglis. Hearing their laughs restored my energy. Perhaps Suffolk could be our new home . . . if I could stay warm.

"Does the moat look as if it has thawed?" Catherine, Madame Clarkson, joined us in the parlor. I felt guilty. We'd taken it over. The girls huddled by the fireplace while I peered out the window.

My hand dropped the gauzy curtain and I turned to Madame Clarkson. "It looks very pretty shimmering with ice."

Her gaze was steady, but she seemed to want to delve deeper into my confidence.

Wasn't sure I wanted anyone to know my thoughts. Could we have waited all this time hoping for a small income only to be surprised with nothing? Henry's trust in others to keep his money safe might've been misplaced.

There I was doubting him again. I needed to have faith in my husband, in the steps that had led us here.

Monsieur Clarkson entered and joined the girls by the fire. When Athénaïre stood with her arms extended and her pearly teeth gnashing dramatically, I knew she'd recount our last days in Sans-Souci.

I didn't know what was worse, the paper's version, which repeated the revolutionaries' lies, or Athénaïre's loud embellishments.

"They came at me, the enemy's guards," she said. "But I picked up my father's sword . . ."

Oh. Henry's sword, this retelling.

The last time she said it was his spurs that she'd looped on a satin ribbon and spun like a battle-ax.

"Extraordinary." Monsieur Clarkson held on to his chair.

Athénaïre swayed back and forth, ducking invisible punches.

She mentioned Victor, protecting him, and I crumbled inside.

I closed my eyes. In my memory, the whole family stood at my feet, laughing and dancing. I remembered all the times I tried to get Henry to join us. He didn't like people looking as we moved to the music.

We didn't dance enough.

My eldest coughed, then sipped from her cup. She surely was not amused, but somehow had perfected a blank smile. Like me, Améthyste had heard dozens of versions of the lies her sister used to comfort herself.

Monsieur Clarkson gaped at me. Was I now a hero in this harrowing version of escaping Hayti? Or a coward for leaving all we'd built?

When I could take no more of his stares, I adjusted the collar of my black chintz gown. "Monsieur Clarkson, have I offended you?"

"Forgive me. You and your daughters amaze me. I corresponded a few times with King Henry. The depth and caliber of his answers astounded me. But I assumed it was one of his aides writing to me."

It was, but dear Vastey conveyed Henry's thoughts in great detail. "My husband had many learned men in his company, but trust that the sentiment was Henry's."

"To meet you and your daughters . . . It's inconceivable what education can do."

"I appreciate your frankness. I'm sure you've rarely met Negroes with a command of both English and French—"

"Latin, too, Maman," Améthyste added.

I chuckled. *Ita, quomodo possum oblivisci*, I thought but said in English, "Yes, how can I forget? But, Monsieur Clarkson, has not your country celebrated the poet Phillis Wheatley and Olaudah Equiano and others? The Christophes can't be that much of a shock?"

His cheeks glowed pink. "I talk of equality and access, but to see it embodied in such a regal fashion . . . it's hard to believe that your father was a mere tradesman and your mother a slave."

Shouldn't I be used to people marveling at our humble beginnings or how articulate my daughters were? I was tired of the gaping that said, *We don't expect much from you or your kind.*

I knew Monsieur Clarkson meant no harm, but I fought to keep my expression even. It saddened me. In a world still run upon enslavement, we'd never be free of such reactions.

"My père owned the Hôtel de la Couronne, one of the most distinguished establishments in Saint-Domingue. Many of your peers stayed there. Yes, my mother was born enslaved as a laundress. I suppose we soaked up the airs. That's what Negroes can do, clean and soak."

Cheeks now fully scarlet, he said, "I'm sorry. But can't you see, you and your family are what the abolition movement needs. People must see you, know you. Talk with you. Then they'll realize we're right."

"Displayed like Saartjie Baartman, the Hottentot Venus? Or on tour like Princess Caraboo? No, monsieur. My daughters and I will not be exploited."

"Maman," Athénaïre said, "that's not what Monsieur Clarkson means. He has been so helpful, both he and Monsieur Wilberforce. They would not degrade us."

"I know that's not what these gentlemen seek, but they cannot control what the masses think any more than one can dissuade a king—"

My mouth clamped.

My heart raced.

My secret regret I'd almost said aloud. Looking to the smooth plaster ceiling, I wished the roof would fall in on me. I didn't mean to voice the pain that filled every chamber of my heart.

Hadn't been able to remove Henry from danger.

Couldn't make him slow down. I should've tried harder to keep him from things that made us end.

Nonetheless, he wouldn't listen. And I gave up trying to be heard.

A maid entered the drawing room. "Ma'am. Monsieur Clarkson. Monsieur Wilberforce is here."

Surely, he wouldn't have come all the way from London without news from the archbishop. My painted smile held in place as I stood and waited.

The thin man entered with hat in hand. He hadn't thought to leave it with the footman, as was the custom here.

Maybe he did come with bad news.

"Wilberforce," Clarkson greeted him. "Sit, warm yourself by the fire. You look as if you are about to fall over."

"I've just left the archbishop of Canterbury. He's in possession of the gold King Henry entrusted to Sir Home Popham."

"I already told you this, Monsieur Wilberforce."

"Yes, you did, madam, but I needed the archbishop to admit this to the Court of Chancery. He will attest to it and make clear that it was the king's intention that the money be used for you and your family."

Wilberforce appeared earnest. He was doubting not me but whether others would admit the truth.

"Then tell me and my daughters what this means."

"I have it here." He pulled documents out of his coat.

The script was English. I gave them to Améthyste. She was much better at translation than I.

"It says we have funds in the Bank of England on Threadneedle Street. Maman, it's over nine thousand pounds."

Nine thousand was enough to lease our own lodgings.

Yet, I felt my brow wrinkling at the amount. Henry's commission work that had filled the vaults of Sans-Souci. How could he only put nine thousand pounds in the archbishop's hands?

Didn't Henry say he set aside millions?

Can one be both angry and grateful? These pounds were enough money to live for some time, but how long? How many months could I feed all the people who came with me?

I glanced at my daughters, passing the papers betwixt them. Was this enough to keep them secure for the rest of their lives?

"Thank you for the news." My tone was cold, but how should one sound when they knew they'd been cheated, given pennies to keep quiet?

Be grateful. Have gratitude, I said to my dry soul.

"Madame, this is not all of my news or the favor I must ask."

Wilberforce looked agonized. Did his grimace mean I couldn't even count upon receiving this money?

Clarkson walked to Wilberforce. "Nine thousand pounds is a good fortune."

Better than nothing. "Say the worst, Monsieur Wilberforce. I can tell there is more bad."

My messenger hesitated at the dark-stained oak threshold, still rolling that black beaver-pelt hat that reminded me of Henry's and Toussaint's round domes, the ones worn when they commanded the French army. Unforgettable, that complicated time of switching allegiances, then our united Black and Colored forces made the final push that won the colony's freedom. Again the feeling that my peace would end settled upon my soul.

Watching Wilberforce shift in his damp boots, I wondered what stance he needed me to shift to keep my family safe. "Sir, we are guests in this home. We have no secrets. Please tell us what has you so animated."

"Ma'am," Wilberforce stood, rolled the brim in his palms. "Hayti is in chaos. Fighting is breaking out everywhere. Even more executions. Without your help, I fear the great experiment of Black self-rule is over."

Non! The Christophes had given enough. I gaped at him, waiting for strength, waiting for the right words. One peek at my daughters showed young women ready to fight. Non. In a quiet, monotone voice, I whispered, "That's unfair, Monsieur, to disparage a nation only twenty years in existence. It took several centuries of violence to lead England to its parliamentary system. And your monarch still finds faults with its rules."

Améthyste chuckled, then coughed. When all eyes moved to her, she said, "Revolution is not unknown to Europe. After what happened to Louis XVI, I suppose George IV was happy for a nonviolent means of changing heads of state."

Wilberforce's lips flattened; Monsieur Clarkson looked away and took a seat by his slightly amused wife.

Wilberforce came closer. "Can you help reach the new government, or someone in the opposition? I'm willing to pursue representing them to my king and Parliament as I did your husband."

"Non. I'll not be political. Not for Hayti or for Britain's politics."

"When the world meets you, madame," Clarkson said, "and your graceful daughters, it will shore up support."

"Support for what? To do what's right to support a nation and keep its children from war?"

"Right is relative in Britain sometimes." Catherine leaned over and added milk to her husband's cup. Her burgundy sleeves fluttered across the white linen covering the table like spilled blood on sand. "With power, right becomes more convoluted."

This was true, so very true of the kingdom.

"Madame Christophe," Wilberforce continued, "you and your

daughters embody what can be achieved. Britain's abolished slave transport. Now we can build upon this and abolish the whole institution."

Henry had wanted the whole world free. He followed the late emperor, seizing slave ships, freeing the stolen, even buying slaves from America to give the captives freedom.

His private security force was made up of male Dahomet warriors, who were spared enslavement as part of a trade deal arranged with King Adandozan.

"Oui, my king would want abolition, but the girls and I are in no position to take public positions, not while we are at risk."

"Have threats been made?" Wilberforce's lean cheeks tensed. His hands balled. "I'll be in contact with the Haytian government. I'll make sure—"

"That's not what I'm talking about, and I definitely don't want another conversation with the friendly assassins who picked which of my family got to live and which died."

Athénaïre gasped and ran from the room. Her sister glanced at me then followed.

For a moment, I started to lift my hands to beg forgiveness, then for Wilberforce to leave us alone, but my bare wrist, the one without my bracelet, Henry's mark of protecting us, felt naked. I sat, anchoring my arms to my lap. "With nine thousand pounds, I'm not in a secure position. The money in the Bank of England will allow me to lease a home of our own for a few years, but not much more. Our future is still in doubt. I will not risk anything more. I'm all the princesses have left. They are all I have, that and pennies on paper."

"I'll help invest the money," Monsieur Clarkson said. "It can be made into more."

Wilberforce moved back to the fireplace. "I have solicitors looking at the king's transactions with American banks and ones in Europe. There may be more money. On your behalf, I've engaged the firm Reid, Irving and Company."

Those were Henry's men in London. These lawyers sounded expensive, but it would be worth it to gain every bit of what was due to me. My family had paid so much. Anything that could protect Henry's daughters needed to go to them, not murderers or thieves.

The way to avenge Henry was to become again what he had made us, a royal family. That required money, a lot of money, to protect the princesses, to dress them for society, and to give them the dowries they deserved.

Couldn't imagine who they'd marry, but that wasn't the point. If the world would use us as models of what Black rule could achieve, then we needed to be at the top of society, like other royal families.

After putting his hat on the mantel, Wilberforce warmed his hands. "There is some good news. The authorities looking into the theft of your jewels found a group of criminals trafficking stolen items. I think most of your valuables will be recovered."

My heart leapt.

The thought of possessing my bracelet again, having it turn on my arm, made me almost giddy. I wanted to look at it and remember when I was fighting for Henry's good dreams.

Just the good ones, not the haunting ones that turned an ambitious king into a raving despot.

THE KINGDOMS

Britain

Dublin Evening Post, Thursday, January 7, 1813

On the 9th inst. Sir Francis Burdett gave notice in the House of Commons, that, after the Recess, he should bring forward a motion for the introduction of a Bill to provide that the Regency should devolve on the Princess Charlotte of Wales, in case the Prince Regent should die while his father continued in his present state of incapacity to govern.

Hayti

The Royal Gazette, July 26, 1813

Feast of HRH Monsignor, the Prince Royal.

    THE 20th of July, the eve of the birthday of HRH Monsignor Victor Henry, Prince Royal of Hayti, was announced by a salvo of artillery from the forts and batteries of Cap-Henry, and repeated by the ships anchored in the roadstead.

12

1813 Cap-Henry, Kingdom of Hayti

The newly smooth route from Sans-Souci to the capital was crowded. People ran along the side of my carriage, cheering.

"Vive ma reine."

"Vive ma reine."

Impressed with Henry's constructed road, I waved at the citizens, old and young, who attended the parade. It warmed my heart to see them saluting the grand caravan.

Geneviève sat beside me counting. "It has to be thousands. Thousands have come to see the royal family."

In a rose-colored gown, with orange and red flowers in her hair, my sister looked lovely.

When I offered my compliments, her sly gaze cut to me. "The queen's sister needs some sort of crown, since the king wouldn't grant me one."

I winced but said nothing. Henry wouldn't budge, nothing more for my sister. He seemed angered every time I brought up the subject.

"I know you cannot control what he does or who he listens to."

She frowned like Athénaïre when I told her she could not perform during the ballet performance. Though my daughter was talented and graceful, the king said no.

Henry's no meant no, no further discussion. Despite his promises, I had little influence. Henry never seemed to talk to me about anything other than the children. On the rare occasion I could get his attention away from his advisers, he was more interested in the meals I planned for the royal balls or in complimenting me until I blushed.

Well, the blushing, the loving wasn't so bad. The king was a charmer, to his men and his queen.

Henry appreciated me in all other aspects of our marriage, particularly the royal bedchamber. He was a tender, generous lover. I was his equal in that room.

But nothing was the same outside the bedroom door.

The promise I'd secured to have the autonomy to create my role languished for the past two years. Geneviève and I, and even Cécile, had to visit the capital in secret to help distribute food or look after the hospitals. Caring for Améthyste because of her sudden weaknesses stole the rest of the time. Nonetheless, my eldest needed every moment. No one knew how many she'd have.

Another roar came from the crowds. Henry and Victor's carriages had stopped, and they flung coins to the people.

Cheers thundered.

Limbs twisted to get to the gold.

Commotion. Shots fired.

The military shoved back the crowds. Cannon blasts covered up shouting. Someone waved the old black and red flag of the empire, one perforated with bullet holes.

My carriage sped away as if we were being chased.

To calm myself, I thought of the tattered flag of the old nation.

That would never do.

It shocked me that this detail hadn't been perceived by his advisers, to give the people the new flags they'd designed, the red and blue background with gold cannons.

Above the crowd, the hole-ridden, worn thing waggled back and forth. It was a sign. "Something should be done about that. I should see to it."

Whether she heard me or not, she didn't say. Instead, Geneviève wrapped her fingers about my diamond and pearl necklace and spun a silken sphere against her thumb. "Nice new gift. Louise, you have a rich man who loves you, who'll protect you with his life. Can't you use your influence and get the king to advance me?"

"Non. Henry is very busy. His advisers don't see me as having an active role except being the wife of the *august sovereign*."

Releasing my jewels and letting them fall to my throat, she squinted at me as if I were speaking a different language.

"Marie-Louise, how did Maman convince our père of anything? Think. Our mother was a genius." Geneviève winked. "She often convinced him to think her idea was his."

"I'll not be a trickster. I shouldn't have to become a magician to make Henry see the light."

Her eyes went wide, showing the gold of her irises. "Magician? Non. I've seen how the king adores you. It's his horrid advisers. They are leading the king. Again, if Maman wanted something, she'd convince Père. You're more powerful than you think."

She fluffed her curls about her woven crown. "We can plot on these things later. It's your son's big day."

Wondering what ideas Geneviève had made me assume were mine, I turned again to the window. It was Victor's day. He needed my focus. My boy and his half brother had practiced for weeks to perform today's military exercise.

"Cécile and her husband are angry the king has decided that French will be our official language, not Kreyòl. I swear, she's always looking for something to criticize."

My groan was loud, but it was good that my two sisters were seeing more of each other. "French is how the documents are written. Contracts and everything legal are in that language. Our people have to know it. Unlike before, all will get schooling, not just the ones with lucky learned parents."

She nodded. "But it seems the king's getting rid of all the old ways."

On French, Henry was right. For Hayti to take its place in the world, everyone had to know French.

Geneviève patted my hand. "I could be of more help if the king gave me a title. Then I could do more for you—"

"Non."

My sister was just another woman in the kingdom. Henry's advisers wouldn't listen. And I'd become a queen who showed up for special occasions. This new Hayti couldn't become a land where no one wanted to hear a woman's thoughts.

Her lips pursed. "I'm sure the king sees how much I help with the girls. You probably haven't had a chance to ask."

"Non, Geneviève, I have. Several times. He's adamant against your elevation."

She bristled as though I'd poked her with quills. Then she shrugged and sank into the seat.

Sorry wasn't good enough for her, but I had no other comfort to offer. The allowance to dress her in finery was all Henry was willing to do for her.

"Is there a reason the king is punishing you? Have you tried to convince him of something, Geneviève? Did you offend him?"

Her eyes widened, and I saw a flash of something on her face. "Non. Non. I did nothing."

Oh. There was something, something secret, something I couldn't resolve on my son's special day.

She fanned her face. "It doesn't matter. Look at the crowds for Victor."

We settled into a stiff silence listening to the shouts of "Long live the king! Long live the queen! Long live the prince royal!"

The curving road ahead offered me a better view of Henry's gold and black carriage. Eight spirited stallions, shades of white and silver, trotted through the triumphal arches erected at the Haut-du-Cap-Henry bridge.

In another minute, my carriage whooshed under the hibiscus and rose garlands at the Cours de la Reine. The bright red of the choublak flowers, the sweet honey of the rosa cayennes, and the cheers of the people I would remember forever.

I swore again in my heart to be worthy of these accolades.

My sister sat in silence with her hands folded in prayer. I hoped that whatever her secret, whatever she'd done, it wouldn't divide us. Our père had grown tired of tricks. The games ruined our parents' marriage. Before all was lost, before our friendship was harmed, I hoped Geneviève Coidavid remembered this lesson.

MY BLACK CARRIAGE, DRAWN BY EIGHT JET MARES, APPROACHED Rue Espagnole. This was the main route to Place d'Armes, where Victor's ceremony would take place. Then we'd all retire back to the palace for a ball.

I'd been allowed to plan it on my own, so it would have my signature. This woman's work, the queen's dinner, would be a brilliant feast. It had to be. One couldn't ask for more if one faltered in assigned or relegated tasks.

The horses slowed as we turned. With heads rearing, their braided manes became more visible. That must be Souliman's handiwork. He enjoyed decking these fillies with decorative silver halters and fittings. Such a sight. Polished brass cinchers along their brows gleamed like the gold ribbons stitched to the scarlet drapes laying across their broad backs. The detail and care made my heart soar.

"This is a great effort for Victor," I said. I wanted Henry to be proud of our son more than I wanted to be proved right about a woman's role.

The troops of the military household marched to my right. They'd come from the garrisons at the Citadel and the barracks of the palace. With the disturbance earlier, I suspected that this display was more than to show king's power but to protect the royal caravan.

As we neared the final stretch of Rue Espagnole, cannons fired.

My heart lodged in my throat as two sixteen pounders fired again. I forced a slow swallow and convinced myself to be at ease. These cannons were under the command of our prince, Prince du Limbé, the tall General Romain.

Then the caravan stopped.

More brigades of our Haytian guards began marching along each side of us. The glossed boots of glorious brown and sable men in long onyx coats with sharp red lapels drummed in unison.

Red epaulettes swinging, shoulders stiff, the soldiers carried rifles.

Brown stocks rested against their black velvet cuffs as the men high-stepped in place, saluting their king.

Henry.

He'd descended from his carriage in a similar black uniform but with white breeches. His gold brooch, engraved with his crest, shimmered in the bright sun. When he waved his hat, his shako, bordered with red silk braiding and a plaque of his coat of arms, I wanted to clap.

He looked regal and strong.

Nothing like last night or days earlier—the man beset with worries who awoke from nightmares in the midnight hours, when it would take minutes for him to recognize where he was. The dreams of enslavement still haunted him, as did every war in which he'd fought. I knew this.

But at dawn, I realized he feared dying from the wounds he received under fire as a drummer with the Chasseurs-Volontaires de Saint-Domingue. That was the American Revolution, so many years ago, but his scream was as if a flintlock blasted in our bed.

Always proud of his service, Henry kept these thoughts buried inside until a nightmare drew the terror to his lips.

What did you say to a man who barely slept, who chased demons when he closed his eyes?

Another cannon fired.

Jerking forward, I clasped Geneviève's fingers.

"Sœur, it's all right," she said. "We're not under attack."

"Of course," I replied with burning cheeks.

My brother, Prince Noël, the Duke du Port-de-Paix, came to the carriage and thrust open the door. "My queen." He bowed, then lifted his arm to me.

Taking his hand, I descended. Geneviève smoothed my train of white silk with embroidered petals. I winked at her my thanks.

Then she tried to join me.

Without hesitation, Noël waved her back and closed the door. "No, only the queen can come out at this moment. She must join the king alone."

I winced at the hurt rising in her face.

"That's how the ceremony goes, sœur. We can't get this wrong." His low voice pleaded with Geneviève as if something bad would happen if things weren't done properly.

Then I recalled the precision and demand for excellence that Henry's new secretary, Pompée Valentin Vastey, appointed as Baron de Vastey had ascribed to the events. It was a show for the world as much as a celebration of the king's heir. The slender man had replaced Comte de Limonade in Henry's eyes. I thought this was good until I saw tears on Geneviève's cheek.

After hearing Vastey give a roaring speech praising the Citadel as a feat of Black excellence, my husband had leapt up and asked him to work for the kingdom, saying God had designated this man to aid Henry in showing the world what Black hands could do.

"It's for the best. Understand? It's for the kingdom." I took my brother's hand, and we walked toward the king. "For Hayti."

The pull on my train, the unfolding of a crease—that had to mean she understood. I couldn't look back and hope for a confirming wave. Couldn't risk drawing my own tears if she openly wept. The constant reminder of my position and Noël's had to hurt.

"Come on, sœur." Noël tugged a little, but I faced forward with my head high, wondering how many secret hurts I'd have to keep hidden, parked away in my heart before I broke.

13

1813 Cap-Henry. Kingdom of Hayti

Grand-Archbishop Brelle finished his homily to Saint John. He called the saint the holy scribe for being given the privilege of recording the acts of Jesus.

While I stood in the royal pew next to the king, Brelle's message struck me, the importance of keeping the records of the kingdom. "It's good you have the *Royal Gazette*, my king."

For a moment, Henry glanced down at me.

"Then all can see a true record of the kingdom's achievements." I said. "They'll know the exploits of a respected monarch."

His gaze assessed me as if I'd discovered a state secret, but then he cleared his throat a little. "Wise woman."

It was strange, his look, but also welcome. He hadn't looked into my eyes since the nightmare.

THE CHURCH WHERE JACQUES I WORSHIPPED HAD BEEN PAINTED with whitewash. Royal banners of purple silk hung above. I stared at them and at the cathedral's limestone arches, which soared as high as Brelle's lofty prayers. The grand-archbishop offered thanks for Henry, me, the children, and the nation. Then he beseeched God for blessings upon each.

The music began. Everyone sang a hymn. The congregation of no-bles and military officials looked resplendent—fancy uniforms, more imported gowns from Europe. If not for all the brown faces, this could be one of the English regent's assemblies.

A pianoforte and several harps announced the procession. Henry turned the emerald bracelet on my arm. It fitted a little better this year. I thanked his fine chef for that, but there remained enough give in the banding for the gem to turn about my wrist.

His golden eyes seemed tentative. "Shall we, my dear?"

With vigor, I clasped his arm and worked my hand against his sleeve. I'd leave no doubt in his mind that I thought well of him.

When we stepped outside of Notre-Dame de l'Assomption, an anxious feeling gripped me. My baby, my son, Victor, walked to his horse. It was his moment to exhibit himself, in front of everyone.

"He'll be fine, Louise. He won't disappoint me."

My stomach dropped. The bond between father and son seemed tenuous. I remembered how Henry praised God when François-Ferdinand was born. My husband bragged to anyone who listened, "He's strong and strapping, like me. He recognized me. He caught hold of my finger and smiled."

Now Armande and Athénaïre were the ones of whom he bragged. Their brash manner, the air of confidence they possessed, was Henry's.

I couldn't fault a man for pride in these two, but I could wish that Henry would see all the reasons Victor and Améthyste were special, too.

Still I bowed my head and prayed anew to Saint Michael, if he wasn't too busy: *Put a shield around Victor. Let him not be distracted.*

My son was good on a horse. It was in his blood to be so, but to watch him perform in front of the king and all his subjects, knowing how Henry demanded perfection, I had to lean on the saints for help.

"Our son has been practicing the routine, Louise. He and Armande together. They'll be fine."

Those words were my miracle. Hearing confidence in Victor from Henry's lips meant everything. With a stolen glance to his light eyes, I offered my love to Henry.

His Cupid's bow lifted.

For a moment, everyone was away. It was me and my man, against the world.

Before I could say that I was sorry or that I loved him, or merely hold his hand, a few drops of rain fell.

As if I'd drown from a light shower, I was led away to my carriage. Why, when we find our way, must we be separated?

Geneviève climbed in from the other side. Splashes of water kissed her cheek. Well, I hoped it was rain.

She looked a little disheveled. I didn't remember seeing her in the church.

With my thumb, I wiped her jaw. "Are you well?"

Eyes darting. "Fine." She wove her fingers with mine. "Victor will be fine."

My sister and her secrets. I sighed and stared at Place d'Armes and our assembled military. Crowds of dignitaries and peers spilled out of the church and gathered around the perimeter.

My son mounted a black stallion and rode in front of his father. He raised his right arm and snapped a sharp salute.

Then he charged across the cobbles to where one of the battalions had aligned in rows. Circling them, handling his mount like it was an extension of his fingers, he moved in front of the soldiers.

His steed stilled.

Everyone quieted.

"Attention! Marche du bataillon!"

The soldiers listened to Victor's command and stepped in unison, heading to the edge of the cobbles, the area that had held trees before everything in the capital burned.

"Attention. À propos du visage. Mars!"

The battalion turned directly around and marched back to the point where they started.

My son told them to stand down. With his head bowed, he and his steed whipped out of Place d'Armes.

Victor had done it. He'd done it. No mistakes.

I hugged and kissed my sister, pretty much sobbed all over her.

"He will be as diligent as Henry with these commands. He'll make a good soldier and eventually a good king."

The light rain became steady, but it was the turn of Prince Armande-Eugène, the Duke of Mole. The young man was the head of the Chasseurs de la Garde. Marching with a firm step and assured voice, he moved the troops through the square in a tight marching routine, then lined them up evenly between the other battalions.

In the rain, the king walked out into Place d'Armes to his sons and saluted them. Being older and more mature, Armande had done better, but to see the three of them together, a father beaming with pride for both his sons, gave me such joy.

"The *Gazette* should capture this moment."

Geneviève nodded and looked again out the other window. With her hand cupped to her brow, was she seeking something? Someone?

There was no doubt in my head that she was up to mischief, but I couldn't be caught in her intrigues.

As long as tonight's ball was a success, I believed the House of Christophe might sleep well.

14

1813 Sans-Souci, Kingdom of Hayti

From the first level of Sans-Souci, I looked to the gallery above and saw Geneviève hurrying the girls and their governesses.

There was a flurry of slippers rushing to change for tonight's dinner. Athénaïre trailed behind, lifting her hands, gliding like a swan or a lost ballerina. She glanced down, surely seeing me. Exaggerating her frown, she made fast pirouettes until she landed at her bedchamber door and disappeared.

Balancing my husband's wishes, my children's needs, and the things I wanted and desired to accomplish had become so hard. I moved down the long hall, trying to remember that today was Victor's day. Henry had to be pleased.

I lingered a moment in the quiet under an ornate brass sconce. Honey perfumed the air. The yellowish wax in the holder didn't look like tallow.

Souliman lumbered down the hall, fussing with his stiff onyx-colored collar. "It's beeswax, madame. Came with the latest shipment from Hamburg."

Excellent. If goods were arriving from Hamburg, that meant Prussia and perhaps even Austria were winning against Napoleon. "These are brighter than tallow. Maybe too bright. It could expose things that should be hidden."

He frowned more. "Supposed to boule pi lontan . . . burn longer."

I watched him walking away, still scratching the collar of his starched shirt. Souliman was my secret ally in the household to ensure the smallest of tasks were done.

Continuing to the dining room to check on place settings, I heard loud voices from the library.

In the opening, I saw two men in military uniforms steeped in conversation.

Peeking a little more, I witnessed my brother thumbing the leather-bound books on the shelves. With arms folded, grousing Prince du Limbé, Paul Romain, stood next to him. General Romain, as I'd always think of him, remained the greediest, skinniest soldier I'd ever seen. Studying countenances, a bad habit that had stayed with me from my days at the Hôtel de la Couronne, I could always identify all of Henry's men, even after they'd been promoted or aged too quickly from war.

Romain, with his hair salt and pepper and cropped low, said the word *assailant.*

My heart raced, making echoey thuds in my chest.

"Rest assured we've detained every one of the bastards." He pumped his fist. "I cannot believe they made their way to the parade route."

"Pétion's villainy is everywhere." Noël's tone was heated. "If he strikes down the king, he thinks no one will stand up for the kingdom."

This was no jest. On a day to honor my son, someone had come against his père.

Romain whipped his palm to the hilt of his ceremonial sword. "You know I will, but we'll have to win the people, you and . . . the queen."

Sweeping out of the shadows, I came fully into the library, crossing the burgundy tapestry centering myself in the room.

The expression on the general's face wasn't ease but embarrassment for carelessly admitting such things in my presence.

They bowed.

The general rose first. "You're the loveliest of women. Most graceful and discreet of women. All the ladies of the kingdom should take note of your behavior."

I took the hint that I should be quiet about what I'd overheard. Romain bent his head again and left.

Alone in this elegant library with a chandelier formed of fragile globes housing hot beeswax candles overhead, I folded my arms and kept my pitch from rising. "Speak plainly, mon frère. Tell me what has happened."

With hands on his white breeches and wearing a coat covered in medallions, Noël offered me a wide smile. "Nothing for you to fret about."

Noël and I stood in this grand room with gilded mirrors and wall-to-wall shelves holding enough leather-spined books to entomb us. I went and poked in him the rib, jingling medals and blocking his path as if he were a child caught being naughty. "Tell me now what has occurred."

"Now, sœur . . ."

"I'm your queen; I demand to know."

"Oh, sœur, must you be difficult?"

My voice was stony. "These titles and uniforms mean something or nothing. If this fancy dress and rigor is to stir people to defend the kingdom with their last breath, then the words of your queen need to mean everything. I'm asking what has occurred."

His head dipped and he knelt on one knee. "Two assailants tried to attack the caravan during the parade. Our guards saw and stopped them. They didn't get close enough to harm the king or the prince."

Henry and Victor. "Was it when the carriages stopped? When they flung money into the crowd?"

"Oui. The king and the prince royal were doing maundy, the mandatum of the Christ at the Last Supper, tossing coins. That's when the attack happened."

Henry had created our money, the gourde. He wanted to hand it out as the British monarchs did. Modeling himself on European notions could've gotten him and our last son killed. "Were the conspirators citizens or spies?"

"Sometimes they can be both."

There was no smile on his face. He wasn't joking but admitting a sobering fact. The enemy who wanted my husband dead could very well be of our kingdom.

"Your Majesty, some aren't happy with the king. They hate his forced-labor policies. Russia has defeated Napoleon, and it seems Prussia and Austria will do the same. No one feels France is a threat. Many fail to see how the Citadel is insurance against anything."

The beautiful Sans-Souci had been finished by such labor. The cupola of our private chapel was hailed as an engineering feat, but two brickmasons had succumbed to the heat during construction. "And the showiness of today's display just emphasizes the gap between rich and poor. I know, Noël. But that's not what Henry's trying to do."

"Tossing pocket change at poor people is not right. They're dignified, and this reduces them to peasants. Dupuy's idea."

"But they scrambled for the money, Noël."

"Who wouldn't?" He touched his fine coat. The medals tinkled softly. "If not for the king's favor, I'd be scrounging as well."

"There has to be a way to fix this. I must speak to Henry . . ."

"No. You will not. You're the queen, and matters of defense are not for you to know about. Uphold your duties to the kingdom tonight. You cannot be a fretful wife and mother on the evening of a royal holiday. You're a queen representing the elegance of your husband's reign."

He was right. Hayti and my king came first. "Then lift your hand, Prince Noël, and escort the queen to greet her guests."

My brother extended his arm, and I allowed him to lead me to the balcony overlooking a well-lit courtyard. Resplendently dressed officials were beginning to arrive for the state banquet.

Clasping the rail, I held my breath and proceeded to be the queen of the Kingdom of Hayti, not the fear-filled wife who could've lost her husband and son.

THE REDHEADED MADAME LA COMTESSE D'OUANAMINTHE AND THE blond Madame la Comtesse du Terrier-Rouge, the American governesses of my daughters, positioned the princesses on the dual staircases that led to the courtyard.

Henry had given these Blanc women titles to make them feel welcome and important in the kingdom. Our brethren in the south used this kind act to say our peerages were meaningless.

Watching these women arrange Améthyste and Athénaïre like heavenly stars, I had to admire them, brave Americans who'd left their home, their Blanc neighbors, to be in a noir country for adventure. They controlled their destinies.

The governesses, women in their late twenties whom Dupuy unfairly called spinsters, had styled my girls to be like Princess Charlotte, the British regent's daughter. This meant Améthyste and Athénaïre were fitted in long, columnlike gowns, of light blue for my elder and beige for the younger. Each dress possessed sweeping pleated trains.

These muted colors, not the brighter hues that I knew they loved, did look nice. Madame la Comtesse du Terrier-Rouge said off-white gowns were the rage in Philadelphia and London for young unmarried women.

Madame la Comtesse d'Ouanaminthe came to me and bowed. "Ma reine, the princesses are in position. They are well prepared."

She glanced at me as if she wanted to *fix* my hair. My parted chignon with heavy pinned braids crowned me perfectly with curls and waves. No heat was required unless it came from Henry's eyes.

I wanted to see him, him and my son. I needed them safe. Then I'd seek the answers as to how the king would keep our family safe from assailants.

MY NEW MAID STEPPED TO ME ON THE BALCONY AND SMOOTHED MY long train. "There, ma reine. Perfect."

"Zephyrine, have you seen le roi?"

"Yes, madame. He's with his advisers in the throne room."

She spun on her heel to leave. I almost caught her elbow to have her take a message to the king, but the guards had opened the iron gates to allow guests to enter Sans-Souci.

"Princesses," I said in low tones. "It is time."

Looking at me, Athénaïre leveled her shoulders and rose up on her toes as if she would do a glissade, another of her sweeping ballet moves, but she lowered her stance and held a wide smile.

Améthyste glared at her sister, then waved at me. "This will go well. All is well."

More than anyone, she had seen me fretting over the ball. She needed to know that planning made things perfect. Yet I hadn't proved to her or her sister that royal women could do more than create dinners, hide their talents, and be ornaments.

The nobles mingled in the courtyard. Barons and baronesses, dukes and duchesses, counts and countesses scattered across the cobbles and fountain. My memory for faces and my rehearsal of titles would help me tonight to be the perfect greeter.

So many smiles.

Everyone was happy.

Yet I looked for the enemy in the crowd.

Dame Marie-Augustine Chancy, niece of Toussaint Louverture and widow of André Vernet, Prince of Gonaïves, had decided to come. Vernet had died the previous year at the age of seventy-two. She seemed spry, with a healthy ginger-brown complexion. It was good she came, offering silent approval of Henry's court.

More nobles entered Sans-Souci's gates.

Chatter and happy fellowship surrounded me, but I was plagued by fearful thoughts. An assassin could strike.

The girls curtsied as guests passed them on the steps. That wasn't quite protocol with their higher royal positions, but when Lord Limonade passed, he didn't seem too put off. I supposed everyone was still learning the rules.

I waved and smiled and became mesmerized by the finery.

The feathers.

Colorful fiends and fools—that's how Pétion and his southern republic would describe us in their newspapers. That would be the new lie he'd feed European reporters. The beast took pleasure in calling Henry a despot and all of us well-dressed clowns, forgetting that half his republic was starving and his treasury was empty. The truth wouldn't stop his untruths meant to reduce the Kingdom of Hayti to barefoot savages for the *Globe*, the *Times*, and even the Barbadian presses.

Observers filled with envy or hate missed the beauty of a moment without war, the beauty of Black skin in silks and satins. As with our coronation, I'd remember this evening.

"Aunt. What a lovely queen." Henry's beloved nephew, His Royal Highness Prince Jean, Duke of Port-Margot, kissed my cheek. He was handsome, tall, and brown, with thick curls and a mustache; I wondered why he was still single.

"Wait. There's my dove," he said. He dashed down the stairs and clasped the hand of the widow of the prince of Gonaïves.

They ascended arm in arm and stood before me. "Princess Marie-Augustine? Prince Jean? What does this—"

"Oui, my queen, I have convinced Toussaint's niece to marry me. The king should be pleased that I'm keeping political ties with the old guard."

I blinked a few times at the two of them. With the princess at least ten years older than Jean, was this a marriage of convenience?

"This is sudden." I softened my tone. "Are you hunting for love or m . . . mischief?"

"Oui," he said. "A little of both. For what else does love bring?"

It would bring a lot to Jean, for Marie-Augustine was a handsome widow with a fortune. "So marriage is what you want? What you both want?"

Clapping his hands and grinning, he said, "My queen, you and the king make wedded bliss look easy."

There were many words I'd use to describe my marriage with Henry—*complicated*, *rewarding*, *compromise-riddled*. *Easy* wasn't exactly one.

My husband was ten years older than me, but no one considered the age difference bothersome when it served men. I decided it shouldn't matter for a princess.

Her face bronzed with a blush of modesty or sadness. She'd turned toward the round chapel on the grounds where her late husband was interred. Then she glanced at me with damp lashes. "It's good to have another chance at love."

This felt true and hopeful and warmed my heart. Love didn't truly concern itself with circumstances or convenience, did it? "Good for you two. Prince Jean, your uncle will want to personally give the bride away."

Her eyes became big, distant. "That's an honorable gift, but I don't wish to impose upon the king."

Jean's brow rose, but his arm flew to his middle. "What she means is that it's too much trouble for a busy monarch."

The showy prince in the peacock-blue jacket pinned with Henry's royal star kissed my fingers. "Where's the king? I wish to tell him."

I didn't know. I hungered to know. "With his ministers, I suppose, or the prince royal."

"Yes, it's Victor's day. Vive le prince." Clasping Princess Marie-Augustine's palm again, splaying it against the smooth sleeve of his military coat, Prince Jean escorted her into Sans-Souci.

More members of the old guard, Joseph and Louis Dessalines, nephews of the late emperor—now styled as barons—came with their wives.

Before I could ask about their aunt, the late empress, my lady-in-waiting, Madame Dieudonné Romain, presented herself to me in a low bow. With her marriage to General Romain, she'd become the Princess du Limbé. I called her Princess Dieudonné.

Raising her square chin, she glared at me with fine jet-black eyes, eyes that often hid her feelings. "Your Majesty, it's time for you to join the king in leading dinner."

No greater sentence had been uttered, for I was ready to see Henry and learn from the king, a strongman who'd destroyed towns and troops to wage wars, whom he held responsible for today's attack and what were his plans for revenge.

15

1813 Sans-Souci, Kingdom of Hayti

The short walk from the outdoor courtyard balcony to the dining hall, the place where the banquet would take place, seemed like miles. I crossed the threshold with my stomach drumming.

Henry and Victor were not inside. None of his ministers were.

It took everything within me to step onto the parquet flooring of the ballroom. Made of strips of mahogany making patterns of crosses. I walked upon the crosses, hoping this brought blessings. The archbishop passed me.

"Ma reine." He nodded, then took his seat. His white robes matched the linen tablecloths and napkins.

Taking the priest and the flooring as good omens, I prayed we were safe and for myself and my husband to have more peace.

Henry had enough things to occupy his mind. Tonight's celebration dinner and ballet performance couldn't become another distraction.

From the raising of the chandeliers to the polish of the intricately carved moldings hung above windows dressed in light blue silk, I believed it would be hard to condemn what I and my ladies and Souliman had done.

Princess Dieudonné bowed to me and then left to greet more guests. Her education in France before the war was essential. Her Grand Blanc father's investment in Dieudonné's schooling was extremely useful to me. I trusted in her etiquette. Her knowledge exceeded Limonade's.

The princess returned, leading my girls to their table beside the raised podium where Henry and I would host.

Améthyste stopped as she always did at the Glasmalereien art mounted near the taller-than-me hanging wood carving of Henry's crest, a phoenix rising from ashes. His emblem was nicely done, but my daughter seemed entranced by the imported German glass portraits.

On one, the intricate bits of glimmering blues and yellows depicted the Virgin Mary. On the other, the shards formed the extended wings of the archangel Michael. Perhaps as Mary prayed, the angel of war would leap from his perch and fight for God's children, the Haytian children in Sans-Souci and throughout a unified land.

The Comte de Limonade came to me at the raised platform and bowed. "Praise be to the prince royal. Praise be to his virtuous mother for hosting such a beautiful ball."

He might be offering a simple compliment, but Limonade could be testing my response. I might not have traveled or lived a life of sophistication in France, but this innkeeper's daughter could read, be gracious, and remember protocol.

I did not bow or dip my chin, as I'd done with the archbishop. Instead, I extended my gloved hand for him to kiss.

The count did so, then backed away and found his seat.

My brief feeling of triumph soon faded when I didn't see the king walk through the door.

Just about every seat filled, and Henry hadn't appeared.

Neither had my son.

With the servers beginning to fill goblets with sparkling wine from London, I couldn't go looking. I tried to forget that he was never late, either on time or not coming.

I sipped the British version of champagne, wishing to soothe my nerves and slow the worries again building in my head.

Améthyste came to me. "Everything looks . . . Maman, is all well?"

I hated that my face hadn't learned to lie. Needed to work on fixing my smile, but my mouth had become more accustomed to saying less and less my true feelings. "Only thing wrong is that you haven't taken your seat."

She bent low, then joined her sister, and I had another reason to be miserable. Chastising a fretful soul was terrible, but I couldn't share my fears with anyone.

My poor stomach twisted.

Had I become Henry, hiding what I felt?

Turning my eyes to the high ceilings and the sparkling grand chandeliers, I wanted the evening over and everyone out of the palace.

Yet in one glance at my daughters smiling, being admired, I reclaimed my peace. The evildoers had been caught. I couldn't deprive the girls or Victor of this moment to shine in perfect candlelight.

The last of the nobles and military officers of the kingdom took their seats. Silver forks and knives, crystal goblets and porcelain plates lay in front of each guest.

Roasted mallard would come from the kitchen on Wedgwood dishes with kalalou djon, stewed okra and tomatoes and mushrooms.

My servers in gray lit the beeswax candles in the center of each table. The pleasing light beamed on the ring of yellow hibiscus and orchids, the pinkish purple flor de pasmo, picked from my garden. This should please the guests and Henry's observant eyes. Of course, him being happy with my choices required the king's attendance.

Geneviève entered a few moments before Louis Michel, Comte de Valière, Cécile's husband. My older sister hadn't come. I wished she had. She'd know if the conspiracy had the potential to grow.

At least Geneviève seemed to be smiling, enjoying the music. Perhaps she'd made peace with the way things were, at least for tonight.

In the cool air created by Sans-Souci's stream-chilled floors, my breath stiffened like a paste in my lungs, stopping in place, in time. Seeing Henry alive, unharmed, entering the room smiling at my happy Victor and handsome Prince Armande-Eugène meant everything. They were all safe. There was more time for everything.

The king's closest advisers followed and went to the seats I'd reserved for them up front.

The dinner could officially begin.

My husband came toward me. His smooth lips, that delightful Cupid's bow, showed a buoyant expression I hadn't seen in a long time. I felt silly for being fearful. The king was in command—brilliant, even ruthless to the enemy—and safe.

I felt beautiful in Henry's gaze. The glint in his eyes said he was proud of me.

Then I kicked myself under the table. Of course he was pleased. I was acting in the role he wanted, the good wife and hostess of the king. A queen needed to be more. Once this party was done, I would be.

OUR MUSICIANS PLAYED FERDINAND RIES'S VIOLIN CONCERTO IN E Minor in the background of the dinner. As the world awaited the next masterpiece from Beethoven, the famed Napoleon opposer, both Baron de Vastey and Comte de Limonade had assured me this music of his friend would set the right tone. Our European guests would see the kingdom to be both sophisticated and in tune with the times.

Tapping his finger lightly to the meter, Henry sat at my right. He'd cleared his plate of the succulent duck. He leaned close to my ear. "Your cook has done well. The char on the tomatoes is perfect."

The red apple-shaped plate de Hayti tasted amazing picked from the vine, but even better cooked into sauces or roasted. "I'm glad you find dinner to your liking, Your Majesty. The little wife did well."

He reared back and wiped his mouth with a napkin. "You sound upset, Louise. Your eyes say it, too."

My voice was tight, tighter than I wanted, but my frustration remained. Listening to the soft music, I tried to recapture the moment I found relief. Yet, I was greedy. I wished more than air. I wanted the peace that change should bring.

"Louise?"

"What do you know of my eyes? I suspect the king doesn't view anything aside from protocol."

He bit his lip and stared.

I'd kept my tone soft. I'd never embarrass Henry, even if meant my wings would be clipped forever.

"I do know you, Marie-Louise."

Well, well. My full name. "Non. No one knows me but my husband and friend."

"But I'm one and the same, the king and the one you married."

"If that were so you'd know the incident today strikes at a wife and mother. A husband would set my mind at ease at once. He'd tell me he'll take care. But the king and his family are always on display, easy targets for a disgruntled subject or spy. The answer is clearly more protocol."

"Ridiculous." He thumbed his sash and glanced straight ahead. "A husband would lead you away, find out who has whispered nonsense to your ears, then have him jailed in the Citadel. Oui. That's the pleasure of the king."

I choked a little on my wine, then set down the goblet. "Then I guess we are all better off with you being a merciful king."

Before he could respond and cast another blank or withering look, Baron de Vastey presented himself, bending before us.

"Your Majesties," he said, "I would like to offer a toast to our dear prince, our prince royal, for his ninth birthday."

Henry nodded, and I leaned back in my chair prepared to see my son praised.

"Prince Victor, most exalted son of our king, go on and pursue the beautiful and glorious career that opens before you. In our august majesty's example, you see wisdom and power, a heart for the people, and above all, the protection of virtue and modernity."

He lifted his goblet high. It sparkled in Vastey's hand.

My boy, sitting a few feet away, peered up at his father. The magnitude of the day should comfort him, that Victor had Henry's love.

That feeling that I could have lost Henry and my only living son again struck my heart. I wasn't mad anymore. I couldn't be, not with gratitude for their lives overflowing in me.

"Unceasingly," Vastey continued, "before your eyes, the lessons of wisdom stand. The illustrious example of your father and the happiness of the Haytian people are before you. Make the most of these gracious moments of your life."

Moments.

This was a memorable toast, with everyone standing, cheering for Victor. I etched it into my soul, like the moment was fragile. No, I was fine glass or delicate crystal, thinking again how everything like my François-Ferdinand could be shattered and gone.

"Long live the king!" everyone shouted. "Long live the queen! Long live the prince royal!"

The praises for my birthday boy repeated, becoming the refrain of a melody, like how the musicians played the fast movements of the concerto.

"To my beloved son, Prince Victor." Henry stood and toasted his son.

I sipped from my cup and glanced at my boy's apple cheeks blossoming with a grin.

I'd never forget how my son, either of my sons, smiled when they were happy and praised by their father.

The British merchants that Henry had invited stood and clapped their hands. So many of them, and diverse. They looked well pleased, particularly the mixed-race couple on the end. Black-Blanc pairings weren't unusual. Henry offered such men full citizenship if they married Haytian women.

Vastey began praising the poor sick monarch of England and then his son, the prince regent. The approving looks of the British Blanc men were the same as those of the nobles who'd stood and praised Victor. The Americans in our midst clapped, but they seemed stiff. I'd probably be the same if I attended a dinner praising French rulers. The memory of revolution for everyone was too fresh.

Nonetheless, looking at these foreigners approving our assimilation into the Blanc world, our modeling and revering foreign cultures, it broke something inside.

"What's wrong, Louise? Your countenance has changed again."

My husband was observant, too observant.

How did one complain about things being done according to the king's exact wishes? This was Henry's dream, his plan of how to be respectable in the world.

"Louise, tell me. I don't want our guests seeing you frown. And I know you'll not ask me to discuss state business while we are in the public eye."

Again, his conditions, his rules, but in this he was right. Saying what I thought would drive more division between me and Henry.

When I saw him fiddling again with his sash and the brooch bearing his kingly crest, I remembered the caravan and the people and the waving torn banner.

"Your Majesty, I saw an old flag of the empire today. Someone carried it during our procession. I think they wanted to show pride, but it saddened me. It had bullet holes. The sight of it weighs on me. It would make one think the Haytian state doesn't take enough care with its identity."

His brow lifted. Henry hadn't expected these words. He looked unsure, with lines marring his forehead. "What do you believe should be done?"

For him to ask my opinion was an opening, but I couldn't reach for the heavens. I aimed for falling stars. "Ordering our flag to be made in another country doesn't make sense. I think the royal women should be charged with restoring our pride. You should order that we sew new ones, at our expense and labor. Then it will be a source of pride and accomplishment."

"So be it. Anything you need will be put at your disposal. Dupuy will be charged—"

"It should be the women. Let us bring honor to you and to the home of every peer in the kingdom. It will reinforce their loyalty."

"So be it, Louise. Keep me abreast of the progress."

"I will, Your Majesty." Henry had given me a victory, but we fought different wars. He wanted to distract me from delving into the attack on the caravan. I wanted a role outside of meal planning. We both won.

"Prince Royal, time will come when you'll enjoy the fruit of your labors," Vastey said in a booming voice. "Divinity, preserve this dear prince for us."

The singing started for Victor, hymns of grace. Henry reached for me and clasped my arm, rolling the loose bracelet about my wrist.

The choice emerald had come to mean so much. Dupuy told me the king had picked it from a table of gems. He liked the fire in the smooth facets. Maybe that was what he loved about me, the passion trapped inside my respectable façade.

But was that me, or was it who I'd become in order to love a man like Henry?

With eyes locked on me, his fingers slipped to my palm. His strength and warmth radiated. I felt that swirling, spiraling connection to him as much as his power. The notion that I could've lost him and my son today, maybe that was the push I needed to shake my stubbornness.

"Your way, Henry. I'll not fight if you keep being safer and smarter than those who oppose you."

A full smile toyed with his tender lips.

Baron Louis Dessalines and his wife led couples in the minuet. The young couple, he in his long indigo coat with gold braiding and the baroness in her high-waisted gown of pink satin, looked lovely hand in hand, making sweet time to the dance Jacques I had tried so hard to master.

The lump in my throat grew a little as I remembered the impressive dinners Madame Dessalines once gave. I hated that she'd withdrawn from our lives. Was that what my life would be if I were suddenly widowed and our young son were forced to rule?

16

1813 Sans-Souci, Kingdom of Hayti

The ballet dancers finished their performance of *La Fille Mal Gardée*, The Poorly Guarded Girl. The two acts were performed beneath the main chandelier, the candlelight gleaming on the artists. Their Black faces and the expressive leaps and spins of their bodies, like splashing swans on a river, brought everyone to their feet.

Athénaïre had swayed with the music, her pinkies moving with the steps of the dancers. It wasn't her moment to shine, I said to myself. There'd be another.

When I glanced to the king, his eyes sparkled.

"This evening for Victor is wonderful. You're wonderful, Louise."

I loved this—the sentiment, the gaze.

We were again in the same place, the same sphere.

It didn't matter that I'd capitulated to be there.

The musicians began again. The harpists, a pianoforte player, and violinist from London joining with local drummers were inspiring. We needed this talent here, with our people. "We need a music teacher, Henry."

"As you command, it shall be done."

Blinking at the ease in which he agreed, I didn't know what to say. I merely offered him a smile and swayed to the sonata.

As much as I loved to dance, Henry did not. It was a shame, for it was a pleasure to be in his shadow, protected and cherished, with a strong hand holding mine.

The music changed.

The new, lulling tones, the sweetness I'd only heard in worship. My king tapped his finger to the seductive rhythm.

The pitch and clarity reached into my soul. This music was meant for movement. "Henry, take my hand and let us attempt a minuet."

His gaze became wary and he looked away. "Non. This amusement is for the nobles and the young. I'm content here, listening to the tune and sitting next to you."

Couples pranced along to the beat, adding more rhythm to the joyous three-quarter tempo.

"Oh. Look, Henry. Even Victor and Athénaïre are taking to the floor. I wonder how she convinced him. Perhaps she could offer the advice to me so that I can dance with my sovereign."

"Athénaïre can convince anyone of anything given the opportunity." Henry chuckled, then released my bracelet. "Always moving, Louise. Sometimes I'm content sitting still watching you."

He took up the silver chalice that sat near his crystal water goblet. Henry leaned closer. His lips dampening with the berry-smelling wine seemed like an invitation, a plea to live and love in the moment.

I longed to dance with my husband. My royal purple dress of satin had a creamy grosgrain ribbon sewn at the hem. It would billow like a sail as I turned about the room.

"You cannot sit still, can you, my dear? So like Athénaïre."

Trying to calm my tapping slipper, I gazed at his mock-shocked gape. "Henry, it's the fault of the musicians. It must be a sin to waste good music."

"Get up and dance."

"By myself? With everyone watching?" Wanting to pull him to the dance floor, I grimaced instead. "I'm sure Limonade or Dupuy would have something to say. Their admonishment would be correct."

"Not if I've ordered it. Besides, everyone's always watching a queen."

He sat back in the large chair tufted in blue velvet padding, then brushed at his hair, the dark curls ceding ground to gray ones. "But you are right about not wasting music."

Stomach knotting in anticipation, I rose but the king remained seated. "Baron de Vastey," he called. "Come."

His adviser snapped to attention and marched the short distance to the raised stage. "His Royal Highness, the prince royal, and Her Royal Highness, Madame Athénaïre, dance so well, excellent performance."

"Oui, Vastey," Henry said. "Dance with the queen."

Knowing Henry's jealous streak, I wasn't sure if this was some sort of test. I decided to be bold and reached for his star brooch. "I thought we were to dance, my king. We rarely do."

A panic crossed his face. "Non. The emperor lost the respect of many when he did the wretched twirling of the minuet. I'll sit and gaze at the experts. Baron de Vastey, dance with the queen."

Henry's adviser looked as disturbed as I, but he'd not refuse. He came up the steps of the platform. "It would be my honor."

All eyes in the ballroom now watched.

"Your Majesty," Vastey said and held out his palm.

Taking the offering, I let him lead me out onto the floor. The tune changed to something different as the tall lean man spun me.

As with everything Vastey did, he danced with distinction, each step precise, each twirl perfectly timed. The secretary was very light on his feet.

I closed my eyes and pretended this was Henry. Yet the motions felt empty.

"Your frown must mean you recognize the tune."

"Non. What is it?"

"Your Majesty, 'The Ruins of Athens,' Beethoven's Opus 113. It's for a play about the goddess Athena awakening after a thousand years to find her city ruined and her country occupied by foreigners."

I stopped midstep. "Why is the tempo upbeat for such a sad thing?"

"Well, it swells with patriotism. At the end, the goddess and a king swear to rebuild the country."

Vastey was a special man. Strategic even when he wasn't trying to be. Or perhaps he was a fortune teller, a mambo warning of what troubles the kingdom could face. But the king and this pretend goddess for our nation had to unite to protect what the Kingdom of Hayti had begun to build.

THE SELECTION ENDED, AND BEFORE THE START OF THE NEXT,
Henry was at my side. "Vastey, lead everyone outside. Time for the
final cannon salute for the prince royal."

"Of course, Your Majesty," the man said with a bow. "Divine dancing, my queen."

With his head still low, he retreated and I felt Henry's shadow over-
take mine.

I turned, brushing against his sash. "You could've just danced with
me from the beginning and spared the baron a moment of your jealousy."

"Unlike the theme of tonight's ballet, I'll not leave you unguarded."
His head tilted. His gaze fell upon me as if I'd been absent a long time.
"You looked too happy dancing with Vastey."

"I'm happy dancing, and I tried to imagine it was you holding my
hand."

The fury in his eyes disappeared. "I don't want to be embarrassed,
but the sight of another man touching you pains me."

The ballroom emptied, and I held my breath and expected a lec-
ture.

Instead, Henry hummed, laced his fingers with mine, and held me.
Slow and easy, we moved as one to his version of Ries's Violin Concerto. My cheek flattened against his solid chest, the icy brooch, but I
warmed in his protective arms. My ear vibrated with the strong beat of
his heart and whispers of his love.

"I fear . . . I wish to never disappoint you. Never draw shame, Louise."

The openness . . . the hums—

I never wanted this moment to end.

With a swirl, a sigh, a light kiss to my brow, he stopped and stepped
away. "Thank you for the dance, ma reine."

He left me to the parquet crosses. At the threshold, he pivoted. "Our
duties are not done, but neither is my love for you. Let's finish Victor's
celebration on one accord."

Times like this, I'd follow Henry anywhere. We walked side by side, palm in palm until we reached the balcony where the girls and I greeted everyone, of the northern entry of Sans-Souci.

As the king talked to his ministers, I found my son and kissed his cheek. "Nine years old with the world ahead of you."

He wiped his face free of my affection. "It's an awful lot of pomp and circumstance. What happens for a tenth or twelfth birthday?"

Knowing that my firstborn never saw past his eleventh, I bent and put my lips to Victor's forehead again. "Every birthday will be bigger than the last. These celebrations tell you how much you are loved."

"Was a good day, Maman. Did you see me? I did the commands right."

Victor looked over my shoulder to where Henry stood. "Père's proud of me. He really is!"

Wanting to hug him and protect him from all the unseen dangers and the mountains of responsibilities that awaited him, I resisted and straightened his lapel. "We are proud. Keep learning all you can. Be an aid to your king."

After a quick hug to my waist, my boy walked to Prince Armande, who stood with younger sons of nobles.

For a moment, I took in the sight of them—happy, bold, growing in their strength. It was beautiful seeing these Black boys, these wonderful young men, coming into their own with no limits being placed upon their futures. They were part of the fabric of a free Hayti. This ideal was worth fighting for, worth protecting.

"Queen Marie-Louise, Prince Victor," Dupuy said, "it's time for the display."

With my son holding on to the balcony rail, Henry and I stood on either side of our birthday boy.

Like a waterfall spilling onto the courtyard, couples fluttered behind us descending either side of the double staircase. Prince Armande and my princesses came close.

Troops marched in both directions, beating drums.

Earlier I'd been so fretful, I hadn't taken a moment to absorb how vast the grounds looked. Torches were lit all the way to the gates, around the surrounding buildings—the storehouse, stables, and barracks. The round chapel had candles in the window.

It stood proud with its circular walls, its majestic tiled brown dome and white cupola.

Turning to Henry, I leaned into him and adjusted his gold brooch. It had slipped a little from our dance. "Look at what you've made. My husband, my king, the builder. These are your people, Henry. Your kingdom."

"Sans-Souci is for you and my sons and daughters. This is where you should feel safe, always."

"It was nothing but hills. You made it smooth, filled the ravine, and planted fruit trees."

"And a pepper cinnamon tree."

"Oui, you remembered, Henry."

"Always."

We stood half in the other's arms, just existing. No pressure to move or pay attention to the marching below.

Then a cannon sounded. Henry wrenched away from me and clutched the rail.

His golden-brown eyes looked wary, even haunted. I rubbed his back, remembering the paralyzing fear of his nightmare.

"Henry?"

He pulled away and headed down the steps. I had to pretend that I hadn't seen fear in his countenance. Why were his wartime demons returning? I'd never felt closer to him.

I looked skyward for answers, for one of those less busy angels or soaring hymns. Above my head, anchored to Sans-Souci's wall, was a black-streaked sun with the motto scored into the wood, "Je vois tout, et tout voit par moi dans l'univers."

That saying was right. Up high or up close, *I saw everything, and everything in the universe could be seen by me.* I saw all of Henry. I saw his doubts and watched him flee.

I'd give him my strength. He needn't ask, just merely stay.

My king stopped near Dupuy and Vastey by the courtyard fountain that pumped water from the underground streams below the palace.

The cannon continued to blast. Troops marched. The crowds sighed and clapped. All the noise drowned the babble of the spigot.

Yet the water still trickled down, even if its sound was never acknowledged.

Shouts came from the left.

Someone ran toward the fountain.

A sword flashed.

"Lanmò wa a!" a woman cried out.

"Mort au roi!" a man shouted.

Dupuy and Vastey and the king's private guard, the Dahomet soldiers in celestial blue uniforms, surrounded Henry. Others came onto the steps and formed a wall around Victor, Armande, the girls, and me.

The Dahomets held their ground. They'd die before allowing anyone to hurt us.

Our guests scattered as I stood with my children on the balcony watching the soldiers subdue the assailants who'd come to kill Henry, Victor, and countless more.

THE KINGDOMS

Britain

Bury and Norwich Post, Wednesday, July 28, 1813

Grand Festival at Vauxhall

A grand National Fete was given at Vauxhall Gardens, on Tuesday, in honour of the glorious service of the army in the Peninsula. Several of the Stewards attended at an early hour to see that every necessary preparation was made for the accommodation of the company. A range of temporary buildings was erected from the Rotunda to the Pavilion, in a semicircular form, to contain 5000 persons.

Hayti

Government Gazette (India), Thursday, July 29, 1813

St. Domingo—Capt. Lyon, who arrived at this port, in 21 days, from St. Domingo, informs, that there had been a hard fought battle between the armies of Pétion and Christophe, in which the latter was defeated with considerable loss. After the battle Christophe was killed by one of his aides-de-camps at a meeting of his Officers.

17

1813 Sans-Souci, Kingdom of Hayti

That feeling that something would happen, that shaking, quaking premonition that the world would end, came over me, and I knew I'd be dragged by the toes to the middle of Place d'Armes and executed like the brave Suzanne Bélair.

Gasping, I awakened in my bedchamber. Pitch blackness greeted my eyes, but I didn't smell sulfur. I had no hole in my chest.

It was a nightmare.

Turning in my bedclothes, I reached for my husband.

Henry, as usual, was not beside me.

I lit a candle and walked outside onto the terrace that housed his bath, a copper tub. He kept it here to soak in warm water and enjoy the view of my gardens.

Light gleamed on the empty tub. I was alone in our private quarters.

Two weeks had passed since the terrifying ending to Victor's fete. He and the girls were fine. They had questions, but Henry told them to be satisfied that the evildoers had been caught.

They weren't. I wasn't, either, but no one would defy the king.

Two attacks on the same day? The level of dissatisfaction with Henry's reign must be high. Pétion and his minions in the south couldn't be responsible for both, could they? With him planting stories of my husband's death in the British papers, I wasn't sure.

And Henry discussed nothing with me.

Kicking at the empty tub made it clang. The man wouldn't admit to any problem.

Down by the mouth of the stream that cooled the palace floors, where the soapberry trees grew and the wash was done, my maid heard the talk, the envy and hatred of Henry. Zephyrine told me of the unrest to protect me and the children, but I needed to save my husband.

Setting my candle on the bronze table next to the tub, I squatted and dragged my limbs inside the copper bowl. It was dry and smooth to the touch, but solid and unmoving.

Hurricanes could come and this thing would withstand them.

And I could be weak inside, sheltered and protected within its walls.

Tucking my chin along the rim, my mind echoed the cannons of the fete, the gunshots in my dreams . . . the noises I heard long ago when I hid in caves with my children.

Henry's and Dessalines's and Pétion's forces were one and on the run from Leclerc, the head of the French forces.

Prizes had been posted for their heads. If I'd been caught, they'd have used me to capture Henry, then slaughter us.

Somehow after all the chaos, our nation was free and my baby Victor was born, healthy and whole.

There was hope in the darkness.

When he was just a waiter, Henry and I used to talk about everything. I had to remind him of that.

Leaping out of the tub, I went inside our bedchamber and scooped on my robe.

The light muslin covering my limbs warred against the coolness of the room. Yet the smooth linen, the color of goat's milk, gave me a glow.

Pulling my robe tighter about me, I moved to the hall. Torches were lit. A gilded mirror captured my ghostly form. Perhaps a persistent haunting would do Henry and me some good.

My girls' rooms were down the corridor. Victor's and Armande's, too. I made my footfalls quiet. The last thing I needed was to awaken everyone in the palace.

Passing guards at their posts, I slipped to the balcony. No one was in the courtyard or on the double steps, no king or imagined attacker.

The night air was cool.

The wet season would soon start. I smelled the light hint of rain in the low clouds.

Maybe a good cleansing, something beyond a hot bath or a gentle shower, was needed to loosen Henry's tongue. How could I drain the hidden poison the wars had left in him?

With my candle lighting the way, I went back inside.

Looking over the gallery, I noticed more members of the Royal Dahomets. Since they were here, that had to mean Henry was on the palace grounds.

Hesitating outside the throne room, I decided to go against protocol and interrupt his meeting. Flinging open the doors, I crossed the threshold and bowed. "Your Majesty."

Lifting my countenance, I expected to see Vastey and Dupuy, or even Dr. Stewart or Limonade or Romain, counseling my husband. An empty room greeted me.

Was he in one of the other buildings of Sans-Souci that served as offices for his advisers?

Yellow petals were on the floor.

A flower from my garden had been brought inside. I bent and picked it up. It still held a fruity scent. It hadn't been here long and it wasn't from my plantings.

My heart drummed.

Geneviève's warnings—rumors of other women and infidelity surrounded all the leaders, but not Henry.

My chest stung. Why else would he disappear?

Not true. Not Henry.

Zephyrine peeked inside. "Ma'am, you in here?"

Gasping, I answered. "Oui."

She squinted at me. "I've checked on Madame Première. She started wheezing. I made her tea. The princess is sleeping easier. The changes in the air are hard for her sometimes."

Breathing was always hard for Améthyste. "The coming rainy season," I said with a useless nod. "I should go to her."

"Madame, she's asleep. And you look frazzled. Upsetting her wouldn't be good."

This was true. My daughter needed her rest.

"But something is wrong with you." She eyed me and my night-clothes. "Let me return you to your room, ma reine."

For a moment, I wanted to keep my thoughts to myself, but I needed an ally, a discreet woman in the palace. "Have you seen the king? Where is he?" I was beginning to feel desperate. "I don't care what he's hiding. I just need to know."

Her gray-smoke eyes turned soft, and she nodded. Taking my hand, she led me back into the throne room to the window. Pulling back the silk curtains, she pointed to the mountains. "The Citadel, madame. That's where he goes. That's where he always goes."

In the dark, the mountain looked ominous, like a giant. "Is something wrong with the construction, Zephyrine?"

"It's taking too long to build, like everything else for the king. He believes he can finish it."

"But the workers aren't there at night. Nor are the architects or the soldiers or the brickmakers he pays. What can the king do?"

Zephyrine shrugged.

I pulled my robe closer to me. "If he's up there, then I should hurry him along. I should go now."

She caught my arm. "I hear he's not alone up there."

Again I heard my sister's warning, and my stomach felt kicked. "Then I should definitely hurry the king back. He may need a reminder that he's married and his wife wants him home."

"It's miles away by carriage." Zephyrine wouldn't release my arm. "Let me show you the quickest route."

"Lead the way." I didn't think about changing or wasting another minute. Tonight, I'd know whether I could still claim Henry's heart.

THOUGH I LOVED WALKING, IT WAS CRAZY TO VENTURE INTO THE jungle at night to chase after a man. Yet I loved Henry and knew he hadn't been the same since he'd been crowned. I had to get to him. I needed to return him to his senses or to open my own eyes to the corruption that power can produce.

Pushing a branch out of my path, I held my torch up to the starry sky. Perhaps something in the clouds could tell me if Henry had faltered like Dessalines. Ruling, the strain and the grandeur, had confused the emperor. He had loved his wife but also taken many mistresses.

I couldn't believe Henry was as lecherous, but he wasn't acting like the man I wed.

Zephyrine panted, "Ma reine, we're almost there."

We'd walked about an hour along this secret way to the Citadel, but soon the clouds opened and revealed Bonnet à l'Evêque, the biggest mountain I knew. On the forward face poked out Henry's Ark, as I liked to call it. The prow of the Citadel's fort looked like a huge boat, lodged into position by a great flood.

Dark, with mere pops of torchlight, the structure was ominous, looming thousands of feet up.

"It will be morning before I reach the top."

"Non, madame," Zephyrine said and pointed to a makeshift stable.

A soldier was on guard. He recognized me. "More royal visitors."

"Oui. Madame needs a mule to take her to the king."

He shrugged and towed one from one of the pens. "Your Majesty, you intend to go up? It's very far."

"I can ride bareback. I've done it before."

The man hesitated. "Mules kick, madame."

So did stubborn Christophes. I went near the beast and smoothed my hand over his spotted hide, then stroked his ear. "I can soothe him. Wait here, Zephyrine."

Her face wrinkled. "Is that wise, madame, to go alone? They say spirits haunt the Citadel. There are workers who've died here. Their angry ghosts remain."

Over the years, fatal accidents had not been uncommon. The mountain was steep, the terrain treacherous. The heavy bricks were hand carried. The sun had overwhelmed big strong men and women who'd come to build . . . or were forced to by soldiers.

"Mules are sure footed. They don't spook easily. This is all I need to reach the top."

"Are you sure, madame?" My poor Zephyrine looked fretful.

Absently, I'd clasped my bracelet and began rolling it the way Henry did. "I'll be fine. I'm going to see the king."

The soldier held the mule, and I climbed on and took up the reins, headed to the dimly lit path. My maid gave me her torch. "Good luck."

"Non. You keep it. It will guide me back if I return alone."

Fingers trembling, my maid gripped it tightly and I saw her whispering prayers. I needed the strength of the saints to prepare me for what I would find at the top of the Citadel.

AS I SUSPECTED, MY MULE CHOSE THE EASIEST PATH TO THE FOR-tress. It took its time moving steadily up until we'd arrived at the base of the largest military structure in the West Indies, probably the world.

I'd been here dozens of times for ceremonies, but never at night.

The stars and the torches that lit the building emphasized the curving walls as much as the flat ones. This was stone and brick, molasses and lime, and blood, lots of blood to build this frightening structure.

I saw no sign of Henry. The man had his hands in every part of the construction. When enslaved in Saint Kitts, he'd learned the trade of bricklaying, and he had built sections here along with everyday people.

No music was playing. Nothing that sounded of a harem or a mistress.

Yet, it was a possibility.

Had I spent so much time trying to find my way that I'd neglected him? My days learning court etiquette or journeying to Cap-Henry to resurrect hospitals—was it too much time away?

I rapped on my skull. My busyness was no excuse for infidelity.

The mule brayed. I climbed down and wanted him to hush. "Don't alert someone before I want them to know I'm here. Are we clear, mule?"

The beast chewed his lip and I tied him to a post. "Stay."

Walking toward the entrance, I felt my temper flare. Did Henry realize how often he left me alone? Had he thought about his fellow officers who'd tried to take his place in my affections? During the long war, I was faithful despite all the temptations. I deserved the same faith. Being apart or busy or having power was no excuse.

"Calm down," I told myself. I'd convicted my husband before I knew the truth.

If it were true that he had a mistress, what was I going to do? He was the king.

And what of our children?

Would he send me away from them?

Or would I have to be like Empress Dessalines, whose good heart had her raising the emperor's sons and daughters from his cheating? Henry said the country's treasury paid Jacques I's mistresses.

I didn't know how she had lifted her head or found a way to still love the man after such betrayal. I knew I wasn't built that way.

18

1813 Citadel, Kingdom of Hayti

Walking into the central courtyard, I smelled the pitch from torches illuminating loopholes for cannons. Looking up at the six high batteries that served as posts to watch the sea, I saw no movement. The buildings in the Citadel that housed rooms for Henry, a chapel, soldiers' barracks, and stores and stores of munitions seemed lifeless.

The enormity of this place, dimly lit, isolated on the mountain, suddenly seemed daunting.

How was I to find Henry when the path to reach him wasn't clear?

I slipped to my knees, my robe acting like a carpet, and prayed for favor. As I had hiding in caves, hoping for an easy birth without the problems of a breech, I asked the saints to help. "Find Henry. Let him be safe and whatever he has done that's wrong, make him have a repentant heart. If he is wrong, make my heart larger to forgive."

Rising, I dusted my clothes, which smelled of mule's lather. I wandered around the echoey building, finding more stores of weapons, barracks, and even a jail.

It had to have been an hour of aimless searching.

Almost ready to give up, I turned to head back to my mule when I heard noises.

Human sounds. Mumbles.

Edging toward them, I saw twinkling light.

One of the batteries overhead had movement, shifting shadows. I found a darkened passage that moonlight poured into and made plain.

I climbed stairs and kept going toward the noises . . . the conversation.

"Père, are we done yet?"

That was Victor's voice.

"Work harder. You can do it. Just a little longer." That was Armande, encouraging my boy.

Creeping a little closer, I saw Henry. His uniform and shirt were off. In the torchlight, he glistened with sweat. He and his boys were up here laying bricks.

I eased back into the shadows. My eyes were wet. I sobbed. Henry brought his sons to the Citadel to spend time with them.

It was good to see Armande with him, but Victor, too. My heart melted.

Henry came closer to our son. "Very good. That line is perfectly straight. Very good, Victor."

Then he moved to Armande and used a trowel to chip off the last row. "Too fast, son. We'll never have what we deserve in life if we move in haste. Solid dependable action wins."

Armande grumbled a little. Then he said, "Why are we here? Workers will come in the morning. It's their job to do this."

Henry shook his head. "Never ask a man to do something you're not prepared to do yourself. You have to be willing to roll up your sleeves and get involved. It's leadership. I need to make sure you both understand."

"Why, Père? Why must we understand in the middle of the night?" Victor's voice sounded tired. I wanted to scoop him up, but that would ruin what Henry was trying to teach him.

He respected his sons, both of them. They, like the girls, were his legacy as much as the Citadel and the kingdom.

"My princes, if the assassins had succeeded, then that would put Victor on the throne of our new kingdom. We're three years old compared to countries that have existed for centuries."

He took the spade from Victor's hand and pointed to the sea. "You will rule the Kingdom of Hayti. And Armande, you must protect him. You'll be his top commander, someone whom he can trust. In leadership, trust is the most important thing."

All the good feeling I had dissolved in my stinging gut. I was spying on my husband because I'd lost faith in the man Henry was.

He wasn't the person I'd married. Being erratic and given to whims must be the result of the pressure he felt in leading. Loving a driven man was hard. I had to let him be who he was. To support him despite myself, despite the tensions I saw conflicting his spirit, that was my calling.

That had been my role since the tall young man waited tables for my father.

I tore away from the battery. Henry and I had problems, but I'd never again doubt him. By the time I made it back to my mule and down to Zephyrine, I'd finished crying. The mule must have thought me a fool, too.

My maid helped me down. "Well, is all well?"

"He's with his sons, preparing them to lead after his death."

It struck my heart, chilling the blood in my marrow. What was the Kingdom of Hayti without Henry?

"Madame? Let's go back to Sans-Souci." She put her hands to my shoulders and led me back to the jungle. I stayed silent, couldn't put to words this feeling—that the king knew assassins would try again and this time succeed.

I WAITED FOR HENRY, SITTING UP IN OUR BED. HE RETURNED AT SUN-rise, dragging into our chambers, probably expecting to see a covered-up lump on our soft mattress.

His face filled with surprise when I lit a candle.

"Louise?"

"I stayed up, waiting for you."

"I was at—"

"I know you were at the Citadel."

With a nod, he took off his jacket and laid it across the Chippendale chair in the sitting area. "You should be asleep."

"And you should be honest. Henry, I know those who want you dead aren't going to stop trying."

"They'll not be lucky enough to do so. As long as there's strength in my body, I'll crush them. No one will come against me and live."

His tone was dark and resolute.

His confidence thrilled me.

Throwing off sheets, I leapt out of the bed and went to him. "I'm glad you're confident, but I'm scared, scared of more war, scared of losing us."

He kissed my brow. "I'm right here, Louise. I've not gone from you."

"Yes, you have. Every time you turn from me and I don't know your thoughts, you've left. Remember before the war . . . when it was just us sitting under a pepper tree."

"A pepper cinnamon tree."

"Oui, and you talked with me. You shared with me your plans. I knew you inside and out."

He dipped his balled fists into a washbasin. "You don't want to know all anymore. My hands aren't clean."

Water drizzled down his bare forearms, sculpting his beautiful, scarred skin. "They'll never be."

His confession had to be about the wars—the ones in the past and the one with Pétion. I cared not for what he'd done, just that he'd survived.

Gripping his fingers, I pulled them to my bosom. Warmth radiated, the coolness of the water—it all seeped through my nightgown.

I shivered and drew closer.

"Got you all wet, Louise."

"Oui. I like water. And I still believe in you. You have to believe in us."

"I've done things to protect the kingdom. I'm guilty. You can't know. I can never tell you—"

"Non, Henry . . ."

The glare in his eyes made him seem possessed. For a moment, he bit his lip. "I must protect you from everything, even me."

"Whatever is done is over. You and I, we're forever."

He dropped to his knees and wrapped his arms about me. "Does that mean I have your forgiveness for everything?"

Wasn't sure what sins he referred to beyond politics and war.

Again, I didn't care. With my fingers in his short, curly hair, smoothing the fine texture, enjoying the spring and life in his graying locks, I blocked all my questions and blurted, "Oui. Of course. Because you're alive, we have another day to do things right."

Henry stood and kept me in his embrace. "You're my queen." He kissed me fully and tenderly, like we'd newly wed, like I was still that fifteen-year-old girl who was completely besotted.

A knock at the door separated us.

Servants came in with his hot bath. I'd told Zephyrine to have them do so the moment he arrived.

They filled the tub with the steaming water and arranged fresh thick towels on the table.

"Thank you" was what he said with his lips. But his eyes were on me. "Now leave me, me and my queen."

He held the door for the servants who would've stayed and helped him dress and shave.

Once the lot of them had fled, Henry kissed me again, so sweetly, and then he went out to the terrace.

I followed him outside, where he stirred the bath with his fingertips. "This will feel good. You go on back to bed. I'll join you when I'm done."

A new bride might be obedient.

I wasn't new. And I refused to sleep and dream of the people that wanted my husband dead.

Henry began unbuttoning buttons, tugging off his shirt, beginning to undo his breeches.

It took him a moment to realize I hadn't moved.

"Louise, is something the matter?"

"Did you know when I and my sisters were little and it was a hot day, we went to the river, the Rivière Mapou?"

"No, but a lot of children I suspect went there."

"Yes, but I didn't want to get my clothes dirty, so I went in bare."

Letting my robe fall, I stepped close to him. Offering him a kiss, a strong embrace, I left him panting and climbed into his tub.

Sinking down, I braced against the walls as the hot water flooded my skin. "It's good and warm, Henry."

My husband looked confused, then amused, but he stayed still, gaping at me and his copper tub.

"Why am I alone, Henry?" I stood. As though I'd emerged from the river, water dripped down my neck, making my nightgown translucent.

His breathing hitched, but he hadn't moved.

With the water ebbing about my knees, I beckoned him with my pinkie. "Come, Your Majesty, the water's fine."

He stretched and lifted me up as if I could touch the sun. But I wanted none of it, none of the light, only Henry. We needed to be so close that nothing would separate us.

With a big splash, he put me back into the tub.

Undressed, he stuck one foot in and then the other. "You summoned, my queen."

I smiled, fully and truthfully with all the love in my heart. Then I went into his arms.

We sank into the water and ripped away muslin and silks. Stays and corset sailed over the balcony, and I laughed and kissed my king. No trappings of this royal life or power could come between us. Never again.

This was the man I knew better than I knew myself—so decent and caring, making me feel beautiful and safe, always so safe.

Then we were as one, soaking in his copper tub, loving each other as we looked toward my gardens and forever.

Death stalks the good and the bad. Perhaps
Saint John or his reaper should spend more
time with those who deserve the company.

— MADAME CHRISTOPHE, 1847

Glasgow Courier, Saturday, May 8, 1847

Death of the late President of Hayti—Jean Baptiste Riche, the late president of Hayti, who died at Hayti at Port-au-Prince on the 27th February, was about seventy years of age and literally covered with wounds.

19

1847 Florence, Italy

The notes of the grand pipe organ of Santa Felicita Church filter into my open window. My leased rooms are a warm orange with pretty mosaic-tiled floors. Close to my favorite bridge and river, I feel at home. The Ponte Vecchio, a living stone monument, crosses the swirling Arno. People have built homes across the span, small dwellings, each a poor man's lively palace. At dusk, the busyness settles. I hear life and love and laughter, then witness the sun lower and wash in the waves.

At noon, a breeze enters the window. Loving the music, I sit back, wrap my cream shawl about my shoulders, and allow the sunshine to dance along my cheeks.

High, extended pitches of today's choir rehearsal of Handel's *Messiah* touch me. "Sunday service will be wonderful. This area of Florence about Santa Felicita is known for immigrants."

"Does it feel like home?" David Michelson, the *Globe* reporter, has asked questions all morning about Victor's fabulous fete and more aspects of the kingdom.

I sip my lemony chamomile tea. "Honey here takes the taste of mildly bitter thistle and earthy heather. In Sans-Souci, it's more vanilla and oranges, for the bees fed on citrus blossoms from my garden."

"No sugar for you? King Henry revitalized the economy of Hayti because of sugarcane. I thought you'd appreciate that more."

The dapper man, in his pleated indigo tailcoat and his expensive check-patterned waistcoat, is hinting at something that sounds like disapproval, but my mind drifts to the saintly choir's singing.

He was despised and rejected of men, a man of sorrows and acquainted with grief.

"Handel's words are gripping. His musical notes pierce, remind me of things." All the doubts, all the damnations that haunt my dreams about the past.

"You're crying, Madame Christophe." The reporter whom I've invited for caffè the past two days offers a handkerchief.

When I wipe my eyes, I notice how soft the linen is. I remember such quality from goods Henry had imported from Hamburg.

Monsieur Michelson has the tip of his quill in his mouth. Probably a nervous habit, like my rolling of a bracelet, but why is he so nervous when we've spent hours talking of my life?

"Madame Christophe, I know it is hard to discuss the kingdom, but I want to get every aspect as correct as possible."

"Do you know difficulty? You're young, strong, a man, and even handsome for those who wish to ignore the tint of your face. Maybe you do know difficulties. Most can't ignore differences in skin."

Setting aside his quill, he stares at me. "You're either very honest or too direct."

"I'm of the age where I get to choose my words with very few consequences."

"We've spent pleasurable mornings discussing the beginnings of the Kingdom of Hayti. I want to talk of the decline."

I rise and return his handkerchief. "Another time. As you say, it has been a good morning."

The fellow doesn't budge. "We can get back to it later, but there's a great deal we have to cover. You mentioned living in Ipswich and then Blackheath."

"Yes, we stayed with the Clarksons at their home for a long time. They made us part of their community. The Thornton girls, the Inglises, Madame Alexander, Madame Shaw, many others made us feel very welcome."

At this, he sits back with his eyes raised. "Was that odd, moving from a predominantly Black society to a Blanc one, as you would say?"

Walking behind my chair to adjust the curtains, my heels tap the wide pine boards, but I miss the patterns of Haytian parquet. "I love leasing rooms from Monsieur Giligni. We're old friends. Anytime I'm in Florence, he's very amenable."

"You've come back and forth a great deal during the years."

"Oui." The answer is sufficient and direct enough to keep Michelson from veering into areas of my life beyond Henry. He's tried that quite a lot today.

He shuffles through his thick set of papers.

"That looks to be enough for a book on Hayti, not a series of mere articles, Monsieur Michelson. Perhaps you should tell me what you're truly doing."

His big manipulative smile is hung with the largest dimples. The man is a charmer, as Madame Clarkson would say.

"If a book is what it takes to correct the narrative about King Henry, don't you think it's worth it?"

"Non. A book takes a long time to write and publish. But newspapers will reprint the lies now. I've seen them, been pestered by them. That's why I sent my manservant, Souliman, to you. If there's a chance to correct horrible propaganda, I wish to do it."

As he twiddles his quill, making lazy circles in the corner, I see the cogs in his head turning, and I prepare for the new onslaught.

"Madame Christophe, how did you manage when you came to England?"

"I told you. The kindness of King Henry's friends."

"Yes, ma'am. You said this, but I meant financially. A bit of jewelry and monies from the archbishop of Canterbury would only last a few years. You've been living abroad for over twenty-five."

Ah, the means question. "How can exiles live so well? Black exiles? That's your question?"

He sat back, leveling his shoulders. "These rooms are beautiful. Your furnishings are stylish. You are, too."

Oui, a charmer. I toss him a short smile. He's earned it with his flattery. "Monsieur Giligni has a nice eye for pretty things. Most of these are his doing. And this is a modest dwelling. While many wouldn't want to live so close to a church, I find it a blessing."

The choir's voice grows loud.

For the Lord God omnipotent reigneth.
Hallelujah!

Hallelujah!

Monsieur Michelson pushes aside his papers and leaps up. "This is the part where King George II stood. I always do, too. The acoustics here are quite fine. Worth whatever you are paying, four or five francs a month?"

Digging into my pockets so soon. "Something like that, give or take a franc for old friends."

The young man doesn't seem satisfied, but I don't care. I glory in the sounds and the history of the place. "The square shares a cistern with the church. See the covered passageway." I point to the floating bridge, as I call it, something Henry would've built from Sans-Souci to his beloved Citadel.

"I believe the ruler Cosimo made the structure, the Vasari Corridor, so that he could work and then go home to his wife at the Pitti Palace. The passageway goes through the beautiful church. Cosimo could hear the pipe organ and the hymns as he left his work for his wife."

Pursing my lips, I think of the love, the weddings I've witnessed staying so close to Santa Felicita Church. "Those who find that one perfect person are loath to let them go, even for a day."

"Odd to do so, building something just for himself and a spouse." Michelson retakes his seat. His brow furrows deeper and deeper. "Selfishness from centuries ago."

"Selfish or selflessly loving? I suppose commitment is another relic for the old. A cynical man would say the rich Medici, Cosimo, just wanted a measure of comfort on his journey. We are always travelers, exiled from something. Some, like Monsieur Giligni and the Clarksons, welcome visitors as if they're entertaining angels. Others don't. They are selfish."

"Is that why you've offered me tea and biscuits? A sort of generosity as I ask deeply personal questions?"

"Perhaps. But can't we be civil?"

"Have many been civil to you, being foreign and exotic?"

I could ask a Colored man the same, but he's still a man. The elephant in the room is how can Black women live well at all. "Our treatment by the Clarksons and their neighbors was not odd at all.

I've gained lifelong friendships. And I left the places where I wasn't wanted."

His lips purse, and I hope that means he understands. In countries designed by Blancs, ruled by Blancs, they have no problems assimilating other Blancs. Occasionally they make room for the unusual, the exotic, but only occasionally.

"For me and my daughters, we kept moving, kept trying to find a safe spot in the world where kindness and generosity were the norm. Some places, we were more successful than others."

The reporter sits and sips his tea, which has surely gone cold. "Madame, you and your family have lived quite well in Europe. You have several attendants. There have been reports of even more, including interpreters—"

"If everyone spoke tolerable French or English, there would be no need for someone else to make sense of things."

His round eyes drift before snapping back to attention. "How have you survived? Where has the money come from? How much of Christophe's illicit treasury did you bring with you to England when you escaped?"

"Are you in need of money, Monsieur Michelson?"

"Everyone can use a little more."

"Then why didn't you say that was what you're after?" I trudge to the door and hold it open. "Leave, sir. At least you didn't pretend to be a nephew or Henry's brother or one of a thousand other invented relatives to gain money that doesn't belong to you."

He caps his ink and gathers his papers. "I want nothing but answers. I'll be well compensated when I submit my assignment. But the question of Christophe's fortune is a true one. He had enormous wealth, and by your lifestyle, even your silk clothes, one can see you haven't suffered."

I point again to the corridor. "Leave now, and quietly. Do not disturb choir practice."

He steps across my threshold. "I don't mean to offend you, but I'm running out of time. You've given me the niceties. It sounds as if King Henry was a misunderstood sensitive genius. That everywhere you've gone in exile everyone has treated you with respect. I know that's not the truth."

Michelson takes his handkerchief and mops at his neck. "You're painting everything to be rosy. I know it wasn't. You have to tell me everything. Then I can help."

"What can you possibly help me with? As you said, I live comfortably. And I have had generous spirits with me."

"But you've had sorrows. And King Henry was no angel. For people to believe what I write, it has to be balanced."

"You want more honesty? Or you want my story to have pain? Why? You want Black people to seem tragic to engender pity amongst your Blanc readers? The Christophes do not need pity."

"Madame. Like to come . . ." He wipes his hands and coughs, covering up that familiar accent. "I'd like to come back tomorrow. I'd like to start again."

"To ask me more questions whose answers you'll choose not to believe? I'm not one to waste anyone's time."

Pushing at the door, I start it moving, but he puts his boot in the way.

"Tell me of the downfall. That's honest. That will touch my readers and preserve the king's place in history. Unless you are happy with your husband being labeled an illiterate, unhinged despot. Are you content with the narrative that Marie-Louise Christophe uses his ill-gotten gains to live in splendor in her exile and gives to charity to assuage her guilt? That will be the story unless you continue talking to me."

My hand flies to my mouth. Now I've become the story, not merely Henry. Zephyrine knew Michelson would be trouble. I should've listened.

"Madame, shall we continue with this interview tomorrow?"

"You wouldn't print such lies."

"I'll have to if you don't talk with me. I know that you and King Henry deserve better than what this report says. Think on it, ma'am. Send for me."

"Make it lunchtime, two days from now. I think I'm done seeing you in the morning."

"Yes, ma'am. Two days." He bows, and I shut the door in his face.

"Thank you, Queen Marie-Louise." His voice carries, echoing like the choir, but this reporter's performance isn't over. It won't be until he knows everything, and I'm not sure I can keep hidden all the sins Henry and I committed.

EXILE

Northampton Mercury, Saturday, May 4, 1822

Madame Christophe, ci-devant Empress of Hayti, is about to take up her residence at Blackheath. It is generally understood that she has saved about £1500 per annum from the wreck of her deceased husband's fortune.

20

1822 Blackheath, England

Staring through the sheer curtains, watching carriages and gigs go by, had become part of my morning routine. With everyone but the servants sleeping in their beds, I'd had a cup of tea and counted wheels of vehicles passing down the lane—two-wheeled gigs, four-wheeled carriages, and one wheelbarrow.

Our leased town house—well, that's what they called these things, buildings that shoot upward instead of sprawling across acreage—sat off King George Street. This residence afforded a nice view of a park with beautiful trees and ponds with daylilies.

One could get lost in there.

I often did.

With the warmer weather, it was a treat to walk alone, just me and my thoughts. In another hour, I'd don my bonnet and do just that.

The girls, particularly Athénaïre, were upset at leaving the friends they'd made in Ipswich and Suffolk. The Thornton daughters' visit to Blackheath next week would brighten everyone's spirits.

"Maman?" Améthyste came down the stairs to the parlor. "Why do you still get up so early? Ladies here don't breakfast until ten."

"When the sun comes up, I'm up. Old habits." I waved her to come to me, but then I saw her bare feet. "Améthyste, we both can't keep getting sick. You need your slippers."

She sat on the light-blue sofa and curled her bare toes into her embroidered pink nightgown. It was something we brought from home . . . Le Cap . . . Cap-Henry . . . Cap-Haytian. Self-correcting my thoughts was a point of gloom.

"Your face. Whenever you made that face, Père . . ."

"Non. Dearest, you can talk of him. The fact that he's chosen not to be with us doesn't matter."

Her face wrinkled; her eyes became wide. "That's an odd way to put what happened."

It was.

My anger or hurt at Henry not being here—not guiding us, not humming, or telling me all will be well—escaped. I covered my face with my hands. "I mean if he lived, he'd want your feet covered, too."

"Maman." Améthyste put her arms around me. "I don't mean to make you sad."

"Then let's not be. I won't dwell on thinking of the king gone. I'll focus on his benevolence. My dearly departed husband provided for me and his princesses."

The archbishop was good to his word. The nine thousand pounds was safely deposited in my bank account. Henry's former money managers were now mine. Reid, Irving and Company would continue to invest this sum, advise us on financial matters, and look into Henry's holdings in the United States. It seemed there might be much more money being held because of the way Henry died. No will. No directives.

"Maman, is there money enough for charcoal and some canvases?"

"Of course. I'll have Zephyrine get some for you."

A huff blasted from her lips. "I ran out and was fretting. I want to draw so badly, but I didn't want to take our last penny."

This time I drew her into my embrace. "I need you to listen. We have access to money. That's why we no longer have to stay and burden others. We have our own again. There's enough for supplies."

"Then why don't you smile more, Maman?"

Maybe the many false ones I wore exhausted me too much, but I couldn't say that. Easing from her, I took the teapot and refreshed my cup. "There's beautiful red sorrel in the park. I wonder if local honey here will be tangy."

"Maman, confide in me. Let me help. I'm almost twenty-four. Not a little girl. Not being demanding or difficult, but I'm no delicate princess, either."

Oh, the arguments the word *difficult* had spawned. How many times did I tell Henry I wasn't that, when my attitude and stance said I was? "Améthyste, we've enough to live on for several years, maybe tens of years. But dowries, and things I know your father wanted for you, we don't have."

Her dark eyes hadn't moved from mine. "Thank you for the truth. I want you to depend on me. And we're doing good. Blackheath is good."

"I wish it had water."

"What, Maman?"

"It's a silly thing to miss. But when you've seen rivers and the sea, the beautiful sea, almost every day of your life, you don't understand how you'll miss it."

She sat again on the sofa. "I miss the salt in the air."

"Améthyste, I don't mean to sound ungrateful. And it's not as if we could return to Hayti—"

"Never, Maman. Not until everything changes."

Carrying my teacup and one for her, I sat beside her. "What if nothing changes? What if it gets worse? How do we help? Those are still our people."

"Are they?" She shook her head and clutched her robe as if caught in a windstorm. "They murdered my brothers and all of Père's allies while others who could help stood by and did nothing. If they think money made it out of their clutches, those Haytians could send someone after us."

We were at risk.

With our every movement and the disposition of our money printed in the papers, I wasn't exactly sure how we'd remain safe. I blew into my tea, making little waves in the clear brown liquid. "You're right, but I wish things could be different. You could be married now. Maybe Athénaïre, too."

My daughter peered into her cup, not at me. "I don't think I want to marry. It would be an unhappy affair."

"You don't want a family of your own?"

"To bear another target? Non." With a shrug, she sipped her tea.

My tongue soured. Bitterness filled me. Having lost her father and her brothers, Améthyste knew the consequences of our loss of power. A leaf floated in my tea. It must've escaped the pot. Would my daughters and I have been allowed to flee, if the traitors knew we'd have money?

Packing away my questions, I caught the leaf with my spoon and carefully flicked it onto a saucer, a common porcelain set I bought for our use. Modest, dependable, but nothing like what we'd had. The bad taste in my mouth returned.

"Sir Home, the Admiral Popham proved to be honorable," I said and set my spoon aside. "He took the money Henry gave him and deposited it with the archbishop. Honor among English gentlemen, I find that appealing."

"Appealing for me or you, Maman?"

That was a ridiculous question. "I'm a settled widow. No one can ever mean more to me than your father. But you and your sœur are young. Love is for the young."

"It's for the healthy and lively. That's you."

We finished our tea in awkward silence—me wanting her to have the world, but a realistic picture of it. We were here, not in our homeland where beautiful Black men were plentiful.

Yet this made me face my future. I, too, would grow old alone. That stung. And as unfair as it was, I blamed Henry for leaving me.

Clinking her cup on the small table, Améthyste stretched. "I forgot. We received a note from Madame Clarkson. Monsieur Clarkson is bringing some friends to visit us today."

The Clarksons were dears, but tonight? That was very soon. "Then I should go take my walk now. Have Zephyrine prepare."

She nodded and turned to the stairs but came back inside the parlor. "Is there anything you miss, besides Sans-Souci?"

I missed the palace and how my whole family lived there. "I miss Cécile. I miss a sky with low clouds."

"If we ever go back, Maman, it would be for our family, nothing else. The people didn't stand up for the king. They didn't have Popham's honor."

I listened to her receding footfalls, then pulled on a coat and bonnet, headed outside, and prayed that I'd live to see to all the threats against my family gone, and that I'd never have to acknowledge the ones who betrayed my trust.

Tying the strings of my bonnet, I hurried on my walk. If the Clarksons were coming for an earlier visit, the news they'd bring couldn't be good.

PINK, CRIMSON, EMERALD GREEN, GREENWICH PARK BLOOMED IN colors. This warm season was unusual, with intermittent rain showers springing up, but today was vibrant with sunshine.

I walked to my favorite path of red sorrel. The arrow-shaped leaves pointed with the light breeze to a young couple. Hand in hand, with a chaperone or maid not too far behind, the young people promenaded.

The party passed me, and my thoughts drifted to walks with Henry. Then I pondered if Améthyste and Athénaïre would ever know the joy of love, of lovers strolling in each other's confidence.

My heart raced. I glanced at my empty hand balled tight at my side. My eyes stung. I headed back to my town house knowing I'd never again have that feeling of an intimate shadow covering me.

Refusing to slow down or listen, Henry had chosen this path for us. That was the truth I'd keep forever.

WHEN I RETURNED TO THE RESIDENCE, A CARRIAGE AND DRIVER were stopped outside. The sadness I'd been feeling changed to confusion when I heard high-pitched giggles.

Up the steps, I pushed inside.

Then I stopped.

The archbishop and Monsieur Clarkson were having tea with my daughters.

I dipped my head to the priest and clasped Monsieur Clarkson's hands. He greeted me, then said, "I've come with news."

My breath slowed. "The church wants the money back? But Sir Home gave it to you for my benefit."

"No, Madame Christophe. That's not why we've come."

Tall and portly, wearing a long dark jacket and breeches, the silver-haired archbishop of Canterbury, Monsieur Charles Manners-Sutton, was not a fussy man. I knew him as being direct and to the point. This silence and stillness must mean another setback or tragedy.

"Let me . . . let me send the girls away. Then tell me the bad news from Hayti." The words barely came out, but I suspected these men were here to reveal the names of more dead. Tears puddled in my throat. "Send them upstairs, then tell me the worst."

"It's not that, Maman." Améthyste opened a silky sack and dumped the contents onto the white table near the sofa. Out rolled gold and sparkling gems. Then I saw my bracelet, my emerald bracelet.

My knees gave way. I dropped to the pine floor. I'd been complaining and feeling sorry for myself, and here was proof of the good love that Henry and I had shared.

Clarkson helped me stand. I lunged toward the table, stretching my fingers toward the emerald as if it, or I, would disappear.

My daughters led me to the sofa, but I gawked at the jewelry the maids had stolen from the Osborne Hotel. Each piece held a memory, a moment of laughter and grandeur and love.

"It's not all returned," the archbishop said, "but a good portion of it."

I reached for the table and, as if it contained fire, tapped the bracelet with my finger. When lightning didn't strike, I greedily scooped it up onto my arm.

"What happened to the thieves?" Athénaïre seemed angry. Her eyes fixed on the fireplace poker. She wasn't going to grab it and use it as a weapon acting out the last scenes of our kingdom. My youngest girl wanted to seize it and beat a villain.

"Will the maids pay for this crime?" She asked in a voice clogging with tears.

The archbishop lowered his chin. "The one that confessed will be spared imprisonment."

He didn't mention the others who hadn't confessed. I wondered if the British dealt with such crimes as Henry would—capital offenses worthy of death.

Or did offenses against exiles mean nothing because a handful of things had been recovered? The lump in my throat became three sizes bigger.

Monsieur Clarkson picked up a brooch, a gold one with Henry's crest. It wasn't the one the king always wore, just an old one that had French inscriptions. I had left his favorite in our bedchamber.

"This is beautiful, ma'am, solid gold. The diamonds you described were sold off. I'm sorry we were unable to retrieve those."

The necklaces, the earrings, even the small tiaras we'd smuggled out were gone forever. I'd been hinting that Améthyste should move forward. Yet these treasures were symbols of our past, all the things lost.

Rolling the bracelet about my arm, I forced a smile. "We have something. Monsieur Clarkson, I'd like you to sell some of these, as we'd discussed before."

"I'll work with your solicitors at Reid, Irving and Company to invest the monies."

The emerald necklace I slipped over Athénaïre's head. The pearl one I offered to Améthyste. A little shaky on my feet, I took my time scooping up each remaining jewel. Putting twelve pieces in the sack as if I were counting stars, I handed it to Clarkson. "The jewels that mean the most are the ones I'll keep. Please take these and make good investments. It was good to see them again. Give the first hundred pounds to benefit the church."

The archbishop clapped his hands. "Thank you, but you should think about this. I know these mean a lot to you. You agonized over their loss."

The times I spent looking in a mirror after Henry had draped gold along my neck had passed. That image of our love would be what I'd keep in my heart. "The pain of the theft was immense. My fledgling peace had been violated. You've restored it, but I need to focus on our future, not the past."

I paused. "But the note said you were bringing friends. I thought it would be the Thornton girls."

Monsieur Clarkson stuffed the bag into his leather pouch. "My plans changed when I learned of the recovery of your stolen items. Madame

Clarkson and the Thornton girls will arrive to our London residence this weekend. We're having dinner with some interesting characters. Why don't you and your daughters join us? Then all the young ladies will travel to Blackheath for their extended stay."

Back to London? Except for my walks along the river, my time in that city hadn't exactly been the best.

"My wife is looking forward to taking tea with you. And Marianne and Patti Thornton can't wait to amuse your daughters."

I didn't have to look back at the girls to know they wanted to go. With a nod, I acquiesced. "Of course, sir. We'll be delighted."

Full of smiles and offerings of blessings, the gentlemen left. I turned to Améthyste and Athénaïre, who were admiring each other's necklaces. They would have pretty jewelry to wear and be admired at the Clarksons' dinner. It was enough. Hopefully, selling the rest of Henry's gifts would generate enough money to protect my girls' future.

21

1822 Tonbridge, England

Our in-town visits went so well that against my better judgment, I allowed my friend Catherine Clarkson to convince me to accept an invitation to Wilberforce's Marden Hall, an estate about an hour and a half away from Blackheath.

We hadn't seen much of Wilberforce last winter. His firstborn girl, Barbara, had died. The family grieved deeply. I understood mourning and loss. I looked forward to seeing him and offering solace.

In new dresses of light muslin instead of thick bombazine, my daughters chatted on the carriage seat. I'd have loved to see them in bright colors, but they wore shades of light blue. I wore gray, which was appropriate for half mourning, according to the customs Zephyrine had learned. Just about two years had passed since I became a widow. This was well beyond the British period of grieving, but I mourned a king. He deserved more.

"We've had intimate dinners with friends," Athénaïre said in a giggly voice. "But this will be our first social excursion. Peers, politicians, and abolitionists, the ones in the newspapers, will be in attendance."

Athénaïre hummed and swished her skirt along the tufted seat. She craved society. She wanted to dance.

My big talk with Améthyste about moving on with life seemed embodied in Athénaïre. When she had Zephyrine straighten the curls gracing her face, I believed my younger princess might be willing to marry a British . . . a Blanc.

Blanc men had been in the kingdom. They'd been employed by Henry; they'd come as part of military engagements. They'd been his trading partners. Though the king had granted citizenship to Blancs who married Haytians, how would I truly react to having a Blanc son-in-law or Colored grandchildren?

Yet who fought for us now? Who worked to secure our welfare? Who offered friendship?

Blancs.

Coloreds killed Victor.

Blacks and Blancs both stole from us.

Skin color was no indication of honesty or kindness.

Améthyste's pearls set off the silver pins in her chignon. Her thick hair was natural and curly above her cream-colored shawl. She coughed and covered her mouth with a handkerchief. "Sorry, the damp air. Summer should be a warmer time."

It wasn't in Britain. Blackheath was greener and more spacious than London but still had the same wet and cold climate. It was beginning to look more and more like this wasn't the place for us.

Warm-blooded Athénaïre wore half-sleeves, baring her café-au-lait arms, as a young gentleman had described her warm brown skin in conversation when he thought no one overheard. Améthyste had a darker complexion than Athénaïre or me but was often pale from being sickly.

"Are we almost at Monsieur Wilberforce's residence? I don't want to miss a moment." My younger daughter fidgeted. "I've read many papers this week. I'm ready to talk to the politicians."

"You'll get to practice your manners and your English," I said. "Peers don't interest you, my dear?"

"Interest? You must mean marriage." She shrugged and twirled her emerald necklace.

Hopefully that was the *non* I wanted. We didn't have the finances to attract and sustain such an alliance. We weren't like the wealthy princess of Gonaïves, who had enough riches and land to sway a royal prince, like my nephew Jean.

"Well, you have time to choose," I said, not actually looking forward to such associations. High pairing would bring our names again to the newspapers. I hated the press as it continued to print lies about Henry.

Améthyste coughed again, then patted her mouth with a handkerchief. "Well, we should also watch the abolitionists. They're looking for educated Negroes to become the face of abolition."

The cause was a worthy one, but neither I nor the girls had been enslaved. Only Henry, and he had fought against France and Spain to end it. "Tonight is for pleasure. No more words about marriages or any other type of alliance, princesses. Then we shall survive the night."

My careless talk of *surviving* made both girls cringe.

The carriage stopped. "I meant that we shall have an enjoyable time."

Leaning less and less on his cane, Souliman stood up straight and handed us down from the carriage. He looked well in his emerald greatcoat and glossed boots. He'd gained weight in his face. He looked strong from his daily exercise and, in his footman's costume, fancier than he'd ever been at Sans-Souci.

"You ladies have fun." He sobered as other carriages arrived. "I'll head to the mews and wait until you are ready to leave."

His weary eyes got to me. The man didn't think this outing would end well.

Maybe it wouldn't. We had to try. My almost-twenty-four- and twenty-two-year-old daughters needed society. I didn't want my gems to be hidden as if they bore a curse.

AS SOON AS WE WERE INTRODUCED, BUBBLY BLOND MARIANNE Thornton embraced Athénaïre, then dragged her and Améthyste off to a noisy parlor.

I hesitated in the grand hall, standing on polished marble.

People moved in and out of the rooms, more well dressed than I'd seen in a long time. Monied people had come to this party.

"Madame Christophe." Catherine waved, then came to me along with our hostess, Madame Wilberforce. With her auburn hair modestly covered in a chiffon mobcap, Madame Wilberforce smiled. "I'm delighted you've come."

Before I could respond with more than a thank-you, her head turned away and then she disappeared into the crowd.

"She's a shy one," Catherine said as she led me deeper into Marden Hall. "The woman never gets involved in her husband's fights or his politics."

Nodding, I twisted my bracelet. Madame's quick retreat made me concerned about the reception my daughters were receiving. "Does she view me as another of her husband's projects, Madame Clarkson? It's fine if that is her prerogative."

"No." She clasped my hand. "And it's Catherine. No formality among friends."

This woman had taken my family into her home. She understood, in ways I wouldn't say aloud, about race and perception. Now she clasped my hands, as if she didn't want to let them go, tightly and with love. Unlike others, she'd never been fearful of showing care, as if my blackness might rub off. "Catherine's a beautiful name. Almost as pretty as Louise."

She started laughing and so did I. It felt freeing.

"But do give Mrs. Wilberforce a chance. She's having problems with her daughter, something of the wrong suitor's interest. She's overwhelmed and only hosting this for her husband."

I could sympathize. Like Henry, Wilberforce was larger than life, dabbling in international affairs. That didn't leave much room for a woman with her own ideas. Perhaps Madame Wilberforce had resigned herself to having no role but a domestic one.

Tucking her arm in mine, Catherine and I began a slow parade about Marden. She introduced me to a solicitor, several barristers, a baron, and an earl. I recognized some of their faces from caricatures in the newspapers.

Soon we'd walked from one side of the house to the other. Without a throne room, official residences could be smaller. "Where's our host? I want to make sure that he sees me so when I leave . . ."

Shaking her head at me, Catherine chuckled. "I'm glad you came. And of course I brought along Miss Mary Inglis to gossip with your girls and the Thornton girls. Marianne and Patti loved spending the week in Blackheath. I hope we will all be lifelong friends."

"Your kindness to me and them abounds."

"Louise, I enjoyed every moment you were in my house. I only wish I could do more."

"You've done enough." Our arms were entwined. It felt normal. Meeting the right people, good people, made a difference.

"Where are our host and Monsieur Clarkson?" I asked before my eyes began to sting.

"Documents came about a half hour ago. They've been locked away in his study ever since. You'd think the host of his party would actually host it."

"Well, not every man frets over each painstaking detail of his wife's dinner or seating arrangements."

Her eyes clouded, her forehead marring with tiny lines. "I'd hope men had better things to do."

Lord Limonade, Dupuy, and Henry had nothing better to do, but if King George were to appear, I'd hope Wilberforce might be a little more attentive to details.

We moved again to a parlor with lively yellow-striped walls and a pianoforte. Madame Wilberforce was chatting loudly about some of their many children—a twenty-year-old Robert, a sixteen-year-old Henry, and a twenty-one-year-old Elizabeth.

Madame Clarkson beckoned me to head with her to another room, but my music-loving heart made me excuse myself and settle into a corner, counting servings of wine and watching how many braved exhibiting their skills on the pianoforte.

Observing conversations suited me. After spending so long with others studying me, this seemed a treat.

THE HEIGHT OF THE LONG EIGHT-HOUR BEESWAX CANDLES HALVED as I held court in the corner. I remembered when nobles had swarmed about my throne. My full court of royal ladies went with me on my missions to Cap-Henry. For my Thursday teas, they surrounded me, in lace and colorful plumes.

Tucked away, distant from the crowd, this had been my private life as a general's wife. As queen, I never hid or cowered to anyone. Henry would hate the timid creature his exiled widow had become.

More wine was poured. The air now smelled of honey and grapes. Upon occasion, a whiff of cologne water or perspiration wafted past, along with a parade of colorful satins. I drowned my mourning in claret, giving it a dunking, as if I'd set it free in the Rivière Mapou.

A servant refreshed my glass with weaker ratafia.

Another young lady took to the pianoforte. The tune I didn't recognize. Whether it was the performer's fault or my tiring ears or too much wine, it was an indication that it was time to leave.

Moving from the corner, I heard conversations puffing from liquor-soaked cheeks.

"Yes, the little Greeks. They beat the Ottomans. Admiral Miaoulis, the smaller fish, won against a world power again."

Thinking of Hayti and Napoleon's fleet, this made me giggle and look into my glass.

The mumbles continued. "Britain . . . and France will get involved quickly to recognize the Greeks' independence."

This sobered me.

The world would rush to recognize a newly freed Greece but leave Hayti dangling? It would've made a difference. If other countries had been brave and proclaimed Hayti's existence, the pressure on Henry would have lessened. We might still be there—our kingdom, our thrones.

The grumbling in my spirit became louder. I eased my glass to a server's tray to avoid throwing it. Through the maze of rooms, I hunted for my daughters.

It was time to go. Then I saw them and froze at the threshold.

Athénaïre was dancing. Her lovely sky-blue gown flared as she turned in a reel. A young man, a young Blanc man, had asked her to dance. She'd bravely accepted and was performing the steps perfectly. Madame la Comtesse du Terrier-Rouge would be proud.

Améthyste's head was turned from me. She was laughing, enjoying herself with Sarah and Marianne and Patti.

Slipping back into the hall, I slunk into the shadows. Being upset about politics, the things I had no power to change, was nonsensical. I grabbed a flute of ratafia and sipped until I felt numb, until my raging feelings drowned.

CATHERINE CLARKSON CALLED HER HUSBAND A CHARMER, BUT SIT-ting with her in a remote parlor with a bottle of claret, I found her con-versation exquisite. For the past hour, she had talked of nonsense—of knitting, summers in the Lake District, and the foibles of George IV.

"It's true. The high collars hide a double chin, and a corset gives him his muscular shape. Your king didn't need such."

"Non. Henry for the most part kept fit, give or take a slice of gateau au beurre. Or was that me?"

We started chuckling again and she refilled my glass. "Have we wasted enough time, Louise?"

"No time is a waste spent living with friends."

She glanced over the rim of her goblet. "Have you thought of living? At forty-four, you cannot want to be closeted away. Your wonderful daughters *will* settle. What of you?"

"Those aren't the questions I ask of the future."

"Athénaïre is beautiful and outgoing. With Mr. Clarkson finding discreet buyers for your jewels, your solicitors will invest the money well. There could be enough for a small dowry. Yes, you could carve out a substantial sum and still not worry about the rent in Black-heath."

Her words bore logic, but that was a whole lot of *could*s and *will*s. "The doctors' treatments for Améthyste are costly. I don't want to choose which daughter gets the benefit of our means. My physician says Princess Améthyste needs a warm climate and to take the waters to prolong her life. She was very sick when we came to Suffolk."

Hadn't we had enough sorrows? My gaze lowered and I sipped the rich claret. "I don't want to think of losing another child, whether in marriage or to an apoplexy."

"I'm your friend, Louise. I haven't lived your life. I don't know how you get out of bed and face the day. But I don't want you surprised or caught unprepared. Wilberforce's daughter died of tuberculosis last year, barely twenty-one. Though she was sickly, her parents weren't prepared. It nearly destroyed William."

For strength, I clasped my bracelet. Didn't want to think of all Améthyste had survived or how much she continued to struggle.

"Louise, your being settled could help. A well-off widow can attract security."

Before I could respond—and tell her non, that I'd find a way to protect myself and the girls, and I'd keep Améthyste alive and with me for as long as possible—Monsieur Clarkson wandered into the parlor. He accompanied a man with wild brown hair. The fellow bowed and introduced himself as Viscount Chateaubriand, in divine French.

"Ladies," Monsieur Clarkson said, "Chateaubriand is the French ambassador to Prussia and sometimes to Britain. He's also a onetime exile and the first man I contacted when I tried to gain France's recognition of the kingdom."

The gentleman had a half-empty glass in hand, which he sipped at loudly. "And I had a terrible time getting anyone's ear, though my friends and I did enjoying dining on Christophe's money."

He chuckled and sipped. "When I heard the atrocities Dessalines's Black soldiers committed, executing French landowners, I had no sympathy. But again, I welcomed every expense the king spent to persuade me."

Though Catherine and I had nearly finished our claret, I was in full possession of my tongue. I bristled in silence at this man denigrating my husband's efforts. Henry had paid thousands to Clarkson, Jean-Gabriel Peltier, and others to normalize our relations in Europe.

Rising slowly, I left my flute on the small table in front of me. "And I think it's time to take my leave."

"Madame," Chateaubriand said. "It is true. The execution of so many was an unnecessary revenge."

"This is a condition I'm unfamiliar with, that revenge is unnecessary." I glared at him. "You're not aware of the conditions in Saint-Domingue, my Hayti. Monsieur, if you knew of the French atrocities toward the Blacks, both affranchi and enslaved, you'd not lift your head. The weight of the shame would crush you to dust."

My voice sounded sharp, but I wouldn't be silent. "Henry believed in decency, something few French had." I nodded to Catherine, to Monsieur Clarkson. When I turned to leave, Chateaubriand stepped in my path.

"Madame, do not go. That was my first opinion. Then I read Baron de Vastey's book. It changed my soul."

Vastey? I hadn't heard his name since the revolutionaries executed him ten days after the kingdom fell. "He was a brilliant man."

Again, I tried to pass, but my fretting friend Monsieur Clarkson blocked my escape. "Chateaubriand, you have offended—"

"I didn't mean to. Vastey was a great orator. His *Le Système Colonial Dévoilé* was eye opening. The suffering reported was horrendous."

"Then, monsieur, you know the crimes done by slavers were numerous. Grand Blancs buried alive, severed limbs, assaults, crucifixions, leaving mutilated corpses on display for all to see, even the children. I believe Vastey wrote of the sins as 'crapulous forms of debauchery.'"

"Crapulous." Catherine snorted, then put her lips to her claret.

"Oui, crapulous forms of debauchery." Chateaubriand nodded. "Truly gifted. Such a loss to the world. I've shared his work with a writer friend. I want her to use the pain and suffering for her work."

I'd inched to the door ready to flee, to rush and gather the girls, but I couldn't. The notion of being used planted my slippers. "What? Sir, you want to use our pain for a book?"

"Oui. Non. Claire de Duras needs it. She's writing a book about a Black woman, a dying nun."

Squinting at him and then back to the glass I'd discarded, I wondered if I was as drunk as Chateaubriand. "Perhaps I should sit down. I'm not hearing correctly."

"Do not be distressed. This is fiction, but the story is based on a real slave from Senegal who died mysteriously in the custody of her owner, Madame de Duchesse of Orléans."

"Mysteriously, you say? Hadn't Vastey's words helped you with these mysteries?'" Should've kept that wineglass, either to fill it again or throw it at Chateaubriand's head.

Yet I noticed the reddening Monsieur Clarkson and the wide-eyed Catherine, who'd never seen my temper. A queen didn't show her rage in public or express the depths of her displeasure. Lord Limonade's or Princess Dieudonné's or even Dupuy's advice repeated in my ear. Vastey, from the grave, admonished me to be everything fine.

But I was a woman still in mourning for a strongman who'd needed help—from me, the world, our allies. And didn't get it.

Raising my sorrowful chin, I said, "I must go. Thank the Wilberforces for their hospitality."

"Wait," Chateaubriand said. "Let me get to the point. Madame de Duchesse of Orléans never freed her chattel." His hands became animated, as if the motion would better explain his thoughts. It merely spilled wine, red as blood on his sleeve. "But my friend is trying to write from the slave girl's perspective. You see, I told her she needs pain, to focus on pain to capture the character Ourika's reactions."

Ignoring the insult of a person as chattel, a thing to be owned, and that my people hadn't fought a war to end enslavement, I offered him a polite smile. "Monsieur, why would pain help?"

Clarkson tried to tug his friend to a chair. "Perhaps you've said enough, Chateaubriand."

But the fool seemed driven to speak his folly. "To write Blacks, my friend must dwell on pain. When Ourika discovers she's Black, and no one will marry her because of her skin, that horror, that pain will guide the prose. We must feel the melancholy."

"To be Black, you assume one must be in pain." I glanced at Monsieur Clarkson. "And if one seems well adjusted, sociable, and well spoken, this must be seen. The spectacle of Blackness is to move people."

Chateaubriand became silent. I think he waited to see me turn into flame.

An angry woman could destroy a house.

A very angry woman could burn a village.

But I was a queen.

Such displays of temper were beneath me.

My hands fell to my sides. "Viscount Chateaubriand, I think your writer friend doesn't understand the experiences of an enslaved woman or any Black woman at all. I doubt she knows love, for I love me. I love the skin I'm in. I'm Black and comely. No Black woman ever has to 'discover' that she's Black. Since birth, she knows she's beautiful. Good evening."

"Wait, Madame Christophe." Chateaubriand grabbed the buttons of his waistcoat and lurched forward. Then he dropped back onto the chair. "Do you think I have it wrong? That marriage and upward mobility are not hindered by your race?"

As much as my stomach hurt, I ignored the bits of truth his words possessed in a Blanc world—the one where my daughters and I now resided. "There have been plenty of marriages for Black women. You know the atrocities you read in Vastey's book are caused by Blanc men's passion to possess ebony bodies. Dark and comely is a torture for those who do not understand. It's a dream for those who lust for it."

"You state your opinions quite well, Madame Christophe." Viscount Chateaubriand lifted his glass as if to toast me.

"Madame de Duras, and maybe all of France, have difficulties imagining Blacks ascending to the highest levels of society. I do not, for I've done it. And our kingdom was beautiful. Excuse me, Viscount. Monsieur Clarkson."

I left the room with my head up, imagining my old crown of rubies and diamonds tilting upon my braids.

ATHÉNAÏRE OFFERED ONLY A LITTLE PROTEST WHEN I GATHERED her and her sister. We waited at the door for Souliman to return with our carriage.

Améthyste squinted at me. "Maman, are you well? You look flustered."

"I'm fine." I rolled my bracelet, tracing the raised emerald with my thumb. "I just miss Baron de Vastey's forthright speeches. He was your père's greatest defender."

"And his dancing." Athénaïre scampered around me swinging her arms to an imagined waltz. "Père made him your dance partner on more than a few occasions. I wished Père loved music as much as we do."

Henry loved our music. In quiet, in private, just a great Black king humming to his queen.

"Don't go." Catherine rushed to us, almost running. "I'm sorry. We're sobering the viscount."

I put my arms about this woman, this Blanc woman who understood me. "All is well. I'm tired and I know when it's time to leave."

She pulled back a little and caught my gaze, her silver curls bobbing. "Then we will visit Blackheath before we head back to Suffolk."

"I'd like that. I'll enjoy company tomorrow."

Wilberforce, our host for the evening, entered the hall. "Oh, goodness. You're leaving? I must get Clarkson. Then we'll both tell you the news."

"He's busy with a viscount." Catherine wouldn't release my hand. "My friend has had enough talk. I'm sending her home."

"Not yet." He padded closer; his shoes making squeaks as he did. "It's all settled. I've reviewed the papers myself."

"Newspapers?" Améthyste coughed and moved closer to our host. "Have they printed that the rebel government has fallen, Monsieur Wilberforce?"

"Calm yourself, Miss Christophe, until I tell you all the news. Come with me to my office."

In the casual way he shuffled, I saw Dr. Stewart, Henry's doctor.

"The king has done it." I heard two voices saying the exact same thing.

"He's protected you . . . left you . . ." Wilberforce's mouth was moving, but in my mind, I pictured Stewart saying the worst.

"It seems the American banks, as well as the British, had transactions in which the king extended credit but was never paid. Your solicitors have prepared a settlement which will give you access to the money. Lots of money."

"When?"

Hands clasped mine and shook me. Blinking, I saw Madame Clarkson, then my daughters. There were tears on every cheek. Did they know what Henry had done?

"I think the poor dear's in shock." Madame Clarkson's arms tightened about me. "Let's take her to your study."

Tugging, towing, I was drawn into a room. Sconces lit the room brightly. The girls helped me sit, but the two portraits sitting on golden easels caught my gaze and my heart.

Henry and Victor.

The paintings that Monsieur Evans did, that made Henry look strong and in command, sat on easels. Deep-blue coat with buttons of gold, crisp white shirt with a high collar. His hat and crown and star—all images the European monarchs would understand, that my king insisted upon—were before me.

Then I looked at Victor—his horse, the coco palms, and his brother Armande. My heart broke all over again.

"Handsome." It was all I could manage.

I took a long breath. "Victor posed for hours. His brother's there. See the brave young man in the background. So wonderful."

"King Henry sent me these paintings." Wilberforce steadied my shoulder, then passed me and went to his desk. "These will be going to the National Gallery."

Améthyste moved closer to the canvas. "Such a good likeness. Père seems casual, holding court with the crest of the kingdom behind him. Monsieur Evans was a good teacher. He showed me so many things about color and texture and shadow."

"The king had a set sent to Alexander I, Emperor of Russia." Wilberforce flipped through parchment. He seemed oblivious that I was breathing hard, almost falling apart. "The emperor helped with diplomacy, dissuading France from trying to seize Hayti in 1818."

"King Henry had made some allies. If he'd lived . . ." My throat closed. Henry's eyes, his Cupid's bow, his expression seared my mind.

Fingers curling on the easel, I wanted to scream.

Why? Why didn't you listen? We could've done so much more. And you could've been here with us.

"You just need to sign here." Wilberforce put papers in front of me. "Madame. Madame Christophe. That's how you accept the terms and agreement."

Face fevering, chest tightening, I tried to breathe. The smell of old books and sour ink scented the study. "Accepting. Doing as told. Not objecting—that is what I must do again?"

Befuddled, Wilberforce sat on a wide mahogany chair. The arms of the seat were a rich ebony. He bowed his head for a moment as he sank into the padding.

"Madame Christophe," Wilberforce said. His voice rose as if he'd taken the floor of Parliament. "You're afraid of what this all means. You're giving up no rights. Please tell me you aren't afraid to take possession of nearly three hundred thousand pounds. This money will keep you protected and comfortable in the manner befitting a queen."

"Three hundred . . . thousand?" My head became dizzy. The size of the number punched straight through me. "Are you sure?"

"Yes, but do you want me less certain? Madame, did you expect more? I'd heard his treasury was over twenty million. Is a mere three hundred thousand disappointing?"

"Non. Henry commissioned a lot of trades. Of course there would be monies outstanding. I'm glad it wasn't confiscated."

With the quill in hand, Wilberforce pointed to where I had to attest with my name to signify I agreed with the amount.

Taking up the feather he so generously dipped into the ink, I held my breath and signed the document.

"There, now you ladies have no more money troubles."

Catherine clapped her hands. "Forget what I said earlier. Everything is now settled, Louise. You can even think of traveling to warmer weather. You can take to the waters for your health. Even do the royal spa tour to avoid cold winters."

She sounded gleeful, very much a morning bird buzzing about me.

My eyes watered looking at the notations on the paper. I fingered the lines indicating shipments in transit in 1820. "We have enough to live comfortably for the rest of our lives."

I filled my lungs. No choices had to be made between rent and dowries and medicine. Our daughters' futures were assured. "This is Henry's legacy to protect us."

Wilberforce folded the pages. "Reid, Irving and Company will have these in the morning. All the money will be available soon after."

Staggering a little, I stood and again set my eyes on Henry's portrait. "Thank you, sir, from the bottom of my heart, thank you."

Monsieur Wilberforce nodded. "It's my pleasure to make things right for you."

We curtsied to him, and to Henry and Victor, and headed with Catherine to the door.

"I'm so happy for you all," she said, patting my arm, spinning my bracelet. "How will you sleep with such good fortune?"

"I'll tell you tomorrow when you visit." I embraced her and she returned the hug with a firm grip. She probably knew if she let go, I'd smash to the floor like a broken vase.

The whinny of horses made her release me. Somehow I managed to stay upright.

Souliman presented himself and we climbed into our carriage. "Pleasant evening, madame? You stayed longer than I thought."

"It was." Améthyste caught my silencing gaze and crawled under the blanket to prepare for our hour-and-a-half drive back to Blackheath.

The door closed.

The carriage moved and I gripped my daughters' hands. "Not a word of this until I have finalized letters of credit."

Nodding and smiling, they sat back. Athénaïre began telling me every detail of the evening. Améthyste muffled her coughs, then fell asleep.

She'd pretended again, assuring us she was well so we'd attend tonight. I was glad that we had, but sad that Améthyste put her health at risk for us to have enjoyment. Wasn't right, her suffering in silence.

I extinguished the carriage lantern so only the stars above offered light. Then I settled on my seat and prayed to find a place with warmth, with sea air. Something perfect for comely Black women who still needed to heal in privacy and to plan the next steps in our far from fairy-tale lives.

THE KINGDOMS

Britain

Commercial Chronicle (London), Saturday, January 27, 1816

Haytian Gazettes to the middle of November have been received. The contest between the rival Governors CHRISTOPHE and PÉTION is carried on with fresh proofs of hostility and rancour. The former accuses the latter of carrying on secret negotiations, both with Louis XVIII, and with BONAPARTE, for the purpose of sacrificing the independence of the country.

Hayti

Royal Gazette of Hayti, February 8, 1816

The present issue also rather fascinatingly documents how the US Black northern abolitionist Prince Saunders brought smallpox vaccine to Hayti for the first time and has begun to vaccinate many children at Sans-Souci.

1816 Palace of Sans-Souci, Kingdom of Hayti

Awaking alone on this third day of Henry's visit to his troops in Saint Marc felt peaceful. Henry's highs and lows of maintaining the peace with the south drained something in me, something that the quiet of our room and my garden replenished.

Today, instead of thinking of the next fete, I'd do something different, maybe very different.

Once dressed, in a light-gold high-waisted gown sporting a two-layer embroidered hem, I swished about the palace. Before taking my usual walk, I checked on my daughters.

One governess had Athénaïre playing the harp. My daughter's fingers seemed nimble, plucking at the strings, pulling a sweet melody out of the air.

Her gaze lifted to me. Then the show-off scrunched her brow, pushed up her silver lace sleeves, and played Ferdinand Ries's song from Victor's fete, the Violin Concerto in E Minor.

She was good, plucking away, increasing the tempo.

Proudly backing away, humming like Henry, I went farther down the corridor to the library. Curled in close chairs were Améthyste and Madame d'Ouanaminthe.

"Shakespeare's *Othello* is the greatest of his works," my daughter said and pointed to something in her book. "Othello's a heroic general in the service of Venice. He chooses the right lieutenant but underestimates Iago's destructive power. In the end, his jealousy destroys everything Othello loves."

Her governess's cheeks paled. She seemed distressed. "Why, mademoiselle, is it the greatest?"

Leaning forward, with a light-green satin gown tucked nicely about her ankles and sleek slippers, Améthyste winked at me, grinning. "Because we never learn Iago's motives. Was it always hate? Was it jealousy for being passed over for a promotion? Was it lunacy? The reader must fill in the cause from what they believe the darkness of their own hearts might possess."

"But the villain is alive at the end. The Black general and his wife aren't. And Iago killed his own wife. How is that good?"

"Never said it was good." Améthyste grinned. "The unexplained actions cost everyone so much—that's why it is important."

My heart swelled. My daughter stood up for her opinions in the sharpest French. Her reading selection was questionable. *Othello* was a tome that the Blancs bandied to warn their women, their pretty, hapless Desdemonas, of the Black generals. Never was fond of that Shakespeare play, though numerous guests at the Hôtel de la Couronne were.

Yet many times I felt a kinship to Desdemona, loving a warrior who was given to jealousy.

Retreating again to my chambers, I found my maid stripping the bed.

"Madame, is there something I can get for you?"

She wasn't looking at me studying her. She kept at her job.

Then my own madness struck. "Let me help you today. I want to go to the river with you and wash the linens."

Her kerchief fell and her glorious thick hair, parted in two braids, came down. "You must not be well. The heat has gotten to you."

"No, Zephyrine, I'm quite fine. But I'm feeling useless."

"The king will be back soon. That will occupy your time. Think of the next fete."

"Is that what everyone sees the queen is good for? Balls?"

"You dress well, too." She dropped the folded sheet. It filled with air, then sailed down onto the mattress.

My hands slid to the delicate buttons of my gown, painted with meadows and flowers. Something I'd chosen because it made me happy. "Can't I be more than a fancy gown?"

"The wife of the king belongs in a castle, not laboring at a stream." Under her breath in Kreyòl she said something that sounded like "fanm sòt," stupid woman.

"I wasn't always a queen. I used to be pretty good at helping my mother in the Rivière Mapou wash the laundry of the hotel. There were a lot of rooms. Take me with you. That's an order."

She put her hands to her wide hips. "Not like that. I don't want to try to clean mud off that gown."

Running to my closet, I looked for my plainest cloak. Everything was long, embroidered, or studded with lace.

Then I found some black drapery, something I used to cover my satin gowns to keep them from ruin.

Jumping out of my airy muslin, with yards of fabric falling to the floor, I wrapped myself in black and cinched a belt at my waist.

Taking a colorful scarf of red silk, I wrapped my hair like my maman used to do. Approving of this look in the mirror, with my chestnut cheeks already blooming, I returned to the bed.

Zephyrine shook her head. "This isn't wise."

"Sometimes the wise thing isn't the right thing."

She scooped a bundle, and I took the rest. "We'll head the secret route. Don't want to get caught with you like this. It's not wise at all."

She fussed a little more until we were on our way to the stream. I'd use the energy of this honest labor to fuel my thoughts. I still needed to find a role for the queen, for future queens, and it couldn't be a helpless Desdemona or a menu planner.

ZEPHYRINE AND I TRAVELED THE BANKS OF THE STREAM UNTIL IT widened. The humid day made the shelflike clouds seem lower. The emerald grasses and trees covering the hills served as the canvas for this perfect day.

The baskets were heavy, filled with sheets from all the bedrooms. Athénaïre's courses had flowed and slightly soiled the ones from her bed. The horsehair and wool mattress, one of the ones Henry imported from Italy, hadn't stained.

At sixteen, she was a young woman. I marveled at how time kept moving, even if I wanted things to slow and stand still.

Soapberry trees lined the banks. The shallow water ran fast along the rocks.

Zephyrine and I set down our bundles.

We weren't alone. Other women washed clothes. Littles one ran around playing, stopping every so often to gather fallen soapberries, the little orange marbles that lathered up well enough to wash linens or even skin.

Far from the lavender soaps Henry procured from London, the trees' offerings smelled a little like vinegar or soured wine, but they left cloth scented like a breeze. This fragrance was fresh and honest and Haytian.

Scrubbing at my daughter's sheet, I loved the coolness of the water.

A hum started with the children, first low then loud and full of joy. The words surrounded me. Then washerwomen took over the children's song.

Sa sa ko ma
Ne ne o
Ko ko ma
Sa sa ko ma
Ne ne o
Che che
Ko ko ma

I hadn't heard this since I was a child. It was Kreyòl. At Sans-Souci, this language was only spoken in the servants' quarters. When Henry made French the official language of our kingdom, the only time anyone spoke anything else was to entertain the British or other foreign guests.

"Ne ne o. Che che, ko ko ma." I sang it, too, as loudly as I could.

"I remember this, singing it with sisters by the river. Was it about who has the stone?"

"The lyrics are older than you," Zephyrine said. "It's from Ghana, where my grand-mère was taken. It's supposed to be 'Sansa Kroma.' It's about Sansa the hawk, who snatched up unsuspecting chicks. He sees you've strayed. 'You are an orphan,' the hawk calls out, and then snatches up the babies straightaway."

Then Zephyrine began to sing with her melodious alto voice, beating the linen along the rocks for rhythm.

Sansa kroma
Ne na woo aw
Che kokoma.

When I finally removed all traces of the stain, I wrang the sheet to show Zephyrine, but her face had streaks of water.

None of the droplets came from the river.

"Did you get soap in your eyes, Zephyrine? How can I help?"

"Sadness, madame. You and me and all you see, we are orphaned like the baby chicks because we strayed. The hawks, the people with power, have forgotten why we are free, and they lead us the wrong way."

But Henry was leading. I held her palm with mine in the water. "Keep talking, Zephyrine. I'm here."

"They've forgotten the dreams of our grand-mères. We don't want to be African, just like the Coloreds in the south. Everyone wants to be an orphan to become like the Blancs."

"No, Zephyrine. We are proud of what Blacks have done. The kingdom . . . the king is trying to give us something to be recognized by the world. That's why he's pushing for education and building things for us."

"Pushing for things so we'll be like Blancs and not our grand-mères or grand-pères."

"Is that how you feel?"

"It's how everyone feels." She dropped my hand and began scrubbing a pillowcase. "I know you love the king. And I understand he thinks that Britain is the way. But can't we have both? Non. Because there's no compromise. That's why we have two Haytis, two wrong

Haytis. And the truth is if it weren't for the old, the things that we brought from Africa, the combat, the warfare, the pride, we wouldn't be free."

Suddenly I felt like my disguise had been ripped away. Everything I wanted, that I knew Henry wanted, was wrong. "I have to do something. I have to prove that we want a family, a proud, unified family of old and new."

"What can you do? You're an orphan, married to the hawk who snatches up baby chicks and sends them to the Citadel's prison or Gaffe's blade." Zephyrine started working the pillowcase between her palms. "That Gaffe, he's an expert executioner. Takes off a head and doesn't soil the collar."

Louder than my tears, the song of the children grew. More came. They joined the harmony like wildfire, owning the lyrics. It was blood and bone and fire. And I wept more. I understood the sorrow of forgetting, of making our rich past an orphan, for that was what Henry and I had shown the people with our rule.

23

1816 Cap-Henry, Kingdom of Hayti

Cécile had slipped into the back of the classroom, one of a dozen that Henry had allowed to be set up in Cap-Henry. This one had a wall painted red and black, the colors of the kingdom, with one of the flags my ladies had stitched hung beside the window.

I'd come to welcome Prince Saunders back to our capital and arrange for him to be received at the palace to inoculate my children against smallpox.

My sister, though wearing an eye-catching head wrap of gold and red and a matching vibrant tunic, still had a way of appearing and disappearing. Could still remember waiting for her to return to the Hôtel de la Couronne the day she ran away. My père wasn't mean to my half sister, but he had no use for her. Like Henry, he demanded unquestioned obedience.

That was hard on Cécile, who was gifted from an early age with a defiant mind and a will of iron.

She slid into a corner, one of her favorite places to observe people. When our eyes met and her smile radiated, I could be nine again, thankful to see my big sister's countenance.

My face turned to the resonant voice of Monsieur Saunders explaining what must be done to protect the children from the ravages of smallpox, a disease brought to these shores by merchants and European visitors. God knew we already had enough sickness with yellow fever.

I moved closer to my sister.

Anticipating my questions, her head cocked to the side. "I came to see American royalty."

"His honorific is what his mother named him to ensure that even if he's hated because of his skin, the evilest of men must call him prince. I think it's clever."

"Indeed. They say he's the first Black to receive a degree from a university."

Didn't know about that, but Vastey said he'd received credentials from a place called Dartmouth College. From the way they talked, it must be impressive.

The king walked in with Dupuy.

All the children rose. "Vive le roi!"

Cécile and I bowed.

My husband looked well, very put together in an ebony jacket of military styling and gold braiding on his shoulders and the Henry star, the symbol all the peers of the kingdom had begun displaying.

"Your Majesty," Saunders said. He dipped his sable head with its short, curly hair. He lifted his wide forehead. "Children, this is the man whose foresight will show all the world that Blacks are just as intelligent as whites. This is the man who'll give you every tool to succeed. Hayti needs to be looked upon as a symbol."

"You shall have what you need to make the children as smart as can be." The king turned to the baby chicks. "You must lead this world. Everywhere, they'll see your example and know that all should be free, all should be able to lead and control their destiny."

"As my spiritual guide, Minister John Wesley, says, 'Liberty is the right of every human creature as soon as he breathes the vital air.' What you, King Henry, will show here is the vastness of our intellectual capacity. Hayti, under your leadership, will show the world the way. Black can rise like Blanc. Each can rule and coexist."

Dupuy stalked around the room, his face beaming, taking pride in this work. He strutted around the children's oak chairs, his bootheels clicking on the pine boards. "This is the future, Your Majesty. The world needs to know. I'll send notice to the newspapers. Britain needs to understand what you're trying to do."

Patting a little fellow on the head, Henry drew himself up. "That's my mission. We'll have a heritage that everyone will recognize and revere."

"That's a big ambition, my king." Cécile said, her green eyes flashing. "Especially when the discontent of being forced to labor for the treasury seems to be rising."

No one could dispute her words. The people working in the fields according to Code Henry would agree. The women I met at the river on wash day would, too.

No one understood Henry's genius. How did one translate it so men and women at all levels understood? Saunders and Dupuy and Vastey couldn't be the only ones.

And no one felt Henry's pain but me. It kept him up at night. It kept him hungering to push for more.

"Cécile, let's go into the hall and allow the teacher and his students display for His Majesty what they've learned this past week."

Before she could protest, I had her arm and pried her stubborn feet out the door.

"Be contrary to me. Don't embarrass Henry. He's trying to do great things."

"Is it great if no one wants his vision of Hayti? Sœur, the hearts of the people are being lost." She fingered the pearl necklace at my throat. "They see the king's riches, the finery he gives his family while they wear rags."

"Henry is very generous to me and his children. That's a good father."

"He's the father of this nation. He must take better care of the people. Many don't want to become a darker version of the mulattoes and the Blancs. We love our African heritage. Henry has turned from it to kiss the European kings' feet."

"That's not fair, Cécile. He's bringing the people science and education and pride."

"Our king's actions are for naught. All the colonies of Spain, our neighbors in this part of the world, will become independent and be recognized by Britain before Hayti. No one cares for free Blacks. We are still dogs to them."

"Henry has men working on the kingdom's behalf. And unlike ours, these countries aren't split by a traitor who'd make deals with their former masters."

With her thumb, Cécile plucked my pearls and let them swing back, swatting my throat. "Meanwhile, he's enriched himself and the nobles on the people's backs."

"Your husband is a peer. A count. Geneviève says Louis Michel is being considered for another elevation for his valuable service to the king. Is he guilty, too?"

She looked away for a moment. "We're all guilty. The African story is our story, and we're losing it." Her voice was low, like a sputtering wave. "The Dahomet women taught us how to fight. We are forgetting that. Where's their honor? How do European teachings and languages and fancy dress honor those who bled for our freedom?"

They didn't.

They made many feel important.

Even though I liked the flow of lace and linen on my skin, it hadn't made a difference in the life of a single soul. "We are Sansa the hawk. How do we save the ones we've orphaned? How do I help the people and Henry?"

"My sister shrugged. "My queen, listen to your heart and do something. You can make a difference."

I closed my eyes for a long moment, thinking about how despondent he'd been, and how any critique of his approach made him more melancholy, more irrational.

When I blinked, Cécile had gone. She'd left me alone to find my calling, what a queen must do to save her country and king.

THE SAND-COLORED HALL WITH THE INFINITE TAPESTRY OF GOLD and garnet and green threads lay empty.

I looked around to make sure I hadn't taken a wrong turn.

No advisers. How odd.

No curving, out-the-door line of citizens coming to their king to receive arbitration.

No peers.

Today was Thursday. Oui. It was.

At ten in the morning those petitioning to see the king would gather. Long lines typically formed, and like a wise man, the king carefully deliberated on each matter brought before him. Often, he stayed busy until five o'clock. That was when the nobles and their wives would come.

It had to be about four or four thirty now. Very odd for it to be empty.

I crossed my arms as if a breeze had caught me. My arms shivered within the puffy muslin sleeves of my light rose gown. As I paced, the inch-wide pleats fluttered like the butterflies of my beloved garden. I should be out there with my flowers, but I needed answers. I hadn't figured out how to solve the kingdom's problems. This silence, this lack of visitors, meant things were getting worse.

Checking the library, I found it empty. No advisers. The girls were in town visiting Victor, who now lived during the week with tutors in Cap-Henry. Because the king and the prince royal bickered so much, my twelve-year-old son had to be tutored miles from Sans-Souci.

Could this huge palace contain only me, the king, and guards?

The last time Sans-Souci was this quiet, Henry had sentenced Jean-Pierre Richard, Duke of Marmelade and the governor of Cap-Henry, to the Citadel for a week of hard labor. For some trivial offense, the king embarrassed the popular governor.

The duke now despised Henry.

Was my husband deliberately trying to alienate his supporters?

I headed back to the throne room, where a Dahomet guard stood at the entry. Henry must be inside.

"Your Majesty." The soldier dipped his tall stovepipe hat. "Since there are no petitioners for the king, he doesn't wish to be disturbed."

"He'll see me."

"Non, madame. We are not to open the—"

With my head up, I pushed past and went inside.

The soldier followed, bowing low like a groveling puppy. "Your Majesty, the queen could not be stopped."

Henry was at the window. His white sash was off his chest. He wore his emerald jacket sloppily, falling from his shoulder.

He didn't turn. His face stayed pointing to the glass. The sun shined on him. I wished it would brighten his soul.

"It's fine." His voice sounded low and painstakingly slow. "The queen can stay if she wishes. No one else."

"Oui, Your Majesty." The lean fellow kept bowing, almost tripping over his glossed black boots until he was out of the throne room. The door slammed with an earthshaking thud.

It was me and a dejected king, all alone.

Walking closer, I passed our thrones. Multiple colored pieces of correspondence lay dumped on the burgundy tapestry that lay beneath the bigger polished royal chair, Henry's seat of power.

"What's going on? Has something happened?"

My husband never looked at me. Instead, his hand rested on the glass, flat, like he wanted to push through the pane.

"Henry, tell me."

He didn't move or answer.

"Come from the window, my king."

The man didn't budge. I had to go to him. I had to be drawn into his dour world to pull him back to mine.

With careful steps, I positioned myself behind Henry. As lightly as I could, I put a palm to his shoulder. "Whatever it is, we can face it together."

His fingers dropped from the window, dragging a little at the creamy casement. When he turned, his golden eyes settled on me as if he'd been far away. "Sometimes there are too many things to face."

"Never. Non, never."

He wanted to confess to something. He bore a burden that ate at him. "Say it, Henry."

With a shake of his head, the king flew from me to his throne and glared at the door. "The guard shall be punished. I said no visitors."

"Henry, leave him alone. I came because I had to see you."

"Look . . . look at the papers." One by one, he picked them up, then crushed them into balls and tossed them at the thrones.

He slipped to his knees and picked up the crumpled pages that had landed on my velvet cushion. "Victor's tutors say he's belligerent. He won't do his lessons, and he's rude to the teachers. He says he's a son of a king and doesn't have to read."

"I'm sorry, Henry. I'll speak to him."

"My influence. I've done this, Louise."

My husband, the king, began scrounging around on the floor like a madman. The shock of this made my tongue feel thick, but I managed to form words. "Why . . . why take blame for something that's not your fault?"

Scrambling to my slippers, he sat hunched over, inches away. Then he crawled to a piece of light-blue paper. "This is from Clarkson. He says that France will not attack us—"

"That's good, Henry. Let me get you back to our rooms. I can get you a warm bath—"

"Extortion. If I give in to extortion. France will never recognize this country, not without reparations. They want us to pay for defeating them."

"Henry, we won't pay. They fear you."

Beads of sweat dripped from his brow. "There will be war. Death will be everywhere again. I smell the rot. I see the blood."

"Calm down. War won't happen."

"France will send troops if Pétion and I battle. I must live with two enemies always. No peace. Never will have peace."

Henry seemed so disturbed. Had he been drinking? Was he sick? Yellow fever could bring wild dreams.

Kneeling, I fingered his face. His eyes were wide and clear. "Let's get you your favorite tea and some rest. And then I'll find Dr. Stewart."

He flattened the paper, smoothing it with his forearm along the burgundy tapestry. "You think France will go away if I sleep?"

"Non, of course not. But you'll replenish your energy if you do. You need your strength."

"You are my strength, Louise. You've always been."

I sat beside him. "You've overworked yourself. Day and night you go to the Citadel. Then you ride to check on your cities and all your army posts, gone for days at a time. You have to rest."

"How do you know what I do when I'm away? Are you watching me, Louise? Do you have spies?"

With my hands to his neck, I held him. "You need rest. You're chasing villains that aren't here."

"Oui. Oui. Of course." He clasped my hands and kissed my knuckles. "I know that you're with me. It's the lack of sleep talking. It's made me very cross with everyone. I must be sick to ever think you'd abandon me. Forgive me, Louise."

Before I could reply, his lips touched mine. It was a gentle offering, so tentative. The moment I accepted, letting his kiss grow and linger, he delved into the recesses of my mouth. His arms banded about me like iron.

The hold was tight.

I couldn't breathe. He ripped at my painted buttons and divided my pleats. "Be with me, Louise. Here. Now. Make everything all right for me."

The king, my man, was wild, possessed.

"Henry, someone could come. Let's—"

"Non. I've sent them all away. They know not to enter unless I invite them."

I wanted to protest, but his hands were everywhere.

This body that he knew—that he tempted, that he touched with his warm long fingers—rose to him.

Suddenly, it felt right to want him.

This scandalous union on the floor of the throne room had to be.

Trying to help him, I'd lost my mind.

For it couldn't be inside my head with this body giving in to a frenzied love.

I had to be above, horrified, watching, watching him drown in me, watching him pushing away my gown to my hips. His teeth tore at corset strings, loosening the boning, freeing my bosom of its chemise.

With silent lips, he teased me, making me respond, making me yearn for him, not reason.

This was madness.

I was mad with passion, panting for a harried warrior.

"Henry." My gasp was futile. He was a strongman with battle plans. I had no defenses from his touch and this whirling out-of-control sensation.

That mind of mine, up in the air, tried to form words, to will him to talk through the problems, but I was helpless, shapeless, boneless in his palms.

I watched him push and drive into loving me. Our union became some mamba-mambo dance that chased away Obeah and bad dreams.

Henry took me with him, to craziness, to passion and pain and beyond.

If our love was his salvation, how could I deny him?

Non.

"Hold on to me, Louise."

I had to or he'd slip away to the darkness again.

I said goodbye to reason and wrapped one arm about his shoulders and raised his chin from the valley of my breasts. Eye to eye, I surrendered.

There was no escape for either of us, not today.

THE KINGDOMS

Britain

Hereford Journal, Wednesday, July 16, 1817

Mr. Wilberforce brought forward his motion respecting the Slave Trade, and recapitulated several facts that have already been stated, respecting the cruel manner in which this diabolical traffic is still carried on by several nations. He concluded with moving Address to the Prince Regent, the object which was to request that his Royal Highness, in concurrence with the other Powers of Europe, would adopt such further measures might be effectual for the suppression of the Slave Trade; and to this end, that they would refuse to receive the colonial produce of any country which still continued to carry it on.

Hayti

Royal Gazette of Hayti, October 10, 1817

His Majesty's colonial brig, the Prince Regent, had captured the Portuguese schooner the Rodeur, coming from Cayenne, and having on board eighty slaves; the Haytians hastened to remove their irons, telling them that they were free and among brothers and compatriots;

As soon as our benevolent Sovereign was informed of these circumstances, he ordered that linen be made to clothe these unfortunate Africans, who were naked.

24

1817 Palace of Sans-Souci, Kingdom of Hayti

I stood outside our chamber's door, hesitant to go inside. The funeral for Prince Jean had filled Sans-Souci with such sadness. Bereavement and anguish hung in the thick humid air.

Yellow fever swirled heavily in our cities. The plague that had killed off so many French soldiers hadn't spared our people. Our nephew suffered with the sickness for a week. Henry made it back from his tour of the kingdom too late. The young man's eyes had fully yellowed and shut forever before Henry arrived at Prince Jean's house.

It hurt the king not to say goodbye.

It tormented him that the honorable young man would die in his prime.

The funeral ended hours ago. Princess Marie-Augustine, widowed again, looked strong in her black dress and veil, but her eyes, solid black, raged.

I didn't know what to say. How did one go on losing love, again and again?

Outside of my bedchamber, fearing Henry's dark mood, I stayed silent.

Physical sickness killed the prince, but foul self-loathing robbed life, too.

Wiping perspiration from my fingers, I decided to stop cowering. We hurt, but the people seemed unmoved. The few who'd come to wave along the roadside for the prince's funeral procession needed their hearts rewarded. The many who had stayed away needed again to see the monarchy was human and for them.

The solution was behind the door. I had to reach Henry.

Gaining new courage, I knocked and waited. My held breath felt like fire in my chest. Then he said, "Enter."

Inside our chambers, I didn't find Henry resting in bed but on the terrace. The man was at his telescope. The brass thing with lenses and glass wasn't pointed to the night sky or stars, but out at the horizon. "Are you looking at the Citadel or the sea?"

He didn't answer. His posture stayed bent, his face fixed to the shiny tube.

"Henry, I . . . I've come to talk with you."

His groan was loud. "Queen Marie-Louise, what is it you want? Have you come to condemn me, too?"

My mouth fused shut. I gripped my emerald necklace, fingering the chain about my throat to make sure it hadn't knotted like a noose. I had worries. I had fears, but none I could voice and risk Henry's rage.

With a gulp, I came closer. "Wanted to see how you're doing. You've mourned hard for Jean."

He snapped up, making his stance perfect. His palm clasped the telescope with a slap. "Too young. I had his allegiance. And I couldn't return to meet him on his deathbed . . . An argument among generals took precedence."

"I'm sorry. The king has many duties."

"Duty." A laugh left him, merciless, bloodcurdling. "Death should be for those that deserve it. For old men like me."

"Prince Jean knew how you felt. He was so proud of the honors you'd bestowed on him."

"I pinned my star on him. You think Saint John will show him favor because of it?"

Henry had it in his hand. This medallion was the old emblem of the kingdom, the Silver Star of Henry. It had a phoenix rising from flames, was one of the old ones, one of the original ones with the mottos: *Je renais de mes cendres,* I will rise in my ashes, and *Dieu ma cause et mon épée*, God, my cause and my sword. The new ones no longer had any French. Just Latin, *Ex cineribus cascitur*, Reborn from the ashes.

Somehow rising fully formed seemed better than being reborn from blood and tears, having to fight for air and food and care—all the things one needs to start anew.

He closed his fist. "Louise, you rest. I've no need for sleep. I'll go to my study. Perhaps Stewart is skulking around."

"Why should I sleep when you don't?"

Henry shrugged, then started twisting knobs on the telescope.

"What are you looking at? What are you possibly searching for in the dark?"

"The Citadel. Want to see if anyone's working. It's been since 1806 and the thing's still not done."

Tiptoeing, I passed our beloved copper tub and stood next to Henry. "It will be done. Great works take time."

Air gushed from his flared nostrils. "Sometimes there's not enough time."

"Well, it's night. Workers should be home with their families. The construction will continue in the morning."

He glared at me as if at a stranger. "Do you know that France won't wait till morning to attack? Neither will Pétion."

My husband struck the telescope. It spun round and round on its stand. "If they believe us to be weak, that we aren't prepared, they will attack and destroy us."

With my palms, I clasped his hand. The medallion separated our skin. "Henry, what are you trying to accomplish that you haven't already done? The kingdom's shipping more goods than ever. We have economic partners in America, in Britain, in Russia, in Prussia. What is it you still want?"

"Respectability, Louise. They don't respect me. The United States secretary of state sends correspondence for his captains referring to the island as Saint Domingo, like we're still a French colony. They care not for these stars." He flung it into the jungle. "They address me as chief or general. They do not respect our sovereignty."

"What did you do to the captains?"

"Detained them, then released them. This last one, Captain Septimus Tayler, I sent back to John Quincy Adams with a letter expressing my displeasure."

"Displeasure?" My fear dissipated. I started to laugh.

The fire in Henry's eyes extinguished. "Goodness, that sounds pompous."

Then he started to chuckle.

This time it was rich and stirring and very human.

For at least five minutes, we stood under the stars sharing the same humor at how he'd dismissed emissaries of a powerful nation.

I reached for Henry and held him. This was the man I loved, not the other one being eaten alive by rage.

"The world is making up lies about me, Louise. They say I'm a murderous fiend. That I've enslaved everyone to build monuments for my vanity. They print that I'm causing rebellions on other islands."

Turning the telescope, pushing it out of the way, I leaned my back against the terrace wall. "They fear you, Henry. All the lies they've told about Blacks being inferior have crumbled. They cannot stand it. They have to make you look bad to keep themselves looking good."

Putting his hands to his head, he rubbed his temples. "No one honors what I'm trying to do. They think it all the ravings of a madman."

Tugging the end of the telescope to me, I stooped and looked out. I saw nothing.

Henry lifted my chin, spun the brass tube halfway round. "You were looking at the wrong end. Try again."

I did and saw the Citadel and the stars over the sea.

"Louise, I've had visions of what will come. Bad ones. If we let our guard down, this will all end. France will be in that harbor with all their fleet bringing war and enslavement to our shores. I'll die defending you and Hayti."

Standing up tall, I laced my fingers with his. They were rough. One digit had a scar, a new one. "Laying bricks again?"

"Someone has to."

"The Citadel will be ready to defend against France. You don't have to keep pushing. You can give the people rest."

"The ingrates? The ones who can't be bothered to honor Prince Jean? The ones who want me dead, just because I believe in marriage?"

"What?"

I looked at him, my eyes squinting at his golden ones. "You must be mistaken."

"The mulatto women had a service in church to pray for my death."

Horrified, I pivoted from him and stared at the night, as though answers might be written in the stars.

"Did your sister Cécile tell you of the mulatto women's evil plans? Her green eyes would know."

When I turned back, his friendly gaze had become a slow-burning fire again. "She would've told me."

"Are you sure?"

"Yes. I know my sisters."

The sneer on his face suggested I didn't.

His head must be twisting on some new conspiracy, but he'd given me an opening.

"Henry, she did tell me you are losing the people. They don't see your vision, just the hard labor. They think that you are worse than Pétion because you won't admit to wanting to be Blanc."

Rubbing at his mouth as if he wanted to spit, he pivoted and groaned as if I'd stabbed him.

Well, maybe I had.

ON THE TERRACE OUTSIDE OUR BEDCHAMBERS, I WATCHED MY HUS-band pull away, slipping into the dark. This was not what I wanted, to create more distance. I needed the king to listen to his number-one supporter. Me.

With my hand to his shoulders, I leaned against Henry's back. "You are not Pétion. You're not a monster but a patriot."

"Patriot?"

"Yes. And we need to restore a feeling of patriotism to the people. Our citizens think you've forgotten Africa. That you, like Pétion, look down on our roots."

"How can we forget when ships of stolen people from the Slave Coast still float in our sea?"

"I know what you're doing, how you've built the military to keep our freedom, but the citizens must see us honor Africa, not just everything Blanc and European. They must know we remember and honor our past."

He turned, his eyes reddening, burning with thoughts. "If they can't understand what I'm doing, they never will."

"They can, Henry. They need to be reminded that you're not just a king, but a Black king. You're restoring our ancestors' legacy, their pride."

He rubbed again at his skull. "So how do I fix this? I can't stop building the Citadel. It will strike terror in the French."

"Non. It has to be finished. What of finishing the rebuilding of Cap-Henry? Only the church has been restored. The Royal School has been established, but there's much more."

He nodded, and I filled with hope. "That will take time, but I can begin the planning stages."

Henry craned his face to the heavens. "I can't stop courting Britain. We're too close to gaining them for our side. I have emissaries, true advocates in Clarkson and Wilberforce. I won't abandon them. I sent a set of the Evans pictures to Wilberforce."

"He will see you as regal."

"Victor, too. That boy."

I put my palms to Henry's cheeks. "You were saying about Monsieur Wilberforce."

"Oui. He has an elegant picture to see we're not animals, but possessing humanity and dignity just like them. None of the cartoon buffoonery they draw in their papers."

"And he and Monsieur Clarkson need you, too, to help fight enslavement."

His hand slipped down my back. "I wonder how they'd draw you. Probably like the poor creature Saartjie Baartman. Last I heard, they had her on display in a cage in Paris with Frenchmen ogling her buttocks."

Keeping his gaze, I decided to be bold and to ask for what I wanted. "Since you've lost support with the women, they must be part of the solution."

"Oui. And?"

"I believe doing something with women will soften you to the people."

"Louise, I'm not soft."

"Let me build something, Henry. You always build things. It's my turn."

He shook his head and started inside to our bed. "I'm the builder. You're the queen. The queen is not to have her hands dirty. The last thing I need is for the newspapers to picture my queen scrounging in dirt."

Never would I be a feckless Desdemona. "Non. I'm not for show. I'm flesh and blood. I have passions as strong as yours."

He glanced at me, perhaps weighing how much effort it would take to appease me. That slow smile of his arose, the one that said he'd sweet-talk me into submission.

Not this time.

"I want to have a guard of women, women like the Dahomet warriors. The late Duchess Adbaraya led them in battle to break the might of Rochambeau."

Sitting on the edge of the bed, he patted the space beside him. "You want women guards?"

I wouldn't sit. I couldn't relent. "The training the women brought from Africa helped Dessalines. A royal guard of women will be a visible link to our African heritage. When visitors come to the courts, they'll see this connection and report on it to the world. All these horrid newspapers that track our every move will see our heritage and our unity."

His arms folded and he yawned. It seemed my ideas had calmed and bored him.

"Will you allow me to do this, Henry?"

"Sit next to me."

Feeling stronger than I was, I did.

He clutched my fingers, running his thumb up and down my palm. "You have a very long lifeline. And these hands. They're soft, Louise. So soft. Riding horses can ruin them."

"I rode my father's horses. I've ridden mules. I need you to allow this. My royal guard will show you do respect women."

My king's hands moved to my waist. "I revere you, Louise. Your body . . ." His voice was a whisper. "It's a temple. You know how I love you. You know I'd do almost anything for you. But is this right? The British officers who visit will see my wife and think I'm foolish."

"Our heritage is not foolish. It's proud. Let me do this. And I'll show you . . ."

He slipped to his knees with his breath steaming my abdomen. "You don't want to do anything of the sort. You're a queen. I must protect and love you."

My gown wrinkled at his touch, at the heat of his sighs.

I loved him, but I needed his agreement more.

"This is what I want, Henry." I edged out of his reach. "This is what I want, my king. You said I could have what I wanted. Let it be done. This will shape my role."

Glancing at me, frustrated and surely tired, he sat again on the bed. He swirled his finger along the firm mattress, against the soft silver blanket. "Come, ma reine. May we discuss this later. I need you."

Bowing, with my face to the floor, I showed him that his queen honored her king. My braids touched his knee. I was in full supplication to my leader, not my lover.

"Passion cannot distract from what's right." Easing lower in a deeper curtsy, I said, "If I don't try to inspire the women and restore them to your side, I'll always regret it. Then I will live knowing you don't trust me."

Henry lifted me and set me on my feet. "You win, Louise. You can do what you want. At the first moment your troop looks ridiculous, or you falter in your seat, or you give me one moment of pause, the experiment will be done. It will be stricken from every record. No one will know I allowed you to have your way and embarrass the kingdom."

The anger I felt at his words, at the suggestion that I'd do something to bring him dishonor, tasted like acid. I glared into his eyes. "I'll not embarrass the kingdom. I know what I must do. I agree to everything you request, because my idea is right. The women and all of Hayti will know you haven't left us all behind."

Breaking his gaze, I marched to the door. I needed to be away before I said something I'd regret.

Beating me to the threshold, he pressed above my head on the intricate carvings of the door. "Now that this is settled, must you leave?"

He had the gall to have desire sizzling in his light eyes.

"I have to do something, Henry. Lie down. Rest. I'll be back soon."

"Oui, my love." He opened the door. "Do hurry back."

I left the chamber and walked out of the palace, past the bubbling, singing fountain. Soldiers stood guard along the perimeter. When had Sans-Souci become a prison?

I traipsed to my torchlit gardens and stood scanning the new choublak flowers, red and beautiful. Then I looked up at the high mountains.

To love someone was to give more of yourself than you expected in return. To love a king was to expect to lose more of him every day to his reign. To love Henry was to accept all this and still figure out how to keep my soul.

25

1817 Milot, Kingdom of Hayti

Down by the stream that cooled the floors of Sans-Souci, I had ten ladies join me. There were a few from my court, like the Dame d'Atour, Madame Dieudonné Romain, my Princess Dieudonné. The others were women Zephyrine had introduced to me, good horsewomen, and some had been part of Duchess Adbaraya's Minos, her fighting women.

On this jade field edged with mountain soursop, kowosòl, and plenty of scarlet milkweed, our herbe madame, we practiced a routine with horses Souliman had procured from Henry's mews.

My daughters sat in the shade of an evergreen boxwood in the soft grasses. They were laughing, filled with glee, happy to be away from their governesses.

Madame la Comtesse d'Ouanaminthe and Madame la Comtesse du Terrier-Rouge had begun making complaints about the heat, the weather.

They avoided the sun. Outdoor exercises caused them to wilt like the flopping white petals of the milk bush flowers. The poor petals needed a lot of shade to thrive, just like the governesses. I wasn't sure how long the women would continue. I believed they would give up their titles and return to Philadelphia.

Prince Saunders would have to get me new governesses for the girls. He would know smart women of good moral character. Nonetheless, I imagined Henry's disappointment when the day came and he learned what he'd offered these Americans wasn't good enough.

I rubbed my temples. I needed to focus. Only Haytians would be involved in our training. Somehow that seemed appropriate.

"Yay, Maman!" Athénaïre seemed thrilled I mounted my gray

mare without falling. At thirty-nine, I wasn't too old to do this, and even after six years of Henry's reign, I wasn't too soft or out of practice.

Dieudonné rode her silver stallion close to me. "It is rather hot. Perhaps we should cut our practice short today."

We had been out here for hours. "To be presented at court, no one can find fault. We have to be perfect."

"But no one is perfect, ma reine."

This was true, but not a good excuse to slacken my resolve. My girls sat on the sidelines, watching me ride in the specially made gown that split in the middle like breeches. Galloping astride like men—British and American women would be shocked.

The leathers I'd had my maid haggle to obtain weren't in the best condition, but usable or I wouldn't dare have a pommel rip and send one of my ladies crashing to the ground. The Minos had used wide palm leaves to cover their mules. Those women held their seat the best.

Upon proving ourselves worthy, I knew Henry would procure my team the best riding habits and saddles.

Geneviève rode down from the hills. "I'm sorry to be late."

Though she looked magnificent with her braids tumbling down her back, her tardiness could harm my project.

"Sœur, if you haven't the time to practice, you don't need to do this, not for me."

Dieudonné waved the others to the shade. "And now it's time for an official break."

My Dame d'Atour could sense I was agitated. It would be better to argue with my sister in private.

"Take a ride with me, Geneviève."

Her horse followed mine until we came to the widest part of the stream.

I stopped and swung down. She did the same, and we let our horses slurp the water, which looked cold and refreshing.

"It's fine with me if you don't want to do this. Geneviève, I need everyone fully committed."

"I'm committed."

"But."

"It also seems a little silly. You're the queen. Why are you and your fanciful Dame d'Atour, your lady-in-waiting, having playtime with maids?"

"What's wrong with maids? We were maids for our father. We cleaned. We helped out. It was honest work."

She brushed the silky black mane of her stallion. "What are you trying to prove? That you are as common as the rest? That you haven't been elevated?"

My lips parted and I almost began to explain, but she wouldn't understand. "It's something I'm trying to do well. Like your queen, you should also want to strive for perfection."

Flicking her wet nose, my mare drenched me.

The spray felt good, but I wouldn't tell my chuckling sister.

"Seems your horse, Your Majesty, doesn't know this is good, either. Back to plain ol' Marie-Louise."

The next I knew, the devil came over me, and I towed my sister waist deep into the stream. The cool water kept calling, and despite her protests, I baptized her and she me. We became filled with John the Baptist's Holy Spirit of mischief.

Sprawling on the bank, kicking wet feet, I grinned. "Now that we both look pitiful, tell me what's going on. You're never late. And you're not normally so mean."

"I'm in love."

Grabbing her hands, I wanted to hug her, but she pulled away. "I'm preparing for condemnation. He's not someone you or the king would approve of."

I began wringing out my pant leg. "How about you tell me about him, then let me decide if I approve or not?"

"A merchant. My love is a merchant in Cap-Henry."

"We need people selling goods. The kingdom—"

"A Blanc merchant."

I paused. There were more Europeans and Americans coming to the country now. They weren't unwelcome.

"Say something, Louise. I know our père would hate it."

Though he had made plenty of money off their business at his hotel,

Père had always made sure to keep me and my sisters out of the Blanc men's way.

I sighed. "Geneviève, if he makes you happy, then how can I complain? And Père is gone."

She looked back at the stream. "Cécile will hate it. She'll think me a traitor to our race."

The only thing our père and our older sister could agree upon was a general distrust of Blancs. The two had seen too much abuse.

"You and Cécile hardly ever get along. Why would her disapproval matter?"

Her face bloomed a smile. "I want a love like you and Henry have. Someone to encourage me. Someone of my own. Everyone should be happy with that."

Shaking my head, flinging water with my chignon, I gaped at her. "You flatter me, but my marriage is not perfect. Henry loves Hayti as much as he loves me. That means he often has to choose between us. Though he'll always protect me, Hayti always wins."

"You're just saying that to make me feel better. You have protection and encouragement." She pulled me up and dusted my ruined satin. "That's what I want."

Wanting and having were not the same. The distinction was as clear as the differences between Geneviève and Cécile.

None of that mattered to me right now. I had a troop of women I needed to train. We needed to be perfect. Pretty hard to do when I wasn't without flaws or delusions.

ANOTHER STEAMY DAY OF PRACTICE HAD BEGUN. I ROUNDED MY troops, with my mare going at top speed.

"Continue, Maman!" Athénaïre leapt up and down, then began arguing with her sister. "You should get up and encourage her. This is her dream."

Waving a flag, one she'd sewn, Améthyste coughed, then settled. "I love this dream."

Wouldn't exactly call this group of royal women on horseback my fondest desire, but it was a necessary statement.

I slowed in front of them. "It's a symbol. Sometimes a symbol is better than a dream. Women being seen as powerful by all the kingdom will have an impact. The people will view this homage to our heritage and know again where our hearts lie, with Africa and our power."

Both my daughters clapped, and I felt stronger. "Let's try again."

Up and down the flat plain, my troop rode in our costumes, gold-and-black-striped tunics. They were made of the finest silk, with the star of Henry I embroidered on our right shoulders. Word had reached the king of our practices, and he had commanded the royal weavers to make our costumes. I took this as a sign. My husband believed in me and my plan.

"Begin now." I whipped up my horse, making her rise on her rear legs, then I edged her toward the imagined lines that represented the gates of Sans-Souci.

My women trailed behind, mirroring my gait.

We surely looked like a military parade, though wobbly. Even Geneviève weaved a bit. She whistled, then said, "Let's sing hymns to keep in rhythm."

It sounded like a good idea. So we lifted our voices high, singing Handel's *Messiah*, the "Hallelujah Chorus." It had the right meter. We did this over and over until we were hoarse, until we became precise, and until the sun rose to the highest, hottest position.

"Your Majesty," Dieudonné said, fanning. "We should stop. Everyone looks ready to faint. I know I am."

Zephyrine stood in the shade with pitchers of water. "Refreshments."

"Oui, Princess Dieudonné," I agreed. "I think we are very close to perfect. Once we achieve it, we'll decide at which fete our Dahomet Minos will appear."

Relieved, the riders flew off their saddles and dove headlong into mugs of water.

Améthyste started coughing again.

Jumping down from my mount, I steadied Améthyste against my leg, patting her back until she settled. "Maybe you should avoid practice until there's a break in the weather."

"Non. If I stay indoors, I'll miss the fun." She shook her head so forcefully, her cough ramped up, this time deeper than before.

"Améthyste?"

Zephyrine brought her a cup of water and we made my daughter drink slowly.

She gasped and then breathed a shallow breath. "Never. Never let me miss out on the fun. No missing life."

She sounded dire, and it scared me, but I nodded. "Oui. Oui, now still. Rest."

"Maman," Athénaïre said, "if we go in, the governesses will pester us about what you're doing. They're very curious."

As much as I didn't want them to be behind in their studies, I enjoyed the girls watching. One day they . . . Athénaïre might join me in this tribute. I glanced at my older girl and breathed again when Améthyste's coughing stopped.

"Are the Americans untrustworthy?" Geneviève splashed water on her reddening cheeks. "Are they gossips?"

My baby sister loved court intrigue.

"Non, but it's very hard to explain that we are doing something for our culture when they don't understand the significance of our history."

My sister started fanning as if she'd pass out.

I knew Geneviève.

My opinion may have been stated artfully, but I'd struck at a problem, one she surely had encountered with her newfound love. How could a Blanc truly understand our Haytian culture . . . what our Blackness meant?

"Maman, will everyone have military braiding?" Athénaïre interrupted my thoughts as she pranced about. "The Prussian soldiers Père has working on cannons for the Citadel wear it—that is, when they aren't baring their chests forging hot metal."

I glared at her, wanting to ask how she knew about the young men and their naked chests. But then I spied the person I'd been missing for months: my sister Cécile.

"You've heard and you've come to join us," I said to her and waved for her to come.

She walked down from the hills to me. "There are whispers the queen is up to something, something that has our king distracted. I had to see."

"Cécile, these beautiful Black and Brown women and I are part of the Dahomet royal guard. When we exhibit in front of the royal court, King Henry will be proud. The people, too. They'll see we are honoring our heritage."

Cécile nodded. "Interesting."

She looked regal in a green dress and matching headdress surrounding her golden-brown locks.

"Have you come to join us? The Coidavid sisters unified?"

"No, Louise," she said, "that's not why I'm here. I watched from the ridge. You do look good, sister, holding your seats well. All your ladies do."

Probably so used to bickering, Geneviève flinched before offering thanks. "Why not join us, Cécile? I remember you riding well, just like our maman."

"Geneviève is right. You ride better than any. Join us. Your queen wishes it."

"No, Louise, I don't want to be on display."

With a hand on her hip, Geneviève pointed her finger in Cécile's face. "You're on display. Your husband is a count. He'll probably be elevated even further . . . Unless you are one of the mulatto women praying for the king to die."

"Why would I want that? Why would I want anything that would make Louise or my nieces and nephews unhappy?"

"No, just things to make your baby sister unhappy. This is for women, for unity, and you can't even do that."

Yes, the squabbling Coidavids were certainly models of unity. "Geneviève, Cécile, stop. The girls can hear you."

Surely, they saw Athénaïre listening to us. I rubbed my temples. "Dear, go back to your sister and the troop."

My younger girl stomped her feet. "You're always bickering."

"Daughter! Sisters! Please. I can only handle one battle at a time. The fact that the king is allowing women this position of honor is what's important. Women will know he respects women. All our people will see that King Henry I respects our heritage. Can we pretend to do the same for each other?"

With a shrug, my older sister burst my hope. "There've been so many protests recently against his policies, like the push for marriages. I think you have a lot of work to do. Women need to be able to choose who they love and when or if they should marry."

Folding her arms, Geneviève sneered. "Easy for you to say. You're married to a peer, a man who should be a prince."

"Even a prince can be disagreeable, just as disagreeable as a king or a two-bit merchant."

Fanning herself, Geneviève left us, walking with Athénaïre back to where Dieudonné, Améthyste, and the other women were gathered.

Cécile headed deeper into the jungle.

"Ladies, go back to Sans-Souci." I gave my order, then chased after my sister. "Wait."

She pushed at the limb of a kowosòl flowering with white petals, future soursop fruits. "I didn't come to fight with Geneviève, but I don't like her current paramour. He's nothing but trash trying to fleece the kingdom to line his own pockets. Why not bed the king's sister-in-law if it can get you money?"

"Our sister wouldn't be stupid enough to let a man use her. And what type of man would do this for money?"

"The Brits call them fortune hunters. Maman would say fòtin chasè. Papa Melgrin wouldn't have to say anything. He'd run him off."

"She sounded so happy when she told me about him."

Cécile finally stopped fighting the brush and turned to me. "Geneviève is lonely. And there's nothing wrong with enjoying company, but she needs her eyes wide open. And she must leave married men alone."

"What? Non? She'd not be . . . that girl." My head ached. I didn't want to hear more. "Is that why you came? You want me to be the one to tell her she can't marry this merchant because he's already married?"

My sister closed her eyes for a moment. "Non. Geneviève is grown. She can make her own mistakes. Mistakes might bring wisdom."

She reopened her eyes, and her brilliant green gaze became as wide as a cannon's bore. She took aim and fired. "My husband said Henry is truly agitated—"

"Over my women's troop?"

"Louis Michel says he's never seen him in such a state. Came to make sure he's not taking his anger out on you."

Not sure if I remembered to breathe before shouting down the nonsense. "Non. Henry's never lifted a hand to me."

She sighed. A look of relief, as though someone had been twisting her arm and then relented, washed over her face. "Good. Sometimes when men ascend, they treat those closest to them poorly. I saw it in the ranks of the French army, then with our Black troops. They forget that shared struggle brought them to power."

"Sometimes the struggle is too much. Henry's haunted about the past. He's tormented by Pétion and the lies he sends to the European papers. They're making people think he's a monster. No country will recognize a monster."

"Are you surprised at this, Louise, that people choose to believe the worst?"

"Cécile, you came here thinking Henry was being cruel to me."

She closed her eye for a moment. "You're my sœur. I'll always check on you. But the Blanc world doesn't mean us anything but harm. After all Napoleon has done, the Blancs let him rise twice."

Flinging a small green soursop over my shoulder like a toy, I came closer to Cécile. "Hayti needs a space in that world. Oui, right now Blancs have all the power. That's why this nation must survive. We must thrive."

"It's hard, Louise. The cost of the next battle will be paid by you and your children."

Seeing her concern touched me. I went nearer, shortening the distance between us to inches. I smelled cinnamon and nutmeg in her tunic. She must've baked this morning.

"Have sympathy for what the heroes of the revolution have suffered. The wives, too. Toussaint's Suzanne was tortured by the French."

"And Madame Dessalines was left a widow by Pétion. Make no mistake, Pétion wants to do that to you."

I put a palm on her elbow. "And you suffered. You're a hero too, Cécile."

She linked her hands with mine. If we believed the same, praised the same gods, we'd be in worship now for our nation.

But we didn't believe the same. And I thought Henry was right in trying to make allies.

"Louise, it's more than the common people angry with the king. It's the nobles, too."

"Your husband, Louis Michel—"

"He'll not rise up against the king, but he won't stop a rebellion. People in the kingdom and the republic are suffering. They all want to blame Henry. He'll be overthrown if he can't at least win back his subjects."

My sister's bluntness felt like a slap, hard and stinging across my jaw.

"Are you telling me to give up? Then what? My place is with my husband."

Geneviève came through the trees. "Your Majesty, we need to return to practice. Why is she still here?"

"Louise has to know the truth. She needs to protect her family if there's a rebellion."

Geneviève wagged her finger in Cécile's face. "You're just here to torment our sœur while I'm here helping her."

This time my older sister yanked our youngest sister off her feet, tossed her over a shoulder. Then she flipped her to the ground and put a foot to Geneviève's chest. "Never do that again. I'm getting cranky as I get older, and you're still an easy fight."

Huffing and puffing, Geneviève struggled, but Cécile had her.

"Stop, both of you." I gawked at my wrestling siblings. "Get off her before someone sees."

Cécile helped Geneviève up, and I put space between them. "Look, you two may never agree. But we're family. And, Cécile, I thank you, but know that Henry's trying. He really has a heart for the people. I'm fighting for our king."

She stepped to me and bowed. "My queen, I wish you luck. I truly do. I hope things change."

Princess Dieudonné ran to us with her arms waving. "Your Majesty, Madame Première has fainted. Her breathing is bad."

I charged to my prostrate daughter.

Zephyrine rocked her, but Améthyste was pale, gray like the shelf clouds above.

"Let's take her to the palace and get Dr. Stewart."

All the ladies of my troop and my sisters helped carry Améthyste to Sans-Souci.

The whole way, I prayed for mercy and healing.

None of my plans to save the kingdom mattered if my work killed my daughter.

26

1817 Palace of Sans-Souci, Kingdom of Hayti

Clutching my bracelet, twisting it about my wrist, wishing it had magic powers, I paced outside of Améthyste's bedchamber. I'd done nothing for weeks. My birthday fete approached. My royal troop practiced without me.

Hard to plan a celebration or think of my Dahomet tribute when my poor daughter lay gravely ill.

Améthyste had always been sickly, but it had been years since she had an attack this bad.

The hall was full of noise. My royal court of ladies prayed with me. Others had come and shared my vigil. It made me feel not so alone wearing a path from the cracked bedchamber door to the middle of the corridor.

Geneviève stood beside me and let me lean on her shoulder. "Any change?"

"No. Henry and Dr. Stewart are in with her. They made me leave. That's one of the cruelest things one can do to a mother."

She rubbed my shoulders and the stiff part of my neck. "Princess Améthyste will be well. Don't lose heart."

Straightening, I left the touch of her warm hand. She didn't know what I'd always known about my oldest girl, that every day she breathed was a miracle.

"Having Améthyste come watch my ladies practice while the horses kicked up dust, the scorching heat, even the wildflowers—all this choked her lungs."

My fault.

Geneviève said nothing.

Her condemnation made my pulse boom. It echoed in the hall and in my hurting head, like the pounding of the Citadel's cannons.

Was I a bad mother for letting her live life the way she wanted out in the sun?

Or was I merely a desperate wife who put her husband's needs above her children's . . . and even her own?

I peeked through the door and watched the doctor circling the bed, saw the king looking smaller by the hour.

"It's fifty-fifty," Dr. Stewart said to Henry. The physician was a gambler. He knew odds.

Henry folded his arms, then banged the chair. "This one is not like her other attacks."

He didn't know about the worst ones. The war had called him away when Améthyste suffered in the damp woods. I thought she'd die then.

"She'll pull through this time, Your Majesty. Fifty percent is good. If we were in Europe, I could try more treatments. Here, there's not much we can do to shorten these attacks or extend her life."

"What are you saying, Stewart?"

The doctor put his hand to my daughter's wrist, then moved away. "This inflammation of the lungs . . . it will eventually claim her, Your Majesty. One day, her lungs will simply fail to work."

My sister drew me, shaking and furious, away from the door. "How dare Stewart talk to Henry like that? And with Améthyste right there! She might hear."

Henry's shadow covered me.

Geneviève took one look at him and left, backing all the way down the hall.

Turning, I could barely meet his eyes.

"This is my fault, Louise." Pushing at his sleeves, he exposed his rich dark hands. "The blood on these is why our daughter suffers."

"Non."

He looked at his fingers and I clasped them with mine. "I had her outside in the heat. She doesn't want to miss life. Améthyste wants to do everything her sister can. I'm to blame. I should know that she can't do everything."

"Never, sweet Louise. My crimes. My guilt. My blood."

"What things have you done that haven't needed to be done? There's no evil in fighting crime or fighting for freedom."

"You believe in me still? How?" He sighed, his hot breath scorching my brow. "The prince regent's daughter has died giving birth to his grandson. And the prince regent hasn't even been to war. He hasn't done anything like what I've done."

"Henry, stop punishing yourself. Let us share our sins and pray for forgiveness together."

His head tilted and his eyes brightened. "I'm blessed by your love for me."

I did love him, but I pitied him, too. He kept piling boulders on his shoulders. The weight would soon bring him down. If Améthyste died, I feared we'd both be destroyed.

Stewart stuck his head out of the room. "I'm going to bleed her. Then we should see improvement."

Clasping my bracelet tighter, I moved closer to the door. "Améthyste is already weak. Won't that make her worse?"

"Queen Marie-Louise." Henry's voice changed to a command. "We must trust Dr. Stewart. And I will help."

"Non, Your Majesty."

"I'll hold the bucket. I'll catch every drop of my daughter's royal blood."

"One of my assistants, King Henry, can—"

My husband shoved past the man and crossed Améthyste's threshold. "Time's wasting, doctor."

The men shut the door.

Again, I found myself on the outside. I had to pray that they were right.

HOURS DRAGGED AND BROUGHT THE SETTING SUN. THE MEN HADN'T come out. Geneviève left, taking a gloomy Athénaïre with her. All of my court women said their goodbyes and offered last-minute prayers.

They didn't seem hopeful about my Améthyste's recovery. I must admit I didn't, either.

Under the light of a sconce, Victor sat along the beige wall. As shadows played on either side of him, he twiddled his long thumbs while firmly pressing his back into the gilded molding. Perfect posture for once.

"Améthyste is strong like you, Maman," he said. "She'll get better."

Slow and echoey, his words reached me, restoring the missing metal in my bending spine. "She'll not give up, Maman. She won't leave you or me alone, not when we need her."

My Victor, my youngest, was known for his humor and lack of seriousness, but now I heard something different in his tone. My son was gracious. He was strong, even though I could weep at any moment. I'd never seen him like this, a wary young king in the making.

"Améthyste draws very well, you know. Her sketches are amazing. The painter that Père brought to do portraits, he taught her a few tricks."

"Monsieur Evans?"

"Oui. Him. He showed Améthyste something about perspective and shadows. It made her smile. She couldn't wait to try."

I knew she liked to draw, but Dr. Stewart said the paint fumes were bad for her lungs. I'd stopped her from using her talent. She could die without her passion, without using all the gifts God had given her. How horrible.

Guilty. Again, I was to blame.

Glancing at my son, I saw his drooping frown. "What is it? What are you remembering?"

Drawing a white handkerchief from his indigo jacket, something styled like one of Henry's military coats and having large brass buttons, Victor fumbled with the cloth, swatting it against his buff knee breeches. "I wasn't supposed to tell about her drawing. I told her secret. She'll never forgive me."

"No. Don't you fret. I can keep a secret. It gives me great pleasure to know she did something that brought her joy. You should be proud that you enjoyed it with her."

"Améthyste thinks I'm as good as Armande and even François-Ferdinand. Sometimes, she's the only one who thinks anything good of me at all."

"Non. Non." Kneeling in my burgundy walking gown, the hem sweeping the gold India tapestry, I took the soft handkerchief and wiped at his leaky eyes. "Your père wants you to learn everything. You shall rule one day. All the things your père is trying to do will fall upon you to complete."

"Me, a builder? And Père builds such big things."

"That's what kings do. Archbishop Brelle taught us at the Independence Day fete that King David had to store up materials for his son, Solomon, to construct the temple. That's a heavy burden for both father and son."

He took the cloth from my fingers and swiped at his forehead, as if suddenly embarrassed that his mother was cleaning his face. You'd think a thirteen-year-old would realize he'd always be my baby.

Victor looked up at the candle burning overhead.

No honey fragrance wafted, just the smell of Stewart's mustardy potions.

"If she . . . Will you stop her from drawing now that you know? I want another sketch of me beside Père's throne. I'll keep it and have it framed."

"As long as you wait for her to be strong, I'll not stop you. Like I said, I can keep a secret."

His arms went about my neck holding me tight, tight as two children, as if my firstborn had reached beyond the shadows to aid Victor.

I missed the smile of that one son, so much like my youngest. François-Ferdinand was so curious, so eager to learn of the world.

But François-Ferdinand would have to be alone in heaven with my maman and père. Améthyste couldn't go anywhere.

THUNDER MOANED OUTSIDE OF SANS-SOUCI. THERE WAS NO RAIN, just lightning painting streaks in the night sky. Améthyste hadn't awakened. Unable to be idle, unable to be still, Henry had left to review troops at the Citadel.

I didn't stop him.

Though Dieudonné and Cécile tried to get me to move, I couldn't.

Améthyste and I were in this together, just like those times when we lived in the caves.

I couldn't bear to be anywhere else if my daughter might call my name and need me.

I shut my eyes and prayed. Some saint needed to hear the cries of this mother. I was selfish. For how many mothers in this land had also called out in desperation?

Something rustled and wafted a mustardy smell. The perfume of a broken fever was there, sour and musty.

"Maman. May I have something to drink?"

Blinking, I wiped my wet cheeks and glanced at the most beautiful dark eyes in the world.

Améthyste stared at me.

She knew who I was. The fever had truly gone and hadn't left her confused.

"Maman?"

"Oui, dear. It's just so good to have you looking at me."

A pitcher of water and cups sat on her bedside table. I stretched and lifted a cool drink to her lips.

After a sip or two, she pushed the mug away. "Sorry, Maman. I've taken you away from practice."

"Nonsense. My Dame d'Atour, Dieudonné, is leading my royal Dahomet troops through their paces. If we're not ready, we'll wait until next year."

"I may not get to see it. I may not have next year. I'm losing time."

How did one answer such a statement without bawling? Hayti fevers and humid air made the lungs easy targets of sicknesses. The odds were so much worse for someone with breathing problems.

"I'm not afraid of death. Père has faced it so many times. I'll be brave for him."

"Non. You don't have to do anything but get better."

"But I won't. And I'll keep working everyone up into a frenzy. Père has greater fears than my coughing."

"Améthyste, please."

"I could see you all around me. Could feel the love and your pain. I think that's what death is, that awareness and sadness of those you leave behind. But at least then your own pain is gone."

My hand tightened on hers. The slow thud of her pulse curled about mine. I breathed with her. Then I grieved with her that she chose pain over peace. "I love you, Améthyste. And I'm fearful you'll miss the important things. I want you to live your dreams. You should do everything you desire. You're a princess. I think it's part of the role."

She smiled, and I pushed back the tears beginning to fill my eyes.

"Maman, I think I'm more like Aunt Cécile than anyone. I see the truth. I feel it. I know that one of these times my body will forget how to breathe. It will be forever."

"Non. No more of this talk. You'll get better, and you will do or become whatever you want."

"If you say so, Maman."

I held her and rocked her and hoped that my will was strong enough to keep us all safe in the coming storms. The dark clouds would come even if I couldn't see from what direction. The next time, I doubted we'd escape the fury.

THE KINGDOMS

Britain

English Chronicle and *Whitehall Evening Post*, Thursday, May 14, 1818

Death of Pétion

Extract of a Letter from Port au Prince, dated April 1, 1818

The funeral was grand, but we were kept six hours in the sun, which, with the fatigue, incapacitated me from doing any thing more that day.

The appointment of the present President (Boyer) has been unanimous.

It is very possible that Christophe, on hearing of the death of Pétion, might advance. It is also the intention of the merchants to request Sir Home Popham to send a ship of war here, in the event of Christophe's advancing.

Hayti

Saint James's Chronicle, Tuesday, May 26, 1818

The following are some new regulations of Christophe, of Hayti:—A white man who marries a woman of Hayti becomes a citizen; and, after a residence of a year and a day, is eligible to all offices, and may become a proprietor on the island. A white woman, marrying an inhabitant of Hayti, becomes a female citizen of Hayti. A white man, of any part of the world, marrying a Negress in the place where he resides, may come to the territory the Republic; on his arrival the expense of his voyage shall be paid him.

27

1818 Palace of Sans-Souci, Kingdom of Hayti

June 2, the anniversary of our coronation, had arrived. I dressed, met with my attendants, the ladies of my court, and my special troop. The excitement for performing, for paying our tribute, was palatable.

Yet I couldn't get into my carriage without checking on Améthyste. With my crown in place, my train of silver silk straight and pressed, I went to her chambers.

Looking small and delicate on her bed, she had her eyes closed.

My daughter took a long time to recover. I had pushed off my exhibition for months. Kissing her forehead, I crept away.

When I reached the door of her pristine white room, she whispered. "I'm proud of you."

I put those words in my heart and headed to my carriage.

HENRY'S GUARDS WERE ON HIGH ALERT. AS I DESCENDED THE COURT-yard stairs, I noticed how tense everyone seemed, how tightly they held their bayoneted rifles.

My throat tightened, but I continued with my head high. Our mortal enemy was dead. Pétion was gone from our lives. Though Henry's nightmares should have lessened, they hadn't.

Jean-Pierre Boyer, who made the same evil speeches as Pétion, had been named president of the south. He vowed to defeat the kingdom.

Pushing this all out of my mind, I counted the grand cannons blasting from the Citadel. The fortress had over a hundred now. They would intimidate any fleet in our harbor.

Today was not about war, not necessarily, but preventing it. My display of the Royal Dahomet Guard should touch hearts. I hoped it would cause everyone to remember the unity we all had before the nation split in two. With Pétion gone, reunification could be possible.

I tapped my feet on the floor. My sweeping gown of blue and silver imported from Hamburg was long enough for me to wear boots instead of appropriate court dress slippers, but I decided against it. There was no need to do something that if caught would bring out Henry's temper. With the need for everything to be perfect, one flaw could send him in a rage.

Easing down the stairs, I stopped and admired the fountain bubbling water. A little shiver flooded my skin, vibrating the silver ribbons on my sleeves. Here was where my women would exhibit.

"Queen Marie-Louise, wait." That was Henry. "Don't move." He rushed down the stairs and stopped at my side.

I'd caught Henry's eye.

Not as svelte as in the painting done last year, my king had grown a little corpulent, soft in his middle, with more fullness in his cheeks. His lean form had gained weight, but sautéed plantains and gateau au beurre with rum sauce had also taken a toll on mine.

Yet he looked good to me, still handsome and dangerous.

"Happy Coronation Day, my queen." He kissed my fingertips, then escorted me to my sleek onyx carriage. As if it caused pain for him to do so, he handed me inside, clutching my palm to the last conceivable moment. Then he shut the door.

"Henry? We always ride together."

"I have to attend Sir Home Popham. The admiral needs to tell me the latest news. He's just returned from the republic and the new president."

Boyer and his ilk—they could not ruin this day.

Henry seemed agitated, tugging on his sash, his brooch.

"Nothing newspapers or Boyer says can change the progress you've made with the kingdom. Our schools are running. Monsieur Saunders has done wonders. Be at ease."

Thunderclouds in his eyes lingered. "You say his name a little too enthusiastically."

"Henry, please."

He raised his hand, palm flat in the air. "I know. I know. Pétion's death has me addled. The nation should be unified. I fear Sir Home will say Britain will align with the south because they like the new president. All the work we've been doing will be for naught."

"Henry, you've met every challenge the south has brought to our border."

"They've repelled my advances, too. Louise, the divided island is at a stalemate. That puts us under constant threat from our border and from the sea. The French fleet could be—"

"We're ahead. Boyer can do nothing to us. And we'll know if France dares to come. You're winning. Sir Home will recommend you to his prince regent."

Henry's attempt at smiling completely failed. His lips, the faltering Cupid's bow, formed a light grimace.

I wanted to tell him that once we regained the people's love, once they saw and understood what Henry was doing, no force could stop the kingdom.

But I couldn't say that, not until I'd done my part. "Henry, we'll impress Sir Home and the people with our tribute today."

He left, muttering. "We'll see, Marie-Louise."

Words couldn't salve a fretting spirit any more than wishing on stars for a child to be healed. I thanked the saints that Améthyste wasn't gone, but I wasn't sure how many more years she'd have.

Victor and Athénaïre walked past my carriage. I was about to compliment them when I saw how my son staggered.

My daughter steadied him as he swayed. My glare upon her was as good as shouting for a confession. "He'll be well, Maman," she said quietly. "I mean, he's fine."

A whiff of liquor hit my nose. Inebriated? Today of all days.

Cannons pounded the bay.

The lead carriages started moving.

I had no time to see about Victor without alerting others to the problem. Sitting against the firm seat, I had to believe that Athénaïre, jovial, energetic Athénaïre, could keep her brother from ruin.

I forced myself to concentrate instead on the fete and all the festivities, particularly my homage to our heritage. My troop had to inspire the women of the kingdom to rethink their opinion of Henry and his government.

Duchess Adbaraya Toya, the Gran Toya, would be excited to see us remembering her and the Minos.

A final glance at Sans-Souci, and I saw Améthyste's round face from an upper window. She definitely must have felt better to be up and peeking at the caravan.

I prayed again for her and added another prayer for her brother. Henry would be livid if he knew Victor might be intoxicated.

Then I prayed for myself.

My children and my troop of women alone couldn't forge an alliance with Britain.

AS MY CARRIAGE ENTERED CAP-HENRY, I MARVELED AT HOW MUCH of the rubble had been cleared. Some houses bore fresh paint. There was still plenty to reconstruct, but our capital could again be the Pearl of the Antilles.

Henry's frontline soldiers, the Gardes Haytiennes, were everywhere along the route, hoisting their guns, standing proudly in long coats with red lapels and black velvet cuffs.

The ones marching alongside my horses wore short white breeches and bleached stockings.

I thought of that day, Victor's fete, when would-be assassins had struck. My feet jittered.

The huge military presence was to impress Sir Home Popham, not dissuade a revolt. The carriage jostled. Horses whinnied as if straining. Cannons pounded from Cap-Henry's harbor.

My heart roared, wanting to come through my lace bodice.

Then the road became smooth.

People shouted, "Long live the queen! Vive la reine!"

My pulse slowed.

Sitting back, I spied more soldiers. These men had white collars and red epaulettes. Their hats, big shakos, were edged in scarlet silk and embroidered with the king's new coat of arms.

When we turned on Rue d'Esperille, the busiest street, I saw our citizens waving the flags my royal court had made and distributed the past few years. The crowd lifted their strong voices shouting, "Vive le roi! Vive la reine! Vive la famille royale!"

I treasured this. Henry hadn't lost the people. There was still time.

Our party dismounted to salutes and cheers. We went into the chapel, the Church of Champ-de-Mars, where Emperor Jacques had been crowned. It had been restored to its former glory—fresh white paint, polished mahogany pews, and stained glass showering us in golden sunshine.

Father Brelle, our archbishop, raised his staff with the brass crucifix and welcomed the congregation, seating us in the royal section that had silver ribbon draping.

The Latin chant of "Ave Maria" made everyone rise. The song, which swayed from the highest tones to low drawn-out pitches, blessed my soul. I reveled in worship. I thanked the Christ and Mother Mary for my children.

An older British gentleman, Sir Home, and his men sat behind us. Henry was beside me, strong and silent, with his familiar shadow falling upon my shoulder.

The archbishop looked like the pope in beautiful new white robes and scarlet hat. "The goodness of God has been shown to the kingdom," he said. "Mercies have been bestowed upon us. We must be mindful of this. We must be grateful."

In my heart, I was.

Time should stand still and let me enjoy this moment. If Améthyste were here sitting with her sister and the crown prince, everything would be perfect.

Then Victor started to slip forward. Athénaïre held him up.

This was far from perfect.

Again I held my breath, forgetting everything I'd just counted as blessings.

My prayers turned to Henry and his ministers and Sir Home not noticing my son's antics. The admiral had a distinctive nose, pointy and sharp. I never forgot faces. The way his blue eyes grew big as he marveled at our grace, I'd not forget.

The archbishop began his homily. "At the beginning, the faithful were responsible for proselytizing the world. These are the saints we must uphold. Today, we remember Saint Olga of Kiev, who was given the honorific of Equal to the Apostles."

A woman proclaimed an equal?

The priest's tone became brash. "She is the patron of widows and converts. A regent to her son when her husband was murdered, but she reigned and avenged every evil, even as she continued to encourage the spreading of the gospel."

The priest wasn't a stupid man. He knew the people were on edge, but why offer such a sermon and mention a widowed queen, a regency, and a murdered husband? The British representative was here. And Henry's temper was easily provoked.

I looked over at Victor, who could barely keep his head up. He was in no position to lead against Henry's enemies.

My throat started to close. Like Saint Olga, if my husband were murdered, it would be up to me to rule, to complete Henry's vision.

If Archbishop Brelle meant to warn the king, why speak publicly and sound like he was encouraging insurrection?

The sermon continued, moving to safer subjects such as grace and redemption.

One look at Henry—tight lipped, hands balling behind his straight back—and I knew the damage was done.

My husband fumed. Someone would pay.

I prayed to God, to Saint Olga, and to Mary, the mother of peace, to send us some. I needed joy to descend and salve wounds.

The fire in Henry's eyes let me know he was praying for something different.

28

1818 Palace of Sans-Souci, Kingdom of Hayti

By the time my carriage had parked at Sans-Souci, I had a plan to save us all.

Springing out, I ran inside to Zephyrine and told her to get my hat and colonel's braiding that I was to wear for the parade review.

She glanced at me as if I'd lost my mind, as if I would try to wear my lacy court dress with its foot-long train to mount a horse. Grumbling, she went to retrieve the items.

"My Dame d'Atour," I called out as she descended her carriage. I locked arms with Princess Dieudonné and guided her to a secluded spot.

"I need you to lead the women today."

"Your Majesty, it's your team. You have to do this."

"Dieudonné, you're supportive. But there's something else I must do. I can't be in two places at once. The prince royal is not well."

Her mouth pursed, but at least she did not bite her lip. That was when she was very nervous. "Oh, no, and just as the princess is feeling better."

Zephyrine ran to me with my shako and the braiding.

Taking these precious objects from my maid, I pushed them to my lady-in-waiting. I lifted her chin. "Shine today as I know you can. Do this and let the king and kingdom see our reverie."

She clutched the hat to her bosom. "Oui, Your Majesty."

Dieudonné went one way to change for the presentation. Zephyrine and I went the other to scoop up Victor before the king noticed.

PUSHING VICTOR INTO HIS BEDCHAMBER TO BE WATCHED BY HIS SISter, I heard Henry's heavy footfalls. I couldn't let the king discover his inebriated heir. "Keep him here, Athénaïre. Save him from your père's wrath."

"Let me explain," Victor said with a hiccup before falling back on the bed.

My daughter waved her hand. "Go. I have him."

I dashed out and clasped Henry's arm, walking him past our son's door. "Is everything well, my king?"

"Sir Home is impressed." He glanced at me in my silver gown, not the elaborate habit edged in feathers I'd designed. The winning smile that bloomed on his countenance hurt, but I had to pretend to be happy.

"You've decided against exhibiting. Join me with Sir Home." He kissed my cheek, but I burned. Henry was happy, thinking I'd lost courage, that I was being what he wanted in a wife—submissive and for show.

I had to let him believe this lie rather than expose Victor.

Falling a step behind, I followed the king to Sans-Souci's grand balcony.

The courtyard was filled with the best of our divisions—the Corps Royal du Génie, the police and battlefield groups of the Nord. The way the armies gathered in formation, this could be 1805, the moment after Dessalines pushed out the French.

Music meant for marching played in the background. Henry approached with Sir Home, followed by his ministers Vastey and Dupuy. Like Henry, his men were dressed in coats that looked like military uniforms of dark red with black lapels.

Sir Home Popham, in a blue frock coat with shiny gold buttons and ribbon, held that pointy nose high and stood next to Henry. Speaking mostly French to the king, the admiral occasionally slipped in a few English words, which made Vastey's brows rise.

Turning away from the men, I concentrated on the performance.

The parade began.

Soldiers in brilliant uniforms passed in front of the lines of troops that stretched to the edge of the plateau, even beyond the newly constructed church on the palace grounds.

Showcasing their spinning weapons, each man saluted the king as they marched.

"I say, King Henry." Sir Home fanned his head of thick white hair with his moon-shaped hat. "Your people seem well and under control. So precise. They do this often? It's very different than we've heard."

Vastey stepped forward. "The king reviews his men from the Citadel on Wednesdays."

The admiral and his group of fellow officers nodded to themselves and whispered.

I couldn't tell if they were impressed or amused. Time would expose them. Wine at tonight's dinner should loosen their tongues, too.

Our nobles waved flags and cheered. They looked superb in their court dress of fine coats and breeches and boots. Every duchess, countess, and baroness appeared elegant in silks and satins, their hair sweetly coiffed in beautiful braids, turbans, or bonnets with feathers.

The captain to the admiral's right remarked in English, "The women are all wearing shoes. No resemblance to savages at all."

Glaring at him, I hoped that foolishness came from Pétion and Boyer's propaganda, not the British notion of Blacks.

The man blushed, pulled out a cloth, and mopped his fevered face.

Henry smiled as if he hadn't heard, but he understood the English insult.

Vastey sulked more and more.

Dupuy used Kreyòl, the language the king didn't want spoken, to say, *moun fou blan dyab*, calling them something like *foolish white devils*.

Every man on the balcony was foolish.

Princess Dieudonné was at the gates of Sans-Souci. My team fell in a perfect line behind her. On her command they cantered in unison. By the time they reached the top of the plateau, their mounts were galloping like cannon blasts firing across the plain.

Our nobles clapped as my royal troop brandished bronze swords like the ones made on the mountaintops for the revolution. Each lady sported a black-and-gold-striped blousy tunic over long white breeches.

Calling the troops to attention, Dieudonné made four riders stand perfectly still while the other six wove in between, shouting, "Vive le roi! Vive la reine! Vive les Dahomet Minos!"

Spontaneous cries of pride filled the air, echoing about the palace and pounding into my soul. Everyone had to feel the same joy. Every heart remembering the old should be beating a little faster.

Sir Home clasped his palms together. "What is this, King Henry?"

"The queen's tribute to the Africans, particularly the women whose drive and courage live through us. Their dreams spurred our freedom."

The snide talkative lieutenant shrugged. "But such regalia and weaponry on the women? And they are riding like men."

"For the maneuvers the troops are performing, to imitate the skills of warrior women, skirts would get in the way." I raised my chin, wishing I had my larger crown. "Riding sidesaddle could cause one to fall. I know I did when I tried. Astride gives us power."

"The queen rode like an Amazon?" The lieutenant laughed and whipped off his hat, waving it like the rest of the crowd. "I'd like to see the prince regent's wife do that. I suppose Princess Caroline is too preoccupied with other things." He waggled his brows and said in crude-sounding tones, "Exile in Italy must be difficult with her masculine friends."

The man scoffed at his future queen, hinting at something untoward. It was interesting to know that other men, not just the Haytians, were skeptical of women in power.

As if he feared I'd say something unwise, Dupuy coughed, then pushed his way to be near Henry. "Our lovely, gracious, soft-spoken queen is the colonel of this special troop."

It was funny to hear Dupuy boast about my troop when he and all the king's advisers had opposed it.

Sir Home chuckled. "These ladies are pretty good."

"Oui. They are." Henry clapped, but his warm gaze was upon me.

Wanting distance from all these men, I went down the stairs.

The ladies finished their routine, whipping out our new flags.

General Romain, a tall, brown-skinned man, clapped for his wife. I was proud for Dieudonné. Then I saw the hateful way he looked up at the king. The man smoothed his face when he saw me.

Then he erupted in laughter when Victor ran past.

The prince royal had eluded Athénaïre, who chased after him.

"Marvelous, Maman!" Slapping his palms together, Victor kept moving closer, saluting me, the troops, and the king. Then he lost his balance and toppled into the fountain.

Laughter whipped up and down the courtyard.

Dupuy mentioned the word *skit* to Sir Home, garnering cheers from him and his men as if the prince royal were a hired clown.

I fished Victor out of the water, but my world crumbled as I witnessed thunder in his father's face.

WALKING IN MY GARDENS, I SURVEYED THE DAMAGE DONE BY LAST week's troop presentation. Sans-Souci looked a little the worse for wear, but was no longer littered in horses' leavings. The gardeners said the manure would be good for my vegetables.

There was minimal damage to my roses, but my pineapple-smelling frangipani had fared badly. Trampled creamy-yellow petals were everywhere.

Taking up a crumpled flower, I ripped it to shreds. Just like my heart. I still couldn't believe Henry had imprisoned our son.

Vastey approached, bowing before I could fully turn. "Your Majesty, the king would like to see you."

With a shake of my head, I turned back to the flower bed. "My sea lavender has been run over. Look at the crushed white buds. Such a shame."

The man came closer. "Madame, please. Go talk with the king. He's in a dark state. He needs you."

Henry might need me, but I didn't want him. I'd removed myself from our chambers and stayed away from his bed. "Tell him I'm in a dark state, too. My only living son is imprisoned. Summon me when that's no longer the situation."

"Your Majesty, I know things are difficult—"

"You have no idea what those words mean. Do you know how many times I've sacrificed myself for Henry's duty or his difficulties or Napoleon or LeClerc or Rochambeau or Pétion? Or his jealousy of Dessalines or Toussaint or anyone who challenged him? Do you know what it's like to hide in damp caves which are choking the life out of a daughter, or to fear birthing a baby early in the dirt, or to give a firstborn to the enemy because Henry's duties require it? No, Baron de Vastey, you do not know difficulties."

"Pardon, madame." He gaped at me, probably shocked, but I'd thank him later for giving me cause to speak my mind.

He started to leave but turned back. "Queen Marie-Louise, he needs you. The country needs you. Go to him. Hear him out."

"Non. You want his mood to worsen? If he hears how I loathe what he's done, he won't recover."

"Madame, if you don't try, all is lost. The goodwill your royal troop has done, the good opinion Sir Home Popham has taken from our shores—you want it gone? Non, madame. I cannot believe that you will set Hayti backward."

Henry went through these fits like an angry child to get his way, to control me and the country. "Hayti will not go backward. What we've done has to be more than one man."

Vastey stooped in his crimson military frock coat that the king made his advisers wear and picked up a crushed blossom. "I do what I'm asked for the nation. From the lowest in the kingdom to the royal household, everybody must do their part to support the narrative that we want. Europe won't ally with Hayti if they believe we are ignorant slaves playing dress-up."

What Vastey said was true. Britain and Russia had determined that France should not reconquer the island and promised to stay our enemy's hand. "In upcoming negotiations, all could change. Alliances could easily shift."

Casting the petals to the trampled grass, he glanced at the palace. "The king cannot spare punishment for the son when he hasn't done so with his nobles. You see a hard-hearted father. I see a just king who wants his heir to take responsibility like a leader."

"The people don't trust Henry. They're afraid of him. They're afraid of the king."

And I was, too . . .

Fearful of the man he was becoming, fearful that there were no bounds of decency he wouldn't break to enforce his will.

"Sometimes it's better, madame, to instill fear. If no one is afraid of the king, he'll be overthrown. The same will happen when it's Victor's turn to lead. Your husband knows that. He's trying to give the young man discipline, some backbone."

"That's what Henry's doing, maturing Victor?" My slow laugh rose to wicked glee. "Congratulate him. Let's hope he's done it, for he's also ripped out my heart."

"Madame."

"You're not a mother. You haven't disregarded everything that's important to you to satisfy the king's needs. I can't do it anymore."

He dipped his head and sighed. "I know mistakes have been made. I know you're hurting, but you're the queen. And a queen has a responsibility to make sure that people understand the king."

"I tried. Then he put our son in prison." I walked away from Vastey, deeper into my garden, right into a pepper cinnamon tree. The spice of the berries and bark seasoned the air. Just needed the salt of my tears to finish the dish.

The man gave chase. "Please, Your Majesty. Since you've stopped talking with him, his mood is darker. More people are being punished. He's in a maddening spiral. Only you can bring him out of this."

Henry should have some control. It was getting harder and harder to see the man I loved and not the monster the people saw.

"Please meet with him. Talk to him."

If I had spoken up more . . . If I'd appeased him less, our eldest son would be alive. Victor would not be under such pressure. "The king should be able to help himself."

"He can't. That's why I'm appealing to you to please put your disappointment away. He'll order his son released if you ask, but you have to ask him."

"I did. A week ago."

"The prince royal has learned his lesson, but the king needs to know he hasn't lost your support."

"Why must I be his salvation?"

"Maman!"

Victor's voice.

Vastey and I turned toward the courtyard balcony. My son was there—healthy and free. He ran to me, running fast from the king's shadow.

AFTER A MILLION KISSES TO MY SON, I SENT HIM WITH BARON DE Vastey back into Sans-Souci.

Henry hadn't moved from the balcony, and I hadn't inched from my garden.

In the warm sunshine of the fleeting day, I stood clasping my emerald bracelet, with a mountain breeze rustling my black gown. This was the mourning crepe I'd donned for Prince Jean's funeral, and I had worn ebony every day this past week to mourn the imprisonment of my son and the loss of Henry's humanity.

The king stared and I swayed with the breeze that moved blades of fresh-cut grass along the cobbles.

Henry was a proud man. It was hard for him to admit that he was wrong.

But he knew he'd married a proud woman. I couldn't budge, not this time.

So we stood yards apart, like children holding a competition to see who would blink first.

Dupuy came up to him with papers in his hand. The fearless man who always had Henry's ear stopped and stood like a statue.

This was ridiculous, three grown people deciding who'd be the more forgiving or foolhardy and speak first.

That had to be me. "King Henry, go handle your business. I'll wait for you here."

I turned my back to them and again began stooping to pick up petals.

Soon, I felt that familiar shadow cascading over my shoulders.

"I freed him, Louise, because I knew you wanted it."

"How about because you knew you were wrong?"

"I'm sorry, but Victor gave me no choice. He had to be punished."

"So you made him a mockery to the court?"

"His drunkenness did that."

He said it as though imprisonment was a normal punishment. Maybe it was for someone who had grown up enslaved. Like most things that tortured him, he never spoke much of his childhood in bondage. He just relived it in nightmares.

"Look at me, Louise. Let me see your face. Share some of your light."

Casting the petals into the garden bed, I wiped my hands on my skirt before rising. Then I turned to Henry.

I saw struggle in his face. He looked unsure, even tortured.

"Sorry." The words tumbled from his lips. The lowering sun dropping behind him made his silhouette sag on the ground. But his heavy frown sank my heart.

"You're a father, Henry. We already lost a son to France. Victor, I kept him safe in my stomach while I hid in caves with your daughters. I was so afraid I'd lose him. How can you risk one hair on his head?"

"I had a guard with him all the time. He wasn't alone."

That made it better? Was a guard supposed to make me think Henry hadn't succumbed to madness?

"Louise, I'll die before we lose another child. I want to be proud of Victor. And he has made me proud at times. If the vain priest is right, and my days are numbered, then our son will soon be king."

Clutching my collar, I let the shock of what Henry said wash over me. It was like I'd jumped headfirst into the cold Rivière Mapou. Was he waiting for another assassination attempt? "Everyone's days are numbered. We all die, someday."

"The sermon the day of the anniversary fete was a warning. I'm making preparations for you and the children. But here in Hayti, I have to protect you all. I cannot show weakness. Not a moment of weakness."

He raised his balled fist to the sky as if he were readying to fight Saint Michael. "The minute I show any softness, the forces against me will know I can be overthrown. The enemy's knives won't stop with me. They will kill all my children, all the heirs to our kingdom."

I grasped his hand and lowered it. It was our first touch in days.

"You could rule this country well because you have a heart for the people, Louise. You are strong. The country sees it. I see it. I wish I had your grace."

He didn't want my grace. Henry wanted to control it, to control me.

"One day, the people will see what I was trying to do. One day, the nation will be revered. We'll be a model to the world."

I kept his rough hands in mine. "You have to be more patient. You have to be more kind. When you give speeches, take Victor with you. Let the country know that he has your approval."

"But I want your approval, Louise. I need to know you're on my side. That you still love me."

His light eyes seemed so desperate, so tortured. All I had to do was agree and his suffering would be alleviated.

Yet this was still more manipulation.

"I'm not mad anymore. Victor's home. Go on back to Dupuy. Do what he needs."

"No. You need to still love me. I worship you."

His rushed words made him seem frenzied. He took my arm and led me to the round chapel.

Four stone columns supported its portico. The dome was a masterpiece, surmounted by a white cupola and steeple. The magnificent structure was another thing Henry's brilliant, tormented mind had dreamed.

Light glowed inside, pouring out from under the threshold. Henry had ordered that the chapel always be lit, so that one could pray at any moment. Through the arched doorway, we entered. The windows behind the altar let in the setting sun's pink dusky rays.

"There's a crypt below. I don't want to be laid to rest here, Louise. Bury me in my Citadel so my bones will help protect the kingdom."

He'd given up.

He expected to die.

How did you make someone live when they sought death?

"Promise me, Louise. Promise."

"I will, but what did you want to show me?"

"Louise, I worship you. I need you to see that I'm telling the truth."

He towed me to paintings that I thought depicted saints.

They didn't. Each had my brown face, my brown hands, my skin. "Henry, this is sacrilege."

"How can you say that? I worship you. You and the children are my shining stars. It's why I have five points on my star, for you, Victor, Armande, and the girls."

The symbol on his chest, the shiny brooch that he loved—it was for us?

I was frozen, looking at my face as the Virgin Mary.

"You've always believed in me. Even when I didn't believe in myself, you've believed. You've sacrificed like no one else. I worship you."

Didn't notice that he'd knelt before me. When I turned, his mouth pressed at my stomach.

"Henry?"

"I worship you."

His arms wrapped about my hips.

The grip was tight, obsessive, controlling.

"You haven't left me. Have you?"

One glance into his eyes revealed his sadness. He was lost.

I didn't know what to say. This man, my protector, was breaking into pieces.

But I wasn't lost. I wasn't Henry's lifeline. I couldn't be a rope, no matter how much he wanted to cling to me. He had to find his own peace instead of stealing mine.

Cradling his face between my palms, I said, "Everything will be all right."

Then I lowered my eyes so he couldn't tell I'd lied.

EXILE

New Times (London), Monday, February 17, 1823

NEW TIMES. SWINDLER AT PARIS. THE FALSE PRINCE of HAYTI. Charles Wilson, a man of colour, aged 20 years was brought before the Assize Court of Paris a few days ago, charged with a fraud having subscribed his name as Prince Charles of Hayti. From the statement of M. Privet, proprietor of the Hotel des Princes, rue de Richelieu, it appeared that on the 24th of September, obliged to provide domestic expenses for Wilson until he received funds from his aunt, the queen of Hayti, who is at present in England.

The Jury, after a short consultation, found [Wilson] guilty, on a majority of seven to five, of swindling. The Court afterwards sentenced him to three years imprisonment, and to 50 francs damages and costs.

29

1823 Hastings, England

I should blame Catherine for convincing me to follow the pattern of European royals in England. This notion brought my daughters and me here to Hastings. My solicitors haggled and bartered but finally engaged a town house, 5 Exmouth Place, on West Hill.

The unobstructed view of sky and water meant everything to my soul, but it brought danger to my daughters. They were thrust into society alone while I recovered from cold after cold.

Waking every morning and flinging open sheer beige curtains to glance at the sea brought me peace, healed pieces in me that I didn't know were wounded. Yet I feared the intrigues I'd been careful to avoid could seduce Améthyste and Athénaïre.

Dressed and huddled in a blanket, I made my way down to my whitewashed parlor. My bare feet loved the spring of the warm pine floors. I settled into a chair, watching the bobbing of boat sails in the harbor, counting the minutes to Améthyste and Athénaïre's return from a luncheon.

"Any letters, Zephyrine?"

She handed me a bone china cup that bore stenciled roses. "Non. But there's word of another fraud, another fake prince from Hayti. The princesses spoke of this earlier."

Tugging a blanket about my legs, warming myself to the coal fire, I sat back, then sipped my chamomile. My solicitors had told me of the dozens of inquiries after our fortune. The rebels led by Boyer lined their pockets with our kingdom's treasury. They'd not spent a penny on the people's education or well-being. The rebels could rot in hell before they stole my means.

My fist balled around the arm of the chair. I'd not give the killers of my family anything, not even a prayer.

"I'll go see about dinner." Zephyrine left, and I relaxed with my tea and the beautiful fire in the hearth.

The downstairs door rattled open. I heard the girls chattering.

"Souliman, what an adventure we had today. Count M showed us the castles."

That was Athénaïre bragging about another peer, an earl they'd met at a dinner party. This M was a member of the British parliament. I think a Tory.

Souliman grunted. "The village is still standin' outside, so it couldn't have been that great."

The door banged shut. "Go on up. Your maman is in the parlor. She's out of her bed, feeling strong."

That I was. A winter cold and achy bones weren't going to do me in. I had princesses to keep safe.

The good man probably took their coats and rushed them to the stairs as if I were at death's door.

"Count M," Athénaïre said, with her mouth puckering from saying that letter. "He was humorous today. Such a handsome man."

"He's old. In his forties." Améthyste's high-pitched voice sounded annoyed, but she wasn't coughing. "And he flirted so much with Marianne, I'm surprised you think he saw you at all. It was shameless."

Feet pattered on the steps.

Athénaïre danced into my parlor with her mustard-yellow gown that belled above her ankles. I liked these new styles that flowed like rivers and weren't stiff columns. It was good to see her in color.

Turning back to her sister, she flopped onto the Barbel blue-and-white-striped sofa. "Today was memorable."

Améthyste sat by the fire, warming her hands. The hem of her cream satin dress covered her short walking boots. "The count talked to everyone. He's a very charming flirt. He had much to say about the rising Lord Melbourne. Apparently, Melbourne hates Catholicism and supported enslavement."

"At least he's open about his hateful opinions." I sipped my tea and thought of our popular Duc de Marmelade, who feigned his loyalty and then turned against Henry. "It's much better to see who the enemy is, isn't?'"

"Politics is boring." Athénaïre spun and headed to the window. "Travel is illuminating. Maman, we should head to the spas of Belgium. Count M believes it will be beneficial to you."

Shaking her head, breathing easily, Améthyste laid back on the sofa. "I think chasing after the count is something that benefits you. Shameful."

They both laughed. Their faces glowed from the sea and sun and silly talk. I loved this. "I take it you had a good time at the Thorntons' luncheon."

Améthyste wheezed a little, then straightened. "My sister had a much better time, but it was good. Marianne and Patti are as delightful as ever. I didn't know how much I'd missed them."

My younger daughter waltzed about the room, her graceful movements vibrant, striking. She came close to my chair and put her head on my lap. I stroked her thick curls. She'd braided her hair, no straightening her tendrils in the damp air.

"Maman," she said, "tomorrow, Madame Camac, a friend of his lordship, is throwing a ball here in town. Come and let Count M convince you of taking the full royal tour. He says spas and waters of Europe will do wonders for your constitution. Your rheumatism will be better. And Améthyste can have better treatments, too."

The new physicians recommended taking the waters for both Améthyste and me. Hastings's sea was too cold. "Traveling to warmer destinations is something to consider."

"Maman, Athénaïre merely wants to follow Count M and sip champagne as the peers do in Belgium and Prussia."

Didn't know much about those countries, but aristocrats loved sparkling wine everywhere.

Zephyrine entered the room, the fine floorboards creaking a little. In her nervous, jittering hands was a note. The stationery looked like the letters Monsieur Senn sent from his desk at Reid, Irving and Company.

She extended the letter to me. Glancing at a few words, I found my heart sinking. I offered it to Athénaïre. "Tell me what bad news it brings."

Her brow furrowed as her lips moved. She kept turning the pages, but it was minutes before she uttered a word. "The letter is to inform you, Maman, that another claim has been made against the monies Père left for us."

"Fraudulent." I groaned and focused my anger on the flames. "Another dead uncle or mysterious nephew to the king?"

Huffing, Athénaïre kicked out her feet. "Non. Not a relative, but Baron de Dupuy."

I grabbed the paper. An obscenity formed on my lips. Henry's friend, one of his closest advisers who couldn't tell him the truth, was now trying to take away our protection.

"Maman. You're shaking. Monsieur Senn told him that there's nothing for him. We are all right. We're safe."

Athénaïre said this to me. Then Améthyste.

But I chided myself. I'd begun to feel comfortable and safe, perhaps untouchable. Perhaps I needed to act untouchable. "We will go to your ball. Zephyrine, press our best gowns."

My youngest was elated and started singing and dancing.

Améthyste's brow rose. She peered at me as I often did at her, with concern filling her dark eyes.

Being cautious might encourage attacks. The Christophes had been attacked enough. A line had to be drawn. It might as well be chalked on the floor of a ballroom.

SOULIMAN DROVE PAST TALL HOUSES ON ROUTE TO MADAME CA-mac's ball and supper. Beautiful gorse hedges lined the circular drive of her newly constructed residence.

My thoughts drifted to Sans-Souci's construction—the width of the courtyard and how the windowpanes glistened with chandelier light. I remembered nobles in their finery arriving for our fetes and the girls' position on the balcony stairs.

Glancing at my princesses in their crimson capes, my eyes grew misty. Dressed and coiffed to perfection, beyond what we did for the Clarksons' gatherings or even Wilberforce's dinner, they were ready for the first very formal event we'd attended since the fall of the kingdom.

Henry's provisions made this possible. These doors wouldn't be opening to us if we were paupers.

The carriage stopped. Torches burned near the short set of steps leading into the house. Servants in blue satin mantles opened our door.

One young man, the tallest groom, blinked wildly when my daughters and I descended.

Ignoring him, I smoothed my vanilla satin gown and straightened my marabou-feather tippet so that it draped smoothly along my shoulder without creasing the gathered puff of my sleeve.

"Your Majesty," Souliman said in clear, loud English from his perch on the top of our new upholstered barouche. He pounded his cane. "Send for me when you become bored."

Nodding, Athénaïre drew back her cloak to expose the azure frill at the satin banding of her hem. To my surprise, Améthyste did the same, exposing her darker blue bodice, which I had trimmed with silk netting.

Standing behind them, watching the footmen bow and move out their way, I wished I'd kept their small tiaras.

Then I thought differently.

They glowed, with their curly chignons pinned and braided like adorning crowns. They floated up the shallow stairs to the house. Beauty and grace, in addition to my footman announcing their station, announced to all that the most delightful and regal princesses had arrived to the ball.

THE CLAMOR OF MUSIC AND CONVERSATION FILLED THE CROWDED drawing room where dinner was served. I tried not to fidget, to not roll my bracelet about my wrist, but I failed. The gold-and-emerald band slipped up and down my silver satin gloves.

My hands should be uncovered, but I hadn't decided whether I'd partake of the pheasant being served. I'd become nervous, watching Améthyste and Athénaïre and trying to find the mysterious Count M, whom my youngest seemed to fancy.

The girls were on the far side of the room with Marianne and Patti. The gregarious Thorntons made sure my daughters danced, delighted in talks of books, and dodged difficult conversations from the curious, wealthy women snooping into the Christophes' prospects.

Not everyone wanted to know my princesses as friends and peers. Some merely wanted gossip. With Hastings becoming more popular with European exiles, tittle-tattle opportunities were plentiful.

And again, my family was in the center of it all.

From my chair far in the corner, my gaze lifted to Athénaïre. Her peacock fan of sweeping blue fluttered in front of her delicate chin. She appeared to enjoy all the noise.

Améthyste sat beside her sister but didn't seem to be speaking. Was her reserved nature winning? Or was she hiding illness?

"More wine?" A server held a dark glass bottle by my goblet.

I nodded and returned my focus to my table, my surroundings. Cream molding formed picture-frame boxes along pristine white walls. To my left was a wall of windows. Sheer curtains hovered along the sides of the glass.

Outside, the Camacs' torches highlighted their garden. More gorse hedges and an abundance of trees graced their lawn.

I wished to walk.

No banana palms could be spied but lots of oaks and a sprawling cypress that looked a hundred years old. This tree's limbs seemed to stretch to the sea. The trunk was battered, completely brown, and bald in the cold air.

Yet it still stood.

"Have you had a chance to travel, Madame Christophe?" Lady Robert sat at my right. Chubby, with ruddy cheeks and wonderful red hair, she'd kept conversation moving among our party.

"Non, not recently. But I suspect my daughters will want to do more in the warm months."

Talk drifted back to the head of the table.

Breathing easier, feeling that I had passed some test, I relaxed.

Servers carrying entrees of pheasant and partridge entered the drawing room. Madame Camac had them trained well. Not a drop of red wine or mustard sauce dripped on the white-draped tables. The napkin on my lap felt stiff from starch. This dinner could have been scripted by Lord Limonade. Princess Dieudonné's rare smile would bloom at the servers' precision. I thought of her, my lost friend, and wondered how she fared in the new Hayti.

The engaging Lady Robert laughed again and whispered something to Lord Cholmondeley to her left. I feigned ignorance of their English words—the murmurs about my wealth and speculation about how I'd survived the fall of the kingdom.

The last man at our table, a slender, silent fellow, stared at me as much as at the window. The violinist began to play Ferdinand Ries's Violin Concerto in E Minor. My mind drifted to Sans-Souci again, then I looked down to my plate, wishing it held Henry's favorite, roasted mallard.

"At least the music is not Beethoven. I find his work overrated." The fellow window watcher had finally spoken, and his French was divine. He sat back in his chair and lightly fingered his goblet with his pinkie, staring at me or the glass panes or both.

Lord Cholmondeley wiped his fingers on his napkin. "I hear you're very taken with your town house, Madame Christophe. Do you intend to make Hastings your permanent residence?"

Impertinent to ask my plans, having just met, but I offered him a polite smile. "I make no lengthy plans. One never knows what tomorrow may bring."

Our fourth tablemate, the watchful gentleman with slick black hair, lifted his wineglass. "That sentiment is something with which I can agree. To tomorrow."

Cholmondeley, whose gaze passed from me to the other fellow, accepted the toast, raising his goblet. "Count Saint-Leu, I can imagine you feeling that way, with your brother's passing last year."

The chatty Lady Robert gasped, then forked pheasant into her mouth.

Saint-Leu put down his glass. "It was in '21, and unexpected. A pitiful end to a man who wanted the world. I suppose that's the way for men of conquest." Glancing at me, he said, "Many here can agree."

With a nod, the count wiped his fingers, excused himself, then accompanied Lord Cholmondeley out of the room. With his barely touched plate, I supposed Saint-Leu went hungry to join the men to drink liquors and smoke cigars.

Lady Robert and I were left with an uncomfortable silence. We stayed like this until it was time for the ladies to adjourn to the library.

But neither I nor my dinner companion moved.

"I'm sorry, Madame Christophe."

Stomach spinning a little, I was torn between chasing after my girls and remaining still.

"You did handle that well." Her voice sounded soft.

"Am I complimented for behaving, Lady Robert? Would you expect less from a humble widow or a queen?"

"You're very good." Her voice sounded cryptic. "I'd be upset."

"Lady Robert, I've never been good at guessing what makes someone angry. Please tell me what you are talking about."

"You've had dinner with a Bonaparte. Louis Bonaparte, the former king of Holland, is Count Saint-Leu, the brother of Napoleon Bonaparte. Napoleon—it's good he's dead. The fiend tried to take over the world and crush your Hayti."

I gripped the table. My head spun. I'd dined with the enemy. Non. A relative of the enemy. Facing Lady Robert, who looked hungry for gossip, I remembered my station.

"Madame Camac," I said, "has a sense of humor. She's made this table truly one of exiles. What country do you formerly command?"

Cheeks reddening like her hair, my dinner companion shrugged. "You're quick witted. I'll give you that. And very calm."

"I don't fight old wars, Lady Robert." False smile plastered, I stood and headed out the nearest door to find the cypress and chill my fevered brow in the wind.

30

1823 Hastings, England

My garden grew the finest tea roses in summer, but now, steeped in this cold season, my white Christmas roses had started to bud. On my knees picking up fallen leaves and petals, I savored the freshness of the sea air. If it had been warmer and I didn't need to wrap my arms in a wool shawl, this moment would be perfect.

The kitchen door banged behind me.

Startled, imagining the sound of cannons, I stilled until Zephyrine's voice became clear.

"Shame we can't get a decent plate de Hayti to grow, not even when it was warm."

"Cécile writes that they are hard to find back home. The continued chaos is affecting the farmers. The people seem no better off."

"The duchess can't help. Her husband is in league with the new government."

Louis Michel, my sister's husband, whom Henry had recognized as a count, then a duke and prince of the realm, hadn't fought for the king. "He chose to live, Zephyrine. Those who didn't have been executed." Figuring out whom to battle and when was sort of like abstaining from waging war with dinner guests. "Maybe they'll find a way in time."

"Your Majesty . . . I mean madame, you look pale. Do you wish to go inside and rest?"

"I think I need to walk. The girls should be back from saying their goodbyes to the Thorntons. Marianne and Patti have to head back to Suffolk. I'm sure the princesses will need to be commiserated on their friends leaving."

As I tried to step past her, Zephyrine stood in my path. "The Princess Athénaïre is with the count again. They are exploring the ruins today."

Count M, or Comte de Maltverne, or the earl of Maltverne, as he was known in London, was a pleasant Blanc man—widowed, no children, no fortune, but with a smile for days. Lady Robert said he was looking for a wealthy wife. That wasn't the same as seeking love. I had had love. Athénaïre deserved love, not an accountant. "She must tell him goodbye, too."

"He does seem nice." Her bronzed face said the exact opposite. She knew he wasn't right for my daughter. "And he did chase away the newspaperman."

She put a hand to her mouth and fluttered like an errant butterfly back into Exmouth Cottage.

I chased and stopped her at the staircase that led to our upper rooms. "Out with it, Zephyrine. We've been through too much for secrets now."

"A newspaperman came up to the princesses when they were meeting their friends by the docks. He said awful things about the king. He asked questions about how many were killed in the coup that claimed the kingdom. The beast wanted to know if they smuggled the nation's treasury out of Hayti in their petticoats."

A headache lodged in my temples. "When did this happen?"

"A few days ago, after the Camacs' ball."

Moving closer, I clutched the stair rail and peered up, all the way to the third level. Envisioning my daughters' brown hands swirling along the oak banister as they descended from their bedchamber, remembering our first carefree laughs here, I sighed aloud. "This isn't the place for us. We can't become targets again."

It was unfair.

There were other exiles. Napoleon's brother had been ousted as the king of Holland. Why couldn't the newspapers chase him? "We should leave as soon as possible."

"Where, madame?"

Unsure, but feeling that we should disappear, I dashed from the house and trudged up the high path to the hillside view of the gorgeous sea.

Blue-gray waves lapped at the shore. They hummed a soothing rhythm. Clouds hung low, but not quite flat like Hayti's. They comforted me. I needed to find a place that made me feel as free as swimming in Rivière Mapou.

WITH THE SEA AT MY BACK, I WALKED FARTHER ALONG THE PATH, TO the ruins of Hastings Castle.

Big chunks of stone were all that was left of the building constructed by William the Conqueror. At least that's what Améthyste said. She'd sketched it when we first arrived.

Her picture created from a distance showed the foundation and the beauty of the cliffs or mountains that secured the castle. I wondered why the British had let the monument decay. Did they want no trace of what William had done?

The familiar laughter of Patti Thornton caught my ear. The blond woman, my younger daughter's age, strolled with Count M and Athénaïre.

My daughter whipped a painted orange fan in one hand while her other wrapped the count's arm. Patti did the same on the opposite side. The three looked cozy. Count M seemed to be courting both women.

From nowhere, Améthyste tapped me on my shoulder.

I jumped, then braced my hand against my heart. "You scared me."

"Didn't mean to. But now you get to bask in the spectacle."

She didn't mean the ruins. My goodness. Even Améthyste knew these attentions from the count were wrong.

"She's scared, Maman. She doesn't want to be alone. She's not like you or me."

I hadn't thought about being alone as a choice. Henry was gone, but he chose . . .

Améthyste flicked a tear from my cheek. "Love is beautiful." She started coughing. "But it's for those who can see forever."

I drew my daughter into my arms and held her tightly. "Love comes for those it's meant to find. Your aunt Geneviève, she was frightened of being alone. She made wrong choices trying to find her heart's desire."

"That's the first kind word you've said about our aunt in a long time. Have you written her?"

Non. I hadn't found the words.

She hadn't, either.

Before I could tell Améthyste why I couldn't speak to my treacherous sister, my daughter doubled over.

Améthyste clutched her chest and sank, heaving.

The count and his ladies came running.

"Breathe, sis." Athénaïre grabbed her hand. "I knew it was a bad idea to go exploring in the dusty ruins."

We laid Améthyste on the grass.

Patti fanned her, pushing cool air to my girl's paling face.

I cradled Améthyste's slim chin in my palm. "Améthyste. Keep breathing."

Count M stood there with a befuddled look on his countenance. "Is she all right? Should I take Miss Thornton home?"

My daughter was fighting for her life while this man rolled his hat and stared.

"Comte de Maltverne, go get help. Dr. Stewart. I mean Monsieur McKinney. Two houses over from mine. Run."

My tone was sharp. I'd issued the command.

He glared at me. It was only for a moment, a mere second, but something crossed his eyes, like I'd seen in General Romain's: How dare a woman command him?

But that was what queens did. "Go now, monsieur. Now."

Patti got up. "I'll show you, Count M."

"Yes. Sorry, Madame Christophe. The shock." He and Patti began up the path.

Améthyste took up the fan and swatted at us. "Just give me time. I'll be fine. No bleeding."

"The doctor won't do that. Your mère won't let him."

She relaxed against my knees.

Athénaïre patted her sister's cheeks. "You will be well, and I'll tell you my latest folly. I want to dance under the stars at the Géronstère spa. Count M says that's where all the royals of Europe visit on their grand tour. Get well and help me convince Maman that we should do as the other peers do."

A dance.

A tour.

Somewhere different didn't sound so bad. Nothing did as long as Améthyste kept breathing.

Her chest opened up. Her lungs whistled, but she stood on weak legs. "It wasn't the walk that exhausted me. It's the reporter. He's back." She pointed to a tall fellow coming up the path. "He won't go away."

If I'd known, I'd have acted sooner. Later I would persuade them to be honest with me. To not be like Henry or me. They had to say what hurt them. "Ladies, hold your heads high. Ignore him. Let's get back to the cottage."

"Madame Christophe! Madame Christophe, do you have any comment on Hayti's proclamation? Its navy will no longer disturb slave vessels from friendly nations."

"No such thing as a friendly nation if they enslave people." Athénaïre lifted a finger to the man's face. "King Henry faced down evil. He freed many people."

She was right, but we were in no position to make political comments. Grabbing Athénaïre's hand, I pushed the girls forward.

"Madame Christophe!" The newspaperman chased. "This proclamation will undo what the late king did. Do you have a message for the Hayti government?"

"My daughter is ill. Do not bother us."

Souliman came toward us shouting at the brash Blanc reporter. When he neared, he held his balance and swung his cane at the reporter until he fled.

I put a palm on my footman's shoulder. "If you injure yourself, we can't carry you back to the cottage. Please be calm. The fiend's gone."

"Wish I had a bayonet. I need to protect you."

"Non. I need to protect us. And I will."

This type of harassment would continue. We needed to find our safe place in the world. Somewhere where we could be free, without limitations. Somewhere all my household would be happy. There had to be a place that would fully accept three dark and comely queens with the money to pay for peace.

EXILE

Morning Herald (London), Friday, July 16, 1824

PHILADELPHIA, JUNE 19. When our private citizens visit Hayti, they are treated with every mark of respect; but a public agent of the Haytien Government, who has visited our country for the purpose of facilitating the emigration of those [American] coloured persons, has received a public insult. The agent in question is Citizen Grandeville, who, during the short time he sojourned in Philadelphia, gained the esteem of our citizens, by his correct conduct and gentlemanly deportment. He is an intelligent man, and the only thing that the most fastidious can object to in him, is his complexion, which is that of a dark mustee.

On his passage from this place to New York, he met with most ungentlemanly treatment from a Lieutenant of the Navy, and behaved on the occasion in a manner which does him honour. Being seated at table, Citizen Grandeville was rudely spoken to by a Lieutenant from the south, but took no notice of him, until he was addressed in a more public and insulting manner.—Upon this he immediately rose and observed, that—"When in his own country, it was his province to take into custody those Haytiens who insulted strangers." He then in a very handsome manner apologized to the company, and thereupon left the table. Eighteen of the passengers rose simultaneously, and ordered another table to be spread, which being done, Citizen G. was invited to dine with them, and the Lieutenant left at the first table alone!

—

31

1824 Weymouth Street, Marylebone, London

Zephyrine brushed the sheer yellow curtains framing the big window of my parlor. I waited at the threshold for her to finish dusting.

"Morning, madame." Her cleaning cloth could be a weapon the way it eliminated minute specs—the enemy of Améthyste's lungs. "Almost done once I attend to your desk."

"Take your time." Back in London to be closer to the doctors who treated the Clarksons' lung sicknesses, I felt the move was a good interim solution. Hiding in London until Améthyste's strength returned would give me time to make a wise, unrushed choice.

It would also provide Athénaïre the time to give up her Count M.

He had followed us to London and dined with us here on many occasions. Lately, we'd seen less and less of him.

"Only another moment, madame. Won't keep you from your favorite room."

Footsteps overhead sounded like music. A recovering daughter getting out of bed to embrace the day, that was my heart's best gift.

Leaning against the threshold, I stroked my fingers against the waves of molding surrounding the door. The way the wood lined up like a ribbon tying an expensive present made me think that our family was cinching up the loose ends that tied us to Britain.

"When I finish, I'll bring you tea."

"That would be lovely, but take your time, Zephyrine. I'm moving a little slowly."

Her warm gaze crossed over me. "You sat up with her again, but now Madame Première is much improved."

Hadn't heard anyone use her exquisite title in years. It still sounded good. Perfectly prim and thoughtful, that was Améthyste. Though her fever had broken, she couldn't seem to get warm. Odd to have chills and yet burn with fever. This needed to be our last winter in England.

Zephyrine spread the curtains wider and stretched to dust the carved rosettes at the top of the window.

The clear panes exposed the street.

No gigs, drays, carriages, or pedestrians. In another hour the coal man might come. I heard a wealthy Black owned the service and his carts had both Blanc and Black workers—good to see.

The kingdom would've achieved this level of mobility, where all could succeed.

Gripping my fawn sleeves, long thick ones with a ruffle at the wrist, I shook my shoulders, forcing myself to stop lingering in the past— what could've been, what should've happened.

"Madame, number twenty has the same visitor again. The man with the top hat. Such a hat."

Last week, I saw a fellow in an illustrious chapeau, an inky dark one that looked like a taller stovepipe version of the ones Generals Toussaint and Dessalines wore before the War of the Knives. That fight for freedom brought distinction to Henry. He beat Pétion. I wished Dessalines or Henry had finished him in 1800.

Then the differences between light skinned and dark skinned, between those with Blanc paternity and those without, wouldn't have been exploited.

We weren't of divergent races.

We were all Black.

Certainly, the rest of the world saw no distinction, unlike the small-minded men and women of my soil. The tint of skin, the proximity to whiteness mattered in Hayti.

Stretching to touch my beloved doorframe, I could rip off this molding if that would tear the scales from their eyes. And Henry wouldn't have suffered so many pressures. He might've still been alive. My Victor, my baby, would live, too.

"Madame. Your fingernails will leave dents in the trim."

I should stick to twisting my bracelet. Everything—the wars, the split, the ruining of Henry, my sons—was the past.

"If you are fretting about Princess Athénaïre, she was in earlier. Her mood was brighter. She will soon be over Count M."

Time does heal wounds, most of them. "Where is she?"

"I believe she went to mass."

There was no mass here. Oh, Zephyrine meant the Anglican services. The pageantry of this faith was like ours, with the processionals and bishops in decorated robes. When Henry accepted Wilberforce's teachers into the kingdom, he allowed their faithful to gather and hold to their practices.

"I hope Athénaïre takes comfort in the hymns." They could salve an abandoned heart.

Shuffling through papers, opened and unopened correspondence, I could see my daughter had searched my things, probably looking for notes from Hayti or Count M.

Nothing new had come from him in weeks. Though I wanted to protect her, I'd not hide a letter, and Count M should beg off with dignity.

Zephyrine moved on to fluffing pillows, and I looked out the window to see if Souliman had returned with the carriage. We weren't that far from St. George's mews, but he might rather wait here than there. Our town house, at number 30, resided a little way from the expensive mansions of Mayfair and Grosvenor Square.

"You lookin' for something, madame?"

With a little shake of my head, I said, "Non. Just staring at Weymouth Street's wide pavement. It's made for pedestrians."

"And peddlers. Turned away another coal vendor yesterday."

"Perhaps when Athénaïre returns we'll go shopping on Bond Street."

"The season's most illustrious modiste has enough of your money, madame."

True, but we had a lot. My money managers seemed pleased that I was spending on sofas and chaises. More things for my friend to dust and more fees earned by Leghorn, and Reid, Irving for the procurement assistance.

Nonetheless, Monsieur Senn became more aggressive in keeping others from getting my money, even having Athénaïre attest to who was actually a relative for the courts.

"Perhaps I should take her to Hatchards for a new novel. That should cheer my daughter."

"The princess likes to read. She left with a book under her arm." Zephyrine swatted at the smooth harplike back of the tufted chair with her rag. "All ready for you, madame."

After lifting the chimney glass of my oil lamp and lighting it, she strutted away. With her gray gown swinging, a big white apron tied about her waist, and a lacy white mobcap covering her new shorter brown curls, she looked like all the other servants working in the neighborhood. "Zephyrine, if you need to return to Hayti or stretch your wings here . . . I'd understand."

She put her cloth in her pocket and peered at me with her wide eyes. "I made the decision when we stepped on that boat, madame. I'm with you as long as you need me."

"Then that will be forever." My gaze locked with hers. We were more than employer and maid. We were confidantes, allies, old friends.

"Fine with me. I'll go check on Madame Première."

"Take her some broth. And the crusty cheese toasts she loves."

"Oui, madame." Zephyrine left me to my stacks of papers.

Flipping through the foolscap and parchment, I found bits of a parcel from Monsieur Chateaubriand.

Curious man.

The onetime rebel against the French government continued to be in great favor with the restored Bourbon kings. When we met at Wilberforce's Marden Hall, he was the French ambassador to England. Now he was France's minister of foreign affairs. Perhaps our continued association would improve his view of Hayti and discourage France from going after her.

Fingering the brown paper, I searched for the novel he'd sent, the trash-filled *Ourika*, written by his friend Madame de Duras. When the poor Black nun saw her dark hand as cloven like a beast's hoof, I'd tossed the book to the floor. It would do well in the firebox.

Scooting pages here and there over the chestnut surface of my desk, I didn't see it.

Maybe Zephyrine had seen it on the rug and known it to be garbage. I should've dumped it in the coal bin so it would touch actual blackness.

Noise outside. Sounding like a shout.

A thud hit my window. Looking out, I saw a young Black boy throwing pebbles, waving.

"Souliman! I need you to chase . . ."

Non. He was with Athénaïre.

Another pebble lobbed against the glass.

"Auntie. Auntie?"

I was no one's auntie. Geneviève had no children, and I knew Cécile's would be older than this fellow.

The young boy kept shouting. There were no other possibilities, none who could rightfully call me a relation. Another liar.

"Auntie," he said again, staring at me through the glass.

Knowing better, that I should ignore him, I went outside my front door.

In my best English, I asked. "May I help you?"

"Yes. I heard a Black queen lives here. I wanted to see for myself, cause Black ain't ever been queen."

The light-skinned boy had a mark on his forehead and a cockney accent. He had to be from these shores. His words sounded like the tongues I heard at the docks.

"Is it true? Does a Black queen live here?"

He didn't know who I was. He didn't seem to be up to mischief. Maybe he thought I was Zephyrine.

"Auntie, is it a lie?"

"No. She came to Britain."

His brown eyes grew big like silver guineas. "It's true. A queen does live here on Weymouth."

From the stunned look on his face, I could tell he didn't know any-thing about Haiti or Henry.

Maybe that was good.

Maybe it was best the young didn't know our failings.

"Where is she? Where did she go?"

"She's used to having a kingdom," I said. "She got in a fine carriage and left to find a new land."

The fellow nodded. Then he smiled. "Good to know one of us made it to be like King George."

"Which King George? The third or fourth?"

"Doesn't matter, really. They're royal. And a Black woman made it to be one."

With his head up, the young fellow went on his way. I wished I had something to give him to keep that chin lifted.

I went inside, feeling lighter, but my mood slowly shifted to melan-choly. If I hadn't talked to this young man, he'd never know about me. In a world that treated Black skin as a curse, there needed to be a way for every Black girl and boy to know our faces were once royal.

Then everything in me shattered.

Athénaïre had come in from the kitchen, the fastest route from the mews. Her lip trembled and she held the awful *Ourika* book with her white gloves.

The horror on her face I'd seen before, when she thought her sister would die, when the taunting men led Victor away.

I understood what had to be done.

Not only did the world outside need to know about the good that Henry and I had done, my daughter had to understand that it was possible to be royal, Black, and have a happily-ever-after life.

EXILE

Bell's Weekly Messenger (London), Sunday, September 12, 1824

The Americans are very anxious to clear the country of the free people of colour by encouraging them to emigrate to Hayti. For this purpose, the invitations of President Boyer are advertised in the Papers, and the inducements appear to be so strong, that we should think they could not fail to produce an extensive emigration.

32

1824 Weymouth Street, Marylebone, London

The girls sat with me in my parlor. The bright oil lamps gave Athénaïre's sad countenance a warm glow. She hadn't been her talkative self since Sunday, since reading *Ourika*.

My hope to entice her with conversations about travel for the winter and the royal tours she'd gushed about failed. Athénaïre wanted nothing to do with any plans.

It had taken sweet biscuits and her favorite mulled cider to coax her from her room.

Sitting on the plantain-colored sofa of tufted velvety fabric, I scoured the papers, as I often did. "Hayti's in the news again. Cécile said the government loves giving reports. This time they are pushing for free Blacks to leave America and come to Port-au-Prince."

Athénaïre stared at the fire. She wore a purple shawl about her arms. Her gown possessed an iridescent sheen along the peach satin. It was made for movement, but she sat stiff as a statue.

"He's getting support from the Americans, apparently, to relocate the Blacks." Améthyste chuckled. She looked healthy in her evening-primrose gown.

Athénaïre sulked and slurped her cider. "Free men from America like Prince Saunders were an excellent addition to the country."

"Your père appointed him to lead our educational system. The king was right."

My daughters looked at me as if my head had been cut off by Gaffe's knife or a French guillotine.

"What?" I put down my cup on the Italian carved-mahogany table. "What's wrong?"

They blinked at me and remained speechless.

Then I realized it was the first time I'd spoken of their father aloud in his royal capacity. I decided to speak louder. "The good that Henry did needs to be talked about more. Perhaps then it can inspire the young and the ignorant."

"Count M taught me many English words for ignorant." Athénaïre's tone sounded harsh. Her eyes darted back to her cup.

"There are many words for many things." Améthyste glared at her sister as if to silence her. Then she bent her head to the sketchbook in her lap and began re-creating the room and the beautiful molding of the door's surround. "More people coming to Hayti, people with education and insight, would be good."

"Perhaps we should go back and be with our own kind," Athénaïre's grumbling continued. "With the papers saying free Blacks are being recruited, maybe we should consider returning."

"Athénaïre, do you think the people who overthrew the kingdom, killed your brothers and so many others who supported your père, would leave us free? It's only been three years since we left."

"Maybe we should pay for our safety. Then I could be admired by men of our own race. The odds of finding someone with a gentle heart here are minuscule."

She covered her mouth, that Cupid's bow dripping with sadness.

"Daughters, I would love to return to the kingdom, to a Black nation dedicated to education and science and medicine, but that's not Hayti. If they could gain our means, they'd leave us to be beggars. If we are on that soil, the people who plagued our king will torment us. They'll use any vile tactic to defraud and imprison us. There's nothing there for us. Nothing at all."

"Here, we are safe," Améthyste said. "We have friends here, sœur."

Athénaïre swiped at her face. "Do you think the Thorntons laugh at us? The pretty little things who don't know they're Black?"

"Stop. Athénaïre." I moved closer to her. "Stop."

"Just getting started, Maman." She stood up tall and faced me. "The Blacks with upturned noses. That's what some say. The Blacks who don't understand their place. The Blacks who stole Hayti's treasury. Les négresses, or as the Americans say, the nig—"

I clapped her mouth before another low word slipped her lips. "The Blancs and the Coloreds used insults on Blacks. They tried to call your father and Dessalines and Toussaint horrible words, but the Black generals kept winning. Never say any word to lower yourself."

My palm stung, but I refused to move it from her mouth. "No more evil will be said in my presence."

It seemed an eternity before my fingers left her darkening cheeks.

We remained close like this, my shadow devouring hers. Then I bent to her ear. "You're a princess, but I'm your queen. I demand this."

"A queen with no country."

"Whether exiled or on the throne, I am a queen."

"Because of Père, who's dead."

"Not just because of him. I was crowned. I accepted the possibility of ruling in his stead, being a regent like Prince George, until Victor could lead. I was made a queen. I carry myself with respect. I demand you respect yourself, too."

She rubbed her wet cheeks. Tears flowed. "Do you know how hard it is? You see what they write. Can you imagine all the things they whisper? If I just accepted it, then maybe the hate wouldn't hurt so much."

Self-doubt was as sharp as a bayonet. It bled out all the good. It smothered lungs. "You, Athénaïre, and you, Améthyste, are beautiful. You two are none of the fool words penned by Dumas. Neither she nor Chateaubriand have lived in our bodies. Neither know the dignity of our existence or of our joy. You're angels."

Athénaïre wrenched away. "It's hard for me, Maman, to see my wings when the world tells me I'm nothing but a cloven-hoofed devil. Those are words in your book—"

"The copy you had, I burned. I sent a maid to Hatchards to buy all the copies. Each night this week, we've fired them with the coals for the house."

"Well, Dumas is still popular. Hatchards might reorder. If Blancs hadn't thought us low before, they will now. I should've fought to be with Victor. He understood how hard it was to try to live up to expectations and fail."

I gasped as she stomped away, her short boots pounding the pine boards.

Wanting to go after her, I couldn't move. Victor was dead. "How could Athénaïre want to do that to us, be away from us?"

"Maman, she doesn't mean it. She's just angry and hurt."

"Can't she see how she's loved? We've made true intimate friends in the Clarksons and the Thorntons."

"It's the business with Count M," Améthyste said. "He hurt her heart."

How did I tell her the pain would pass? That her heart would move forward?

Yet to give my child those guarantees, I'd have to lie. I still awakened to nightmares. I still reached for what wasn't there.

Améthyste stepped to me with a small smile. "You burnt the books. Good."

"Not sure if it helped. But it felt cleansing."

"Maman, if we did go back to Hayti, you believe we'd be at risk? I love seeing the world. Everything is new. It's a gift for me. It's not the same for Athénaïre. I don't know how she'll be happy here. Lord M is engaged to an heiress. In a few weeks, they'll wed in the church we attend."

"St. George's?"

"Oui." She put her arms about me. "Write to Tante Cécile. Her husband is with the new government. They'll know if there's any way we can safely return."

Améthyste moved to the threshold. "I'll go comfort Athénaïre."

Letting her go, I stumbled down the hall to my study. I picked up a quill and tried to think of how to ask, how to beg killers to let us return to Hayti, but soon tossed the pen into my fireplace.

The flame spat sparks and bits of cinders and released a sour scent of burnt ink.

Then I sobbed the way I had when we first came to London. I had to get it all out, every drop of sorrow and pain. Nothing could weigh me down. I had to plan how the Christophes would rise again from the ashes.

EXILE

Morning Advertiser (London), Friday, September 24, 1824

By Mr. M'SHANE, on the Premises, No. 30, Weymouth-street, Portland Place. All the genuine Household Furniture and Effects removed from St. Stephen's, Twickenham, the property of Madame Christophe, leaving England.

The Furniture comprises lofty 4-post and other bedsteads, with rich hangings, capital seasoned down and goose feather beds, best horse-hair and white wool mattresses, clean bedding, elegant drawing-room chairs, sofas and tables, brilliant chimney glasses, Spanish mahogany dining tables, ditto chairs, French stuffed in morocco, sideboard, excellent chamber furniture, elegant china and glass, large India china jars, French lamps, etc. May be viewed the day previous and morning sale.

33

1824 Weymouth Street, Marylebone, London

My ivory mattress of the best down feathers had been carted away by Monsieur M'Shane's apprentices. I stood in the parlor near the trunks and the final chairs awaiting sale.

Zephyrine brought down another bundle. This one looked heavy, like a sack of coal, but it was my books, the fairy tales I'd ordered from Hatchards to match the ones my father had gifted me from his library.

Copies of these precious pages I'd saved when Henry set fire to our house in Le Cap. How they survived in the damp caves in the forest as we hid out during the rebellion was a miracle.

They didn't outlast Sans-Souci.

There was no time to grab "Ancilotto" and "Biancabella" when the madness came. Everything happened so fast. I wondered if the looters scooped the pages up and knew they'd received a blessing in those books.

I'd never think of them as a curse. They made us believe in the impossible. I was ready to write the next chapter, how to keep fairy tales alive.

"Madame, it's almost all done," Zephyrine said. "But I can't believe we're leaving. I thought we'd be here forever."

I'd ordered furniture as if we'd travel back and forth with Weymouth as our London home. Non. Everything I'd bought was for our comfort, from the best horsehair mattresses to the softest embroidered linens.

And books, plenty of them, for the girls. To travel great distances, one had to fit their lives in a trunk.

After tapping the bundle, I stood. Wrinkles fell out of my carriage gown, colored the red of autumn maple leaves. "The auction house says there has been a great interest. People want a piece of a queen. I should make some of my money back. Maybe half of what I've spent."

That sounded like robbery, but we had to choose what came on the journey.

"You're not fretful, madame?"

"Oui." Of course I was.

Though I didn't see the Clarksons every day, they were reachable. We could share a tea or coffee with them. They could dine with us and we could stay with them without hesitation. Wilberforce and the Clarksons truly cared for me and the girls. Then there were the dear Thornton girls. Athénaïre and Améthyste had bonded with Patti and Marianne.

They'd shared.

They'd fought.

They'd always found a way to laugh together.

There was true affection between them, like sœurs.

A longing for Cécile and even Geneviève cut at my soul. My eyes stung a little.

"Madame. Madame, don't cry. We'll be blessed when we go. I shouldn't have mentioned anything."

"Non, Zephyrine. I'm just overcome for a minute. Leaving does that." I mopped at my face and willed the wetness to dry. Folding my arms, clasping my elbows, I made the puffy sleeve caps at my shoulders pull tight. "I want this move to be right."

"Madame, it's not too late to contact Monsieur M'Shane. We could stop this. We could stay in this place which has given you peace. Or return to Hastings."

This British coast wasn't for us. I needed better weather for Améthyste's health. And Athénaïre required new adventures. That would help her heal. At least I hoped it would. "Our plans are firm."

Zephyrine nodded. "Seems a lot of risk. Dr. Stewart didn't think Améthyste would improve anywhere but here. London has the best doctors."

"He doesn't know everything."

Zephyrine's lips drew to a tiny dot. "And the sulker shouldn't be indulged."

I forgave Zephyrine's outspoken words and put my hand on her checked gingham sleeve. Her relationship to me was sometimes servant, sometimes truth sayer, always friend. "Shouldn't she be indulged? She's the king's princess. The girls have sacrificed and suffered. They should have everything Henry wasn't able to give."

As if they'd heard us talking, Améthyste and Athénaïre sauntered into the study. They'd finished packing their trunks.

With her eyes sparkling, Athénaïre danced her sister around the empty room. "I can't believe we're leaving."

Then Athénaïre twirled away in a perfect ballet move, the pirouette. Kicking off her slippers, she arched her feet and leapt on her toes, doing an échappé. Again my beautiful black swan danced.

The moment I told her of our voyage, her happiness had returned. Now, she jumped about like she had at Victor's fete. She'd perfected these spins and wanted to join the ballerina who was to perform that night.

I should've let her.

I should've freed her desires rather than keep her questioning her talents.

Athénaïre's glissade came now; I think that was the movement, sliding her foot back and forth.

Hallelujah. I rejoiced. She was herself again, the flamboyant girl I'd always known.

Améthyste held her hands out as she framed each wall for a future sketch. "We won't be here when all is sold. We won't see whose home will get these beautiful things."

Why stay and see looters be blessed? "Non, my dears. We will be gone."

"Hurray. Travel by boat." Athénaïre floated.

With my arms outstretched, my sheer sleeves stretching like a net, I caught her and Améthyste, my delicate birds. "Onward to our future in Europe."

No returning to Hayti.

Not now. Not until real change came.

Cécile had informed me that some of the generals who'd had a change of heart, seeing that Henry was right, had been executed. All the nobles who'd turned on my husband had paid with their lives.

The assurances I offered, that we'd not rally the people against President Boyer or establish a rival court, meant nothing. The new government felt that people still loved their queen. With France beginning to pressure Hayti again, more people wanted a return to the time when they'd had protection, when they'd had Henry's kingdom.

Améthyste clapped her hands. "We're going to do this."

"Oui." We were. The princesses and I were off to Brussels, on our way to the thermal spas of Europe. We were destined to find our place in the warm sun.

And I prayed we survived bouncing barges, fast-moving ferries, and the snares the world set for Black queens trying to live.

Why should the truth stand in the gossip's way? The fairy tales we share are better.

—MADAME CHRISTOPHE, 1847

Kerry Examiner and *Munster General Observer*, Tuesday, May 18, 1847

A report prevails that a general of the Dominican Republic, at the head of his regiment, has declared for Hayti, at Port Flat. This may, or may not, be true but it is certain that the inhabitants of that part of the island are suffering great privations, and that business of all kind is nearly at a standstill.

34

1847 Tuscan Countryside, Italy

Hens clucking and scratching and wandering about the Giligni vineyard make me chuckle. If birds could possess human emotions, I'd say the chickens, the little red-and-black things yawling, are rebelling.

Unfortunately, a few will lose today. The Gilignis love roasting birds for dinner.

As I stroll uphill, the breeze blows my woolen mantle like a sail. My cloak, of a soft mint hue, feels too light for the sudden chill. I almost exchanged it for my trusty shawl, but the lacy knit never blocks a thing. After so many years, the poor threads aren't strong enough to provide the warmth I need.

The cloudy day has dimmed my mood. I didn't think disappointment could bring me such sadness anymore. A delayed visit isn't the end of the world. I'd left Pisa early to come to Florence, but my friend might take a few more weeks to arrive.

"Madame Christophe."

Sighing, feeling a little more of my peace dissipate, I try to ignore the excited voice of the reporter from the *Globe*.

"Madame Christophe."

I see him coming up the hill along the lane of vines. If I don't answer, he'll get louder, more insistent.

With a wave, I summon him, then continue my inspection of the plantings—the bud breaks and new growth.

Then my view becomes shadowed.

That hasn't happened in years, a man standing so close to me that my light is dimmed.

"Monsieur Michelson, don't crowd me or the vines. It's not good for either. We shall not dishonor my friend. Monsieur Giligni puts a great deal of effort into the health of his vineyards."

"How does my being close to you damage the grapes?"

"I might lose my balance from being choked by your Cologne water."

He laughs and takes a step back. "Of course," he says as he looks over his glasses. "We're not done with our interview. I came to remind you."

"I'm done. At least for now." I walk away.

The reporter follows, this time at a respectable distance. "Mister Souliman said you were thinking of leaving."

"Oui. I live in Pisa now. I had expected . . . a special delivery that's now delayed. I could go back for a few weeks and return closer to the new arrival date."

"Must be a significant delay." He folds his arms and thumbs his lips. "You've gone to the trouble of leasing rooms. That seems a wasteful expense."

I'll keep the rooms. I won't inconvenience Monsieur Giligni by shortening the arrangements, but I miss my house and my girls. "Why have you followed me?"

"You're a fascinating woman, one who doesn't seem to mind trouble or expense."

"Money talk again, sir? I mind both. But sometimes you have to settle for what you can get."

His gaze sweeps over me, touching my face, warming my cheeks. It is nothing indecent, but nothing I want.

Perhaps it's time to intrude upon his life. "How did you get the scar on your temple?"

His tanned skin reddens on his cheeks and along his neck above the tied ebony stock about his collar. "Fight at a pub. Someone said the wrong thing about my mama and my aun . . ." His jaw stiffens and winces as if he'd been struck again. "My mother and my aunt."

"For any man, to hold on to anger is dangerous. For a Black man, it's lethal."

He nods and accepts both my words and his stature, as a young Black man, not Colored. Perhaps the world has progressed.

"Madame. I can't stand someone disrespecting the women in my family." His words are slow, measured. "My mother and my aunt, the Black women who raised me, they sacrificed when my father died. He was a merchant. A very successful one. That's how he and my mama went to Hayti. His family cut off my mama. Wanted us to disappear. Wasn't supposed to make nothin' of myself. Here I am interviewing a queen."

Honorable. Volatile. And yet vulnerable. That was Henry before the fall. "Do something enjoyable today. Remind yourself that you're young and alive and have time to make magic. Care not if it be a success or a glorious failure."

Smiling like a happy puppy, he's at my heels. "Enjoyment later. Madame, I have a job to do. I've more questions."

"Monsieur Michelson, you came to do an article on Henry, and I've given you the information you wanted. My visit to a vineyard is none of your business."

"Don't mean to offend you, ma'am, but you're as much a part of the story as the king. I need to give the readers a glimpse of your life. That will help them understand you."

"You mean him."

"No, you. Why does a woman stay in a marriage to such a driven man?"

"I was married. A woman can't just leave. My word, the commitments I make, are as important as my peace."

"You've left your country and came very far to be in exile. You could've found a way."

Michelson doesn't know what he's talking about, and his baiting won't prompt me to respond.

I move down the line, looking at the clusters of flowers beginning to bud. I love the way the young grape vines curl along the posts. "This will be a good harvest. The sap is now running through these branches."

Wrapping my palm against the gnarled bark, I breathe in the scent of the floral buds. "These are young." The flower clusters slip through my fingers. "These will bloom into the fruit we love and eventually make it to our glasses."

"Madame Christophe."

I blink my eyes, hoping he'll disappear.

The annoying fellow stays, looking like a magazine advertisement with his checked wool trousers and flared double-breasted coat. That's the style of the fashionable young rakes.

"Madame Christophe, please."

"Why are men so persistent, particularly ones born in Europe?"

"Madame," he says standing beside me, "what are you hiding?"

"Everything, Monsieur Michelson. I'm protecting my peace."

"Is that why you are here, ma'am? To escape scrutiny?"

I stop short, my boots dusted in the gray, powdery dirt. "How much do reporters get paid for the drivel you research?"

"How much did the king steal for you?"

I hold my breath and bury my hands in my empty pockets. "You need to go away."

"Don't you see that this is what they'll say, madame? They'll tarnish you with such venom." He lifts his arms as if to show the width of the headlines. "While Hayti flounders paying massive debts, the former queen lives in luxury."

"I do not live in luxury, but comfort. There's a difference."

"Next headline." His palms spread again. His voice booms. "Queen enjoys riches while Haytians starve."

"Boyer would have me starved. A beggar if not for my king's fore-thought. My husband provided for me. That's love."

"I don't mean to be offensive, but that's exactly what those who hated the king are leaking to the press. Help me to help you. Then the article will be balanced, fair."

This man before me acts as if he's come to my court on a Thursday hoping to be heard. He seeks a fair arbiter about the past. That's not me, not for any subject involving my children or the men I loved.

The reporter kneels, an exaggerated, ridiculous motion with his arms dragging on the ground. His knees soil, ruining his fancy pants. "Please, Madame Christophe. Help me complete this article and restore the king's reputation."

Why is he so persistent? Righting this wrong seems like a very personal mission to him. "Get up, Monsieur Michelson. No need to be in a position of supplication. You sound sincere."

"I am," says the pesky man, dusting his trousers as he rises. "The king was a good man. He cared how the world saw him. He'd want you protected from the noise bad press can bring."

That's Henry. The protection part. I wish I could've helped . . . Maybe this is my way now. "This is an old friend's winery. His Chianti is the best. But he knows I like to walk and enjoy the countryside. I'm allowed to come whenever I choose."

"Allowed? That must be something. A queen having to get permission."

"Women of the world always have to ask permission to do anything. I guess that's why I don't like to answer unnecessary questions."

He brushes at a speck of dirt on his lapel. "Yes, you love escaping your problems."

"If that were true, you'd not have found me."

I chuckle and so does Michelson.

He pulls off his top hat and fans it. "You've told me about the old days, but not how the kingdom ended."

"I don't feel like discussing that today."

"We need to discuss it. I need to know how the kingdom fell. Why didn't King Henry fight harder to keep what he had?"

The ghosts of the past swirl in my head. My brow is hot, fevered like Améthyste's. "Not today. Go find an accident to chase. A cliff to jump . . ."

I clap my lips. The aggravation has made me say the wrong things. Regret brings fresh tears to my eyes.

"How did the king die? How did you get him to the Citadel, to the lime pit?"

"I'm here because some dates, some fetes, are hard for me. I come here to escape."

"Last week, Princess Améthyste's birthday?"

"Oui. I miss spending it with her. I wasn't in Pisa to be with her." I move away at a slow pace.

The reporter stays behind me like an entourage, following at a distance as if to avoid my gown's imaginary train.

He touches branches, even plucking a white petal, as if it's completely natural for an annoying reporter to follow a queen.

Ignoring him becomes harder. He shortens the space between us. His shadow entangles with mine. If I turn I'll be in his arms, dancing a waltz.

I do like to waltz.

I love being turned about a dance floor.

"Madame Christophe, then tell me about your life in Europe. You left Britain in '24. Where did you go? What did you do?"

His voice sounds earnest, and his plea tugs at something deep in my chest. "This exposé, will it talk about Henry's family? Will it talk about our princesses?"

"Yes, of course. They're a part of the king's legacy. Their inclusion will humanize the Christophes."

Humanize? It's 1847, and the world still looks at Blacks as subhuman. I guess a Black royal family is an anomaly, the subject of fairy tales.

"People want to know how you survived, the type of lives you built away from Hayti."

Found the mountain I've been looking for. "This part of the vineyard, the highest part, offers a view of the Tuscan Apennines. The tops, the places that touch the heavens, are obscured by clouds."

"Madame Christophe. I'll put in the article enough details so the world will understand your choices and your dignity."

We did live fully, quickly, with joy and sorrow, didn't we?

The world should know.

Shrugging my shoulders, I start walking again back to my friend's house. "Let me show you the olive grove. Did you know a whole tree produces only three or four bottles of oil?"

"So much fruit for such meager results." Michelson quickens his pace and is again at my side. "Let's talk about your travels, the princesses. We'll discuss King Henry later."

My lungs swell with pride and the scent of good earth. I miss seeing my girls every day. Miss Athénaïre's dances, how her golden eyes lighten when she waltzes. Her dancing and Améthyste's drawing in Pisa are my fondest memories.

"Let's go to the main house, monsieur. I'm sure my friends will find a nice Chianti, some bread and olive oil. We can have a little repast and I'll tell you about the most ridiculous times of our lives."

He holds out his arm to me.

I grab it as Athénaïre would, as if this fellow, a half or a third my age, is a suitor and has called me pretty.

Perhaps he has by wanting to know about my treasures, my girls. "A little Chianti will loosen my tongue."

"I look forward to everything." Michelson's smile is broad, giving him the appearance of an angelic little boy or a sly fox. He might be lying, but I don't care. I suppose persistence pays. I want to talk about the girls.

The Tuscan countryside is always meant to be shared, and being with an attentive stranger has to be better than walking alone.

EXILE

Morning Advertiser (London), Friday, October 8, 1824

Taken from Brussels Papers: Madame Christophe, widow of the late Emperor of Hayti, has arrived here on her way to Florence, where she intends to pass the winter.

35

1824 Liège, Belgium

Our first stop after leaving London was enemy territory, Calais . . . French Calais. When we landed, I panicked, discovering my feet trod there and not neutral Belgium. It took every ounce of strength to appear calm, serene, and not expect the border soldiers to chase. Papers with the name Madame Christophe on them shouldn't cause alarm. I was another traveler, an exile, no longer the queen of France's enemy.

I was stone, rubble brick made of molasses and blood, when my daughters and I boarded a crowded carriage. It was to take us to our lodgings, but would it lead to a hotel or a prison? Enchanted by the white cliffs, the girls had no idea of the danger. Perhaps that was best, for my thoughts flew to François-Ferdinand, knowing this was as close as I could come to his soul.

When we crossed into Belgium, I rejoiced, but wished we could go farther. New papers were needed to keep going on our tour. If we didn't get them where would we be sent? Hayti? Back to London or Toussaint's vacant prison cell in Napoleon's Jura Mountains?

I FORCED MY SOUL TO STILL EVEN AS TIME PASSED AT OUR INN, THE former Thermae Boetfort castle. Though I'd assumed some royal had once lived here, it was now in need of repair. The clientele was common, even coarse.

Leaning on the windowsill of my bedchamber, I waited, pondered philosophy, and watched for the enemy. For a week, we stayed here. Upon occasion, the girls and I ventured downstairs to dine. The talk of politics, particularly France's desire to reconquer the Haytians, made us quit public spaces.

The hateful voices were the loudest. The travelers saw me and my Black daughters and wanted us fearful.

Lifting my hand toward the molded ceiling, I swore to the baroque carved rosettes strewn above, like hibiscus draping a coffin, I'd not travel again in the open, where common ignorant chatter could target us.

How was I to show Athénaïre we weren't lowly, that we were lovely, when my frugality seated us among rabble?

We had means. I had to stop acting as though the money would be taken by some new pretender or lawsuit . . . or Boyer.

Feeling cold and alone, I wrapped my arms about myself. It wasn't just the gawking that upset me. I'd been around fools before. I didn't want to accept that France was on the verge of seizing Hayti. Henry's nightmare would become true.

Sweaty hands. Fast breaths.

My heart started to fail. The things that torched his dreams, his every waking minute that I thought crazed, would come to pass.

How does one say sorry to the dead?

How does one begin to make amends?

My stomach clenched, and I dropped to my knees. My cheek bobbed along the windowsill. "Sorry."

Gone four years, and I missed Henry, missed him leading his army, missed him patrolling the Citadel.

Missed him looking at our children with love.

Missed him in my bed.

At forty-six, I should still have my love. This should've been our time to enjoy the world the wars of independence had wrought. But I'd failed him. "So very sorry."

Footfalls echoed in the hall. I wrenched myself from the floor and swiped at my eyes. My station. My station. A ready queen.

The heavy oak door creaked, moaning like a ghost.

Zephyrine entered.

Relieved, my posture sagged, but I straightened when I saw how red her eyes burned.

When she came near, I thought she'd forget herself and bow. I'd dispensed with that the moment we left the Citadel that last time.

My gaze, begging her to remain erect, surely interceded. She straightened her shoulders and laid a garnet gown with wide brass buttons on my bed. "If they turn us over to Napoleon, you will look like a queen."

"It won't be to him. Napoleon Bonaparte's dead. I had dinner with his brother. The family no longer means us harm. They're exiles like us, people with means but no power."

Zephyrine's eyes bulged. I hadn't told her about my interesting table mates in Hastings.

With a sigh, I plopped against the window frame. Leaves rustled in the distance. "The change of colors of the leaves, I didn't see that with banana palms. Here, maples turn orange. Birch, gold. Aspen, a lovely red."

"Trees, madame? We are in trouble. Hayti is in tr—"

"Fools see free Blacks and wish to make us uncomfortable. They are exaggerating the dangers to Hayti."

"The papers the girls read say differently."

So much my pretending. "We must trust Monsieur Senn. We'll have our diplomatic papers soon. My money pays my solicitor to keep us protected."

"And Hayti? What of her?"

Though storms raged inside me, I had to lead. I had to be the picture of calm. I had to wish out loud. "Our people will not be enslaved again."

"But they could be betrayed by the Coloreds. Boyer will put Blacks in chains just to be recognized by France. He's no different than Pétion. Chains, madame. I still have family there."

The tears dripping down her face brought mine. "I have sisters there, too. We must have faith in the people."

"Even the ones who turned on the king?"

The fears I had for our lost home welled up in my throat. But none of this I'd speak aloud. I had to be a silent queen about my nightmares. My duty was to lead and to instill calm. "We are all Black. All Haytians know this. They'll not put any of their brothers in chains."

Zephyrine wept in my arms. She didn't believe.

I didn't blame her. If President Boyer had continued arming the Citadel and all the forts around Hayti, France wouldn't dare touch the nation. But he hated everything Henry had built. He'd discounted the politicking, the necessary influence that would keep the country safe. Couldn't he see how France aligned the world against Hayti?

"Madame, I've spoken out of turn. Forgive me."

"You spoke truth, Zephyrine." Even if I couldn't, those who needed me, they had to say what troubled them. "You can speak your fears. It's not wrong. It doesn't diminish your strength. Hear me. It doesn't diminish you."

She mopped her smoky eyes with her dark-gray sleeve. "You're strong. I keep remembering the crimes of LeClerc and Rochambeau. The tortures."

My fists clenched; my fingers dug into my palms. Why did she number all the evils? The images, the cries in the wilderness. I couldn't admit to the same doubts that Boyer would save all of Hayti. I was Henry.

"Ma reine?"

I still dreamed of the slaughtered Royal Dahomet troops who had tried to protect Sans-Souci against the rebels. Then Armande's round face, trying to look proud, like Henry. And always, always, I see my poor Victor with his lips trembling.

Boyer's guards kept me from touching my son's warm face one last time. They stomped him with their boots and bled him and Armande, those two boys with bayonets.

Their crime was possessing the king's blood.

Mine was not helping Henry more.

These useless hands of mine vibrated, but I refused to be Desdemona again. I offered my friend truth. "I've no confidence in Boyer, but I still believe in the people. They won't submit to terror."

Zephyrine embraced me, and I her, again, calming her shakes, feeling the spinning top of my insides slow.

She took a deep breath. "I believe in you. If you have hope, then I do. Let me get you tea."

"I welcome your care."

Propped against the window ledge, I listened to her slippers slapping the stone floor.

That familiar echo, that sound of marching away—I noticed her footfalls were denser and deader on marble than parquet.

Maybe that was the difference between castles and palaces.

A palace was for life, brimming with meetings and movement, all centered on a vibrant family. A castle seemed a stony memorial. The slightest movement echoed, mirroring the emptiness. It might as well be a headstone for the dead.

Boyer's bloodlust should be done, so he can rally his courage. He'd better not let Hayti become another castle, with our people made to be broken as slaves, living monuments of death.

EXILE

Saunders' News-Letter (Dublin, Republic of Ireland), Thursday, October 14, 1824

The Ex-Queen of Hayti arrived at Liege on her way from Brussels on the 24th ultimo, and alighted at the Black Eagle Hotel. She was accompanied by her two daughters, a lady companion, and some servants. The passport which was given her by the Neapolitan Ambassador Extraordinary to London, designates her under the name of Madame Louise Christophe, tenant in St. Domingo.

36

1824 Baden-Baden, Germany

My private carriage rumbled over the rocky trail heading away from Brussels to Germany. The view outside my window was a glorious sunrise coming through the trees, glistening on the snow-capped mountains. It was different than our quick viewing of Liège's citadel. Hundreds of years old, it towered above the city like Henry's master-piece on Bonnet à l'Evêque.

My heart saddened again. Ours had been abandoned.

Turning from the glass, I tugged up my short leather gloves and caught Athénaïre glaring at me. She pouted like a girl of twelve, not a woman of twenty-four.

"I know you wanted to remain at Black Eagle Hotel, but too many people stared. Remember the rude man who interrupted our dinner. We had to get away."

"They thought we were Russian princesses," she said. "I liked that."

The Gannibal legacy again. "We're not related to Tsar Peter's god-son. We're not Ethiopian. We're Haytian royalty." For what that was worth. Boyer could be surrendering the country as we spoke.

Améthyste stretched, then turned her face from us. "The Haytian-Russian princesses will be going to Baden-Baden. The spa will be good for me, and for your sour temperaments."

She pulled her plaid blanket over her head.

The poor dear slept most of the way with her head on my lap. It was another rough night of coughing and tonics.

"The white ice, Maman. It looks very pretty up on the mountains."

"You know it's snow, Améthyste," her sister said with a yawn.

We'd spent several years in cold England. Horrid stuff everywhere. Nothing like the warmth of a walk about Sans-Souci. Seeing my name on official papers but with my residence as the old colonial name, St. Domingo, made it feel as if France had already won.

"Maman? Are you well?" With dark eyes peeking through the blanket, Améthyste glanced at me. "You're frowning."

Leaning forward I tugged off her cover. "Merely remembering the heat of a free Milot, dear."

"Europe will never have a warm season like Hayti's." She sat up, adjusting the frill of her long, blush-colored sleeve. "But at least it makes wearing long sleeves a joy, not a torment. Remember some of the dresses Père imported. One had fur trim."

Nodding, I chuckled, my first laugh in days.

Henry wanted us to look like European royals, how they posed in their paintings. Now we dressed like them, traveled like them, and went into exile just like them.

Athénaïre groused and leaned back against the seat. "Sleeves do stop the men from looking at my arms."

"It's your sweet face they're seeking, dear. You're beautiful. Both of my daughters are."

"Maman, no." Her voice sounded both sad and resolute like Cécile's. "I need to look at things honestly."

Améthyste seemed to ignore her sister's melancholy. She curled her blanket closer to her chin. "It's more common for African blood to be in Russian nobles under the tsars than anywhere else. I don't mind being a Russian princess. As nomads, we should be able to choose."

"I'm Haytian," Athénaïre said. "I'm a proud Haytian. Père gave us a world that everyone wants to forget. If we're nomads, I guess we don't want to remember, either."

No, I didn't want to forget, but so many things I wanted to do over.

Améthyste began coughing. It took a minute or two before she settled. "I remember moving about, fearing Père's enemies. That's what this feels like."

"We never hid in castles or expensive inns," I said. "Our accommodations in Baden-Baden will be far from caves."

"Maman, that's not what I meant. I'm talking of that feeling that we'll always be hiding."

The plainspoken resignation in Améthyste's words stunned me. I braced for a moment of complete honesty. "I'm hiding news of Hayti. The whole island may fall to France. We're in exile. We must be cautious, but we must also live."

A tear drizzled down Athénaïre's cheek. "How do we live? At least, Maman, you had children and a husband. You know those joys."

"And I've lost much. I'm trying to live, just like you."

"I'm sorry, Maman. I sound so selfish. I don't mean to be." She kissed my hand, but I pulled her to my side and snuggled her close. Athénaïre wasn't a child, but she needed a mother's love. I prayed to Mary to send Josephs to my girls. Men who would love them for who they were and not for their riches or any political purposes. They never needed to make the choices I had.

Améthyste peered at us from her blanket. "Don't fret, sœur. I heard the dancing and intrigue of Baden-Baden are as good as the medicinal water. You'll soon be in high spirits. Your troubles will vanish."

Then she closed her eyes, her breathing slow and labored, then stopping. It started again after two beats of my heart. Améthyste didn't have the same desires as her sister. My eldest wasn't looking for the love of her life, just life.

Sometimes, I didn't think she fought hard enough to keep living, thinking it bothersome or disruptive to her sister's entertainment. With politics following us, finding the right blend of adventure and health treatments had grown tougher.

Feeling Athénaïre clinging to me, I knew I needed to do everything to make sure we won.

THE TILE FLOORS OF THE SPA WERE WARM BENEATH MY BARE FEET. It was like walking on the cobbles of old Le Cap on a lazy afternoon. Of course, that was before the war, when Hayti was Saint-Domingue and the Hôtel de la Couronne was the fashionable place to be.

The maid leading us down the path seemed confused by our English bathing costumes—long indigo dresses of muslin with short, puffed sleeves, and white cotton wraps about our braids.

She shrugged, muttered something in an unintelligible language, and opened a door at the end of the corridor. "Madame, you'll be in complete privacy in this room. You can bare yourselves to the waters. It is the best way to absorb the minerals."

Bare? Oh, naked.

I refused to gaze at Athénaïre. I wanted her to feel up to this adventure, not embarrassed.

She needed to see that her sister and I weren't ashamed of our bodies. Améthyste's deep caramel skin and my bronze flesh were as beautiful as Athénaïre's reddish-brown glow.

After glancing at the blue-painted walls and the crisp white trim rimming the room, I acted the part of a confident woman. Raising my nose high, I turned to our escort. "It's a little small. The Rivière Mapou was much bigger."

"I have not heard of that resort." The attendant put towels on the table. "I assure you the measurements are intentional, to concentrate the heat."

With plenty of Baroque scrolling in the corners, the pool was a large rectangle. One could swim across.

The woman moved closer to the water, stooped, and scooped up the crystal-clear liquid into a marble-edged basin a priest could use for baptism. "The temperature is perfect, Madame Christophe. You'll love it."

The pool glistened. Little sparkles circulated against the gray stone bottom. "Minerals?"

"Yes, ma'am. The same as in Fräulein Améthyste's tea treatments."

In addition to bathing, the physician's protocol included drinking the spa tonic several times daily. The carbonation and nutrients were supposed to improve the health.

Yet in front of the opulent pool, I wondered if this bath of crushed rocks would hurt my supple skin or badly swell my chignon.

Athénaïre looked as if she'd melt in the steam. Having again taken to straightening her locks, she looked confused.

The attendant went to her. "It will be fine. Shall I help you disrobe?"

"Non." Athénaïre clutched the buttons of her tunic.

Chuckling, Améthyste waved the lady to the door. "Thank you, ma'am. We'll be fine. Return for us in two hours."

"Very good, ladies." The door closed. Her soft footfalls disappeared, drowned by the babbling fountain dribbling into the pool.

Steam rose from the middle. This was very different from Henry's copper tub or the bathing machines, the odd carriages we'd used in Hastings to take to the waters.

"Impressed, Maman?" Améthyste's voice carried, echoing like a morning bird.

The stone rosettes on the door moldings indicated an old structure. A holy place, perhaps? With the number of visitors waiting to come to this baden, it had to be a palace teeming with life.

Definitely not a castle. So many fashionable people—royals, peers, exiles, and the wealthy—buzzed in Baden-Baden. From Zephyrine's report, the nightly entertainment was as busy.

We were a part of this world. We could enjoy it all if we were brave enough to take the leap.

Améthyste walked around the pool, touching the carvings, the ridges in the moldings. The stonework and glass paintings at Sans-Souci sprang to mind. "I think this used to be a church. I read something about how the princes of the town repurposed old buildings."

Well, I was close in my guess. And it was a place for the living.

"Too smooth to be rubble stone." Athénaïre stuck her toes into the water. Even with her hair up and protected, my girl would go no farther. She stuck her hand in, then drizzled a few drops over her pouty lips. "It feels nice."

Barely wet and in the shallow end, Athénaïre hardly offered a comforting endorsement.

Améthyste started in. Water came up to her ankles, then she moved a little deeper. Waves swirled at her knees. Then she went back to the edge with her gaze turning to the walls, the etchings of fleurs-de-lis and crosses.

"Maman, are you going to join us?" Athénaïre waved at me, her eyes daring me to be young and carefree. "Stick your toes in. It will warm your old bones."

It did look inviting, and I certainly was dressed for the part of a bather, an old British woman.

Didn't feel old or British.

Maybe there were minerals in the air making me drunk, making me want to be free and show the girls how to fly. "When we were young, my sisters and I, we swam in the Rivière Mapou. Once, on a hot day, we wrenched off all our clothes and leapt into the water. Oh, we had fun."

"Aunt Geneviève, too?"

"Oui. She had a glorious time. We all did." The three of us didn't argue the entire day. Cécile sang beautiful songs. Geneviève told stories. She'd laugh at my hesitation now. She might even try to push me in, as I'd done to her. I missed my younger sister. Hadn't let my heart do that for a long time.

As if ghosts taunted me, I undid my cuffs and worked away a thousand buttons on my gown. I let the muslin fall to the marble. Standing gloriously naked with the steam greeting my skin, I walked out to the middle of the pool and baptized myself.

Face fully below, luxuriating in the hot water, I relaxed until I heard Améthyste scream.

An attack.

It couldn't be.

Not here.

I stood and ran toward Améthyste, but now both girls screamed.

That's when I saw the commotion. At the door, a group of men stood gaping, even as the attendant attempted to shoo them away.

Too late to cover up or pretend to be demure, I glared at them and pointed. "Leave this bath. The room is occupied."

The tallest man I'd seen since Henry said something garbled about foreign queens.

The three bowed. I think I heard "sorry" as they left.

Then I descended into the deep waters of the pool.

"Maman," Athénaïre said, "are you not embarrassed?"

Acting as if nothing had happened, I shrugged. "I'm embarrassed for the spa, to allow something like this to occur."

She nodded. Then my rebel went into the water fully, no more hesitation.

Améthyste splashed in, too.

The girls had been made bold by my exposure. My body was whole. I was glorious in my skin.

With two months to stay in Baden-Baden, I became amused thinking the gossips would attribute this immodesty to the Black Russian princesses and not the Haytian queen whose former nation was preparing for war.

37

1824 Baden-Baden, Germany

Souliman grumbled as I asked the innkeeper to send for a driver. It was dusk, on its way to a dark night, and my part-time protector didn't know the roads well. Accidents in carriages were becoming more common with the increasing amount of travel on the roads.

"Don't like this, Mad'me. I drive for you and the princesses."

"We shall be fine." I adjusted the collar of his dark mantle, the color making his wavy curls seem ebony.

He lifted his cane. "It's because of this. You don't think me capable. An injury doesn't make me lesser. I'm strong. I keep fighting."

"Of course you are, Souliman. Not once have I ever doubted your ability. But we're new to Baden-Baden. It's dark. I need you to take your time. Learn the streets of this city."

"Wi, rèn mwen." He grumbled a little more under his breath, but then he leaned on his cane and made a low bow. "Oui, ma reine."

With her tendrils straightened and pulled tight, Athénaïre joined us in the hall.

She seemed determined to follow patterns of European beauty. In my prayers, I asked Rose of Lima, the saint of beautification and blooming, to restore my daughter's confidence. My girl, my precious hibiscus, needed to flower again.

Fumbling with my reticule, I turned back to Souliman. "I need for you to be of help to Zephyrine. If Madame Première . . . Princess Améthyste begins to get sick or feels like she needs—"

"Zephyrine good," he said. "She knows what to do."

That was a high compliment, because I didn't. The water treatments had made Améthyste feel worse. Now her bowels were upset.

My hand pulsed as I tried to put on my silver gloves but couldn't manage. My knuckles felt tight, my palm slick.

"Mad'me, she be fine. Wants you to show her sister a bit of the world. Older princess feels like a . . . tankou yon chay . . . like a burden. You doin' for the other gives peace."

Frustrated Kreyòl and all, I understood. If I hadn't been ready to step into a carriage with Athénaïre, I'd be crying. How do you balance going on adventures with one while wanting to sit still with the other? Any moment could be Améthyste's last.

Imagining the texture of the mineral water—the sands, gritty and salty, draining through my fingers—I dusted my palms, wiped them along my mantle, and wished Améthyste lived forever.

Athénaïre swirled to me in her new gown, which had a white-striped muslin bodice and full ivory skirt. "Have you changed your mind? Is sœur worse?" She bent her head. "She did look very pale this afternoon. We don't have to go. It was nice dressing up."

My younger girl looked forlorn, and that made my conflicted heart feel guiltier.

"Non." My tone was low. I locked arms with her and towed her to the door. "I spend every moment fretting about Améthyste, but she's well enough right now. That's all we can ask for."

Once we settled onto our seats, Athénaïre leaned down and brightened the carriage lantern. "We truly don't have to do this."

"Nonsense. I want dinner. You want to hear music and dance. That can't be accomplished in our suite."

"The dinner part could, Maman."

"Athénaïre, this is not how I pictured any of our lives. But we must make the most of it. Time is a gift and so are you. You're special. Don't feel guilty because you are healthy." And alive.

"Maman, I feel selfish."

I reached for her hands, wanting to save her from the same grieving spiral I'd just endured. "While your sister is feeling good, resting well, I'll indulge you. You wanted society. We'll have it. And who knows what may happen if you smile."

"I expect nothing more than a dance." She started to hum.

"Athénaïre, we never talked about Count M. Did he break your heart?"

She drew her fingers into her lap. "He was a gentleman, but he made it plain that though I cared for him and he was fond of me, he couldn't bring a wife like me home to his family, no matter how big my dowry was. He wanted a mistress only. When I rejected him, he said that all my Negro stylings and education were perfect for the queen of a brothel. Then I read that book and understood why he'd say such awful things. That's what he truly thought when he looked at me."

Her tone was low and hurt.

I lifted her chin. "Non. Not true. None of that is true. Men can be horrid when rejected."

"But it felt true."

Never had Athénaïre's golden eyes looked so like Henry's. Again, I was choking on silent tears, wanting to lie about how the world saw grace, not colors. "When Hayti was Saint-Domingue, the Grand Blancs lusted for Black women. Instead of admitting we were beautiful, they lied and forced themselves upon the enslaved. Now we're free. We have choices. They still crave us, and some will try anything to manipulate us into their beds. I hope you told him off."

"I didn't. I kept my dignity. He never saw me cry."

Souliman should get a mule to kick the count or hit him with that cane. "Living well is the best revenge."

"I shall try, Maman. I will."

Our carriage stopped at Promenadenhaus, a place for dancing on the other side of the River Oos. No bricks, just a wood-framed building. I supposed that meant dancing would be a temporary amusement for Baden-Baden.

Before the door opened, I straightened the emerald necklace about Athénaïre's throat, then slipped her my emerald bracelet.

"Maman, you've never taken this off since we recovered it."

"You shall wear it. Especially when you need to remember you're wonderful and deserve love."

She spun it on her wrist the way I did when I wore it. The facets of the gem shimmered in the lantern's light. "I'll wear it tonight and know you love me. That's enough."

We were handed down by our grooms, men in cranberry liveries. A servant led us into a room filled with linen-covered tables.

"Will it be crowded tonight?" I voiced the question before I could stop myself.

"Oui, madame," he said. "It's the season for dignitaries and royalty across Europe." That meant exiles, too. I wondered who I'd see.

A fine oak table in the corner, with a sumptuous crisp white table-cloth and folded napkins, was our destination. Out of the way of most prying eyes, we still had our share of stares, especially from a group of gentlemen across the room.

"You'd think that peers or royals would know better than to gape, Athénaïre."

She laughed and picked up the goblet of water. After a sniff, she put it back down. "More of the mineral water."

I was tired of it myself. When the waiter came, I'd order champagne.

Music began to play. A string quartet. I thought this tune was Beethoven's, or was it his friend? Dear Vastey would be able to tell me. He'd also be here to dance with me until Henry found that perfect moment for us—husband and wife, a king with his queen, lovers.

"This is like our fetes, Maman."

Her whisper returned me to where we were, alone in exile.

"Maman, are you upset? Do we need to go?"

"Non. But we should look for a partner for you."

"Don't look so sad, Maman." With my emerald twinkling on her arm, she reached for my hand. "I'm happy just being here."

When did I teach her that merely showing up was enough? That was how life passed one by. Henry would never allow it. He'd order someone to dance with her, as he had for me. "If I announced to every-one in Baden-Baden that you're a princess with a handsome dowry, I think it would make a difference for your dance card."

Her head shook "no" as if it had been caught in an earthquake. "Non, Maman. Keep your voice low."

"What, it's embarrassing to tell the world who you are? A Russian princess?"

Athénaïre's chortle was musical. Standing, I grasped her hand and we whirled in the minuet. In the corner in the dark, we danced and giggled until we both were breathless.

Then we sat back down and drank champagne. "To you—"

Two men came to our table.

The younger bowed to my daughter. "Puis-je avoir . . . cette danse, mademoiselle?"

His struggle with the universal language of French made no difference to Athénaïre. My daughter lit up. "Mademoiselle Christophe."

"Major Dieterich Ernestus, gnädige frau." The tall blond man nodded, took my smiling daughter's gloved hand in his, and escorted her to the floor.

They began moving together in a minuet, showered in candlelight from crystal chandeliers above.

Beautiful. Stately. Her arm extended, Athénaïre swept about the major with perfect steps. She'd not forgotten a moment of her instruction. The balls in Hastings, the dinners in London had kept her moves sharp.

Then a shadow fell upon my arm, my neck.

The older gentleman, the companion of Ernestus, stood by my table, staring. Not exactly indecent in a roomful of people dining and dancing, but not exactly polite, either.

Black hair tinged with silver indicated that age didn't account for his manners.

"Sir." I plucked my fan out of my reticule. "Is there something you need? I believe your table is on the other side of the room."

He stated something in a very foreign tongue. When I shrugged, he said, "Quelle belle mère et fille. La princesse russe est glorieuse."

This time I understood, not just that he'd called us glorious and Russian royalty, but that his gaze was of admiration.

My memory for faces alerted me. This was the man who'd stared the longest at my bare body, emerging from the steaming bath.

38

1824 Baden-Baden, Germany

Trying to seem unbothered, I looked away to the dance floor. Without asking, he sat down in Athénaïre's empty chair. His constant gaze, which reminded me of a restless blue-gray sea during Hayti's wet season, bore down on me, making my covered skin moist.

He waved for a waiter and ordered something. The next I knew, two goblets of purple wine appeared. "A toast for my Russian princess."

"I suppose you must drink alone, unless you can point one out."

The fellow chuckled, picked up the glass, and sipped. The candlelight showed full, thick sideburns and a mustache, too. "Non, Madame Marie-Louise Christophe, I prefer to drink with you."

It had been years since someone addressed me by my full name . . . and four since a man stared so deeply into my eyes.

"It's a good blend," he said, his gaze not wavering. "You'll like it."

The man wasn't leaving. I was out of champagne. The musicians played Beethoven's Piano Sonata Thirty-Two. I still remember my harpist waiting for his new music long ago.

Surrendering, I lifted the new goblet, swirling ruby waves. One sip left berries on my tongue. A half glass made any embarrassment flee from my spirit.

"Would you care to dance now, Madame Christophe?"

"Non, thank you." I offered him the politest smile I could muster.

His eyes never left my face. He put his wide palm out to me.

I'd said something to Athénaïre about being brave. Perhaps that was why my fingers found his. Then the world slowed. I rose from my seat and joined a stranger on the floor.

My palm lifted to begin the minuet, but he waggled his finger to me. "That's an old dance. Try something new."

He took white gloves from his pocket, slid them on. He kissed my silver glove and put it to his broad shoulder. Then, timed to the start of new music, he scooped up my other hand and slipped his free arm about my waist. "A Russian or Haytian nymph should know the waltz."

It was scandalous, the way he held me close, with inches between my bosom and his wide chest.

"And now we move and spin."

My hips decided to follow, and I allowed this tall gentleman to whisk me across the room, around and around. He taught me to waltz, taught me to not think, taught me to laugh at myself again.

AFTER THE THIRD SONG, I CURTSIED AND WENT BACK TO MY SEAT.

The dancing stranger followed and again took Athénaïre's chair.

"I'm glad you don't embarrass easily. The human body is art. You're a masterpiece of shade and color. Wunderschönes meisterwerk."

"You're charming. And I thank you for the dance, but—"

"Meisterwerk," he repeated. "I want to spend another moment worshipping you."

"Idolatry is wrong, monsieur. Does the blasphemer have a name? Or shall I merely call you the dance master who stares?"

"Hermann Ludwig Heinrich von Pückler-Muskau."

That was a mouthful.

He didn't look like a Hermann, someone I pictured as loud. Definitively this man seemed quieter. A Ludwig, like Beethoven. "Mister Mus-kau? Is that how to say it?"

"Prince Pückler-Muskau, or just Pückler." His tone was strong, prideful. His simmering smile expected surprise in my countenance. Perhaps other ladies had swooned at such attention, but I'd known many princes. My husband had created them. In Hastings, I'd met a former king, but the thought of dancing with Napoleon's brother never crossed my mind.

"There's a crease in your brow, madame. Do you prefer my company better with no name? You wish to remain intimate strangers?"

My mouth dropped open at his clear invitation, and I lifted a glass to my lips. Should be shocked. Should ask him to leave. Shouldn't gape into turbulent sea-gray eyes that darkened to blue-black.

Squinting, turning to hunt for my daughter, I couldn't believe I was sitting with a prince and allowing his flirtation. But it was nonsensical to dance with him merely because he'd seen me naked.

"What's that look, madame?"

"Me trying to explain my evening to my daughters."

He chuckled. "Your princess is still with my friend. They've not stopped dancing."

"Well, well. Count M might be forgotten."

"Excuse me?"

"Nothing. Tell me, Prince Pückler, are you another exile or merely enjoying Baden-Baden as part of the royal tour?"

"I'm Prussian, from the town of Muskau. I was a soldier. Now I'm a traveler . . ."

And a lover.

Those were the unspoken words hanging from his lips—thin ones, with no notable Cupid's bow. I picked up the crystal goblet, swirling the last swallow, wondering if it was the wine making my thoughts scatter. "I don't think I'm myself this evening."

"You are you. I've taken the week to learn of you, the former and only queen of Hayti. Now a fabulous early-morning walker of Lichtentaler Allee. Perhaps we can meet tomorrow."

The prince had studied me? I wasn't Athénaïre, flattered by the attention, but I hadn't had such eyes on me in years.

"Madame Christophe, you've not answered."

"Typically gossips and newspapermen pay people to follow me. Which are you?"

"A man smitten by an incredible woman who has survived the unimaginable and is sitting in a ballroom in Baden-Baden holding court."

It was Friday evening, not Thursday. According to Limonade, one didn't have to be shown to the public any other day. Did I want to hold court . . . to be viewed as a desirable woman again?

Pückler's eyes turned toward the dancers. "I said too much. I apologize."

"For being honest? Non. That's refreshing. It's tiresome, always having to figure out what someone means. I wish more people said what they thought."

"You don't want that. It would be shocking."

"It's freeing to unburden yourself."

Athénaïre whirled past on the arms of another gentleman. Where she'd lost the major, I wasn't sure, but my girl looked enraptured.

Then it dawned upon me that this might be the prince's doing, manipulating the situation to maneuver a conversation. "Have you done this? Encouraged young men to dance with my daughter so that you could have a moment of my time?"

"No. It was your minuet with your daughter that enticed her partners." His smile returned, lusty and full. "Yet now that I know how beautiful your smile is up close, very little will stop me from wanting more of your time."

Sounding serious, with no hint of a jest, he lifted his glass to me. "A fine Tuscan Chianti and a queen are a perfect match."

Hmm. "I'll have to remember this when we head to Florence."

"Stay. Stay a little longer." His confident tone became rushed. "I owe you an apology, madame. A gentleman mustn't admit so soon to . . ."

I saw his mind turning to come up with the right word. His pause, that thoughtful look in his eye, searching for what was right and acceptable, brought new warmth to my skin.

I'd not let him know this. Our conversation needed to be light. "Was the word you searched for 'ogling' or 'admiring'?"

"A gentleman can't help but do a bit of both." He stood. "I hope to see more of you, a great deal more, during your visit."

"You've seen enough. We came only to enjoy the waters, then we'll be on our way."

He pulled the chair closer and sat back down. "Are you ill, madame? You seem very vibrant."

I was, wasn't I? "One of my daughters needs the baths to grow stronger."

"Europe has many beautiful health spas. Even some remote, less populated ones. Baden-Baden is always crowded. I'd love to share my thoughts on travel. What of dinner tomorrow?"

"Non, sir. I'm at my daughters' beck and call."

"Who's at yours?" His dark sweeping gaze kept searching my countenance.

"Don't be concerned. I have plenty of people managing my household."

"Managing with a precise schedule?" He finished his wine and let his thick fingers caress the delicate stem of the goblet. "Sounds as if a queen in Hayti is the same here. They are to be waited upon. They are to be treasured."

"A treasure? I'm neither fragile nor delicate, or only to be noticed at special occasions."

"Non. You're the type of woman to be admired always."

"Why are you saying this? To embarrass me, to find out if brown skin can a hold a blush?"

"We both know it can . . . and it did. You're beautiful."

Again he stood, towering over me. He was quite tall, intense, and dark—dark hair, stormy eyes, midnight tailcoat. And very Blanc and royal. "I'll start about seven on the allee. I've been trained to diligently escort queens." He bowed his chin. "Looking forward to our next talk. I cannot wait to listen."

I kept gazing at Pückler until he left the ballroom.

Athénaïre returned.

She looked at me with cheeks blushing. Her spirit bubbled, adding a glow to her bright eyes. "Maman, I hope you weren't bored."

"Non. I met Prussian royalty. He listened and kept me entertained."

She chuckled as if I were joking.

Then I did, too, for part of me looked forward to encountering a prince early in the morning at Lichtentaler Allee.

In a world of tricksters, gossips, and fortune hunters, sensible me hoped Pückler would be entertaining, providing me with weeks of laughter before I figured out his scheme.

39

1824 Baden-Baden, Germany

After checking on everyone in my household, from my daughters to my servants, I started for my daily stroll to Lichtentaler Allee.

Our accommodations, the top floor of the three-story Auberge a l'Arbre Vert, were quite comfortable and very private. The rest of the city offered fairy-tale adventures. From operas to the finest bakeries, Baden-Baden had every pleasure.

This morning Zephyrine brought back fresh Brötchen. These rolls fit in your palm and had hearty crusts. Another favorite, the thickly cut grain bread, Vollkornbrot, when basted in fresh butter and cream made the tongue rapturous.

Nonetheless, it wasn't food from home.

I lusted for true cassava, the toasted Haytian flatbreads, which, when layered with peppers and onions, returned me to my mother's cooking hearth. Oh, good onions, onions with bite that only a Haytian sun produced, had me weepy and homesick and remembering the man who'd eaten cassava with me in Maman's kitchen at the Hôtel de la Couronne.

I missed the intimacy of quiet moments with Henry. The soft whistle of the wind along the great river of Baden-Baden, the Oos, stirred me like a hum in a room that holds two.

Perhaps that was why I never missed my walks.

And why I allowed a Prussian accent murmuring perfect French to greet my lonely heart. Trying to figure out his gambit was no longer as important as having him present. It was scandalous thinking of a Blanc prince. In a world devoid of Haytian kings, I gave grace to my heart. As Saint Ambrose said, "In Milan I do not fast on Saturday, in Rome I do."

Crossing the bridge, I stopped, inhaled the fresh air, and listened to the river.

Like clockwork, a shadow, a welcomed presence, covered me.

"Guten Morgen, ma reine." Prince Pückler doffed his top hat, a sleek thing of slick beaver felt.

I nodded and said nothing, savoring the smell of nutmeg and cherry cigar ash in his cloak.

"How's the princess?"

A quick glance at his thoughtful countenance made me smile, but I safely returned my gaze to the gentle river. "No fever, Prince Pückler, but she's still weak. I thought this place would help."

"Patience, madame. Patience heals. All problems are solved with patience."

The prince parked beside me and let nature serenade us. The splash of a frog. The call of an orange-crested grebe.

"He's preparing for his mate. The bird is practicing. He must get everything right to win love."

"That's beautiful and depressing. Love should be more forgiving."

He nodded and stepped closer, his greatcoat sleeve touching my shawl.

For a half hour or more, we stayed like this, silent, listening to the river sing.

It wasn't uncomfortable.

It was pleasant to be in this man's shadow and not have to guess his mood or determine in advance how I must act or speak. I owed Pückler nothing. Perhaps that was the draw: no debts, no history, no reasons to say sorry.

The sun beamed above. The prince sighed and drummed his hands along the stone walls of the bridge. "'Nah am Wasser gebaut sein' is a saying inferring unstable things are built near the water. But this bridge looks sturdy."

My thoughts went to Sans-Souci. Its foundation had been laid over streams. It sounded like a good plan. The water kept the rooms cool, but didn't keep the palace from falling. It became a castle, a place abandoned, only visited by looters. "Looks can be deceiving."

"You think the bridge will tumble, madame?"

"Non, Prince Pückler, just remarking about appearances. They deceive."

"They can be honest. One can tell at a glance everything one wishes to know. A mere look can be open and accepting. I can tell you're hurting. The pain is fresh in your eyes."

Was I now a wine bottle, keeping everything, the sweetness, the bitters, trapped inside?

Would I burst?

Who would pick up the pieces?

"What causes you pain, ma reine? Is it merely the princess not doing better or the French fleet heading to Port-au-Prince?"

On this bridge I only wanted the river to know my weakness. I leaned farther, trying to see the foundation and the water's banks. "I've lost two children. I can't lose more. Once I was the mother of a nation. I can't lose my orphaned people to France or a new hawk. Though I'm exiled, my broken heart bleeds red and black, even red and blue for a unified Hayti."

A strong arm embraced me, but not for a waltz. It drew me to comfort. The prince, my friend, held me securely. I should've pulled away. I should've said he hadn't been given permission to touch me. But my gaze, the honest one, exposed my heart.

I wanted to be held.

I wanted to feel warm and heard.

I wanted my loneliness hidden, gone, even for a moment, a minute, a river's murmur of time.

My scarlet bonnet tipped backward. My braids tumbled forward as I clung to his chest. The thin wool of his Carmelite-colored coat tickled my jaw. Yet I wasn't satisfied. I remained too far from his soul.

Below the waters swayed and swished, chanting peace. The Oos could be Beethoven or Ries, but my tears trickled, adding to the melody.

When I felt I could finally string a coherent sentence together, I tried to push free, but the prince refused to release me. "No, schöne königin, beautiful queen."

"We're in public."

"This is Baden-Baden. Gossip stays in ballrooms and on bridges. And what's wrong with a man supporting a queen?"

Maybe logic in a heavy Prussian accent was what a French-speaking woman needed to hear, for I clung to the prince and wouldn't let go.

Soon the river's song became whispers. Footfalls sounded in the distance.

"It must be ten. The city's awakening. I must leave, Prince Pückler."

His hold loosened. Fixing my bonnet, I stepped from his heat.

"If you're here tomorrow, ma reine, I'll show you the best tree in Lichtentaler Allee. At the beginning of the season, it's surrounded by crocuses and daffodils and dahlias."

"What are those, dahlias?"

"They are beautiful flowers with numerous petals. Reminds me of the many facets of beautiful women. Come tomorrow, I'll show you. Nature helps me sort my thoughts. Perhaps it will convince you there's nothing more natural than friends. A queen and her escort should be the best of friends."

"You sound sad about someone you'll forget in months."

"Doubtful. You've burned in my mind for weeks and I've only just caressed you."

He bowed and left.

I ran back to my lodgings, trying to figure out how to return to normal, without a Prussian prince lingering in my thoughts.

WALKING WAS SOMETHING I HAD ALWAYS ENJOYED. HERE IN BADEN-Baden, it lifted my spirits.

Head up, I paced down the stone steps of the inn and lightly traipsed to Lichtentaler Allee. Stopping along the bridge, I said a prayer over the Oos. Becoming more comfortable outside of my rooms while my daughter grew sicker in her bed made me feel guilty and helpless.

Coming to this park and spending time with a prince who enjoyed gardens and flowers as much as me was a godsend.

"Louise." He waved to me.

The man must've been here fairly early. Yet his black breeches and white waistcoat, his evening clothes, said he'd been out all night.

My arms crossed. "I think you should make your way to your lodgings and get some sleep."

"Will you come and tuck me in?"

I shook my head. "Prince Pückler, I think you should go get rest and then we can try again tomorrow."

"Gambling, Louise. No other woman."

The admission should mean nothing, but it did. "And call me Hermann."

"Non. Ludwig."

His dimples showed beneath his curly mustache. "So you do think of me. I'm not alone in this."

He took my hand, clutching it tightly as if to prevent me from slipping away. "Come with me."

Rushing, not quite running, he took me to the huge sequoia.

"I made art at sunrise. Look."

The sweet crazy man had carved his initials into the thick bark along with mine. "But it's not finished."

He pulled a short knife from his evening coat and cut the first letters of my children's names, V, A, A, and then he added F, for my first, François-Ferdinand.

This mother's heart exploded. "How can you be so thoughtful? And you've listened to all my babbles."

After stuffing the knife back into his pocket, he brushed at his handiwork, making the indentions in the bark more noticeable. "Yes, I've listened and learned. You need to tell me more of King Henry. I want to know how to clear his shadow and find my path to you."

"Non. I loved his shadow. I loved being in it. I'll not lose Henry for anyone."

"Then share him." Stepping closer, Ludwig angled me under the tree's canopy. "Then we both shall be in the shade of greatness. Just know in the dark who's loving you."

Turning away from his eager, light face, I was lost. I could think of Ludwig as Colored, but even that wasn't right, changing him to be something he wasn't. So much hate had come from differences in race—how did I make sense of these feelings?

With a finger to my chin, he turned me, spinning me back to his stormy gaze. "Louise, perhaps if you let yourself desire me, then the confusion will go away."

Non. "That will make things worse. I'm not ready."

He kicked a pebble and groaned. "I've never done something like this before."

"Stay out all night gambling? You must've had a good time."

His lips formed a slight smirk. "You should know why I didn't turn in at a sensible hour. I'd rather be up using my mind counting cards, looking for luck, than wanting a woman in my bed who won't visit. I'm not used to empty sheets."

"Does anyone ever get used to being alone?" It was wrong to say. I shouldn't encourage him to think we could be more.

Ludwig took my hand and kissed my fingers. "Seems two people who enjoy each other's company should do something about it. That would send me straight to my lodgings, the anticipation of being with you."

Men who didn't sleep scared me. Though Ludwig was different from Henry, he was also very similar—tall, intense, brooding. But he was also truthful with his emotions. That made my pulse race, my thoughts more scandalous, my heart more open.

His tongue flicked between my fingers at the soft flesh, the webbing. The sensation sent warm vibrations down my arm. I'd been touched by fire and was growing less afraid of being burned.

I drew my hand away and stuffed it into the safety of my pocket. "Ludwig." I cleared my throat, hoping my voice didn't sound pitchy. "The carving is lovely."

"What else do you get a queen who has everything?"

My smile faltered. "What do you mean I have everything?"

"I know all about you, Louise. And you need to know about me. I'm searching for a wealthy bride."

My mouth flew open. The Virgin Mary hadn't protected me. She'd gifted a friend who spoke too much truth. "Prince Pückler, you're a fortune hunter?"

"It's Ludwig." He sighed. "And you say that like it's a bad thing? Rest assured, it's not. I could do a lot with a fortune."

I pushed at my turban, knocking its dropping egret feather out of the way. I'd hoped the hat looked regal, aloof, but I felt my lips drooping. "Explain or tell me goodbye."

"Everything there's to know about you, you've told me, or I've read in papers or heard rumors. I understand about the banking settlements, and that you'll never want for money. Madame Christophe is an excellent candidate to marry."

"Oh, I see."

"No, you don't. You've enchanted me for weeks, madame, worked my soul into a fever, but I know you'll not marry me. You'll only toy with my listening skills. You'll cast me aside, and I haven't tasted your lips."

The man was serious and passionate about declaring his intentions. He withheld none of his truth. The openness of his speech was seductive.

"Say something, ma reine."

"I don't know what I should."

"Louise, say the truth does not make you run."

He wrenched at his loose cravat. A half-hearted chuckle fell. "I'm desperate for you, Queen Louise."

It must be hard to be this transparent. It should be rewarded. "I'll not abandon you. A warier woman would, but I appreciate a very honest friend."

"A friend . . . If the queen knew my heart, she'd not be just a friend."

He bit his lip for a moment. "I don't want you to stop seeing me, but I had to tell you my intentions."

"Baden-Baden is for a season, Ludwig. Nothing more. And these walks are purely platonic, no passion." I said this because of my daughters, and Henry being larger than life, and the gossips looking for me to stumble.

There were thousands of reasons. But they all hid my dishonesty. I was scared and unwilling to risk my heart again.

He whisked his hands to his head, sinking his fingers into his thick dark hair. "Of course, madame. Thank you for allowing me to say this."

Polite but visibly pained and disappointed, he looked to the sky.

Before I could stop myself, I clutched his arm. "That doesn't mean I won't savor our walks. This will be my favorite season because of you."

His hand covered mine.

Time stood still. Hope shone in his eyes, not storm clouds. "Some seasons can be the greatest, especially just beginning. And when we do come together, you'll know it will be wonderful, full of care. We must have many seasons."

I didn't mean . . . I didn't think . . . Touching him was an invisible line. I'd crossed it. The roar of my beating heart announced I wasn't ready to let him go.

In silence, we walked through the park. He pointed to more dahlias, so pretty and purple.

"Madame Christophe," Ludwig said in strong formal tones, "I value this time. I won't give up the chase."

"Sir, you'll charm a wealthy wife. Forget me and go chase others."

Sighing, he stopped. "I wish to pursue you. Are you saying that's not allowed?"

My lips pursed and shut before I agreed.

He flipped the white feather from my eyes. "I think I'll have to ask you again later. For now, what do friends do? Can they lie in each other's arms and listen to the river?"

As hard as it was to move from his shadow and the tension in his body that jolted through mine, I stepped away. "Ludwig. Save this passion for your future bride. Let's keep strolling."

His head bent close to mine. "Only talk and walk? Why should I be used by a woman who won't admit to what she truly wants?"

"The begging me for more seasons is a good indication that you'll find time for our walks."

Supple and smooth, his mouth graced my fingertips, then the back of my hand, then my wrist, where Henry's bracelet should be. I hadn't been wearing it, not for these walks.

"I beg well. Princes do. We have good breeding, schöne frau."

Palm against palm, we started down Lichtentaler Allee. And just as in fairy tales, we talked of weather and politics and other nonsense. Nothing of how it would hurt me to see him with another woman.

SWAYING TO THE VIOLINS AT OUR LAST BALL BEFORE THE SEASON ended, I watched my daughters enjoy themselves.

Améthyste lightly clapped her hands. "The Promenadenhaus is lovely. The chandeliers remind me of the drawing room of Sans-Souci."

My eldest had improved so much these last few weeks, my fears of losing her had subsided. With her hair in a tight bun laced with pearls, like my chignon, she lifted her hands, framing images to sketch. My darling was drawing again. I had Zephyrine buy all the charcoals in town.

The Vienna-green gown, close in color to my emeralds, wrapped about Améthyste's slender form. It made her skin seem brighter, not sallow or sickly. More weight and sun would do her good. The way her appetite for toasted Brötchen had grown, I was sure she'd gain.

Major Ernestus's gaze followed Athénaïre's every movement. He sat with us this evening at our preferred table in the corner of the ballroom, watching her dance. The man seemed very attentive, but my daughter hadn't decided whom she liked best. My butterfly in a mazarine gown floated here and there, from partner to partner, fluttering her purple wings—the decorative rolled hem of her skirt.

I felt for him, the quiet young man struggling to learn better French to converse fluently with Athénaïre. Part of me wanted such a devoted young man to ask Améthyste to dance, for she had the patience her sister didn't.

Then I wanted to kick myself under the table.

No intervening in my daughters' affairs.

"Madame Christophe." Lady Robert from our Hastings days stood before me. "I had heard you were taking the waters here."

"Oui. Baden-Baden will be a place I'll always visit."

With her sweeping titian hair topped by a ruby tiara, she looked lovely. Nonetheless, I'd heard from Zephyrine that such an intense robin-red hair color was obtained from dyes. Though the red was beautiful, I wasn't tempted. The pearls woven in my braids made errant gray strands appear glorious, like fine silver.

Lady Robert sat and chattered about Hastings. I listened as intently as I could while looking for Ludwig. He'd disappeared after dancing with a lady from Austria. Before her, there was an British widow.

When Lady Robert mentioned him and some shocking behavior of years ago, I merely listened. Zephyrine kept me in tune with the gossip. Laundresses here were the same as in London or Milot. They knew everyone's business. Though Ludwig was a favorite of many, there were no rumors about the prince and me or his designs on anyone else in Baden-Baden.

Ludwig and I still had our morning walks, but he seemed more distracted lately. Our exchanges—"bonjour" and "guten morgen," "au revoir" and "auf wiedersehen"—would end. I had to prepare that he'd soon announce his future bride, perhaps a woman back home in Prussia.

"And Count Saint-Leu is here tonight." Lady Robert's words snapped me to attention. "He's joined my party; you must come and say hello."

The brother of Napoleon was in the Promenadenhaus? Surely, he'd kept abreast of politics. The man must know what was going on in France's war of words with Hayti. "Take me to them."

My voice sounded pleasant, revealing nothing of the anxious heat flooding my middle.

As I rose, Ludwig appeared at my table. "Madame Christophe, a dance for your last night in Baden-Baden?"

"Oui, in a moment. Lady Robert, this is Prince Pückler."

He kissed her hand, but his gaze returned to me. "Is something wrong?"

"Prince Pückler, will you chaperone the princess and the major while I say hello to Count Saint-Leu?"

My friend's stormy eyes knew the distress in my spirit. "Ma reine, are you sure you do not need an escort?"

"Non. Keep your friend entertained, or dance with my daughter. She's another young, beautiful heiress."

Améthyste squinted at me, then at Ludwig. She coughed, covered her mouth. "I'm fine with just a discussion, Prince Pückler."

I'd exposed myself to my girl and Ludwig—my jealousy, my distraught state, my care for a man for whom I shouldn't have feelings—and I had to go see my enemy's brother.

"Princess Améthyste," Ludwig said, taking my seat. "Your mother says you are fond of architecture. Let me tell you of the things you must see in Florence. Major Ernestus can attest to it. My old friend and I have seen plenty together."

"Ja. I mean oui." The poor man rubbed his temples, then went back to his prior occupation of watching Athénaïre.

Ludwig's heated gaze followed me as I locked arms with Lady Robert and went to meet my fellow exile and learn firsthand about the looming confrontation between Hayti and France.

40

1824 Baden-Baden, Germany

Lady Robert led me through the crowded Promenadenhaus. We stopped several times and she laughed with delight telling me of Hastings gossip. Then she peered over my shoulder at the Christophe corner of the ballroom. "Warn your daughters that Prince Pückler has a woman in every city. He's hunting for an heiress, you see, to bulk up his fortune."

Men. Peers. Their leisure was pursuit, pursuit of women, cigars, and gambling. Zephyrine had even overheard a rumor that he had three wives. The gossip was rubbish. "I'll be sure to warn them, but what's so terrible about harmless fun with a prince? How would fairy tales be made without them?"

Her chortle sounded musical. She folded her hand tighter along my glittering silver glove. "Oh, you are missed in Hastings."

I spied the Comte de Maltverne, Athénaïre's infamous Count M, seated with his wife and a few other British peers. He waved, but I kept walking and hoped my daughter didn't see him.

Lady Robert finally stopped at a table filled with many familiar faces and a few new ones. Gentlemen stood, as the custom demanded. She introduced me again to Count Saint-Leu, Louis Bonaparte, the former king of Holland. Then she motioned to his brother the former king of Westphalia, now Prince de Montfort, Jérôme-Napoléon Bonaparte.

The prince, the youngest brother of France's old emperor, wore sideburns like Ludwig's and a mop of curly hair. In his forties, he was fit and flirting with the ladies. He turned to me and with all the tact of a smelly tallow candle asked, "Do tell, how much of King Henry's treasury did you abscond with? I heard it was sizable."

Count Saint-Leu rolled his eyes and jabbed his brother—a little knock on the knee. "Prince de Montfort, that's impolite. Next, you'll be asking Madame Christophe to pay reparations on behalf of her former nation."

"That would be the same as having your former countries sacked to return you to stolen thrones. Then you could demand the peasants' blood. You'll be winners again. Wouldn't be right for losers to demand anything."

"Funny madame. Leu. Prince de Montfort," Lady Robert said, "you said you'd be cordial if I brought our old friend."

Keeping my false smile intact, I waved my delicate ostrich fan as if I were inhaling a fishy stench or worse. "Why would you expect manners from . . . French exiles? That's a crapulous endeavor, I believe."

The count sat back, folding his arm across his jet jacket and crisp white cravat. The way his hand hooked onto his lapel, it reminded me of how Henry touched his sash and royal star. "Forgive me and my brother, madame. We are all part of the exile community. No one is held to account for past sins or revolutions. Pardonnez-moi."

I took a seat near the count. Conversation resumed, with talk of other kingdoms and war. The British fighting in the Burmese empire for control of northern India animated Saint-Leu.

The British loved their tea, and Assam made the finest. As in Saint-Domingue, a foreign power always sought to control the land and the people who created the goods.

Lord Cholmondeley lifted a glass. "A salute to Dom Miguel. He may be joining our community."

I looked to Lady Robert. She whispered, "Miguel is the third son of the king of Portugal. He opposed his father, King John VI . . ." Then she looked at Cholmondeley. "And was banished to Vienna. Who gets banished to Austria? Is the punishment to see bad opera?"

A new round of laughs ensued. Amid the folly, Saint-Leu caught my gaze. "Madame Christophe, I apologize for my brother's impertinence."

"Sir, we can sit here and converse without animosity."

"Oui, madame. We've both lost because of the wars."

"Then why can't our countries coexist?"

"Madame Christophe, I'm not in favor in Paris at all. But no one likes to lose. The defeat by . . ."

"The enemy."

"By someone you've subjugated and thought of as lesser than you is deeply humiliating. Britain started the war with the Burmese. Because it's been costly, they'll force reparations to be paid. Burma will pay millions of pounds."

"But that is the victor punishing the loser. Hayti won. It shouldn't be punished."

"Perhaps President Boyer is as diplomatic as you. If he can figure out how to give the Bourbons in Paris something to allow them to save face, that will settle things."

"And if he cannot?"

He put his glass down and looked again directly into my eyes. "There's been enough war over a small island that's struggling to find its footing. Let us hope the new chief, or shall I say the surviving chief, knows what he's doing. If not, it will cost more blood and treasure."

A frank answer, one that filled me with the utmost dread.

Conversation flowed about me, but I spiraled, feeling lost, until Ludwig came.

"Madame Christophe, I can report that the princesses have been taken back to your residence, shepherded by Major Ernestus. There's a dance that I've come to claim."

"Oui, of course." I put my hand in his and bade farewell to the table.

In Ludwig's arms, I danced the waltz. My steps were slow, then I let him twirl me, guide me about the room. I was glad this spinning kept me close to him, for I didn't know how to stand up without his power.

"I think now your friends see you enjoying your night under lights of the chandelier—"

"Sweet beeswax candles."

"Oui. Now you'll leave with me, Madame Christophe, and no one will know they hurt you."

"But you know."

With a nod, he stopped dancing, tucked my hand under his arm, and led me from the ballroom.

"Won't your heiress mind that you're taking me to the Auberge a l'Arbre Vert?"

"A queen outranks a commoner. And who said I'm taking you anywhere that I can't be with you?"

He sounded serious. I didn't care if he was or wasn't. I needed to leave Promenadenhaus with my dignity. Ludwig would transport me from these troubles. Lord, help me survive the ones stirring in his stormy eyes.

THE MOON WAS PEEKING OVER THE MOUNTAIN AS LUDWIG'S CAR-
riage raced to the River Oos. I relaxed against the prince's shoulder. Light kisses to my brow made me realize I was too comfortable, too vulnerable to be alone with him. "Take me to my inn, Ludwig. There's packing to be done."

"That's tomorrow. By my calculation, that's at least an hour from now." His fingers dipped into my curls. "Princess Athénaïre was a little miffed I clipped her wings before midnight. Then she saw the Comte de Maltverne. His visit to our table helped convince her to leave with the major."

I groaned. "Duels are illegal here? That man should be dealt with."

He shrugged. "The major's a good shot. All Prussian men are. The Princess Améthyste was tired. Perhaps my friend Ernestus will finally tell the younger Christophe of his admiration. I think it's easier for him to think of what to say if they are away from a ballroom. He's quite taken with her."

That knowledge would lift her spirits after seeing Count M. "I believe Athénaïre likes him as a friend."

"Pity that's catching. Must be a condition when men are enraptured by Christophe women."

I rested my head more heavily on his shoulder. "Don't make me laugh. I want to hold on to this rage for just another moment. It will help me think of what to do."

He had his driver stop close to the River Oos. "Come with me, Louise. Let's take a final walk."

I pulled my tippet of black-edged white feathers tighter about my shoulders and followed him. We ambled arm in arm onto our bridge and leaned on the rail.

"What did the Bonapartes say to the widow of the man who bested their brother? I know they said something. I kept watching to see if I needed to come to your defense, but you assigned me to the tisch für kinder, the kiddie table."

"Well, you are young."

"Thirty-nine is young enough. It's old enough as well. Tell me, Louise."

"They confirmed what the newspapers say. France wants Hayti to pay for winning. Count Saint-Leu thinks that until a sacrifice is made to assuage Paris, there will be war."

"War would be unfortunate. The loser is taking a horrible attitude. But Hayti won before. Surely it can again?"

"Maybe, but Boyer hasn't been building the military. He's abandoned the defenses Henry put in place. The strongmen who would stand up to France are gone."

He put his hands on my shoulders, rubbing them to warm me or shake me from feeling helpless. "What will happen will happen. Boyer's not your pick to lead, but he's leading. He has generals and people supporting him."

"What if there were something the French wanted besides war? What if someone could be surrendered to them? A high-ranking prisoner might help France feel as if they had won something?"

With palms to my cheeks, he bent and peered into my eyes. "And you think *surrendering* a queen would do it?"

"Maybe. That might keep France from enslaving Hayti."

"You've lost your mind."

"Don't say that."

"That's the most arrogant thing to think, that the French would recognize how smart and brave and honest you are. That those fools would know you're a worthy sacrifice. No, Louise. They'd take you, put you through a sham of a trial. They might even execute you, then still send their fleet to attack Hayti."

Shaking, I stepped from his reach. "I have to do something."

"You don't have to do anything for the people who betrayed you." He clasped my hand and murmured words I didn't understand. Then his lips briefly brushed my wrist. "You don't have to suffer another second for the generals and the army who slaughtered your son and all the friends of the court who turned away. Not another thing."

The truth, said aloud, stung like a slap. I broke free, tried to find my way, but stumbled. Hearing his footfalls, I headed off the bridge and down the path to where the sequoia stood.

"Louise!"

It was too dark to stop, to turn back and be reminded of my pain and my pride.

Arms came about my middle. I started to fight, tried to struggle, but why resist what felt so right?

"You have to accept that you're not all powerful. Louise, you can't control the good or the bad. The world keeps turning. You can't stop it."

I spun in his arms, poked at his chest, his chest with no medals. A chest with a silky white waistcoat and painted buttons like Toussaint used to wear. "Then you make it stop, Ludwig. Make everything go away. You're man. A prince. Do it. Do it now."

He nodded. "Oui. For a queen, I'll make the world stop."

Lifting me up, with hands seeking my bottom, he held me securely. "Touch the sky. Touch a cloud. Touch me."

He lowered me against his trim body, making me feel his muscles, those buttons, those naughty fingers.

Then he dipped his head and kissed me.

Kissed me until everything felt warm and wet in my lonely body.

Kissed me until my arms settled about his neck and I whispered never let go.

Kissed me until his buttons undid and my tippet fell away.

Kissed me until we were against the sequoia making love in the moonlight.

Kissed me until I promised to return to Baden-Baden the same time next year.

EXILE

Berkshire Chronicle, Saturday, September 10, 1825

A letter from Port-au-Prince, from the 12th of July says an entertainment was given yesterday evening by the President to the Baron de Mackau, and the officers the French squadron. The toasts after dinner were—[King] Charles X and the President of Hayti, that "France and Hayti are mother and daughter [again]."

41

1825 Baden-Baden, Germany

Standing on the steps of the Auberge a l'Arbre Vert, I welcomed the sunshine. I had become like the rest of the exiles and royals in Europe, taking the waters for the summer.

For my Améthyste, it was necessary. Every time we went back to London for business, the rainy weather proved to be too much. Baden-Baden provided the perfect balance of treatments for Améthyste and society for Athénaïre.

And a little company for me.

Zephyrine came outside. "You forgot these."

"Oh, did I?" I took the soft sand-colored gloves from her. My voice sounded innocent, not as if I'd purposely left them behind to aid in the scandalous holding of a gentleman's hand.

"Madame, I hear Princess Athénaïre's friend keeps writing her."

"Oui. Major Ernestus writes very good letters. His French has improved."

I could usually read her emotions like newsprint, but not today. "What is it?"

Zephyrine put her hands in the pocket of her apron. "Princess Athénaïre will marry, eventually. It will be someone from this society."

There was every indication of it. The major seemed smitten, but she'd caught many men's eyes. "Is there something wrong with her finding love here, not in Hayti?"

A bitter chuckle fell from her lips. "Hayti, the one we knew, is gone. I don't fault the princess for living. Especially with her sister not doing well. She's . . ."

With her voice dropping away, I could finish Zephyrine's sentence.

The treatments weren't working like last time. My sweet Améthyste was growing weaker. I didn't know what to do anymore.

Zephyrine put her hand on my shoulder. "We've been to many places. You enjoy it here. Think of yourself. You're flesh and blood. You can be loved again, too. A widow can marry again. Even a queen."

She knew I was fond of coming here and walking in Lichtentaler Allee, among the flower beds and trees and the river that whispered of peace. The look in her smoky eyes said she knew of my secret affair. Can one call it a love affair if you only stole moments a few months a year?

"Go on to your bath, madame. Enjoy yourself today."

Chin dropping, I started down the stone steps, to relax and wait for my friend from Prussia to arrive.

I FOLLOWED THE ATTENDANT DOWN THE HALL TO MY FAVORITE SPA in Baden-Baden, the first one my daughters and I had visited when we first came the previous year.

The prince had encouraged me to have a day of decadence, to not fret about a thing. He'd arranged this baden and a private nuncheon later.

To take care of myself was easy for my Prussian friend to say. His thoughts weren't on daughters and their welfare. He had no countrymen who'd sold his homeland to the enemy.

Fanning as we came to the room with the large pool, I took deep breaths of the minerals in the air. The situation in Hayti wasn't something its former queen could do anything about.

I hadn't signed papers agreeing to pay 150 million francs to France. That was Boyer's failing.

"Madame, the instructions said to make this as steamy as possible. Something about replicating the conditions of the Rivière Mapou?"

Ludwig had given instructions? I smiled to myself. I treasured his concern for me. "Rivière Mapou. Oui. That would be nice."

She opened the door and steam rolled out, thick and white and slightly sparkling because of the minerals.

"We did our best, madame."

Sauntering inside, it felt as if I'd stepped into Le Cap. I could picture my sisters with head wraps and towels running with me to the riverbank.

"I'll come back to check on you in a few hours." She held out her hand for my robe, but I kept it on.

"When I'm done, I'll find you. I don't want to be disturbed."

"Oui, madame."

The confused but kindly woman left. I stood alone imagining my river.

I took off my mobcap, unpinned my chignon, and loosened each long braid. My hair would swell, even knot. But no one who dove into the Mapou cared about such things.

Slipping my robe to the floor, I took a deep breath, then leapt into the pool.

The warm water covered me.

I swam through the heat to the bubble fountain. It troubled this river, making small, lovely waves.

Oh, this felt good.

Eyes closed, I floated and let the heat relax every muscle. "This is perfect."

"I thought you'd like it."

Hearing Ludwig's voice, I began to sink. Feet dipping to the marble bottom, I bobbed in the pool searching for him. "You really needn't sneak up on a person."

"You shouldn't hide yourself. You're wunderschönes meisterwerk, a masterpiece."

Crouching, resting above the water's surface, I glared at the naked man coming out of the steam.

His tanned white skin, darker than porcelain, richer and warmer than alabaster, shimmered in the fog. The prince strutted with a wooden tray of berries in hand.

I only glanced at the fruit for a moment.

The attraction of sculpted legs made strong by long walks, horse-back riding, and a life of holding himself erect as he proudly entered all rooms.

Dignity.

Intrigue with a wide hairy chest.

His crazy mustache sagging in the heat needed my fingers to part it and curl it about my pinkie.

Ludwig wasn't what I expected to be in my life.

Yet his care, his need to surprise me and to listen, always listen—this was joy.

He held the tray over the pool. "Do you approve of what you see?"

Face feeling hot, not from the bath but from being caught gazing, I merely laughed. "My eyesight might be fading. I'm a bit older than you. Perhaps you should come closer."

"The sweetest wine is made with grapes left late on the vine."

Easing into the water, he splashed and strutted to me, still carrying the tray aloft. "Treats, luscious ones for a queen. To enjoy with this baden, my compliments."

"This is too much—"

"Ah, a poor prince can do this."

Squinting at him, I waited for him to say more. Men needed to talk of things that were uncomfortable. A woman having more was difficult.

He blinked then put a berry to his tongue. "A friend commissioned me for a garden design. And I was paid to edit some pages for a new acquaintance in publishing. Seems I have talent."

"Ludwig, you're very talented. Your letters, they preserve me."

When he set the tray on the water, it floated.

"I have himbeeren. That is raspberries. Then there are stachelbeere, the tangy gooseberries. And to finish off, lovely quince jam with fresh cream."

He dipped a raspberry into the sweet spread and put it to my lips. It tasted good—tart and sweet like honey.

Then he kissed my mouth, a quick peck before stepping back.

He steepled the fingers of his left hand with mine, heated ivory and fiery bronze, and drizzled the jam on our knuckles.

"Such a treat," he said, tasting my skin, cleaning it of quince. His touch quickened my pulse, my breathing, my desire for this moment to last.

"Ma reine, you're silent. You need a berry on your tongue?"

He took his time, picking the perfect raspberry. Rolling it against my lips, he slipped the berry into my eager mouth.

Wiping my lips, I asked the question I dreaded. "Did you find your heiress this year while we were apart?"

Flinging water from his hands, he gave me a withering look with his dark eyes. "Do you truly want to know what I do while I'm away?"

Swallowing the berry, I offered him nothing—no emotion, no evident care. "Ludwig, you and I have no understanding. You're a man of leisure. A man of the world. I'm a busy person, too."

"I worked on garden designs. I consulted with architects for the park at my estate."

"You're a builder as well as a lover."

His lips pursed. "The only heiress on my mind has beautiful *Eurafrican* blood."

Célestina Coidavid, my mother was enslaved. Her skin was lighter than mine. She didn't talk of her father, but many born of such conditions didn't.

Ludwig came closer and ran his thumb down my throat to the valley of my breasts. "No other heiress fills my thoughts."

"Oh. I've met no additional princes or reigning kings. A few out-of-power ones, but kings are always falling out of power."

"What of princes?" He bent his head and licked my wet lips. "Do we lose our power?"

There wasn't time to answer, not with his hands roaming my skin, counting every rib, tracing everything that led to my heart.

"You can stand up fully, Louise. I've seen quite a lot of you."

"But it's warm being in the water. The perfect temperature when you're fully immersed."

A dimple appeared beneath his curly mustache. "Can't have a cold queen."

Sinking a little, Ludwig reached for me, embracing my spirit in our oasis. He kissed me until I purred and opened my love to him.

He lifted me out of the water and put his hands in my hair.

"Careful, Ludwig. It will tangle when wet. I didn't give permission for you to be tied to me."

"But there is no better way to hold on to you and keep you. My soul is tied to the most beautiful queen."

This time I kissed him. He drew back as if he were searching for something.

"What's wrong?"

"I'm watching the water bead on your skin. I love how it drizzles over you. It's intoxicating. Drops of heaven on silk—I believe that was when I first knew you had to be mine."

My lotions kept me soft. I liked to be supple and touched.

I slipped below the water's surface and then rose like a mermaid from a fairy tale, shaking my head. My loosed hair splashed water on Ludwig's chest.

It ran over his flesh, making my prince shimmer.

"I think we are well matched, Ludwig."

I kissed him, embracing the man who lived, who reminded me that this sensual part of my life hadn't ended.

The Rivière Mapou—I might never see it again.

Nor Cap-Henry, the Citadel, or Sans-Souci. They had become old memories—castles.

No more frets or regrets. I'd found a palace in me. I had peace knowing living for the moment was not wrong. I deserved happiness.

The question of how we could continue outside Baden-Baden and beyond our summer world began to swirl about me like the steam.

"My wunderschönes meisterwerk, my Louise."

Prince Hermann Ludwig Heinrich von Pückler-Muskau claimed my mouth and took me deeper into the water.

No need to think of the future when Ludwig loved me now.

DAWN SHONE THROUGH THE WINDOWPANE OF THE BATHING CHAM-ber. My neck hurt. I lifted my head, arching my back against the cold metal tub in the center of the room.

"Maman, you look so uncomfortable. Go to bed, you don't have to watch me."

Améthyste cleaned the nightgown she'd stained in a basin of water. The treatments had loosened her bowels. She lacked control. "Please go to bed."

Lunging to my feet, I went to her and poked my finger in the luke-warm water of the basin. "Guess I fell asleep."

"You did." She worked a spot that truly needed bleach.

"Stop. Zephyrine can finish it."

"Non. I can do it."

She scrubbed at the lace and the fine embroidery of flowers on her nightgown. The biggest stain lifted, but she kept adding soap as if she'd picked hundreds of soapberries.

"Améthyste, you've gotten most of it—"

"It's not clean."

She lathered the garment again and kept working.

I put my hands in the water and grabbed hers. "It's clean."

Tears fell from her eyes. She rarely cried.

"Maman, I don't want these treatments anymore. I don't want to live like this, with no strength or control. I don't want to do this any-more. This is not living."

The bowl dumped its water when I reached for her. It hit the ground, spilling its soapy contents. "Non. Améthyste, this is to make you better. Then you can live a full life."

"This is no life. I finally understand Père's choice. If I can't control my limbs, my lungs, my ability to keep down food, I want no more of this. Death is peace. Death is freedom."

I pulled back in horror. This wasn't like Athénaïre, who was full of emotion. Or Henry, given to moods. Améthyste had a logical mind.

She used words carefully.

She wanted to die.

"Non. Non. Non. Améthyste, I can't lose you."

"What is left of me? To be so weak I cannot draw, that I cannot taste a peach or a tomato? I'm not living, Maman. I'm existing for you."

Sobbing, I wanted to tell her no, that this wasn't right. That the Holy Father wanted us to fight. But I looked in her dark eyes and they said non, no more.

"What do you want? Have Souliman go buy a pistol? Do I find a bayonet and let you run yourself through? Poison, as your aunt and the Voduns taught?"

"Non." She freed herself from my grasp and tugged her robe about her thin limbs. "I know if I drink any more of the tonic water, I'll drown myself in it. You know that one day the sickness is going to win, but if I have no life now, I don't want to be here."

She expressed my greatest fear aloud. It wasn't her lungs claiming her, it was Améthyste surrendering to death.

So many in my life had surrendered. Henry had yielded his throne, his legacy.

His nobles had given up on the king and the ideals of Black power.

Boyer would soon hand over Hayti's independence to France—all surrendering.

I wiped at my mouth. My bare feet were in the slippery suds, making it easy to fall. But I chose to dive in headfirst, yielding. "Then no more tonics."

"What, Maman?"

"Listen to me. I won't push anymore, but you have to keep living."

Améthyste wrenched off her mobcap and flung the yellowish lace against the wall; it fell to the slate floor. Her long braids came down. "Help me wash my hair this morning. Then I want tea, tea from regular water, so chamomile tastes like chamomile, not medicine."

As if she'd been holding in an ocean, she broke down and sobbed.

I knelt beside her and held her. "That's your truth. Here's mine. You make every day special. You haven't lived enough to be done with living. We don't know what life will bring. Only the brave find out. And you are brave."

"Brave people tire, too."

That was true. A sad and miserable truth.

I wanted to say that those who took their lives by their own hands were cowards.

But that wasn't true, either.

Brave people wanted their dignity.

Brave people wished to control their destiny.

Brave people could become bogged down in the depths of depression.

Brave people died.

"You inspire me, Améthyste."

"One day, I'm not going to win, Maman."

"All of us will die, but when Saint Peter reads the entries of your life, let it be a long list of things that brought you joy. Let him say well done, that you lived every second, that you did more than you were called to do."

I held her, scooping up this thoughtful girl to cradle her. "Keep filling your brave body with air for as long as you can."

She nodded and sobbed down my shift.

This day I would no longer count the years of Hayti's independence or the years since we lost the kingdom, I'd count the sunrises that greeted Améthyste. That number plus one would equal the sum of days until my heart again fell to the floor and smashed to pieces.

EXILE

Public Ledger and *Daily Advertiser* (London), Wednesday, July 19, 1826

The American Papers draw a gloomy picture of the state of affairs in Hayti and add that nothing but the personal influence of General Magny, who commands in the North, has prevented the Blacks from breaking out into open rebellion against the Government, and seizing the property of the Whites and Mulattoes. The state of things might arise as destructive as the wildest scenes that were exposed during the insurrectionary war between Christophe and Pétion.

42

1826 Baden-Baden, Germany

Walking into the parlor of our rooms in the Auberge a l'Arbre Vert, I saw crates and packaging paper. This sight in the sunny-yellow room meant we'd be leaving soon for Tuscan sunshine. With our treasures wrapped, we'd be making the trip as soon as tomorrow.

It all depended on Améthyste. She had to feel up to the drive and have no fever.

I wasn't up to it. It was hard to say goodbye to my prince, knowing it would be a whole year before I saw him again.

Creeping into Améthyste's room, where she lay on the bed with eyes closed, I touched her forehead. Cool.

"Just tired, Maman. I promised not to die yet. I'm keeping my word."

"Rest, and soon we'll start our journey to Florence."

"The rooms near the Arno?"

"Oui, Monsieur Giligni has them ready as always."

With a kiss to her sweet cheek, I tucked a blanket about her shoulders. "Write to the Thorntons. See if Patti or Marianne might visit."

"Marianne married. I believe she is a Smyth now."

Such a sweet girl, both of them. "See if they can make the trek. It would be lovely to see them."

My daughter smiled and closed her eyes again.

Backing out, I closed the door. It made a gentle thud. She needed to be in the warm Tuscan sun. Today marked thirty-six sunshines. Tomorrow would be thirty-seven.

A fidgeting Zephyrine found me in the hall. "Souliman has finished shipping the biggest crates of dishes. You think they'll make it mostly unbroken?"

I chuckled. "I think he is determined to save every cup this time."

"Madame, Princess Athénaïre has gone walking. Though not alone."

With the major? Was that why she'd borrowed my emerald bracelet again? "Do you think Major Ernestus will propose?"

Her frown became bigger. "Non, madame."

"It's fine that she's with him, Zephyrine. It's the middle of the day, and he's been a friend for years. No need to look anxious. This is no ground for scandal."

She wrung her hands against her blue checked gingham skirt. "She's not with the major. It's Count M. He came to visit. He's sent her letters. He still wants her to be his mistress. He sent his wife back to England early."

The man who broke Athénaïre's heart was toying with her again. "Let me go find the princess and hurry her back."

Tugging on my red Terre d'Egypte–colored mantle, I went to find my daughter, to keep her from folly. That was hypocritical, the notion that I could keep her from falling for the wrong man. I'd fallen for a waiter turned king with war in his eyes, and I'd risked my own scandal for a fortune-hunting prince with storms in his.

Yet I wouldn't deny my heart.

And I couldn't live in the past. I wanted Ludwig to come with us.

We'd walked all over Baden-Baden. We could have adventures other places. I selfishly wanted to lean on him when we might not have a reason to come here next year. Adding to our party instead of taking away would be—

Athénaïre?

She was on the bridge crossing the River Oos. Count M stood with his hands animated, talking, fighting . . . perhaps not getting his way.

The closer I came, the more heated the conversation looked. He stepped to her with white-gloved hands and touched her face.

She wrenched back, but I saw her playing off the movement, adjusting her rose silk bonnet in front of some onlookers.

Still too far to hear the conversation, I prayed she was taking this opportunity to disparage him to his face without apologies.

Don't stop because more people are gawking. A woman needed to say goodbye to pain, to move forward for power or pleasure or anything that pleased her.

I slowed my steps to give Athénaïre every opportunity to stand in this moment. My princess should know her worth, her beauty, and that a fool count was never meant to have her.

With more people stopping, she mouthed goodbye. Lifted her head and began to leave.

Count M put his hands on my daughter's shoulders, shaking her. I started running.

How dare he manhandle a princess!

Before I could get to her, Major Ernestus slipped through the crowd. He glanced at my daughter. Said nothing. Asked nothing. Then proceeded to punch the count in the jaw.

It wasn't French, but the language of good old fists. Blow after blow, he left the count's nose bloody.

"I think you broke my nose." Comte de Maltverne fell backward. "Stop."

"Must be drinking to think you can treat Fräulein Christophe like this." The major picked up the fool and struck him again. "Debauched fiend."

I watched as Ernestus beat all the crapulous hubris out of a fool. "What's going on?" I asked as I approached them.

Holding his face, Count M got off the ground and searched for his fallen top hat. "Madame Christophe, she's crazy. Crazy like her father, and she's found crazy people to protect her."

The major charged at the British buffoon again.

I held my hand out, to make him stay back, but he addressed the count. "If you look at Princess Athénaïre, I'll kill you. If you follow in her direction, I will kill you. If you ever write her a letter that doesn't begin or end with an apology, I will kill you. Je vais vous tuer."

That was perfect French.

The count took his dusty hat and trudged away, deeper into Lichtentaler Allee.

In minutes, the crowds on both sides of the Oos began to thin.

"Athénaïre, are you well?" I said. "Did he hurt you?"

Pushing at her rosy cloak, she glanced at Ernestus as if she were seeing the tall blond man for the first time, then back at me. "I'm fine, Maman. Just fine."

"Madame Christophe," Ernestus said with his chest puffed up and the military braiding on his uniform shining. "May I escort the princess to your inn?"

"I can answer for myself, monsieur." She rested her hand on his arm. My bracelet sparkled on her wrist. "Oui, Major Ernestus, I'd love for you to walk me back to the Auberge a l'Arbre Vert. And we have no need for a chaperone, Maman. I believe the major can keep me safe."

A blush tinged his cheeks, warming his peachy skin. He loved Athénaïre. The military man would fight for her. "Oui. I believe you are correct. Thank you, Major Ernestus. Perhaps stay for dinner as we finish packing. My daughter will let you know where we'll reside in Florence."

He nodded, glowing in sunshine, and I watched the couple walk away.

If Athénaïre could love him and forget the buffoon Count M, they would be happy. This man would make sure of it.

Leaning on the bridge, I listened to the swirl of the Oos. After an hour, I heard the familiar footsteps, then a shadow fell on mine. Seeing our dark silhouettes entwined in the leaves, stretching to the water, made the tension in me rise.

"Guten Nachmittag, Queen of the Oos."

If it were early morning or late in the night, I'd clasp Ludwig's hand. I'd fall against his chest and breathe the fragrance of cherry and sandalwood in his greatcoat.

I gasped a little when he boldly kissed my hand and let his lips linger.

"Madame Christophe. I seem to have missed some activity."

"You did, Prince Pückler. Quite a lot."

A feather fan waved in the distance. The prince started to move away, but I shook my head. There was nothing wrong with meeting friends on the bridge.

Lady Robert came to me, looking as spry as ever in a fur-trimmed hat and long cape of violet-dyed wool. "It's you. They said there was a fight over a Russian princess. Who did you get into a frenzy? Count Saint-Leu? His brother? Was it over the hundred and fifty million francs Hayti must pay to France?"

It was like being kicked in the stomach. I dwelled on the amount, which would take my nation decades and decades to pay. "Non. I've not seen the brothers. And you know me well enough to know that I don't discuss politics in public."

"Oh." She put her hand to her mouth.

"Lady Robert," Ludwig said, "the commotion was me. I was acting out a scene from . . . ah . . . *Othello.*"

"Guess I was Desdemona again."

Ludwig stepped forward and kissed Lady Robert's hand. "If we do encounter some ready gossip or a fight, we'll find you."

She dimpled and hit him with her fan. "You'd better. Safe travels to Florence, Madame Christophe. I shall see you there in a month. Too much intrigue in Baden-Baden to leave right now."

Titian hair perfectly coiffed, Lady Robert sauntered away. Heaven help the trouble she found.

In synchronization like waltzers, the prince and I turned back to face the water.

Ludwig sighed. "I was on my way to visit you Christophes. I received the latest papers and wanted to break the news about Boyer."

"A hundred and fifty million francs. I received word from my solicitors yesterday. They wanted me prepared if reporters discovered me here and wanted my reaction. Will there ever be a day when I'm not asked what I think of cowards?"

"I'm sorry, Louise."

"Boyer's going to take the people's money, their children's and children's children's money, to pay that ungodly sum."

"Governments always use taxation."

For a moment, I closed my eyes, reliving the foolish glee Boyer and his government must have felt surrendering Hayti's future. "I told you he stole Henry's gold from the palace and all the kingdom's treasury. That was at least twenty million. He could've used that to bargain with Baron de Mackau, but he and his minions kept it for themselves. He'll burden the people for these reparations. They've paid enough."

"Millions, you say?"

Ludwig's tone was light, but if that was meant to put me at ease, the prince didn't understand me.

"You're liberal and eccentric. I've told you everything about King Henry, how much we achieved. So don't be stunned that he had more cash on hand than King George IV or even your king."

"Everyone has more money than Frederick William III. But my king was a lover, not a financier. His first wife, also named Louise, was the love of his life. He mourned for a decade before marrying again . . . although his second marriage was for money, not love."

My prince's eyes softened when he mentioned love and Louise. Then he turned to the Oos when he mentioned money and a second marriage.

I supposed Ludwig was still a fortune hunter at heart. A repentant one.

The river kept talking. People floated by.

Not the crowd of before but a significant few. Yet most were used to seeing a prince and a queen dining or dancing upon occasion. Would Florence be as casual?

"You're clutching your wrist. Something else is upsetting you—not Boyer or the young fighting lovers."

He held up his palm, walked down to the brush by the edge of the river, picked a brown weed, and returned. It wasn't dahlias he'd brought me. Ludwig twisted thin twigs, braiding them until he formed a bracelet. "This is a feather reed, a natural grass used for baskets or flower arrangements. To cheer you up and remember me until next year."

Slipping off my glove, he slid it onto my wrist.

I touched the bracelet, spun it, then held it close to my chest. "Come with us. Join us in Florence." I blurted this out as fast as I could. Then stopped breathing, waiting for him to say non or oui or I love you, too.

He adjusted his dark top hat, which was wobbling in the wind, while staring at me.

"I . . . I should go see about Souliman. He's probably double-, triple-checking our route."

"Florence is nice this time of year." His voice became lower, even hypnotic. His hands touched my arms, sliding up the puffed sleeves of my mantle. Then he pulled back. "Why do you have this power over me, Louise? Why must you make an honest man of me?"

"You're the most honest man I know."

"Non. For I would've told you everything. And you must know everything. I can't come, not right now. In the morning, I head back to Muskau to formally seek a divorce from my wife."

I blinked, felt faint. Wealthy men had mistresses. Peers in England had them all the time. I didn't know Ludwig was married. Hadn't known, these past couple of years, that what I wanted belonged to someone else.

"There were rumors about you. That you had women in every city. I didn't think that included wives. And you said no one else. No heiress."

I brought my hands to my eyes, tears drizzling. "I'm so foolish."

Stepping away from him, feeling brazen, I was disgusted. I had once condemned Geneviève for this sin. Now I was guilty, too. "I must go."

Ludwig caught my hand. "Lucie and I have been estranged for years. Ours was not a love match. It was for money. We are friendly. I promised her that I'd never be faithful, only discreet. I've kept my word."

"Why are you telling me this now? Not when we met, when I could've guarded my heart?"

"Because I sensed you'd avoid me. And this fever I have for my Louise, that would only be my torment."

"So I must be tormented, too?"

Clasping my wrist, trying to hold to my sanity, I gave him what he needed to hear. "We shall part. We're not obligated."

A smile settled under his mustache. "We are obligated, madame. I'm in love with you."

"I must go, monsieur."

Not budging, he blocked my path, standing with his unbuttoned coat waving in the breeze. The exposed ebony waistcoat denoted a gentleman, one who should be respectful, not a cad.

"Goodbye."

"No, Louise. We can't end like this."

"But we must, Ludwig. Prince Pückler. We have to."

"You've told me everything in your life. I know what it means for you to love. I know what you suffered loving a king, but you love me. Let me make this right."

"You could've protected me."

"From love? Never. Admit what we both know is true."

I remained silent. The wind grew, rustling leaves at our feet, whipping at my frilly hem. I was a lady, a queen, a sinner.

"I have to go. I have to think."

"Promise me that you'll wait, Louise. That when I'm free, we'll be together. That you'll marry me."

"Not marrying again."

"Then we'll marry in our hearts and do what we must to be in the same place. We share one heart."

He claimed my palm, but I jerked my fingers away.

"Please forgive me. There's a word in German, 'frieden.' It means peace. I gained that from you. When you lose your anger, you'll see I've given you frieden."

"Peace based on a lie is no peace."

"I wasn't truthful, but I didn't think you'd leave the past. When we met, you were still married to the memory of a man. King Henry loomed everywhere in your thoughts. I know his edicts, his habits, his nightmares, and how it all weighed on you. Didn't know if I was enough to break you free."

I wanted to deny what he said, but it was true. I turned my back to Ludwig, hating that I'd told him about Henry. Hating that I wouldn't be the same if I hadn't.

With my grass bracelet sliding into the spot of my absent emerald, I asked, "So your wife will let you go? Will she be devastated, or do you intend to stay friends?"

"Yes. She's delightful."

"Delightful, but not enough to stay wedded?"

"It was her idea that I should find an heiress. But what can I say? I love the act of falling in love. I did that, then I met you. Now I know what it truly means to love."

There were no guarantees for us. He'd shattered my confidence. "I don't know what to say or think."

"I was timid. I'm sorry I didn't confess before this. But then I never would have known your love. Schöne frau, that would be the greater crime." He sighed. "Let me walk you back to the Auberge a l'Arbre Vert."

Ludwig led. His knuckles grazed my hand often, as if to encourage me to reclaim his.

I couldn't.

I needed to be away from Baden-Baden, from Ludwig.

"May I write, Louise?"

"You're married. Non."

Desperation spun across his countenance. He whirled me about as if waltzing. "Please, Louise."

"I do not control the post."

A dimple appeared, curled under his long mustache. "After the winter in Florence, try the spas in Bath and in Ireland in the spring. They're not as fashionable or as crowded as Baden-Baden, but there I can see you. I can't wait a year to see you. We can be together. We can be discreet. My divorce should be finalized."

"So the papers can blame the empress, ex-queen of Hayti, for ruining a prince's marriage. Non."

"Then we'll wait more time after my divorce to be together."

"I've tried to be a respectable widow. I'm done taking risks. Our time is over. My princess is not well. I can't make plans for next spring."

"Louise, plan on our being together. Marry me. You're an heiress. I like accomplishing goals."

Shaking my head, caught between crying and laughing, I became bold, leaned near, straightened the lapel of his greatcoat, and kissed him in the open on our bridge over the Oos.

"We'll just be a Baden-Baden intrigue. Au revoir, Ludwig."

"Glad you did not say goodbye. Never goodbye, Louise."

As if my sisters and I raced, I outpaced Ludwig toward the inn. He didn't turn away until I was inside.

Out of bed, Améthyste sat with her sister and the major enjoying tea. Head lifted, I went to my room and wept as I hadn't since the soldiers led me away from Henry.

With no plan for how to recover my heart, my eyes remained wet until the morn.

EXILE

Berkshire Chronicle, Saturday, March 17, 1827

Letters from Prussia say that Prince Pückler-Muskau, who was married to the daughter of the late Prince Hardenberg, has divorced her to marry the widow of King Christophe, a negress of Hayti, who is still young!!

43

1827 Florence, Italy

The hard wooden bench beneath me was carved from oak, sturdy and solid like Haytian mahogany, like the pews Henry made for the chapel in Sans-Souci. I sat in the cathedral of Florence, the Duomo, grateful the gossip linking me to Ludwig had at least called me young.

We weren't engaged. The letters he had penned remained unopened, but someone like Lady Robert had finally put all the clues together—our early walks, our public dances in the Promenadenhaus—to discover my lengthy romance with the prince and why now, after all these years, he was seeking a divorce.

Perhaps the friendly Lucie leaked our affair to the press to embarrass him or me. I deserved to be pilloried.

The priest spoke his prayers of forgiveness in Latin. I had mine written in my heart. I was humiliated and hiding but couldn't stop thinking of Ludwig.

Améthyste clasped my shaking hands. "This is impressive, Maman. If Père had seen this, this would be how he restored the church in the capital."

I nodded, for I wanted to encourage her.

"The marble is as exquisite as the high arches."

Sitting in the nave, we had the perfect view of the curves of the ceiling, the stacked stone that formed columns. We were told it had taken centuries to build.

"Do you suppose what Père built will last?"

The question snapped me from my guilty fog. "If it survives Boyer, it will survive anything."

She pulled on her thin cream shawl, the one made of Haytian cotton that she had taken with her from Sans-Souci. Though it was a wonderfully warm day outside, the temperature inside the church was cooler.

"Maman, you're frowning again. Is your first scandal upsetting you? Or the truth?"

I groaned. "Does your sister know?"

"Athénaïre is too busy preparing for the opera next week. Major Ernestus will be joining us."

Reveling in the major's attention, my younger daughter seemed preoccupied. She and Zephyrine had gone shopping for lace for a theater gown.

"We're living the life of the wealthy in Europe, Maman. We attend balls with kings and peers. It's like it was at Sans-Souci. I'm sickly, not blind. I noticed every time Prince Pückler looked at you, it was the same as Père, with love in his eyes."

"How can you say such, Améthyste? We're in church."

"Church is love, what better place to talk of it?"

"Améthyste, I'm mortified about the gossip."

"About the gossip, not about the truth that you've found love again?"

"This morning I went from our rooms to my bridge over the Arno. The walk is spectacular from the cobbled roads to see the mountains, and then this huge dome. It is part of my heart."

"Of course. We always love Florence."

"On my way back, I ran into Lady Robert. She congratulated me on my impending nuptials with Prince Pückler. She said everyone is talking of it, and she peppered me for details. I refused to admit to adultery on a public street. I can't do it in church, either."

"You're human, Maman. Père loved you, but his ambitions put you on the world's stage. You've had to be stronger than anyone. How could someone see your light and not admire you?"

I gripped the bench to keep from lowering on my knees and repenting. "We represent your père and the kingdom. I need to be beyond reproach."

"Restricting our lives won't bring back the Kingdom of Hayti. It won't resurrect Père or my brothers or anyone else we've lost. Being respectable didn't make world leaders ally with Hayti. They've turned their backs on the people."

My daughter whom I sheltered because I thought her weak had

become a forthright tower of strength, a citadel. "I've watched you, Maman, fighting for us, for money to live, making a space in the world for our royal Black family. I admire your strength."

The Duomo's priest bade the congregation stand. He offered a blessing. Yet it was my daughter's words that made me feel pure.

"*Sanctus, sanctus, sanctus, Dominus Deus Sabaoth.*" The singers' voices loud and strong repeated the hymn I heard so many times in Le Cap, "*Holy, holy, holy, Lord God of hosts.*"

The sweetness of the swinging incense, the rich frankincense, and cedar reminded me that faith kept us moving, kept us safe. The Lord made a way even when the path was obscured, when I was unsure of my footing.

The doors of the cathedral opened. The sun came inside. For a moment, I felt earth and heaven embrace, tightly and safely and bright. Blinking, blinded by the light, I felt seen and absolved. I breathed easier because of Améthyste.

One scandal, one season of living, hadn't destroyed me or Henry's legacy.

I was a good queen, one who'd find more ways to uphold the principles upon which our kingdom stood. "I'll serve the poor, Améthyste. The empress fed the people. I'll work with the church here to clothe and educate the humble. Those things mattered most to your père."

The congregation thinned, but my daughter and I waited. She busied herself studying the frescoes on the ceiling. "*The Last Judgment* again, Maman. This one isn't like James Barry's *Elysium, The State of Final Retribution*, but it's richer in color. You remember? We saw it at the Osborne, the first hotel we stayed in London."

"Oui. The murals. Then you found us, our place in that painting, the West Indian women with the angels."

Améthyste grabbed my hand, turning the bracelets I wore like bangles, the reed one and the emerald. "I promised you I'd live. You promise me, too. You're not a still painting, frozen and unmoving. You're not a marble column, cold and supporting the weight of the world. Even if you're my mother, you don't always have to be so strong. But you are a beautiful woman, Maman. A Black queen, Maman, forever

young and free. Your role, the thing you'd searched for, hungered and
wept for, is to be a proud woman with joy. That's it."

I hugged her tightly.

Her tender arms clung to me. "My wish is to build like Père, to make
something lasting that will live beyond me, that will honor him and all
I've learned."

Swiping at my eyes, I released her and saw the seriousness in her
countenance. "A church," she said. "I want to build one. They bury
people aboveground here."

If we did that, then at least I'd know where one of my children was
buried. And I could visit, bring flowers or burn candles. "I'll ask the
priests. They will know of any such projects that need funding. Now let
us get lunch. No more sadness for you or me."

"When Prince Pückler's business is finished, you should invite him
to Florence. I think he'll come."

"A year from now. With society knowing he's divorcing, I'm sure
some heiress will find him. Princes are good at being found."

She shook her head and hummed.

Nearing the exit, we passed the four-hundred-year-old clock steadily
ticking. My gaze went from Améthyste's proud face to the slow-moving
hands pointing at the passing hours. Thinking of the years it took to build
temples, palaces, or citadels, I'd have to make inquiries soon. My darling
daughter couldn't run out of time before our builders set a cornerstone.

THE OPENING OF A NEW OPERA ALWAYS HAD FLORENCE BUZZING. IN
the lobby of the Teatro della Pergola, known to all as the Pergola, we
waited for seats.

Adjusting my turban, tugging the sleek ostrich plume to the back, I
watched the others gathering for the performance of *L'ultimo giorno di Pompei*, *The Last Day of Pompeii*. I saw many familiar faces. It amazed me how
many I knew—kings and former kings, dignitaries, and revolutionaries.

Like the Christophes, many were representatives of opposing countries.
The slaughter and rampages had all been pushed to the side for polite con-

versation and evening gloves. The blur between right and wrong simmered to ambivalence. The stew became as tame as the soothing Arno.

"He'll be here, Maman," Athénaïre said. "Major Ernestus will arrive soon."

Her countenance seemed marred by worry as she flitted about in her gold Apollo dress. The silk sculpted her figure at the waist, but four petticoats made it float above the floor. The marigold silk ribbon embroidered about her hem announced she was special. This was a princess, one ready to accept an engagement. She'd taken a fancy to Major Ernestus, but there'd been no talk to me of marriage. If they had an understanding, it was a secret kept between the two.

"Don't be jittery, Athénaïre." The major worshipped the ground she walked on. His attention might start at her spectacular hem, but the lace of the bodice modestly covering the reddish-brown swells of her bosom would keep his gaze.

Decent, fashionable, beautiful—Athénaïre should be calmer, more assured of her gentleman.

Améthyste's slim figure looked well in an ethereal silk. This blue, the color of a sunny sky, had puffed taffeta sleeves trimmed with a satin band below the shoulder. The rest was sheer to her cuff, allowing a bit of caramel skin to be seen.

I loved how my girls weren't hiding anymore. Being here with people in this circle, our circle, our royal-exile community, meant I wasn't hiding, either.

Améthyste claimed her sister's hands. "The major will be here before we go to our seats. Maman, where will we sit? In one of the balcony boxes or in a row?"

In old Saint-Domingue, the Affranchi—the free Blacks and Coloreds—had boxes, up high and away from the Blancs. Glancing at her, I had no answer. "The seats will be good. I haven't fretted about chairs since our last fete at Sans-Souci. Let's not begin now."

Athénaïre kept pacing. The light of the sconces made her shimmer. So pretty, too pretty to be beset with nerves.

"Dear, when the major arrives, he shouldn't find you anxious."

"Oh, oui. I'll be calm." The poor girl kept jittering—so unsure of him or herself.

The street doors opened and the Bonaparte brothers entered, Count Saint-Leu, the former king of Holland, and Prince de Montfort, the former king of Westphalia.

With a nod to me, the count headed in our direction. "Madame Christophe, I'd heard you'd taken to Florence."

"Oui, Count Saint-Leu. Is that all you heard? I thought I traveled more."

He laughed and stood up straighter. "I see Boyer and the Bourbons have found a way to avoid war." He tugged at his white waistcoat and slipped his hand into the gap between two buttons. A king missing his sash?

"Both sides get to save face, madame."

"I suppose that's something, Count Saint-Leu."

With a nod, he walked back to his brother. That line of ambivalence seemed wider and clearer. There was no need to help him understand that though cannonballs didn't rain down on my island, paying reparations meant destruction. Schools and hospitals wouldn't be funded. Doctors and scientists my husband had brought to Hayti wouldn't stay to teach and educate and heal.

Unless something changed, Hayti would remain in poverty, while a world of riches kept advancing.

Lady Robert came to me, gazing through her quizzing glass. "Madame Christophe, you sly girl. Looking well as always."

Before I could respond, she waved to Madame Camac. The wealthy woman, now widowed, traveled the royal tour but still maintained her Hastings home.

With pleasantries exchanged, Lady Robert embraced Améthyste and Athénaïre. "Your daughters are as pretty as ever."

The twinkle of pearl and diamond pins in their chignons surely caught the woman's discerning eye. No longer did I fear spending money, particularly on my girls. They deserved the world.

Madame Camac gasped. "The gentleman coming inside. That's Prince Henry of Prussia. He's the brother of the reigning king. What a turnout tonight, all the royals. Not a nation skipped."

"You should go introduce yourself," Lady Robert said to me with a wink. "It's exciting when these families mix."

"Tonight's exciting. Plenty of ambassadors and politicians, and exiles of all sorts." I didn't take the minx's bait. Then I spied another acquaintance speaking with the Bonapartes. "Look, Viscount Chateaubriand came for the opera."

Wondering if he had another writer friend who'd need Greco-Roman pain for a novel, I turned my attention back to these ladies. "Spending Pompeii's last moments with this select group will be interesting."

"To be sure," Madame Camac said. "To witness and to belong."

Henry, my Henry, had wanted this, wanted our nation recognized by the people in this room. Though he had defended Hayti on the battlefield, he had failed at diplomacy. Nonetheless, his business acumen made it possible for my daughters and me to be here.

The king's widow and children were accepted by the elite of the nations.

Major Ernestus burst through the door. His normally pale face looked cherry red as he huffed air.

When he looked our way, he seemed relieved and blew out big breaths. Straightening, rising to his station as a man who led troops, he marched toward us. In uniform—red epaulettes at his shoulders, gold braiding edging a blue jacket above crisp white trousers—the tall man looked the part of a blond Adonis.

Stopping to bow to his Prince Henry, he conversed. Suddenly, the major's face turned redder.

Wanting a moment with the major, I stepped away, leaving the princesses to Lady Robert's questions.

A young page boy bowed in front of me.

"Madame Christophe," he said, "I'm to escort you to your seats."

"In a moment. We're waiting for Major Ernestus to finish with the prince."

The young fellow dipped his head and moved to the side.

With the speed of a hare, the major left his Prussian colleague and came to us.

"Guten abend . . . I mean bonjour, Madame Christophe. Sorry I'm late. I had a mission." From his jacket, he pulled dahlias fashioned as a small bouquet. "For you, from our mutual friend."

I took the beautiful bouquet and stroked the many petals. "How is Prince Pückler?"

"Managing. Doing what he can to minimize talk. He's traveling, writing, and finding things to do. When things settle, he wishes an invitation to Florence."

Ludwig's letters lay unopened on my vanity. Perhaps I should read them, but for now I had to do as Henry would. "What I must say is overdue. If the king were here, he'd have spoken to you about your intentions. It's obvious to all that you like—"

"Love, madame. Worship Princess Athénaïre."

A chill swept over me. "Worship of another isn't . . ." Staring into his blank eyes, I decided to be direct. "When will you ask for my daughter's hand?"

"I must make colonel. I know she's wealthy, but I'm not for her fortune. I wish to make a good home for her."

"And you cannot do that until you are promoted?"

"Some of my superiors will not approve."

"And you care what they think, sir?"

His lips became wry, and his eyes smiled. "Non. I know happiness, but I'm my father's son. Prideful. I must do all to be worthy of him and the princess."

"These superiors will disapprove of the marriage and any Colored children. Are you prepared to protect them?"

"I will love my Black children." His voice sounded strong, resolute. "The princess has told me much."

When his brow dipped and he glanced in her direction, I saw tenderness and understanding. He surely must know that skin color divided my nation, tormented my family, and made a princess feel lost. "Are you sure? Your superiors can be bothersome."

"Our children will be part of Athénaïre," he said. "They'll be the manifestation of the joy I have with her. On my life, I'll protect them. I swear on my life, madame."

This blond man could've been my dark, larger-than-life Henry, all the good parts of my husband. "Then Princess Athénaïre is blessed. When the time comes, I give you, Major Dieterich Ernestus, my blessing and support."

Athénaïre peered around his shoulder. Her hand looped about his. "It's time to go. Is everything well?"

"Perfect," the major said. This time his cheeks reddened because of my daughter's smile.

Feeling hopeful, I led the others behind our page.

Inside, the beautiful opera house bore painted ceilings and moldings along walls housing boxes.

"It's like Drury Lane," Améthyste said.

"Non. Like Saint-Domingue's Comédie du Cap." Sadness tightened about me; the arts, the ballet, the opera would struggle under an economy of reparations.

We passed doors that might lead to the upper balconies, and the page headed toward the stage. I grew warm under the chandelier lights. No boxes or seats in the back. We followed the smooth burgundy carpet to the front row, near the Napoleon brothers, who sat a few seats away.

Behind us were more dignitaries, more retired rivals on the battle-field. Farther away, toward the middle of the theater, were Lady Robert and Madame Camac.

With a thud, Prince Henry took his seat near ours.

I pushed upon my chest and sniffed at the scentless dahlias, wishing the flowers could be restorative. Realizing that the audience was seated in order of precedence, with former kings and a queen arranged first, shocked me.

Then it made me weepy.

My king's desire to be recognized as belonging to the reigning class, to be admired as much as the kings of Europe, had been accomplished in a Florence theater.

My gaze, which had blurred too often with violent tears, almost did so again. For strength, for clear-eyed optimism for the future, I fingered the tiny petals of the purple flowers, looked at my princesses, and savored the performance, *The Last Day of Pompei.*

EXILE

New Times (London), Saturday, September 20, 1828

He [Viscount Chateaubriand] descants upon the laws of nations as if he were an Envoy at the Court of Hayti.

44

1828 Rome, Italy

Viscount Chateaubriand met with me a few times during his visits to Florence. On his last, he invited me to Rome to meet the father of my faith. The stirring in my spirit, the unrest in Hayti, made me decide to go.

Having donned black velvet capes and mobcaps, my daughters and I walked with the viscount across the echoey marble of the Vatican. Chateaubriand was older, his hair wilder, but we'd come to a meeting of the minds.

I didn't understand French politics, and he still didn't understand the Black experience—let alone what it meant to be a Black woman.

Across the floor, a colorful marble mosaic of green and orange and burgundy, a man entered wearing white robes and a miter, a sleek pointed headdress wrapped in ribbons. I bowed to Pope Leo XII.

My whole party did.

Humble-looking, a little taller than me with a bent posture, the man from Genga, a little town north of Florence, peered at each of us.

Were we unusual to him—wealthy women of our stature and color? Maybe not. The Papal States were invested in advancing the gospel around the world. That included Hayti and Africa.

Still, it must be odd for this Blanc in his sixties. He'd lived through the times the church sanctioned the persecution of Blacks in old Saint-Domingue. Until our independence, the church put heavy restrictions on our participation in the faith.

"What is it that you pray for, Madame Christophe?" Pope Leo asked, his voice soft, a whisper. "Take a moment, then tell me."

This man commanded the Papal States. The ornate surroundings showed might and wealth, but he stood motionless, waiting.

Quiet strength.

The realization struck me that as queen of our kingdom I had had power all along. I kept looking for permission, asking to speak. Yet I hadn't used my voice enough to state the truth to Henry or his advisers when it mattered.

Quiet intercession.

"I ask nothing for myself, but for my daughters. I want them to find happiness and live long lives."

"Nothing is promised, Madame." His tone became lower, and it felt as if his soft brown eyes prayed for me.

"Then I . . . I . . . I beg for Hayti. I want it looked upon with kindness, accepted in the community of the world. I want Hayti to be sovereign and a blessed sœur in the family of nations, as King Henry I tried to make it."

Quiet action.

The pope held up a frail hand and prayed aloud. "Strength and peace to you, Madame Christophe and Hayti. Persist with faith in the hour of need."

Chateaubriand bowed.

We lowered our faces as Pope Leo withdrew.

Améthyste took ahold of me. "It's time for us to go. Thank you, Viscount Chateaubriand. We shall never forget it."

Athénaïre looked at me, her sharp gaze piercing my heart. She didn't see the blessing, she saw that, as Souliman would say, Dèyè mòn gen mòn, beyond mountains there are mountains.

She had to be wrong. That feeling in my gut of another gen mòn had to be wrong.

Our slippers tapped the tiles as we navigated the halls heading to our carriage. Remembering that last night in Sans-Souci, the sound of our feet fleeing echoed along the parquet floors. My work, our work, our suffering wasn't finished.

SOULIMAN STOPPED THE CARRIAGE AS CLOSE TO THE PALATINE HILL as possible. The man had done his homework. He liked learning the streets of a city. Europe provided an endless supply.

We shed our robes as he handed us down. "Madame, be careful. Lots of rocks here. But no better view of Rome."

"History says this is where the emperors built their homes. They would rise and see the Forum and the Colosseum." Améthyste pulled her sketchpad and a piece of charcoal from her long pomona-green coat. "Look how big it is."

Athénaïre came down, tying her bonnet into a big bow under her chin. "You see it, Maman. The columns lying down look like cannons." She ran to one, then another. "It's like the ceremonial ground of the Citadel."

Even the brown stacked stone looked like rubble bricks. My daughters followed me to the edge of the plateau. Scanning the horizon, I saw all of Rome, more buildings of stone, statues of marble around the Palatine. "This is glorious." If Milot had continued to grow and thrive, the view from Sans-Souci would be like this.

But it hadn't.

I wanted to blame Boyer and the others who had turned their backs on Henry.

But I was at fault.

The blame must be shared. The woman behind the man should've spoken up.

Athénaïre grabbed my hands and whirled me with her in a circle. It was glorious. "Major Ernestus says this is his favorite place to visit. His last letter talked of . . ."

Her voice trailed off as she ran down the hill. She kept switching from holding the hem of her light-blue gown to keeping her bisque bonnet in place. She stopped twenty feet short of an arch. "Look at this."

Souliman and Améthyste stayed near the carriage while I chased Athénaïre. She yelled and pointed like a child. "The inscription, Maman, 'To the Emperor Caesar Flavius Constantius.' This is over a thousand years old."

The Latin words etched in bronze said that the emperor was pious and fortunate and inspired by divinity. Other parts read of avenging the republic and triumphing militarily.

If Henry's military had fought for the kingdom, so much could've been different.

"No one fought, Maman."

"My Dieterich said visitors come every year to marvel at what the Romans built. This would've happened with Père's Citadel. This is what he wanted for us, for all Blacks. He wanted to build a legacy in stone. People should be awed by our accomplishments. One day Blacks won't only be known for shackles."

If only that could be true. In a world where the poor paid reparations to the rich, I didn't know.

"Look, Maman. Look."

Stepping closer, I saw raised panels that looked like frozen scenery. There were images of soldiers fighting an enemy. Another showed a ruler feeding the people.

My daughter turned to me. "Aunt Cécile says the Citadel is vacant. Cannons rusted. Aunt Geneviève writes that Sans-Souci is ransacked. Only the chapel was spared."

My brow furrowed, but I forced it smooth. "You've received letters from Geneviève?"

At first Athénaïre looked like she wanted to shove pillows into her mouth. Then she stood up tall, ready to take punishment. "Oui, just because you and Aunt Geneviève had words is no reason to cut away our relationship. If you haven't noticed, we're running out of family."

"That's not fair, Athénaïre. I made the right decision at the time."

"Have you never made a mistake, Maman?"

My heart raced. "I have, but I never betrayed family. Geneviève betrayed my trust, then she twisted up your father for favor. How can I forgive her when she hurt people I love?"

Athénaïre shrugged. "She wants forgiveness. Sometimes hurt people are the ones stumbling, hurting everyone, including themselves."

I didn't want to argue, but venom swirled in my gut. Pivoting to Flavian's amphitheater, which everyone called the Colosseum, I counted rubble stones, then broken slabs and ruptured columns. It calmed me and kept me from dwelling on how conniving and vengeful Geneviève had been. And oui, she'd hurt herself and others.

"With all of that damage, Maman, it's still here, still strong and standing up in this square."

Oui, I had survived her betrayal. Cécile and I—all of us had. "I'm not perfect, Athénaïre. Your père thought I was, but I wasn't. Some things are very hard to forget."

"Maybe you should try. Things go wrong and people get desperate."

"Do you think that's the reason she tried to take advantage of your père's madness? Desperation?"

"What?"

"I tried to protect him. I tried to protect our family, but everything worked against us."

"Père went mad? You're saying the man, the genius who could've protected everyone from France—"

"Couldn't protect himself. Henry wouldn't listen. Dr. Stewart wouldn't intervene. Vastey and Dupuy let him spin, faster and faster, until the top crashed."

She put her hands to her face. "Non. Non. He was strong. This is a lie. You say this so you won't feel guilty wanting Prince Pückler."

Athénaïre tried to run, but I held her fast.

"I didn't want to face it. I still don't want to talk of Henry's decline. It has nothing to do with any man. But I drown in guilt, for I watched your père drift to a place where my love couldn't reach."

"Non. It's not true. He was strong."

"Strong men break, too. Strong men hurt. And so do women."

As if we were dancing a reel, I turned her to Constantine's Arch. "Your proud père will be known for his buildings. For the way he brought education and science and art to Hayti; that's his legacy. Yet, if there were a way to take the whole man, the genius and the sufferer, and save a life or help someone heal, that would be Henry's legacy, too."

Athénaïre stopped fighting my hold. She turned in my arms and embraced me. "Don't tell, Maman. No one will understand."

Couldn't make that promise to be silent. That kept the pain roiling. "Non, Athénaïre. I cannot commit to anything that makes my voice go away. That's my legacy. That's how I'm learning to heal. I'll write to Geneviève and forgive her."

I smoothed the tears from her cheeks. "The Citadel will last. His princesses being happy is the legacy I want to remember when I think of your père."

The frown on her face meant she didn't agree with my choice, but she'd heard my words.

"Now dry your eyes. The major will meet us for dinner. Can't let anyone see you've been crying."

"Is that why you never cried for Père?"

"Just because you didn't see it doesn't mean it didn't happen. I grieved the man I loved. I grieve every day for what we lost."

"But you let your heart move forward."

"That was last year's gossip."

She pushed up my coat sleeve and exposed my woven reed bracelet. "I gave you back the emerald bracelet a year ago. You rarely wear it, but this is always on your wrist."

Sighing, I let her traipse back up the hill, with her anger puffing out of her mouth like steam from a teakettle.

Twisting my bracelet, I didn't chase. She was right. I enjoyed every one of Ludwig's letters. I hadn't been brave enough to return them, but now I would. No longer keeping silent about the things that mattered applied to my heart, too.

EXILE

Edinburgh Evening Courant, Monday, June 30, 1828

A singular circumstance took place Saturday evening, which has not been noticed in any of the daily papers. On the morning of that day Madame Buonaparte Wyse ordered her carriage early, and proceeded to the Horticultural Society's Gardens. There she met Prince Pückler-Muskau, with whom she walked about for some time and appeared to enjoy everything with great zest. At seven o'clock Madame Wyse left. On alighting from her carriage, she dismissed the coachman for the night, saying she would not go out anymore. About nine o'clock, a hackney coach into which the lady got, she ordered the coachman to drive to Green Park. The lady entered into the Park, and forthwith flung herself into the river.

45

1828 Dublin, Ireland

From the moment I read about the attempted suicide in the papers, I had to see Ludwig. From his letters, I knew he'd left England and spent the summer in Dublin. He was running, hiding from the guilt one felt for living when someone close had chosen to die.

With Zephyrine in tow, I took up lodgings in Dublin's Gresham Hotel, in a suite of rooms on the third floor with a view of the River Liffey. My bedchamber was a peaceful place, a large space with peach-painted walls, perfect to pace, to pretend I was near the sea. And wonder if Ludwig would see me in the morning.

It was a gamble.

I'd had no time to write in advance that I was coming. With the Thornton girls visiting my princesses and getting along well with the newly promoted Colonel Ernestus, my daughter's fiancé, I was assured everyone would be well entertained in Florence.

Améthyste had made my arrangements. Feeling stronger, she convinced me. She believed I still had a chance at happiness. There was a sense she was tidying up loose ends. The Convent of the Capuchins had accepted our assistance with their building fund. My daughter was getting to help with a chapel. Her goal to be a builder like Henry had started to come true.

"You are unpacked, madame. I've canceled dinner downstairs. I should've known after a full day of travel, you'd not want to eat."

"That's fine. It was different this time traveling without the girls. We won't be the same much longer. Not with one married."

Zephyrine put her hands to my shoulders. "Prince Pückler will visit in the morning. When he looks at you, you'll know if you have his heart and a future."

"At fifty, to a man in his forties, what will he see?"

"A queen. The vibrant woman he loved." She loosed the sash ribbon of my Damascene-purple dinner gown. "Get rest, madame."

She left the room, and I sank onto the bed.

Tugging at the front tape ties, I worked the bodice free and hoped sleep would be kinder to me than I'd been to myself.

HOURS AFTER I'D RETIRED, A LOUD KNOCK SHOOK MY DOOR, MY heart. Too heavy for my maid's delicate hand. I got out of bed, pulled on a creamy silk robe. "Just a minute."

"Madame Christophe, my fabulous Madame L, are you inside?"

Ludwig.

My pulse ramped. "My note said to meet for breakfast tomorrow."

"If you're not alone, breakfast at a café will be nice. If you are by yourself, breakfast in bed is better."

When I opened the door, my friend leaned across the threshold, dressed in an ebony tailcoat. His breath smelled of champagne.

Thicker sideburns framed his face, but his stirred-like-a-stormy-sea blue eyes remained the same. "I heard a Russian princess was here. I couldn't rest. I had to investigate."

"My note was hours ago."

"Meetings, balls, other heiresses who aren't as difficult had to be dealt with." He sauntered in with a big grin, sort of like Victor's when he'd done something he shouldn't.

He stepped closer. His thumbs fingered buttons on the cuff of my robe. "You were actually sleeping, your first night in Dublin?"

"I expected you tomorrow." Curling papers were in the locks I let fall on my forehead; my braids were wrapped in a scarf.

He lifted my cuff and exposed the reed bracelet. "What about us is expected?"

Oh, hell.

I reached up, pulled his pliant form forward and kissed him.

He tasted of sparkling sweetness. Or perhaps it was us. Our romance had been too long on the vine. I decided it was time to harvest.

Up in his arms he lifted me, whirling away satin and silk, wool tail-coat and pin-striped trousers, until skin met skin.

And I loved him and he me.

Generous, sweeping kisses took me back to Baden-Baden, to the moment my soul allowed Ludwig in. I chose to be worshipped, to give all to a prince. I chose my happiness.

A WEEK PASSED BEFORE I MADE IT OUT OF MY SUITE TO THE CAFÉ near the Gresham, on the river. I hadn't starved. Breakfast in bed was quite good.

My companion's freshly pressed evening attire didn't seem so odd. It was astute of Zephyrine to remember how to clean men's clothing.

"I can't believe you're here. I can't believe old Ernestus has come up to scratch and won the princess's hand."

"They've taken their time. They know each other quite well. They have no secrets. In fact, I'm sure Athénaïre knows when her Dieterich is in pain."

Ludwig's eyes turned to the river.

"Madame Bonaparte Wyse. I hadn't thought her so delicate."

"Bonaparte? I'll have to tell her uncles the next time I see them."

His head dipped. His wild curly hair held a sheen from my lavender soap. Or was it my lotions?

"Madame Wyse and I were friendly, but nothing serious, Louise."

"On your part, perhaps. But to attempt to drown herself after breaking with you, that's very serious."

"It's the trouble with her husband. She says he's mean to her, argumentative, even cruel."

The way he proclaimed this, the indictment ripped into my soul. "Was Monsieur Wyse well? Illness can account for changes in behavior."

Ludwig sat up straight, glaring at me as if I'd said something wrong.

"I came to help," I said. "When you're the one left behind when someone commits suicide, the guilt is tremendous. I didn't want you to face that alone. I know how illness can change a person."

"It's no excuse. Men can often be thoughtless to the ones they admire, like not admitting truths. I regret nothing but losing two years with you."

My hand covered his. "Ludwig, I'm sorry. Trust is very hard for me."

He placed our joined hands on the frill of my neckline, close to my heart. "I understand. You mentioned Henry's erratic behavior and the men he killed for looking at you."

"Monsieur Vilton was taken to the Citadel straight from the fete. The man was dead in his cell the next morning."

"Louise, the king had him killed. You've told me everything about Henry. I know you weren't able to help him and how it pains you. And I know you left him at the Citadel. You even described the lime pit up on Bonnet à l'Evêque. A caustic, nasty substance that can effectively hide what you never want to see again. You don't want Henry anymore?"

"The Henry I love will always be with me. As will you. Our time together will keep me happy."

"So you've come here to torment me. To tempt me. To give me anything except what I want: to have you always in my life. It is good I've taken to writing. I'll pen a novel of all my woe."

"Your letters, even the ones I couldn't answer, are divine. Writing is your passion."

His thumbs inched their way past my squared neckline, slipping through gauze and blush-colored satin to my heated skin. "You are my passion."

"Mine are consumed. You're free, Ludwig, but I've one daughter about to marry. One on borrowed time. I've seen that you're well. I think this trip has been successful."

"You've succeeded in being frustrating and divine. But do not break my heart again. Tell me we can continue."

In broad daylight, with the river calling, I felt brave. I wanted passion and him and to be happy. I leaned to Ludwig and offered a kiss, a long one with people watching. "Finish up your business, come be a part of this exile's world. Help give my princess the wedding of her dreams."

Fingers laced, Ludwig and I walked along the river and talked of flowers and the future.

EXILE

English Chronicle and *Whitehall Evening Post*, Saturday, December 12, 1829

The suite of Madame Christophe, the Ex-Empress of Hayti, who is at present at Dresden, consists of her two daughters (the [youngest] of whom is promised in marriage to a Prussian Colonel, who is a very handsome man, and enjoys a high reputation); the father of the Ex-Empress's nurse, and two waiting-women, who are all quite black. They are said to live in the greatest retirement, scarcely ever going out except to church, and employing the remains of their former greatness in acts of beneficence.

46

1829 Florence, Italy

We left Dresden for Florence shortly after meeting Madame Ernestus, the colonel's mother. She didn't approve of the marriage and made Athénaïre feel unwelcome.

It was odd, that feeling of rejection.

We'd been accepted by the aristocracy and peers, yet this woman from a lower class refused. The colonel stood up to his mother. Nothing but death would separate him from the woman he loved.

"A wedding on New Year's Eve, la fête de Saint Sylvestre, in Santa Felicita Church will be lovely." Améthyste started coughing again. She lay on a chaise in the front room of the lodgings I leased from Monsieur Giligni.

"Sœur, I hate to miss your ceremony, but you don't need me barking like a dog." Améthyste hit her chest, as if that would make her lungs work better. "Can't steal attention from you. It's your day, and you're too pretty."

"Dieterich thinks so." Athénaïre had tears in her eyes. "He should be here by now."

A silver veil was pinned on her thick braids, and pin curls adorned her brow. She was beautiful. Did she still not know this?

"If he comes . . . when he comes, you should be with us, sœur. We've been through so much together." Athénaïre paced across the colored tiles, wringing her hands. "After today, we'll be separating."

Standing in the window, listening to a nervous bride and her sister say goodbye, I adjusted the curtain and let the breeze inside. "Athénaïre, calm yourself. The choir will begin singing for you soon."

The wedding was to be a small gathering of guests, a few from the colonel's side, but not his stubborn mère. Lady Robert, Madame Camac, the Thornton women, and Marianne's husband and family were inside.

Moving up the date meant Ludwig wouldn't arrive in time. His meeting with publishers in London couldn't be changed. The weather might be conspiring against us, keep him there until spring. Both my daughters could be gone, one in marriage, the other . . .

Améthyste wheezed, then said, "Sœur, that's enough. Colonel Dieterich loves you so much. I saw your hearts come together."

Rushing to her, I knelt at the chaise. Her face was so pale. "You need to move more, Améthyste. Perhaps you should try. We need to get that blood pumping in you."

She put her brow to mine. "Time's almost drained away. I know it, Maman. You both do. Let there be peace between us."

Sniffling, Athénaïre slipped to the floor, taking no care for the yards of delicate lace used for her wide skirt. "What can we do for you?"

"Love each other fiercely. Love when you fight . . . when you laugh. Just love each other as I love you."

I wasn't prepared for the long goodbye—days or months of my flower withering. That time in Sans-Souci when her life hung in the balance, she'd almost left then. At least we'd had thirteen more years. "Remember, you pledged not to die."

She shrugged. The motion was so slow and stiff. "Some promises can't be kept, even to a queen. I'll live in your memories, and we've had so many."

Tears leaked over Athénaïre's face. "Who'll keep the peace when Dieterich and I visit Maman? Who'll help me get used to someone loving her who's not Père?"

I lifted her face. "My business, Athénaïre. And oui, you have the colonel. Know that he knows your worth. He sees that light in you."

"But he's not here . . . yet."

Her gaze went to the window. A hymn floated in and she whirled away from me.

Agnus Dei, dona nobis pacem.

Lamb of God, grant us peace.

The girl, my princess, had doubts. She hadn't learned. "I thought you had taken the time to heal, to learn your strengths. Why are you marrying a man if you have doubts?"

Her golden eyes lifted to me, exposing deep fear.

My pulse gonged in my ear like church bells. How did I not see this? Too caught up with Ludwig and Améthyste, I'd missed the deep wounds still puncturing her heart. A mixed marriage would be difficult, with every old prejudice still existing. Self-doubt could make it crumble.

Mopping my neck with a handkerchief, I forgot about the scandal of delaying a wedding or even disappointing a man I knew adored Athénaïre. "Perhaps we should wait until your sœur is a little better."

"Non." Améthyste craned her face toward a flickering sconce. Colored globes lit these rooms in a yellow-orange light. "Waiting is for fools who think they're promised tomorrow."

She took the sketches she'd tucked close to her chest and handed them to me. "My life has been well lived. I can truly say I lived."

I stretched the pages out on the floor. All the places we'd been were etched in charcoal. In the house in Hastings, she'd drawn me sitting at the big window looking out at the sea. The ballroom at Baden-Baden showed Athénaïre dancing. Another had Souliman lifting his cane at the Colosseum, marveling at the size.

She'd even captured Zephyrine peeking inside Hatchards at the book display. The last was a self-portrait of Améthyste admiring her completed chapel in Pisa. It was my daughter's design. She'd become a builder like Henry.

I flipped back a few pages and viewed images of Victor, Armande, and Henry, handsome Henry at the Citadel. I wish she'd drawn the night I'd found the three there, the king explaining leadership to his sons.

"He loved going up there." Athénaïre's voice sounded watery.

The lump in my throat grew bigger when I focused on the sketch of Henry by my daughter's bedside. His uniform jacket and sash and star hung on the chair back. The old brooch with the French, near the good father holding Améthyste's hand.

When I managed to swallow, I glanced at my girls. "We're whole.

Our memories have filled our holes. We do love each other fiercely. That's how we've survived."

Athénaïre picked up a page and held it to the light. "One of me and the colonel. It's of me in this dress and him in his uniform in the church. He hasn't come. You haven't seen him."

"He loves his military service, just like Père. We've seen plenty of soldiers on our travels. Lots on our trip to Dresden were heading to Russia." Améthyste took the sketch from her. "And I have pictured this day for a while. You're a beautiful bride and sœur."

Athénaïre gave the drawing to me. "Black and beautiful, my daughter Athénaïre. Remind yourself daily. Say it over and over until the sentiment becomes the melody you hum. Black and beautiful. You're worth every sacrifice."

I straightened Athénaïre's veil and smoothed her puffy sleeves. "Pray my words never leave your soul—Black and beautiful."

We were silent for a long time listening to the choir.

"When he comes, I'll be a perfect bride," Athénaïre said. "I can't disappoint him."

The door crashed opened. Colonel Dieterich Ernestus stood in full dress uniform—bright-blue jacket with a double row of gold buttons, gray pants with a long crimson stripe, white epaulettes, and a gleaming sword.

He charged directly to Athénaïre. "Non. No changing of your mind?"

A smile bloomed on her face, sweet and serene. "Non, Dieterich, my love. We will marry today."

A gasp fled his lips. He scooped up my daughter, swirled her around and around, then kissed her. Her arms cradled his neck. Time stilled as they enjoyed a tender embrace, a slow waltz, the blond Adonis and his Black princess.

He had enough love and care for both their souls. I coughed. Then I sighed. This was right. We had a wedding to start in Santa Felicita Church.

When he finally put her down, he kept holding her fingers. "I'm late because I have the minister coming here. He'll marry us twice. Once for my new schwester, I mean sœur, to see. Then in the church. We'll be man and wife and go to Stresa for our wedding trip."

"Stresa's part of the royal tour, Dieterich?"

"Where else would I take my beautiful princess but a place that is special to me? My father and I visited often. Good memories. I'll make more with you."

Athénaïre squeezed his hand. "That's perfect. Améthyste, draw this moment."

"Oui," my oldest living child said, then she settled again in the blankets.

To clear a path for the minister, I picked up the sketches, flipping through them one more time before handing them back to Améthyste. "I'll get them bound. We'll keep them forever."

Gratitude for the life we had, for how we rose from the ashes to make new memories, swept over my soul. This time I'd store up the good and not let it go. I'd not look for the next mountain.

At least, that was what I told my heart as I tried to concentrate on vows of love while my trained ears listened for Améthyste's last breath.

*What is due any man is in the eye of the
beholder—the dangerous abuser, the
desperately abused, and the deranged.*
—MADAME CHRISTOPHE, 1847

Kerry Examiner, Tuesday, May 18, 1847

Three deputies arrived via England from France by the last packet
[steamer] to make arrangements for the liquidation of the arrears
due of Hayti to France.

47

1847 Pisa, Italy

Monsieur Michelson's gig stops in front of the church, Chiesa di San Donnino. I look at the marble that Améthyste had picked from a local quarry. "My eldest daughter chose the stone. She liked all the different shades of gray. She noticed the little things."

"Do you want to walk, or are you tired?"

"It was a long drive, but it's a lovely one from Florence. Wide open spaces. Mountains and vineyards."

"It's beautiful." Michelson put on his sleek top hat. "And you've been a good tour guide."

"Well, no one respects the old as much as an old builder. We passed ruins and aged churches. Pieces of them last on those hills with minimal care. There was something comforting about things living beyond the builder."

My hands tremble.

They always do when I come here. Stalling, I start thinking of the sights of Pisa. "When we head back, we should pass the Leaning Tower and the Battistero di San Giovanni. You know everything leans over there, but the bell tower leans the most."

"Wasn't aware—"

"We should stop on our way back. At the baptismal, I can tell you the wonderful story of how Améthyste was baptized in an octagonal font. I dressed her in white. We sang hymns. The echo was amazing. It had to have reached to the heavens, to the Holy Father's ear."

Michelson steps down and adjusts his indigo coat before heading to my side of the carriage. "Let's take a tour of the church you built."

I don't budge. My body feels chained to the carriage seat. "I funded the convent, the Capuchins. One of the first revolutions in Saint-

Domingue was the Capuchins over the Franciscans. Did you know that?"

"Madame Christophe, why are you delaying?"

"If I go through those doors, then my daughter is gone again."

The reporter's hand covers mine. He steadies me as I weep. "Keep talking, madame."

"Améthyste held no grudge against anyone. She prayed for Hayti to be reborn. That all her father's good works, in education and science and medicine, be renewed. Those were her final words before she died."

Gasping, I look again at the church we built, made of the finest marble I could buy. Will it last as long as all the other monuments? That will be the ultimate testament of forgiveness and rest. We all need that in the end, to rest, to be at peace.

Michelson digs into his pocket, wrinkling his silky blue waistcoat, and offers a coarse cotton handkerchief. "I'm sorry for your daughter, madame."

"Don't be. Améthyste went to God with grace."

"Did she see what happened to King Henry?"

The reporter is back to pushing, and I'm back to fleeing. Wiping at my face, half-blinded with tears, I step out of the carriage. Then I stop and admire the carved frieze. It sits above the elegant threshold formed from contrasting green and gray marble. "Améthyste sketched the carving. It's *The Last Judgment*. The focal point in the middle is Saint John."

John with Henry's gaze and royal goblet. Hayti's nobles are on one side begging forgiveness and Boyer is being eaten by a wolf on the other. That was appropriate for the betrayers of the kingdom.

"What happened to King Henry, Queen Louise?"

"A king goes away when the kingdom falls. I'm Madame Christophe."

Michelson looks deflated, as if steam has escaped his stock and collar. "We've danced around this for days. You haven't told me what I need to confirm. This report says he was left for dead on the streets. He was left for the rain and jungle to decay and reclaim him."

"None of that is true. Boyer's lies. His final betrayal was to rob Henry of dignity," I said. "Did you know that fiend fled from Hayti? The pompous fool went into exile three years ago to avoid being slaughtered. He should've stayed and faced his sins the way Henry did."

"I'm not writing about Jean-Pierre Boyer."

"Perhaps you should. That man has no heart, no compassion. He could've spared Victor. He could've spared Armande. He executed boys, the young men who had futures. He killed most of the nobles who fought by his side against Henry, even the generals who'd have fought against French reparations."

I feel a sudden wave of heat. I pull at the cream shawl wrapping my shoulders, the smooth Haytian cotton that had been Améthyste's. I always wear it when I come here.

"Madame, are you ill? Do we need to stop?"

"Aren't you running out of time for the news article?"

"Yes, but I don't want you suffering."

That makes me chuckle, as if I can choose when sorrow comes. "Follow me."

We go into the church. It's quiet and cool inside. "The marble ensures it always feels like this."

My gaze goes to the altar. Two candles are lit. Someone has already visited. "Many Pisans came to love Améthyste. She did good works for the poor. Volunteering till her strength gave out. At least I know where this child lies; I can't visit any of her brothers' graves. I can leave them no flowers."

"I'm sorry, madame." His words are slow, heavy. "So sorry."

I go to her plaque on the wall. "My daughter's bones. They don't put you in the ground. They seal you in a wall. We live in a world of walls. Constructing them, painting them, hammering and even demolishing them. These things order and protect our lives. They maintain our privacy and secrets, but here we become part of the things we build."

Monsieur Michelson walks to the other marble marker and fingers the etched lettering.

I've had enough and go to the door. "I need some air."

"Of course, madame." Outside in the bright truthful sun, he says,

"We still have gaps. Many things to clear up. Help me. Do it for the king's princesses. They want the truth told."

"Insistent fellow. Let's walk a little. Then I'll tell you the rest."

He holds out his arm for my hand. This strong young man's shadow covers me. It's a good way to begin talking about the kingdom's end.

THE KINGDOMS

Britain

Morning Post (London), Monday, January 31, 1820

Death of King George the Third

Windsor, January 29, His Royal Highness the Duke of York "My Lord—It becomes my painful duty to acquaint your Lordship, that it has pleased Almighty God to take unto himself the King, my beloved Father, and our most Gracious and Excellent Sovereign. He expired at thirty-five minutes past eight o'clock p.m.

Hayti

Morning Herald (London), Monday, February 14, 1820
A Haytian Sermon—From the *Royal Gazette of Hayti*

"Let us sing the Te Deum, and raise our voices to Heaven for the King, the Royal Family, the Nobility, and the people Amen." The Court returned to the Palace to a sumptuous entertainment. The King drank to his brave and faithful Nobility. Nothing was wanting [for] the joy of the occasion.

48

1820 Church of St. Anne, Kingdom of Hayti

Not too far from the palace, our carriage approached a small parish that serviced the town of Milot. The high bell tower loomed above as Henry readied to descend.

"Wait," I said and took his hand. "You could say you're not feeling well."

"It's your birthday. It's a holiday for the kingdom. I live for the days to honor you."

"Last night you dreamed of my brother Noël." Noël had died in a violent storm. He was struck by lightning while on guard at the Citadel.

"I tried to save him." Henry's voice sounded gravelly and sleep deprived. "Couldn't get to him."

I didn't know if he was talking about trying to save my brother in 1818 or in the nightmare. Couldn't tell anymore.

"Henry. You need to rest. Listen to me."

He shook his head. Dressed in a dark coat and buff breeches, he put his new bicorne on his head. His hair, graying from worry and fits of temper, made his fifty-two years look so much older.

"You're working too hard. Let's go back inside the palace. Let me put you to bed."

His brow rose. "Will you join me in my repose?" His hands went possessively about my waist. The embrace was tight, crushing, wrinkling the ivory gown that Zephyrine had taken hours to press.

"You've avoided my bed—"

"Since you had Gaffe, your executioner, kill a harmless drunk and the archbishop." I glared at him.

"Monsieur Vilton caressed you. He came to my palace and tried to make love to my wife in my ballroom."

That wasn't what had happened. "He bumped into me by accident, then steadied me so I wouldn't fall."

"No one is to touch you. Being drunk is no excuse."

"And Brelle, our archbishop? He was a servant of the pope, a man of God, and you slew him."

"Louise. He was a traitor. I was given evidence that the priest was working with Boyer. They want to overthrow me. That's a crime deserving capital punishment."

"It was hearsay. The archbishop never confessed."

"They are all like Pétion. They will kill me."

"Henry." I put my hands to his face. "Pétion is dead, too. Boyer took his place, but no one in the south can harm you. Listen to me. You're not well."

He drew me close and kissed my lips, but I pushed him away, forcing his shoulders to the seat back. "This is not the time."

"You love me. Tell me you still do?" The man trembled. His eyes looked glassy, and perspiration trickled down his forehead. Had my show of strength unsettled him?

I gripped his hand. "Please, Henry. I need you to take care. Please go back and rest."

His rapid breaths slowed. This time his embrace was easy and true, not frenzied. "After your birthday celebration, I'll rest. I promise."

That was the most I could hope for.

I wouldn't protest or nag. Against my better judgment, I gave in to the king's need to be showy.

He fingered the strand of pearls that he'd given me that morning. "This is perfect. The people will know I love you as much as they do."

The pearls were perfectly sized and shone in the light. The sweet gesture hid the jealousy I knew was simmering in his gut. While I was lauded by the people, Henry had become more hated. Only his newspaper and close advisers didn't vilify him.

"Ready, my dear?"

Non, I wasn't. But I stepped from the carriage and clasped his arm.

The simple church we entered was dedicated to Saint Anne, the mother of the Virgin Mary, the patron of married women, maidens, mothers, and women in childbirth. Seemed odd to have service here when women in the kingdom remained angry at Henry for edicts forcing them into marriage.

Henry jerked as if he'd heard a gunshot. I steadied him as he stumbled. "You need to sleep. You haven't in days. You're either at the Citadel or looking out of your telescope searching for French ships."

"They'll come, Louise. They aren't done with Hayti."

Side by side, we stepped into the church and took our seats in the front pew.

Dupuy and Stewart and his other close advisers were here.

"Cécile has come?"

Her husband, Louis Michel Pierrot, formerly Comte de Valière, had been elevated to Duc de Valière and a prince of the realm. He irritated me. Sometimes he didn't seem kind to Cécile, even jealous that her name was celebrated and his was not known.

Louis Michel beamed, adjusting Henry's silver star on his uniform. Did power and money make men change?

My sœur waved at me. Cécile wore a red and green tunic with matching turban. Her outfit was very pretty and regal and yet unlike the Eurocentric costumes of Henry's court.

Henry looked straight ahead. He rocked back and forth with his arms folded.

I put my palm on his knees to calm him. "This shouldn't take long. Then sleep."

The choir began singing a hymn, "Agnus Dei."

It was beautiful—Lamb of God.

Agnus Dei, qui tolis peccata mundi,

Lamb of God, who takes away the sins of the world,

miserere nobis.

have mercy on us.

Agnus Dei, qui tolis peccata mundi,

Lamb of God, who takes away the sins of the world,

dona nobis pacem.

grant us peace.

Marching to the slow rhythm of the song, the priest came up the aisle holding aloft a golden crucifix. The glint of the sun on gold made me squint.

Henry covered his eyes and shook in the pew.

My heart thrashed. He couldn't control himself. "You're not well, my king. People will understand. Let's go."

"They never understand, Louise. Never."

His skin paled. His mouth stretched wide, and he screamed with the terror of his worst nightmares. "A ghost, Louise! He's come because I slew a lamb of God."

He slipped my grasp and leapt up. "Brelle, go away!"

Saint Anne's priest fell silent.

The choir hushed.

"Brelle!" Henry kept shouting and pointing to nothing. "Brelle! Brelle!"

"My king, he's dead. The archbishop is not here." Trembling, wishing to awaken from this nightmare, I was at his side, ducking his swinging arms.

"A conspiracy," he said. "Some sort of conspiracy. Your sister did this."

"Cécile has done nothing. This isn't Vodou. It's exhaustion. You're confused."

"You're confused! It's Geneviève who's done this!"

A gasp at the rear came from my younger sister's lips. What could that wild girl have done involving the archbishop? Witnessing her running out of the church made my mind conjure everything from stealing tithes to bedding Brelle on the cathedral's steps.

People glared at me, at Henry, then the church doors slammed.

"Brelle is here for revenge, Louise!" Henry whipped off his hat, then tossed it toward the baptismal font. "He's come for me!"

Mouths opened, countenances looked stunned. Brash advisers became limp—Stewart and Dupuy were nailed to their seats. They let the king rant about a ghostly vision only he could see.

"Do something!" I commanded them. "Stewart. Dupuy, help your king!"

"Oui, Your Majesty." Dupuy, the thick pumpkin of a man, leapt up and commanded the choir to sing louder.

"Agnus Dei." The robed men and women chanted. "Agnus Dei"— Lamb of God.

Their voices covered the king's shouts.

Then Dupuy turned in the opposite direction and cleared the gawkers out of the church.

"Agnus Dei." The choir kept repeating the Latin lyrics. "Agnus Dei"—Lamb of God.

The doctor finally moved, stepping in front of the altar. "Your Majesty," he said to the wild, swatting Henry. "Let's get you back to the palace."

Stewart tried to touch his arm, but Henry leapt away as if he'd been set on fire.

"Agnus Dei." In robes of white, belted in black, the singers lifted their hands. "Agnus Dei"—Lamb of God.

The priest bowed to Henry. "My king, please forgive whatever we've done to offend you."

The crucifix in his hand glimmered in my eyes. Blinking, blinded, I couldn't get to the king.

Henry screamed louder.

"Agnus Dei," the choir sang. The hymn sounded so loud that it seemed the roof might collapse. "Agnus Dei"—Lamb of God.

A thundering crash exploded on the parquet-tiled floor.

The choir shrieked. Footfalls fled all around me.

I fought past the priest to find Henry lying in front of the altar unconscious.

AS FAST AS POSSIBLE, STEWART AND DUPUY PUT HENRY IN MY CARriage. With Henry's head in my lap, we sped away from Saint Anne's.

Stewart checked for a pulse. "His heart is still beating, Your Majesty. I'll figure out what this palsy is."

"Can you restore him?"

He gave me the same look that he had when I asked about Améthyste's care.

Glancing down at a silent Henry broke my heart. "He'd just started rebuilding the capital. The programs . . ."

"Your Majesty, if the king doesn't recover, you may have to rule as regent with Prince Victor."

"My son is only sixteen! He can't be the king."

The doctor knelt and put his head to the king's chest. Stewart's fingers tapped as he counted. Then he said, "The prince is not ready. That's why you have to consider being the regent. You're popular, ma'am. The people will follow you."

Me? "Non. I wanted a role in shaping the kingdom, at Henry's side, not as his replacement."

"You have no choice. The nation is King Henry. It will wither if he dies. Everything he tried to do will go away if you fail to lead."

Cradling the listless king, I wondered how any of us would survive.

HAVING TEA IN THE BLUE PARLOR NEXT TO HENRY'S BEDCHAMBER seemed like it should be a respite from the chaos—his ministers and generals coming in and out for updates between Dr. Stewart's bleedings.

Yet it wasn't.

Geneviève sat opposite me in a slate-colored chair, offering comfort. How could I be soothed when I didn't know what was true and what was lies?

"Louise, you're quiet."

Leaning back against my chaise in the same dress I'd worn to church yesterday, I nodded and added more sugar into my tea. "Good of you to come."

My sister played with her fork, tapping a slice of my birthday cake, the gateau au beurre I'd served to my sister hoping she'd think I was calm, even happy to see her. But I seethed. What had she done to Henry?

"Cécile said the king cried out like a madman before he fell ill. Dupuy is telling everyone it's a fever. He says the king will be up in days. The way the doctor looks, it has to be more serious."

"You had a civil conversation with our older sister? Miracles are real."

"It's easier to talk with her with Louis Michel around."

Flexing my finger along the handle of the teacup, I failed at sounding calm. "That's good you appreciate our sister's husband. But what of mine? You haven't gotten along with Henry in a long time. Are you hoping for him to die?"

"Non! Never!"

All the things Geneviève had said about neglected husbands turning to other women echoed in my ears. "What have you conspired to do?"

She forked a huge piece of cake into her mouth. "I don't know what you are talking about."

"You know what I'm talking about. He shouted the archbishop's name . . . and yours. Brelle and Geneviève. Why? What did you do?"

"Non. Nothing."

"Tell me what you've done," I groaned at my baby sister—the one I'd always tried to protect, to encourage—forcing her to meet my eyes.

For a moment, her lips trembled. Then she looked away to the ceiling as if she could hide in the whitewashed trim.

"You tell me now, Geneviève. I demand to know. Your queen must hear your sins."

A fragile gaze fell upon me. She twisted her fingers in her lap. "He caught me in adultery."

I swallowed, waiting for the gut punch. "With Brelle? The man was holy. He's married to God."

"Non. With Louis Michel."

I felt as though she'd kicked me in the stomach. "Cécile's husband! Your own sister's husband."

"Oui. On one of his tours of the kingdom, the king found us. Louis Michel confessed everything to Henry. We've been lovers for years, starting when Cécile was away helping the old empress. That's why

Louis Michel was only made a count at first, and I was made nothing. We both had done this, but I paid more."

My cup clattered as I dropped it onto the saucer. I should have been stunned at the admission, but I was silenced by Geneviève's lack of remorse. She had no sorrow for how she broke our sister's trust, only over being caught and not elevated.

"Say something, Louise. I fear your judgment more than anything."

I coughed and rubbed at my dry, dry throat. Her wide fiery eyes held no contrition. I knew there was more. "Henry said Brelle's name, and then yours."

"Brelle was turned in by my lover—"

"The Blanc merchant, the one you won't let any of us meet?"

"Oui. He discovered Brelle traveling to meet with the south's new president. The archbishop was plotting against the king. My lover thought if I gave the information directly to Henry we'd be rewarded from the treasury. I broke with the merchant and decided to use the information to secure an elevation for Louis Michel. That's why Louis Michel is now a prince of the realm and a royal duke."

"Was the archbishop truly plotting to kill Henry, or was that a lie?"

"The king's guards found documents in the archbishop's possession that the enemy might use. I think Brelle was guilty."

"And the elevation would again gain you favor with Louis Michel, your sister's husband? You want him again?"

"I had to make up for my carelessness to him." Her gaze dropped to her lap.

"You're still in love with him? Your sister's husband!"

"Does it matter? He's not leaving her, and she gets to be a duchess. Cécile doesn't love him, not like I do."

Slamming my hands to my sides, I wanted to throttle her. "You aren't sorry for the hurt you caused our sœur or a man's death."

"Louise, I'm not a bad person. I fell in love with the wrong man. And Louis Michel, he—"

I put my hand to her mouth with a forcefulness just shy of a slap. "I don't want to hear any more. Get out, Geneviève. You've broken my trust, our sisterhood, our family's bond. If Henry had been weak like Louis Michel, would you have committed adultery with him, too?"

"Non. I love you too much to hurt you."

Lies. All lies. I saw her clearly for the first time. "You should've loved our family more. More than money, more than a title. Go from me so you can't hurt me again."

She drew back. "Louise, please."

I clapped for the guards. Two of the Dahomets came with bayonets drawn. "Oui, Your Majesty."

"See this woman out."

Geneviève pushed past them. All headed into the hall, then she turned back. "I'll leave. Know that I'm sorry. Tell Cécile—"

I rose, ran to the door, and slammed it.

Then I cried and tried to reimagine my world without my closest friend, my little sister. I had once laughed at the court intrigues surrounding the prince regent of England. Now, I understood that wherever there was ambition, a royal court, and regal women, there would be pain and pride and punishment circling for power.

THE KINGDOMS

Britain

Morning Post (London), Friday, September 1, 1820

France in 1813, under the Continental System, consumed only 14 million pounds of sugar, and at this time uses 80 million, nearly sixfold [more] through the reduction of price by importation freed from restraint.

Hayti

Morning Chronicle, Wednesday, September 13, 1820

I have lately conversed with a most respectable merchant who has had several interviews with his Majesty, and assures that his Majesty may be considered as absolute Monarch, yet he pursues every means in his power for the education, improvement, and eventually, the independence of the people. As they are prepared by education to form a correct estimate of law and political economy, it's his Majesty's intention to establish a more liberal and constitutional system of Government.

49

1820 Palace of Sans-Souci, Kingdom of Hayti

I sat by Henry's bed, holding his hand, waiting for him to wake up. I had the door to the terrace bath open. If he sat up, he could see his copper tub, his telescope, and my gardens.

Pulling a jade rosary, a gift from my maman, out of my pocket, I draped it onto our linked hands. "You have to wake up. I'll read to you one of our old fairy tales, something with a castle and a handsome king."

Améthyste came inside. "Maman, can I bring you something to eat?"

"I'll eat when your father does." I tried to smile but couldn't.

Victor's voice boomed, howling, calling my name as he barged into the room. "Maman! Make him stop. Baron Dupuy says I need to be ready. He's trying to say Père won't make it. Command . . . command him, command them all to never use those words again!"

His shaking voice grabbed my heart and squeezed it still. My son was disheveled, frazzled, and fearful of the future.

Leaving the beads with Henry, I waved my children to me. "Your father is strong. Don't believe anything else."

"Was he raving, Maman?" Améthyste asked. "I know when I'm sick the fevers make me see things."

Patting their backs, I sat down again in the seat I'd occupied for days. "We just need to keep praying. Now go on. I'm sure you need to study."

They went to the door, but Améthyste spun back. "I'd like to sit here for a while. Père has done the same for me. I know it comforted me."

If it eased the worry lines in her brow, I'd take the risk. "For a little while."

She pulled the mahogany chair closer, the match to mine that Dr. Stewart used when he kept watch.

An hour dragged by, then another.

When I stood, about to send Améthyste away to her bed, Henry's eyes opened.

His gaze at me looked angry, almost accusatory.

"Améthyste, go get Dr. Stewart. He's asleep in my parlor across the hall."

My daughter smiled. "Père's awake! Oui, Maman."

She left the room and I returned to Henry's side. "Thirsty?"

His jaw worked from side to side. Then he turned his face away. "Get out, Louise. You can't see me weak like this."

"Henry, you're my husband. In sickness and in health."

He grunted and cried out, dragging his arm toward me. Pained, groaning, he made a fist. "Go!"

Dr. Stewart came inside wiping his eyes. His shirt was undone, and he wore no jacket. "You're awake, Your Majesty."

"Stewart, make the queen leave. Then tell me how long before I die."

"Now hold on, Henry. Nobody said nothing about dying."

"I can't feel my legs. I can't feel anything below my chest."

The physician looked at him, then turned to me. "Your Majesty, please. Let me examine him—"

"Just make her go. She can't see me like this."

I fled the room, running back to my parlor. Inside, I flopped to the floor. Neither Victor nor I was ready to lead Hayti without Henry. If Dr. Stewart couldn't fix the king, all would be lost.

DUPUY AND VASTEY LEFT THE KING'S BEDCHAMBER LATER THAT night. It was all Henry's now. He'd kicked me out, saying the queen shouldn't share a bed with an invalid. The man was filled with rage.

I didn't know what to do, but his men did.

"Gentlemen," I asked, deliberately keeping my voice low and calm, "do you think the king can rule in this state? Does he need more time to recover?"

Vastey looked tearful. "The hope of a free world, one of power and equality, is in that room, and he wants to die." He shook his head and went down the hall.

"Dupuy, we've never seen eye to eye, but we must for the kingdom. Tell me what to do."

He rubbed at his brow. "Victor should reign, but the king won't say the words to allow it. He won't give up the throne."

"Then what is to happen?"

His handkerchief went to his perspiring neck. "He must let you be regent. We have to forestall rebellions. The gossip is out that the king is impaired. Our enemies are planning attacks. Boyer's looking for an excuse for a military offensive. The kingdom will crumble. Everything we've worked for will be gone."

He started to walk away, and I caught his shoulder, right where Henry's star glimmered.

"Please, Dupuy! Help me help him! I'm frightened."

"The king, my friend, told me to take off this star and to plan an escape for you and the children. He's given up." To his credit, Dupuy kept the brooch on but continued to walk away.

This couldn't be happening.

One man wasn't the kingdom.

I turned to the closed bedroom door. Muffled curses filtered through the wood.

A crash sounded.

Barging into the room, I saw Henry's food tray on the floor. Tea and soup had sprayed everywhere. "Henry, are you all right?"

He bit his lip. "Get the doctor and servants. I soiled myself."

The odor of urine hit me when I bent to pick up the tray. "Henry, I can wash you."

The proud man threw back his head. Tears trickled down his face onto his embroidered nightshirt. The gold star near his collar had stains from the soup. His dominant hand quivered. "Please go, my queen. You can't see me like this. And I can't be in this world and not be able to defend you or the children or what I've created."

Taking the tray, I did as he asked. "I'll send the servants and Stewart. But remember it was we who made this, Henry. I supported you. I tried to help. Maybe if you let me help now, then we could share this burden."

"You can't love me like this, when I can't do anything. The rebels will come. My soldiers are already surrendering and joining the enemy. France and Boyer will pick over the kingdom like scavengers."

"Then you have to keep fighting. You're Henry Christophe. You helped liberate our world."

His head sank into the pillow. "Send servants. Do this one thing. Act like you still respect me."

Carrying the tray, I left Henry and went searching for Stewart and Souliman and the royal valets. I did respect Henry, even if he still didn't realize that the love I had for him was for him, not his ability to walk. It didn't matter.

Henry had chosen to die and take the kingdom with him.

DRUMS POUNDED ACROSS THE KINGDOM. IT SOUNDED LIKE SAINT-Domingue during the last months of the war. Those rhythms had kept the people organized and in contact. I'd heard them in the caves where I and the children hid.

We had waited for Henry to tell us it was safe to emerge.

Now these heavy drums summoned the people to rise up and attack Henry's dwindling forces. Sans-Souci stood silent, motionless, vulnerable. All the servants but my faithful two, Souliman and Zephyrine, had fled.

My Dame d'Atour, my lady-in-waiting, princess of Limbe, Madame Dieudonné Romain, had resigned with her regrets.

That hurt.

I'd thought her a loyal friend, and maybe she was but couldn't defy her husband. Romain had joined the rebellion.

Dupuy came out of the bedchamber. His face was red, his fists balled in anger.

"What has happened? Henry?"

"Your Majesty, we received word the enemy marches tonight. Boyer is coming from the south. He will take Sans-Souci. Too many of our Dahomets have been slaughtered keeping our own nobles at bay."

"Our Duke of Marmelade, too . . . he's turned as well?" He was one of Henry's first supporters.

"Oui," Dupuy said, "and add Limonade. The only ones left are your sister's husband, Noël Joachim, Jean-Philippe Daux, and the Dessalines. No one else is willing to fight."

Leaving me with my mouth hanging open, Dupuy pounded down the hall, then stopped. "Your Majesty, what's left of the Dahomets will hold off the traitors long enough for you to take your children and go. Get out of the country. The king has given Sir Home Popham money for you to live. He does love you."

"I can't leave my husband."

"Go pack. Now!" The king's faithful friend trotted down the stairs. "I'll see how the lines are holding."

Everyone knew more than I. I ran to Henry's bedchamber.

Stewart had gathered the children—Victor, Armande, Améthyste, and Athénaïre. They stood around the bed.

Henry was propped up on pillows. His nightshirt was clean. His face was freshly shaved, with his star cleaned and shining on his chest. Beside his hip was a silver box.

"I want you all to know how much I love you. I want you all to mind your mother. You go with her, Armande."

They all had wet eyes. They knew this was goodbye. With the terrace door open, letting the drumming inside, Henry had to know his forces were surrendering or dying or both.

"Go, my children. Know I love you. You're all my legacy. Show the world your pride."

They piled on the bed kissing his face. His arms worked enough to embrace them. He prayed a blessing on each one. Then they left, but not before glancing back.

Didn't know what they thought or if they like me prayed for a miracle to change things. I closed the door and waited until I no longer heard their steps. "You intend to surrender to the mob?"

"Non. I don't want to be torn to pieces like Dessalines."

"Good. Then we will fight."

"We've run out of time, Louise."

"Please, Henry, for me, the children, for everything you championed, don't give up."

"Non. God has taught me. I thought I was invincible." He hit at his immobile legs. *Thwack*. They didn't jerk or twitch or respond in any way. "I don't feel that, Louise."

"Henry. You're not a quitter. You're still strong. Let us leave. We can go into exile."

"I'm not prepared to leave the kingdom."

"We can calm the crowds by saying you abdicate." My eyes stung, but they remained dry. "Victor can reign with a regent."

"He's weak. They'll cut him to pieces. Escape before they touch you. There's money with Sir Home. I sent money with him, lots of it."

Wanting to go to him, but knowing he'd again order me away, I anchored my feet in place, wrapping my arms about me like taut ropes to keep from the bed. "We started this journey together under a pepper cinnamon tree. I'm not leaving you. We'll face this together."

"The mob doesn't care. They'll tear me apart. I don't want that, but it's what I deserve."

"You don't deserve that!"

"Oui, I do. I knew of the assassination plans for the emperor but did nothing to warn him or stop it. I was his second-in-command. This is my punishment."

Hoping this was a fever talking or some sort of babbling, I ignored it. "If you keep living, you can make amends."

"Get out of here, Louise. I don't want to talk anymore. Words don't work. Dupuy brought me something that will."

His fingers jerked and he clasped the gleaming box. "Louise! Your king is asking you to leave the room! I cannot live like this. I'm too afraid of being weak, even for you."

I wouldn't move. My gaze was pinned to him. "Non. We can be strong together. We can flee together."

Henry proceeded to open the box and take out a silver gun.

My feet slapped the parquet of our bedchamber. I ran toward the bed. "Non! Henry, don't! Our children. Me. Non!"

My husband placed the weapon in his mouth and pulled the trigger.

His head reared back. The bullet shattered his skull.

50

1820 Castle of Sans-Souci, Fallen Kingdom of Hayti

I finally washed Henry clean of the blood. Souliman and Dupuy helped Zephyrine and me lift him into the copper tub.

In the warm water, with soapberries, I scrubbed his face and shut his eyes.

"I have spices," Zephyrine said. "Then we'll wrap him and find a place to bury him."

The drums sounded louder.

Dupuy dried his hands. "No, you have to leave. You have to hide. It will take days to arrange a boat to get you to safety."

I stopped kneeling at the tub and walked to Henry's telescope and peered through it. No lights shone at the Citadel. It was as if it was already in mourning. Moving the lens toward the capital, I saw torches lining up. "Do we hide in the woods again? The rebels are coming and the king is already dead."

Souliman grunted. "Rebels want blood, madame. If not the king's, yours and the children's. We all must flee."

"King Henry I needs to be given a proper burial. He's not a criminal. He's royalty. He deserves better than to be abandoned."

Zephyrine sobbed. "The king leveled the ground here. He changed it to satisfy his will. Perhaps there's room in the crypt beneath the chapel."

Next to André Vernet, Prince of Gonaïves—Henry buried him there, like a state hero.

"The mobs will tear up the palace. Someone will notice it's been disturbed," Souliman said as we lifted Henry from the tub and placed him on sheets imported from Hamburg.

I put his star on his chest, then covered his face. "They will find the crypt and rip his body to shreds, like the fiends did to Emperor Dessalines."

There was a voice at the door. "I know where."

I lifted my gaze.

Dupuy gasped.

The last person I thought I'd see stood in the doorway. "Cécile. Does everyone know?"

"Dr. Stewart is in Cap-Henry, trying to leave Hayti. They all know it's a matter of time. I'm here to help, to save you and the children."

She held me up in her arms. I wanted to collapse, but a queen had a duty to her king. "Let's take him to the place he loved the most. Then we escape."

"Oui," she said.

We all agreed. "We'll bury Henry at the Citadel."

SMOKE AND GUNFIRE FILLED THE NIGHT AIR, BUT WE GATHERED what we could from Sans-Souci. I doubted that I or the children would see it again.

Athénaïre held the bundle with my jewels. "Maman, I smell pitch. The rebels are closer."

Victor had a bag of gold pieces. He couldn't get into the vault but took what he could from Henry's study.

Améthyste held the edge of the litter with Cécile. She looked strong, but we had to get away from the polluted air. She couldn't get sick on the night we sought to bury her père.

Zephyrine and I led the way, holding the front of the stretched fabric that supported Henry's limp body. Dupuy, Armande, and Souliman lifted the rear.

I couldn't fold the king's arms about him. Stiffness had set in. The hand he used to pull the trigger had frozen into a fist. Defiant Henry, even in the end.

Like one of our ceremonial processions, we descended the stone stairs of Sans-Souci. In a rhythm that only a mourning soul knew, we moved in unison, step by step. Then we put him in a dray.

The fountain bubbled ahead of me. This courtyard where we'd held fetes lay empty and lifeless, like the king.

One look back at Sans-Souci and I knew it would never be the same. Mobs would torch the stone walls, destroy the art and paintings. Everything that could show the world the achievement of our kingdom would be gone, and there was nothing I could do to save it.

THE DRAY LED BY HENRY'S SILVER HORSE MOVED SILENTLY THROUGH the jungle. Bodies of Henry's guards, the Dahomet, lay along the path. I prayed and kept everyone moving. Carefully pushing away banana leaves and vines, we avoided detection. The warbled song of a trogon, the hiding bird, offered a final hum for my Henry.

It took hours to reach the top of Bonnet à l'Evêque. The ground that bore the Citadel was hard, compacted by the military marches and the movement of heavy cannons.

We left the dray at the clearing's edge and set Henry's litter on the ground.

Cécile lit torches. When light hit her face, I saw what I'd never witnessed, not when she left home, not during the revolution. Fear. It painted her face, darkened her green eyes. "We've been discovered. There are people gathered at the base of Bonnet à l'Evêque. They're coming for Henry and us."

"Maman! What are we to do? I don't want to die." Victor began to weep.

Athénaïre grabbed him. "It will be all right. We do this, then hide. But you are the king now. You have to be brave."

My daughter was right.

Victor was Henry's successor at this moment, but it was obvious to everyone but these two children that the kingdom was no more.

Dupuy shook his head. "I loved the king like a brother, but you're all in jeopardy. I wish you'd left earlier."

"The king deserves a proper burial." My voice vibrated like a mourning trogon. I knew this man was right. I might've doomed my children and my life. "I'll sacrifice my life, a queen's life to stop further bloodshed."

I handed Zephyrine the jewels and gold. "Hide these. Use it to keep all the king's family safe."

Souliman, who'd wandered off, came back running. "There's an open pit of lime. We can put him there. No one will get him out of that."

Lime was corrosive. There'd be nothing left of Henry's body.

The noise of the rebels increased. Some had decided to make the long trek up the mountain.

"The lime will do." I stepped ahead of everyone. "We must finish, then seek safety."

Henry had hated what the apoplexy had done to his body. The acid would dissolve the weakness that had made him take his life. I couldn't forget what happened in the chamber, but I'd never tell that it was fear, fear of the people, of failing that drove him to suicide. This was my promise.

"Together we lift." My voice sounded monotone, but I'd slipped into a new role, an old role, a protector of my king. "March."

As if I were leading the Dahomet Minos, I kept us in rhythm. No part of the litter dragged or hit the ground.

At the pit we stopped. The acid reeked. I looked at Améthyste. She looked furious but in control.

Souliman, Dupuy, Armande, and Victor lifted the litter on one end. I moved the linens from Henry's face and gaped at him. He looked asleep.

Then I pushed his body forward.

The star fell first. Then the whole man, wrapped in the white sheets, descended like a ghost into the lime. The slurry sucked him down.

Soon all that was left was his face. Then, as if he were offering a final salute, his balled hand flew up, bobbing at the surface.

He sank, the powerful fist sank.

Henry was gone.

Cécile doused her torch and led us another way down Bonnet à l'Evêque.

Halfway down, fire surrounded us. "The queen!"

"And the prince royal, Prince Armande!"

General Romain, our Prince du Limbé, ordered his rebels, who still wore the kingdom's uniforms, to surround us.

"Madame Christophe," he said, "I must place you, Victor and Armande Christophe, and the Mademoiselles Christophe under arrest."

Dupuy stepped forward as if to say something, then he backed away. His duty had ended when a fist sank in lime.

Souliman ran at Romain, but the young hothead was struck in the head by a gun butt. Then soldiers beat him. When one raised a bayonet, I charged forward, "Stop. Leave him. He's no soldier, just a servant, trying to do his job. Let him go."

The men backed up.

Zephyrine got to Souliman. She tore at his shirt and used it to stop his bleeding. He lay in agony, but he was alive.

"Where's the king?" Romain towered over me. "Sans-Souci is empty."

"He's dead." I stood up straight with my shoulders erect, my chin high. "Send your people away."

"Can't do that, madame. Where's the king?"

"I told you, he's dead. He's buried." I waved my arms and tried to sound like someone unafraid, a woman with power. "Under whose authority do you do this?"

"President Boyer. All of the kingdom's forces have surrendered. The two parts of Hayti, the north and the south, are together again. We delight that the despot is no more."

My hand became a rock, hardened with every disappointment I'd held inside. I slapped the general with such force his head whipped back. "King Henry I was no despot. He was a visionary. He's responsible for the clothes on your back and the well-armed military you've corrupted."

He rubbed his jaw. "I can forgive a grieving woman. You'll not be harmed. Come with us."

There was no choice. I had to save my fire to protect the lives of my children. "Oui, we shall, with no further delay. Take us to your new king, the head of the republic that rejected us because of our skin color."

"Things have changed. Nine years have enlightened everyone. Move. Don't be a difficult woman."

"I'm a queen, General. Who do you expect me to be?"

"Move, Your Majesty." He sneered, and I prayed for his wife's safety. Ambition without character would never win.

Men with Henry's stars forced us to move. I watched Dupuy disappear into the crowd, then mouthed my thanks to Cécile. They let her go, slipping around her as if she could call down thunder upon them as she had at Bois Caïman, the beginning of our revolution.

My sister, one of the kingdom's duchesses, was still a legend, a goddess to the people.

Though I thought I'd been good to our citizens, I was the queen of the man they'd betrayed. Since the time I was a soldier's wife hiding in the woods, I had lived in fear expecting the enemy to come. I never pictured the villains as men who had supped at my table.

Burning like beeswax, flaming like kerosene, I walked with my children, Henry's children, and made them lift their chins.

Then I glanced up at the Citadel and hoped Henry could finally sleep among the stones he'd set in place to protect Hayti.

*A spark, a sparkle, a glittering second in the
sun is all it takes for celebration to turn to
agony. Enjoy the moments before the flames.*

—MADAME CHRISTOPHE, 1847

Jamaica Times (Jamaica), Tuesday, May 25, 1847

Dreadful Accident at Hayti

By the arrival of the sloop John Bull Patten, in four days from Port-au-Prince, we learn that the Haytien barque L'President was blown up at twenty minutes to twelve o'clock, on the 23d ult., whilst she was engaged in firing minute guns in celebrating mass for the repose of the soul of President Guirriere, who died two years ago. At the time she was blown up there were 80 convicts in chains on board in the hold, who all perished. The captain, in going on shore, left the first lieutenant in charge, who followed afterwards, leaving the boatswain in charge, who, at the time the accident happened, was engaged with others on board smoking, drinking, and playing cards. The accident occurred from a spark alighting on the powder, which was placed on the deck to be dried.

51

1847 Pisa, Italy

Monsieur Michelson has driven me a second time to Pisa. I've told him all he needs to know about Henry's last days and the fall of our kingdom.

But something still connects us, a sense that there's more to be said.

With my visitor coming tomorrow, I think it only fitting that Michelson entertain me today by returning me to one of my daughter's favorite places.

We walk shoulder to shoulder past the gates built to protect the bell tower and baptistery.

"You're quiet this morning, Madame Christophe."

My palm curls around my bracelet—an old habit of an old anxious woman. "We talked about things I've only mentioned to one, maybe two other people who hadn't lived through them. I'm not free of the pain."

His jaw hardens. His dark eyes look away.

"This place is sacred, monsieur. This is the Field of Miracles. When Améthyste was strong enough, we'd come here and walk. Athénaïre would finish teaching music at the convent and meet us here."

"Then you'd go into the baptistery and study the frescoes?"

"The baptistery has no frescoes. The ceiling is smooth. In the Camposanto Monumentale, the aboveground cemetery, there are some. More than in the Sistine Chapel, but I rarely go. I carry enough of the dead in my memories."

His chin drops.

The weight of everything my family has lived through and survived is all around.

"Perhaps you need to be baptized, Monsieur Michelson. Then you can leave this research behind."

"I would probably be more upset at all the money spent on the baptistery. Marble is expensive. I think of how I grew up and how much of this opulence could have fed the poor."

"Lots of money and time was spent on decoration, but it's important to have something that lasts. It will inspire the young to build. It took years to carve and position the stones. If shortcuts were taken, nothing would be here for our enjoyment."

He covers his eyes, and his chin follows the tilt of the Leaning Tower. "I don't know, madame. I'm not much of an architect."

"The palace of Sans-Souci fell from the damage the rebels did and the horrible earthquake in '40. Yet the Citadel still stands. That will remain a testament to Henry's genius."

We walk a little farther. My steps slow at the cathedral. The singing draws me.

Craning my ear, I hear the hymn "Agnus Dei."

The choir reaches the refrain.

Agnus Dei, dona nobis pacem.

Lamb of God, grant us peace.

"Athénaïre loved to worship here. They performed a requiem for her."

Michelson's hand tightens on mine. "Let's go inside the cathedral and then tell me Athénaïre's story."

"Is this to go into your paper?"

"No. I want to know what happened to the other Black princess. Did she get her fairy-tale ending?"

"Oui. She found her love."

I lean more on the young man as we approach the church. Up close, you can see pink and yellow and green marble that dresses the images carved in the façade.

Three huge cast-metal doors with a green patina greet us. More colors, why Athénaïre loved it here.

I choose for us to enter the door on the far right with the painting of John the Baptist above it.

The yellow of the paint behind the throne of the saint is the brightest, like sunshine.

My heeled slippers clap the marble, which looks like a fine tapestry. The echo is enhanced by the gilded coffered ceiling. "Here are paintings. Many survived the great fire. The Christ seated on the throne is a mosaic. He's looking down at us, sending a message."

"And what is that message, madame?"

"That one can survive the fire but will be changed by it."

Michelson guides me to a pew at the back. We sit, and his shadow stays close to me. I need it, and the warmth. Marble always makes the air cool.

Nonetheless, I feel chilly thinking of my Athénaïre singing here, believing in love and forever.

EXILE

Wiltshire Independent, Thursday, May 2, 1839

The Anti-Slavery Delegates from various parts of the kingdom held a meeting at Exeter Hall and established a new association, to be called the "British and Foreign Anti-Slavery Society," for the "universal extinction of slavery and the slave trade."

Their benevolent objects are thus stated—"To circulate accurate information on the enormities of the Slave-trade; to diffuse authentic intelligence respecting the results of emancipation in Hayti, the British Colonies, and elsewhere."

52

1839 Turin, Italy

While I walked in my garden among the lemon trees, Zephyrine came from inside our house in Turin. Her palm rested on the wooden gate, a rickety thing of olive wood that Souliman constructed a couple of years ago.

Cloaked in her robin's-egg-blue gingham dress and thick knitted tan scarf, she said nothing, just stared ahead.

After all these years, I knew that glance, the tense way she held her neck when she struggled with something to say.

Not wanting bad news, I offered her what had become my joy. "These fruits are beautiful, such perfect yellow rinds bursting with citrus. Souliman will have plenty for his limoncello."

"Madame. I'm concerned about the princess."

Concerned? The word constantly ran through my mind, like a wife trying to convince a husband to keep going, like a survivor trying to keep a dray hidden from rebels as it bumps along a mountain pass. "Is she still in the parlor?"

Didn't bother to ask what made my maid fret. It was apparent—Athénaïre's depression.

"Behold." I held up a lemon the size of a small hearty mango. Setting it in my basket, I began picking again. "This good earth here. Safe ground to grow such gifts."

Zephyrine nodded but came closer into my field. "Madame, it's been years. She should not be in gray. She's still young. She needs color."

I stopped moving away from her, from the truth. "She's still breathing. Isn't that enough?"

My friend wrapped her arm about my shoulders. "Memories breathe, too. It's not the same. My queen, help her get strong again."

If only it were as easy as a conversation . . . I handed Zephyrine my basket brimming with lemons that I couldn't wait to be made sweet. "Let me go see about the princess."

MY HOUSE IN TURIN, A HUNDRED-YEAR LEASE, AS WAS THE FASHION, had the accommodations that we'd learned to love when traveling the continent—comfortable rooms with fluffy mattresses, the softest linens, proximity to natural parks to walk and spas to take the waters. Zephyrine, Souliman, and our other attendants had quarters to themselves. The tomato vines and lemon trees in the yard bloomed with the best fruits.

As much as I adored a hearty tomato, I also craved fresh citrus in my tea and indulging in small glasses of limoncello. Souliman, who used to brew the harsh rum tafia in Hayti, had taken up making the pungent lemon liqueur from the morning harvest.

Humming her favorite hymn, Athénaïre sat near the fire working on her needlepoint. Her dress, like most days, was a perpetual state of half mourning—somber dark gray with stripes. Her jacket was fashioned with epaulette sleeves—a military salute to the man who wasn't there.

"Athénaïre, what if I bought you a pianoforte for your birthday? You love music. I remember you played so well for the governesses."

She chuckled. "Madame Terrier-Rouge didn't think I could carry a tune, but I showed her. But it was the harp that I learned. A piano can't be lugged back and forth between here and Pisa. We can't stop visiting Pisa. We're all supposed to be together. You promised."

The stricken look in her golden eyes took me back to '31, two months after Améthyste passed.

A happy cottage in Dresden.

A door with warning markings.

Drays, the body wagons, traveled up and down the road.

A weak voice.

"Ma chérie, Athénaïre. Go, der liebling. Can't get you sick. My heart must live."

My son-in-law, good Dieterich, lay in their bed. His pearly skin looked gray and had begun turning purple about his fingers.

"Fight to stay with me," my daughter said, her voice breaking. "You can't leave."

She sniffled, keeping her tears at bay, not breaking her promise to the physicians to be with her husband in his last moments. "In fairy tales, love is supposed to win."

"Has won. Got to love you, my schöne frau-chérie."

Athénaïre peered up from her needlework, silver threads of stars for a handkerchief. "Maman, we won't be going back to Pisa yet?"

"Non. We are here for a while, but I do miss traveling. Miss seeing the sea. Maybe we should go to Stresa for your birthday. It's close and you loved it."

"It was my wedding trip." She disappeared again into her stitches.

I wanted to kick myself. "I forgot. Stresa's part of the royal tour, Athénaïre. Lady Robert brags about it in her letters. Perhaps we need to take to the route again. We haven't been to Baden-Baden or Hastings since . . ."

"The year before Améthyste and Dieterich left me."

Left us.

Stole the light we had, that we'd fostered, that burnt as brightly as a cottage infected with cholera set in flames.

The colonel's troops had to defend the border with Russia during the big outbreak. The disease had crossed into East Prussia, ravaging the country and the Christophe family. Was this the mountain I refused to see, the hour of need the Holy Father had pronounced?

Scrubbed clean of disease half-naked Athénaïre wanted to run into the flames.

I held her fast. "You can't go in there."

"Want to die with him. Don't want him to be alone. I don't want to be alone."

She clasped my wrist, her fingers looping onto the reed bracelet. "You sacrificed enough when Améthyste became bedridden."

My only remaining child—I took her into my arms, holding her like a fragile babe. "We'll be together always, always, Athénaïre."

To keep my promise, I said nothing to my daughter about finding new joys, new purpose. I'd become a silent queen again, just like I'd done with Henry.

"Dieterich and I had such fun there." My daughter cut a loose string in her needlepoint. "I'd like to see Stresa, feel close to him again."

Others had tried to court her, here and in Pisa, but she paid no attention to anyone and remained trapped in memories of the colonel.

That could've been me when Henry died. What made me different? How could I make things different for this soon-to-be thirty-nine-year-old woman? She still possessed the beauty, the glow of a princess. "I'll make the arrangements. We'll make it our fete. The resort town that caters to people like us."

"Exiles or those unlucky in love," she said with a shallow breath, sounding like Améthyste.

"Exiles, my dear. We both know what it is to give our hearts and to receive the best in return. That's not unlucky. It's a miracle."

She nodded and threaded her needle.

My platitudes and hope were no better than ashes. "After that, we should go for a short visit to Pisa. See what charity work they need help with. Maybe they have a new outreach for widows."

"The Convent of the Capuchins' work is very important. And Améthyste's chapel is beautiful." Her voice broke. "I want to be buried in Chiesa di San Donnino."

A long, pain-filled silence enveloped the room.

Sitting too long, I had to stand, to move. I poked at the fireplace, praying for something to ignite my daughter's passions.

"Maman, I saw in the papers that your prince is on his way back to England. He went to Egypt."

News columns, from time to time, ran articles about Ludwig's exploits. He had never remarried. The gossips said the prince had affairs with widows and aristocratic heiresses and wealthy women from the merchant classes. He even dabbled in commercial endorsements for razors. Seemed I wasn't the only one who thought his sideburns spectacular.

Sea-storm eyes stared at me in my black crepe. His arms went around me to hold me up, to let me know of his love, and to say goodbye.

"I can never make you choose between things you love, Louise. I'll remember only the good. Remember that in me."

"Non, Ludwig. More time. I have to—"

He kissed me soundly, shutting up my lies. He knew I couldn't have a life if Athénaïre had none.

My prince had left this house in Turin. I didn't stop him.

We wrote letters. Then we didn't.

As an influential author, he belonged to the world, not me.

Athénaïre stood and smoothed bits of loose thread from her skirt, then she went to her trunk and returned with a brown-wrapped parcel. "I had Zephyrine buy a copy of his latest book as soon as it was available."

The prince's first, *Briefe eines Verstorbenen, Letters from the Deceased,* Ludwig had published in 1830. It was full of scandalous tales of his tours in Wales, England, Ireland, and France. I'd scanned it for references to us. He briefly mentioned his love for a "Mrs. L" and his fondness for my dark blood and Eurafrican skin.

And Ireland.

"For you, Maman."

Hesitating, I held the wrapped parcel against my chest.

"Open it, Maman. I want to see your face."

Carefully, I pulled the paper away and exposed the bound book, *Semilasso in Afrika.*

"It's the prince's exploration of Algiers and other parts of Africa."

Ludwig had found a way to make his own money, one that didn't force him into another loveless marriage. "He's kept going on adventures."

Athénaïre sat back in her chair and made knots with her crimson thread. "If I were with Dieterich, you two would be together. You'd be joining him on those adventures. If you had another chance at his love, would you take him back?"

Offering a slow shrug, I turned the pages and tried to find the German word I remembered . . . *frieden. Peace* was the most important word.

The world had changed since I first met Ludwig. Britain ended enslavement in all its colonies. The view of Blacks had begun shifting from chattel and unfortunates to human beings worthy of dignity.

America still possessed the nasty slavery business, but other places had rejected its evil.

If the world would embargo the slaveholding nations, as it had Hayti, the evil practice would end tomorrow. Money always came before morals.

Tugging my shawl about my shoulders, the cream one that Améthyste gave me, I went to my younger princess and kissed her brow. "Thank you. I'll enjoy this. You get ready to travel."

"If you wrote to Prince Pückler, I think he'd come here or Stresa."

He might.

Ludwig was a gambler and a risk taker. "I'm content, Athénaïre. I don't think about what could've been. I think about what we, you and I, have done."

"I would do anything for another moment with my husband." Her voice was low. She looked to be concentrating on her needlework, but the cloth in her lap became wet with splotchy tears.

Hurting for my girl, I searched the bookcase for the binding of Améthyste's sketches. They were what joy looked like. We both needed to be reminded to live.

53

1839 Stresa, Italy

Souliman stopped the carriage in front of the gardens of the Villa Ducale, on the shore of Lago Maggiore.

"Madame Christophe, Princess Athénaïre—"

"Madame Ernestus, sir. Always Ernestus, especially here."

"Yes," he said and tipped his domed hat to cover his sad eyes. "I'll return in an hour."

My daughter and I walked arm in arm until the largest shadow in my life fell upon us. "This tree is bigger than the sequoias in Baden-Baden. It could make support beams in the Citadel."

"It is. Look at the long branches." she said in breathy tones. Her gaze turned to Lago Maggiore. The lake, the second largest in Italy, possessed gorgeous plantings along its sides and views of intimate villas and the high Alps. "I loved it here."

She sighed and stretched her arms, whipping her wide Esterhazy sleeves above her head. The gown I had bought for her birthday, made with silver velvet inset panels, reminded me of her wedding gown. She was wearing the emerald necklace, the match to my bracelet. I should have lent her the bracelet again.

Her sad golden-brown gaze settled on the water. "Stunning blue."

Athénaïre adjusted her silk bonnet that had lace and bows, the fashion of the day. She was stylish, appearing as young as on the day she met her husband.

Should I tell her the colonel wanted her to have joy, to keep dancing? I waited, watching children jump up and down a cobblestone wall that followed the shore.

"The babies, Maman. This is delightful."

At least she smiled. "Let's sit and rest. These old bones were jostled quite a bit on our way here." I was moving slower. If I saw the next decade, or two decades, still moving and enjoying my walks, it would be a miracle, more blessings of my extraordinary life.

At sixty-one, I'd begun to have more reflective thoughts, but I couldn't slow until Athénaïre moved faster.

"You could be a world traveler again. I could engage a companion to help with your next adventure."

"No splitting up. Remember." Anger flashed in her eyes, then she turned again to the lake. "We danced in the moonlight here, Maman. Dieterich talked of the poet Byron, who stayed here. Then we talked of children, and I told him of our fairy tales, how beautiful princesses lived happily ever after."

Maybe that was it.

Maybe I needed to encourage her to talk more of their love.

"The colonel loved watching you dance."

Athénaïre brightened. She twirled around, her gown billowing.

People watched her. Some clapped. "Applause on your birthday is a wonderful thing. You were always elegant on the ballroom floor. But, Athénaïre, come sit down with me. There's a bench——"

"I had the best partners. My brother Victor could dance, and my sweet Dieterich, too." She bent her arm as if she'd found a ghost to waltz with and whirled around and around.

And she hummed,

Agnus Dei, dona nobis pacem.

Lamb of God, grant us peace.

With her hand cupped to her brow, she stopped. "Maman, I wanted to dance along the stone walk. Dieterich thought it too slippery. I'll bet the view from there is amazing."

She dashed to the water's edge. I chased her, but she climbed onto the stones. "I would have taught our children ballet."

Athénaïre pirouetted, then planted her toes and did an assemblé. "Do you remember the day I met him? Dieterich thought me so beautiful. Can't believe I ignored him."

She looked at ease, but her shoes or the rocks might give way. "Come down. You've danced enough."

"There's never enough dancing. And why should I fear, Maman? Aren't you here to catch me?"

"I order you to come down."

"I order myself to stay." She whipped the emerald necklace off and tossed it.

I caught it in my palms. "I've always tried to protect you. Please come down. You're scaring me."

"Should I shout out loud like Père that I see Dieterich's spirit? He's been with me all these years. Been haunting me."

"What's he saying, Athénaïre? Is he telling you to go on with your life? To claim each moment? For that's his voice. He always encouraged you."

"We were supposed to be together. Without him, I'm not beautiful. No one will ever see me like Dieterich." She started to weep. Tears came down. Her hands hovered by her cheeks, but she hesitated, unwilling to wipe the tears away.

"But how do you see you? When you look in the mirror, do you see a survivor, a lovely woman? I do when I look at you."

Sliding her necklace into my reticule, I freed my hands, waving to her like a babe taking a first step. "I'll catch you. I'll hold you until you can stand. Come down, Princess Athénaïre. Please come down."

She did another turn, wobblier than the first. "Why didn't we marry when I first realized I loved him? Maybe I should've had you convince Dieterich."

"I did try. But he wanted his promotion. The colonel didn't want our money, just you. He was a very proud man."

"Well, you tried. I can't even fail on my own." She held up her hand. The diamonds in her ring caught the light. "He was proud of me. We were so happy."

Her weeping became louder. She was distraught, tottering along the wall, which began to look like a knife's edge.

"Athénaïre, carry him with you. You have the best of him, his heart."

Shoulders slumping, she stopped, then lifted her leg in an arabesque. "I miss him."

"Focus on living. Build something with the pain. That's what your père did. That's what your grand-père did with his Hôtel de la Couronne. It's what Améthyste did when she built her chapel. It's what I did when we went into exile. You can be a builder, too. We have to find your passion, Athénaïre. We can find it together."

She lowered her foot back to the stone. "You think I can, Maman?"

"I know you can. My princess, Henry's princess, can do anything. Madame Ernestus can win."

Wiping at her tears, she startled. "The cholera. I wasn't supposed to wipe my face. The cholera. I promised the doctor, so I could be with Dieterich." Her voice ramped up. "It was the only way to stay with him! I promised!"

Frenzied movements.

"I should've gone with him, his schöne frau."

"Come down, Athénaïre."

"Then you'd be free. You could love again. Go to your prince. I send you with peace." Her voice sounded like the colonel's, but I heard Ludwig's words, his frieden.

"Non, Athénaïre. We promised to be together."

"Maman, he's waited long enough."

Her foot slipped.

Bam.

She fell, hitting her head on the cobblestones.

Screaming for help, I picked up my daughter, my last living child, and cradled her face.

My fingers became sticky and red.

Passersby gathered. Someone shouted for a physician.

Athénaïre opened her eyes but was silent.

"A doctor! Please hurry." The tears I didn't have for Henry at the moment of his suicide came now for Athénaïre. "Please don't go. Don't leave me."

In her golden eyes, I saw Henry. The images in my head were of that last moment when he surrendered.

I touched Athénaïre's face, trying to keep her awake, looking at me. "Stay with me, beautiful one. Stay!"

Her breaths slowed, and her lids shut.

If she meant the prince or Dieterich had waited long enough, it mattered not. For on her birthday, Princess Athénaïre closed her eyes, made a wish, and drifted to frieden.

In some eyes, debt and blood are the same. When
I was younger, I'd argue against death being
a debt. My older vision sees I was wrong.

—MADAME CHRISTOPHE, 1847

Morning Advertiser (London), Monday, May 31, 1847

France and Hayti.—We read in Friday's Constitutionnel:—"We learn that, up to the April, the negotiation entered into with respect to the payment of annuities of the interest of the debt due by the Republic of Haiti to France had produced no result; but it is evident that this government desires to keep all its resources to itself and to avoid as long France will allow it the execution of the treaties of 1820 and 1838, to which it owes its independence.

54

1847 Florence, Italy

It is midafternoon when Monsieur Michelson's gig rumbles down the cobbled streets of Florence. The sun still has plenty of hours to hover over the vineyards and mountains.

The slow ride on the tufted seat has given me time to think. To puzzle a few missing pieces together.

"Sir," I say sitting up straight and again reclaiming regal posture. "Do you think the *Globe* will run your favorable article on King Henry I?"

"Yes, madame. I think so. You've given me so much more context about the man and the times in which he lived. And you . . . you're remarkable. Only your words could humanize the king in a way that the average reader will comprehend."

"Good. You have a lot of material. That's much more than you need for a column or two, yes?"

"More or less. Editors have their own minds."

"My maid, she still goes to the bookstore for me. She happened to pick up a translation of a new book called *Aus Mehemed, Ali's Reich*. It's the story of the ruler of Egypt and the Sudan. Some call Muhammad Ali Pasha a despot. Others go so far as to call him a modernizing force. The writer of this book is an old acquaintance of mine."

Michelson takes out a handkerchief and wipes his sweaty hands. "Is there somewhere, madame, you want to be dropped off particularly?"

"Oui. I want you to take me to the author of the new book on King Henry I."

He looks away from me and my scrutiny. "Ma'am. I don't know what you are talking about. It's been a long day."

Like the queen I've always been, I'll not back down. "Monsieur Michelson, you've broken my trust. I'm ashamed of you."

"What? I . . . I don't know—"

"You knew about my husband being buried in lime before I told you. Very few people alive knew how I got him out of the palace. Dupuy died in '26. General Romain died in '24. Cécile Fatiman would never betray me."

"You're getting worked up, madame."

"Victor Christophe, Armande Christophe, Améthyste and Athénaïre Christophe were there. They have preceded me in death. Boyer made Henry's sons confess before he executed them. The poverty that he inflicted on Hayti has made him flee to Jamaica. I heard he's headed to Paris to live out his miserable days there, but he'd rather you think Henry decayed on a road. That no one cared about the king or what he accomplished."

The reporter or traitor picks up his reins. "What if I drove along the Arno to calm you?"

"Take me to Prince Hermann Ludwig Heinrich von Pückler-Muskau."

Darting his eyes, as if trying to become smaller, he scratches the scar on his temple and sinks into the tufting of the seat. "You're mis'aken. 'opefully, you can see that."

Biting his lip doesn't prevent the cockney accent he's hidden from slipping out. It confirms I've been party to an elaborate ruse.

"If I look at you and imagine you twenty years or more younger, I see a boy on Weymouth Street, yelling at my window. Take this auntie to the prince now."

Michelson's stone face breaks. "He said you were very clever. Fine."

He speeds the horse down the road. "To Villa Belvedere to see Prince Pückler. As you commanded, Queen Louise, and he's anxious to see you, too. It was odd, but he hoped you'd figure things out. He wants to know if you're ready for a last adventure."

My lonely heart beats faster. I put my hand to my chest, my sleeve exposing my emerald bracelet and the aged reed one. My romantic Athénaïre wanted me to go to the prince.

She loved romantic tales. Above everything she deserved a happy reunion.

I'm not Athénaïre.

AS THE HORSE CLIMBS A STEEP HILL, THE JOSTLING REMINDS ME OF how bumpy the route to Sans-Souci once was. Henry had teams of men and women working hard to build a smooth road from the palace to the capital. So many improvements, things the king willed into existence, are now lost. The truth should be known.

Monsieur Michelson reaches over to steady me. "The route will become smoother in a moment. I wouldn't want my auntie to be dizzy."

My light head has nothing to do with the ride. I haven't seen Ludwig since he visited me in Turin, shortly after the colonel's death. Ludwig knew I'd never choose him over a daughter in mourning. How could I be happy when Athénaïre had lost her sister and the love of her life?

The years passed. I mourned. The successful writer traveled the world having adventures. I couldn't follow and leave the only known graves of my children.

"Were you ever in Hayti, monsieur?"

"Yes, in my mother's womb. She told me of the glory of seeing you in the carriage, and then on the throne."

I look to the side and see all of Florence. We're up high, and I catch glimpses of the walls of the city, the Duomo, and the mountains. It's glorious. I'd get out and walk if my knees didn't feel like jelly.

"Just a little bit more."

"Stop your carriage, monsieur." I grasp his hand. "Tell me now, sir. Be honest. What's the gambit?"

"I'm a reporter, Madame Christophe, but not for the *Globe*. They haven't let men like me write for British papers. I went to America. I report for the *National Era*, a Black newspaper based in Washington, D.C. When I returned to London to visit my mother, a friend of a friend asked me to work on this. The bits I read, that I learned about you, made me want to know more."

"America? And now you've chased me here to Italy."

"The debate is raging about enslavement. Other nations want to move against America."

"Will they blockade traffic to their shores? Trade is the way to hurt a nation."

"The world needs to do something. It's controversial to present a view of power and excellence in the Black hands of King Henry. Pückler's written an exciting book about him. I was hired to corroborate facts."

"The man wrote a book based on all the things I told him." My hands fly to my face. My emotions run in circles. I'm embarrassed. My memories and trust feel violated.

For a moment, I feel warm inside, remembering what it was like for Ludwig to listen. In my soul, I know whatever the prince has written would have passion, pain, and pleasure. He'd be my Vastey proudly showing the world my complicated Henry Christophe, Hayti's only king. "At least the world will know about the Kingdom."

Michelson leans closer. "He penned every word from memory. Details get a little shaky the more distance you have from events."

"Why not just tell me the truth from the beginning?"

"I wanted to meet you. I wanted to see the auntie who made it to be royalty. But Prince Pückler thought you'd be angry about all your private thoughts being drafted for the world to read."

Ludwig is right about that. I never want to be the subject of scandal. He knows that. The man also understands that for the sake of the princesses, King Henry I should never be slandered. The good and bad must be told aloud, and clearly. That's how change happens.

"Let the prince have his book. Take me to my lodgings at Monsieur Giligni's. Pretend that you fooled me."

"Prince Pückler wants to see you. He thought you'd figure things out. I was supposed to take you tomorrow to meet with him. Ma'am, he still cares for you."

Cares for me? That notion touched me. "Was this game of deceit his way to show me?"

"Ma'am. See him tomorrow. Let him explain."

"I've an appointment tomorrow. If I meet with him, it would have to be today."

"Then today it is, Madame Christophe." Michelson takes up the reins and starts his gig climbing again. We turn down a path that leads to a stone walkway canopied with purple plants. Flowers, fragrant and full, hang like netting or royal banners draped over the path. We've stopped a hundred feet away from pink and purple petals that exhibit a musky fragrance. It's as beautiful as triumphal arches erected at the Haut-du-Cap-Henry, strewn with hibiscus, choublak, and roses waiting for royal carriages to enter. "People should be waving. It's so lovely."

"The owners of Villa Belvedere have cultivated wisteria and created a purple tunnel for romantic walks and promises of forever."

The lovely blooms sway in the wind. Ludwig's at the end of the path—thinking, writing, wondering about a reunion or his next story to tell.

My time of traveling the world has ended. My frieden is soup with the best tomatoes and the company of the friends who've never betrayed my trust. In my heart, it's looking back at the love I had and only seeing the good. I don't have to be fair or balanced with my memories. That's my divine right to rule my peace.

I take the reins and turn the carriage around. "Take me back to my residence. Collect whatever fees you've been promised. You've earned it for entertaining a queen these past few weeks."

His smile falters, then fades. "But, madame. The prince is right there at the end of the path. If I shout, he'll come."

My aged pinkie touches Michelson's full lips. "Shhh. We'll not disturb an artist, nor take away the tools he needs to create. I learned that years ago with Princess Améthyste."

At the bottom of the hill, I slow, reach into my sleeve, and pull off my woven bracelet. "After you drop me home, turn in your assignment and give this to the prince. Thank him for this last adventure. He'll know what it means."

The young man shrugs and places the bracelet into his pocket. "I suppose the queen knows what she wants."

I do, and it is to be left with frieden. My heart deserves no less.

55

1847 Florence, Italy

I sit in the sunshine with my beloved. The person who I want to see most in this world. The person who has always been the most honest with me.

Cécile looks at me from across the table of the trattoria. Then pokes at the sliced tomato. "Not as good as our plate de Hayti, the kind back home . . . your house."

She laughs, then sighs as if she's sprung a leak. "I gave up my old one. That man I married, we aren't the same. His presidency ended last year. I left him then. Been living in Cap-François since. I think he'll marry his mistress soon."

"Marry Geneviève?"

Her green eyes don't look sad or shocked that I know. "Oui. The old man got his younger Coidavid. I had suspected . . . but the cause of freedom, of ending enslavement, seemed more important. Then we had to keep Hayti free. Boyer has wrecked the economy. There was always a reason to overlook my husband's unfaithfulness. I chose not to know who he picked as his lover. When I found out, it didn't matter."

"So you left both of them to come here."

"Oui, Louise. When Louis Michel had a chance to do for the people, he was no better than the rest. He was another feckless politician."

"You should run Hayti. Some woman should. It would be better."

She toasts my words by picking up the glass of limoncello. Her face twists when she puts the liqueur to her lips.

"Cécile, it takes some getting used to."

"I see. Well, that's my sad story. It's why I bought passage on a boat and came to see the one I missed. Besides, I'm too honest to be a politician's wife."

The partner of a man with power has to deal with many competing factions. The wife of a king, or a president, has a lot more pain, hers and his, all amplified by the fears of a nation.

Cécile sits back and glances over my head. "Geneviève is much more suited to the duplicity of politics. I wish her well."

"I'm glad you say that. Our sister will be here next week. She's hoping that I can mediate a peace between you."

My older sister takes a big gulp of limoncello. Then she laughs. "Well, there are problems for the former wife, too." She huffed a long breath. "That means you've already forgiven her."

"I did. We started with a letter. Then our sœur came with our niece in '33. It was a good visit. Athénaïre and I were still in such mourning."

Never asked who my niece's father was. Perhaps the merchant, or Louis Michel. "If anyone could forgive her other than me, it would be you. You're a saint."

"Hardly." Cécile finishes her glass and refills it. "At least you've given me a week to prepare. Is there a river we all can share? I promise not to baptize her too long."

"Sœur. We need peace. I don't want to lose anyone else."

With a sigh, she nodded. "And you've had a time of it. Are you lonely without the girls?"

"Children who lose their parents early have a name, orphans. There's no term for parents whose babes precede them, only sorrow."

Cécile grabs my arm, knocking the emerald bracelet. Without the reed band, my wrist feels empty. "Louise, I didn't mean to make you sad."

"Non. Non. Zephyrine and Souliman do wonders at keeping me company. Today, they are in search of the perfect ribollita. They'll bring back a tale of their adventure. That's enough excitement for me."

She took another swig of the limoncello before putting it down with a clank on our wooden table. "This does get better."

"Most things do."

"Louise, I owe you an apology."

"You owe me nothing. I'm giving you Geneviève and hoping for an impossible frieden—a peace between us."

"Non, I do. I understand what you went through trying to help Henry rule. I understand the burdens to lead, to live."

A shadow crosses me, but it's a waiter carrying a tray. "Henry ran out of strength. I'll never fault him for trying. He did his best for Hayti, and his love protected me and the princesses."

"The country's still in chaos. From the earthquake in '40 to the damned payment to French banks . . . I don't know." She raises her chin toward the Duomo. "Don't know how the nation changes course."

"The spirit of independence still lives. Hayti will rise again, like a phoenix, flying above the ashes. That was Henry's motto, our belief in the people." Clasping her hand tightly, I hold it to my heart. "Wish I could've been in Port-au-Prince to encourage you as you did me."

I order a glass of Chianti, then sit back in my chair. I'm pretty pleased with us. "It takes a lot for two women set in their ways to come to a common understanding."

Cécile smooths the red and blue turban on her straight gray tendrils. "Those fairy tales you read as a child, did they help you become who you wanted, Louise?"

That's a bittersweet question.

More often than I want to admit, I blinked and became what I didn't want to be. "I am widowed, sorrowful without my sons and sweet daughters. Yet, as I walk through the shadows of disaster and death, I've learned to fear nothing. Cécile, I was a wife, une mère, a friend, and a survivor."

"Vive ma reine." She toasted me with another sip of the pungent lemon liqueur. "You were a gracious queen of a proud nation. Then you reigned gloriously in exile."

"I hope the church, Chiesa di San Donnino, where the girls sleep, where I shall sleep, stands for ages, like the Duomo and the Citadel."

"Excuse me, ladies." Monsieur Michelson stops at our table. Handsome in a charcoal tailcoat and dark stock over a pristine white shirt, he has a satchel in his hand. "Going to catch a boat. I'm heading back to America after I visit with my mother. I have said my goodbyes to Madame Zephyrine and Monsieur Souliman. They're enjoying big bowls of ribollita."

"Ah, then they are happy." I chuckle and raise my goblet of crimson Chianti. "A parting drink?"

"Non, but I have gifts for you, madame." He reaches into his rucksack and pulls out a ribbon-tied stack of papers. "These are my notes from our conversations, and these . . ." He tugs out a parcel in brown wrapping. "These are from Prince Pückler. The manuscript he was to submit on Henry I."

Ludwig gave me his writings?

Clutching the papers, I run my pinkie along the dahlia-purple satin bow. "What of his publisher?"

"They'll make a new deal. Pückler's travel books are always in demand."

"The prince went to such lengths. Why did Ludwig change his mind?"

"He said it wasn't worth your trust. He'd forgotten what it meant. That's a quote." Michelson put his hand to the jacket. "I'm a reporter; you can trust me to get the facts right. Oh, one more thing."

Taking my reed bracelet from his pocket, he hands it back to me. "Prince Pückler, when he settles his commitments, said he'll write to request a proper visit. Unencumbered by any debts, he'll be free. He hopes the queen will be free as well."

"Tell the prince the royal schedule can be demanding." I clasp my sœur's hand. "Appearances at my court are filled this season. But make sure he doesn't wait so long to write again. His words have always provided the greatest care."

"I will." Michelson bows. "Goodbye, Queen Louise. It's been a pleasure."

Cécile clicks her tongue, then finishes her glass. "You're blushing. What Ludwig? Who's this prince?"

Smiling, feeling my cheeks burn with the passions of my past, and celebrating the honest peace I'd finally claimed, I put the bracelet on my arm, where it belongs, next to the emerald one. "Someone I met in exile. He still brings surprises."

She stands, takes my hand in hers, and, as she has done so many times, kisses my brow. "Well, done, ma reine, rèn mwen. Well done."

I rise slowly, as though I'm weighted in velvet robes. My golden-yellow dress flows to my sleek slippers. Améthyste's creamy shawl sits loosely about my shoulders. Athénaïre's emerald chain dangles on my neck. I carry them, all of my past, with honor, like a royal sash bearing Henry's star.

Then I reach for my tall sister and enfold her in a hug. "Joy to both of us. And peace to all the Coidavid sisters."

Cécile shrugs. "I will try for you, and because tomorrow isn't promised."

It's not, so I'm glad I've lived—lived through the worst and lived well through the good. "Let's walk. I'll show you the best place in Florence to watch the sunset."

Arm in arm, we follow the smooth cobbles to the Ponte Vecchio, where we'll wait for the sun to dip into the Arno for a heavenly bath.

Afterword

Queen Marie-Louise Coidavid-Melgrin Christophe outlives all her detractors, dying on March 14, 1851, surrounded by friends and family. Laid to rest in Pisa with her daughters in Chiesa di San Donnino, she sleeps in peace, in a church that still stands.

In 1847, a formal tomb is built to enclose the lime pit at the Citadel, to commemorate the resting place of King Henry I.

Prince Hermann Ludwig Heinrich von Pückler-Muskau dies on February 4, 1871. He's buried according to his last wishes: His heart is removed and dissolved in sulfuric acid. His body is encased in caustic lime.

Acknowledgments

Thank you to my Heavenly Father; everything I possess or accomplish is by your Grace.

To my beloved editor, Rachel Kahan, you truly came through on this one by asking the tough questions. I love how you push me to make the story even better.

To Felicia Murell and Isabelle Felix—you help to elevate these books every time. To the couple in 5 Exmouth Place, Hastings, who allowed me to walk inside Queen Louise's house including her bedchamber, thank you!

To my fabulous agent, Sarah Younger, you are always right about which story should be told first. I'll never doubt you. You are my ride-or-die friend and sister.

To Gerald, Marc, and Chris—love you, bros.

To Denny, Pat, Rhonda, Vanessa, and Michelle—thank you for helping me elevate my game, the gentle shoves, and every challenge.

To the Writers of Me and My Sisters, the Divas, and My Friends in Black Authors in Residence.

To those who inspire my pen: Beverly, Brenda, Farrah, Sarah, Julia, Kristan, Alyssa, Maya, Lenora, Sophia, Joanna, Grace, Laurie Alice, Julie, Cathy, Katharine, Carrie, Christina, Jane, Linda, Margie, Liz, Lasheera, Alexis R., Alexis G., and Jude—thank you.

To those who help with the load, Sandra, Rhonda, Angela, and Kenyatta—thank you.

And to my rocks, Frank and Ellen—love you both, so much.

Hey, Mama. I called this queen Louise. It was also to honor you.

Author's Note

Overview

Marie-Louise Coidavid Christophe was born May 8, 1778, in the colony of Saint-Domingue and died in Pisa on March 15, 1851.

After writing *Sister Mother Warrior*, I fell more in love with Haiti and the stories of women who did great things in the name of freedom. Louise played a minor role in that novel as a mere soldier's wife, as her husband began his rise to become second-in-command under Jean-Jacques Dessalines, the first emperor of Hayti.

As the first and only queen of the only free Black nation in the Northern Hemisphere, Louise needed her own book. She led an extraordinary life of heartache and privilege in the Kingdom of Haiti and exile in Europe.

Every newspaper article presented is real, using the exact phrasings and dates from the sources. I use this to show you the politics of the time, the media scrutiny of the Christophe family, and how much of this history has been erased from our present-day discourse.

In *Queen of Exiles*, I want you to feel the level of opulence, beauty, and culture that King Henry's court attained. Right or wrong, he did so in the hope of gaining the respect of the European nations. He believed that if Europeans saw Blacks with dignity and possessing a heritage similar to theirs, they would respect Black people, rally support for Hayti against France, and help Black people gain rights everywhere.

The king was somewhat successful. He gained favor in Britain and with the ruling tsar in Russia. Russia and England pressured France to keep it from mustering an attack to retake Hayti. It should be noted that France did not retake or significantly threaten Hayti until five years after Christophe's death.

Boyer failed to court the alliances that the king had made. Some scholarship points to Boyer and his societal class wanting to secure their personal property rights and means taken from the former habitations (plantations) of the Grand Blancs. Aligning with France to gain the republic's recognition would solidify these leaders' economic positions. Much more scholarship is needed to determine the states of minds and hearts during these volatile times.

I was fortunate to surround myself with Queen Louise's world. Her frame of mind guided me in portraying the men in the book. Napoleon killed her first son. Boyer killed her second. I firmly believe the long war of independence affected her eldest daughter's health and Henry's mental state.

HM Marie-Louise Christophe, née Coidavid-Melgrin [Queen Louise]

Louise is a fascinating woman who endured much heartache but also became a master at reinventing herself. Contemporary references often talk of her as a *sorrowful* queen, but mourning was only one aspect of her life.

Initially, I fell prey to this same convention, until I dug into her life. The evidence is clear. Louise Christophe reigned in exile. It breaks my heart that narratives describing Black heroes focus so much on pain. We need to search our souls. Why is it easier to see the sadness than the joy?

Nonetheless, when you trace Queen Louise's steps, you realize:

1. This woman had significant means.

2. Media attention constantly followed her.

3. There were no public scandals for her or her daughters, except for the mention of her involvement with Prince Pückler.

4. She became well traveled and followed the royal practice of touring spas to take the waters.

5. She kept up with politics in Hayti through her sisters and the papers.

6. She maintained friendships with the Clarksons, Wilberforce, and Chateaubriand.

7. She traveled with her household, which included two daughters and two to four servants.

8. The exiled kings, peers, and diplomats in Europe recognized her status. She was a queen as much as Bonaparte's brothers were kings.

More study needs to be done on Queen Louise. Her papers and letters were destroyed in the bombings of Italy in World War II. This woman was famous. Her movements and her social circles were recorded. I found at least two full-page newspaper articles, the result of interviews in which she reflected on her life.

She lived well, with luxury goods. This indicated her access to money. It is hard to determine the exact amount of money the queen possessed. At the lowest level, her jewelry, valued at £9,000 at the time (over £1,098,222.79 in today's currency), the £6,000 that Clarkson offered her from the money King Henry had paid him, and the one documented settlement of £1,500 per annum add up to be significant. I'm quite sure there was more.

She often used King Henry's solicitors in London, the firm, Leghorn, and Reid, Irving and Company. Receipts due to Henry at his death were outstanding payments for sugar, coffee, and indigo shipments. I firmly believe that once settlements were made, Louise and her daughters no longer had to fret about money. Rumored estimates at the time totaled between three and six million dollars.

Having means, traveling to resorts, and possessing jewels didn't protect her from the tragedies that befell her and her family. All of Louise's children preceded her in death. She didn't get to bury her two sons. Building the church where her daughters would be laid to rest became very important.

The scene in the Teatro della Pergola is based on letters by James Fenimore Cooper discussing his travels in Europe, identifying Madame Christophe sitting in the front row with former kings of Holland (Louis Bonaparte) and of Westphalia (Jérôme-Napoléon Bonaparte).

HRH Princess Françoise-Améthyste Christophe [Madame Première]

Améthyste, sometimes spelled Améthisse, is said to have had something like asthma and later died of congestive heart failure. Because of the limitation of medical treatments in Haiti and the family's quest to take the waters in all the spas in Europe, I interpret Améthyste's illness as terminal. I show a mother of that time dealing with such a condition.

Her governess gave her instruction in the arts and literature. I have let this be her driving passion until the end.

HRH Princess Anne-Athénaïre Christophe

Athénaïre, sometimes spelled Athénaïs, died on her birthday. Unlike her sister, I didn't find any documented illnesses. The briefest reports were that she fell in Stresa and died in her mother's arms.

She became engaged to an unknown Prussian colonel. Prussian soldiers came to Hayti to help construct the Citadel and forge the cannons. The princess would have known them, their uniforms, etc. Colonel Dieterich Ernestus became Athénaïre's unknown husband and a way to evolve the discussions of race, children, and social standing that would've had to occur when she became engaged.

Athénaïre became the model of self-doubt, especially against the backdrop of her privileges. Even a princess can suffer when the world tries to steal her worth.

HRH Prince Hermann Ludwig Heinrich von Pückler-Muskau

Prince Pückler is one of the most fascinating men that I've researched in a very long time. The prince was liberal, honest in admitting his affairs, but a womanizer. He liked a lot of women. He had affairs that were never consummated but conducted by correspondence. His goal at the time he was linked to Queen Louise was to marry a wealthy woman, but he never married again. He became a famous author who used his talents to write about his travels.

In the latter half of his life, he began writing about dictators. As a famous global traveler, he could sit with the rulers of various parts of the world. Stepping into his head, I imagined, after meeting the rare Queen Louise and hearing her story, that he'd be fascinated by this woman. I think he would have been tempted to write the biography of King Henry.

The relationship between the prince and Louise I have based on several things.

The newspaper article indicates he was trying to marry her. Modern sources often discount a relationship, suggesting it would be unlikely because of her race and lack of wealth. These researchers often forget that the prince was near bankruptcy. Queen Marie had more money than Pückler in probably every instance they interacted. Moreover, she was an accepted member of the community of peers and exiles traveling the royal circuit. She would have been a prime candidate for marriage to the ambitious prince.

The prince wrote letters about his attraction and love for Mrs. L. He didn't name Mrs. L. outright, but his description of her as a woman of *Eurafrican* (his phrase) blood makes me believe in their alliance.

Lastly, the Russian/Prussian/German associations with Queen Louise are notable. Russia was one of the first allies of Haiti. King Henry imported goods from Prussia and other parts of Germany. Prussians aided in building weapons at the Citadel. The area's spas were places the Christophes would have been aware of and most likely journeyed to.

Characterization of HM King Henry I

By all accounts, Henry Christophe was a man of great charm and a volatile temper. Reference after reference talks about how he would lose his temper and that only the queen could calm him. The records to better assess his mental state are incomplete, but what I found made me display him as driven, a victim of post-traumatic stress, and very much in love or obsessed with the queen. I wrote him as a man of his time but balanced this account with new scholarship. The political characterizations printed were often sourced from the Republic of the South, which wanted Henry destroyed.

Some say Christophe had a hand in the murder of Emperor Jacques I (Dessalines). Others say that it was ultimately the work of Pétion. The letters that Christophe sent to Thomas Clarkson and to his son Victor show different aspects of the king, which, to me, display Henry as both a victim and a genius. I only saw one accounting of infidelity: a letter by Dr. Stewart to Thomas Clarkson. Stewart offered no specifics, no names. His account could be nothing more than exaggerated man talk or the way the doctor tried to ingratiate himself with Clarkson to gain a portion of the money the king had sent. I defaulted to the overwhelmingly persuasive accounts of the king as wholly in love and obsessed with Queen Louise. More scholarship is needed.

Lastly, dance is a huge part of Haitian society and history. Based on reports that Henry loathed how Jacques I was ridiculed for learning the minuet, I made Henry not want to dance in public. Yet he allows dance and the arts to be part of the fetes. I believe he loved all things beautiful but would never put himself or his family at risk of humiliation.

Cécile Fatiman

Cécile Fatiman was the half sister of Queen Louise. This was the woman who helped lead the big meeting that launched the rebellions at Bois Caïman. There is confusion between the time frames of when Cécile and Geneviève married the same man, Jean Louis Michel Pierrot. Both sisters are reported to have separately visited Louise in Florence and Pisa. There's no indication of them meeting each other in Italy, but it was possible.

Black Excellence in the White World

For the new Black-run nation of Hayti, achievement was important. They needed to play on the world stage. Europe, for the most part, didn't respect Africa. The differences in these societies and the culpability of some tribes in the slave trade have led to confusion. I believe all hands are guilty.

King Henry's desire for white acceptance drove the way he governed.

Yet aspects of the kingdom, such as the queen's guards, the Dahomet Amazons, and the king's personal guards, also called Dahomets, show linkages to African culture. King Henry promoted the use of French over Kreyòl, bilingual education for all, and dress codes to follow London society.

It's a conundrum, having to choose between acceptance on the world stage and the roots from which you came. The leaders of the republic wanted allegiance to France. They wanted France to recognize them. Thinking the people you defeated would give you a fair deal was a short-sighted miscalculation that Haiti has paid for in blood and treasure for years.

Lastly, Boyer and the republic killed off Pompée Valentin Vastey, one of the most brilliant orators of the time. They saw his mind as a threat. His writings served as a vital argument against colonialism. I believe he could've been more of an asset to the nation had he lived.

The Significance of the Kingdom of Hayti

Some think Haiti went straight from gaining independence to becoming a republic. That wasn't the case. When Emperor Jacques I [Dessalines] was killed, the country split in two. The north became a kingdom with a peerage system. The south organized as a republic. The kingdom built the lasting monuments: the Citadel, Sans-Souci, and others. The strides made in education, medicine, and the arts by the north were important. The level of opulence and the acceptance of the Haytian peers on the world stage need to be noted. Even the prince regent, the future George IV, had breakfast with Prince Saunders, because he thought his forename was an honorific. The fiction of wealthy Black peers in *Bridgerton* was a reality for the Kingdom of Hayti.

Suicide

I look for joy and hopefulness in the stories I want to tell. Queen Louise's life is important. She was a hero, a good mother, and a supportive wife, but even as a royal, her life was hard. I tried to balance Henry's PTSD and Athénaïre's depression against Louise's forging ahead and Souliman's moving forward with his cane.

Themes of suicide and being suicidal are relevant to this story. Some suffer in silence. Others hide behind smiles. The weight of expectations and unhealed trauma was as hurtful in the 1800s as it is today. Check on friends. Love in the moment. Don't wait to show love or to know love. As much as you give joy, be your joy.

Bibliography

Accilien, Cécile, and Jowel C. Laguerre. *Haitian Creole Phrasebook: Essential Expressions for Communicating in Haiti*. McGraw-Hill, 2011.

"The American Papers draw a gloomy picture of the state of affairs in Hayti." *Advertiser*, July 19, 1826.

"The Americans are very anxious to clear the country of the free people of colour by encouraging them to emigrate to Hayti." *Bell's Weekly Messenger*, Sept. 12, 1824.

"The ancient Empress of Haiti, Madame Christophe." *English Chronicle and Whitehall Evening Post*, June 25, 1829.

"The Anti-Slavery Delegates." *Wiltshire Independent*, May 2, 1839.

Bailey, Gauvin A., trans. Julian Hermann. *The Palace of Sans-Souci in Milot, Haiti (ca. 1806–1813): The Untold Story of the Potsdam of the Rainforest*. Deutscher Kunstverlag, 2017.

Benson, LeGrace. "A Queen in Diaspora: The Sorrowful Exile of Queen Marie-Louise Christophe (1778, Ouanaminth, Haiti–March 11, 1851, Pisa, Italy)." *Journal of Haitian Studies* 20, no. 2 (2014): 90–101, http://www.jstor.org/stable/24340368.

Bradfield, Nancy. *Costume in Detail, 1730–1930*. Costume & Fashion Press, 1997.

Butler, E. M. *The Tempestuous Prince, Hermann Pückler-Muskau*. Longmans Green and Co., 1929.

Buyers, Christopher. "Haiti: Styles & Titles." *haiti2*, www.royalark.net/Haiti/haiti2.htm.

"Christophe assembled a Council of State." *General Evening Post*, June 13, 1811.

Christophe, Henri, and Thomas Clarkson. *Henry Christophe & Thomas Clarkson: A Correspondence*. University of California Press, 1952.

Cooper, J. F., and R. E. Spiller. *Gleanings in Europe*. Oxford University Press, 1928.

"Death of King George the Third." *Morning Post*, Jan. 31, 1820.

De Vastey, Baron. *The Colonial System Unveiled*. Liverpool University Press, 2016.

"Dreadful Accident at Hayti." *Jamaica Times*, May 25, 1847.

Dupuy, Alex. *Rethinking the Haitian Revolution: Slavery, Independence, and the Struggle for Recognition*. Rowman & Littlefield, 2019.

"Ex-Queen of Hayti arrived at Liege." *Saunders's News-Letter*, Oct. 14, 1824.

Fanm Rebèl, www.fanmrebel.com (accessed June 20, 2021).

"Feast of HRH Monsignor the Prince Royal." *Royal Gazette of Hayti*, July 26, 1813.

"France and Hayti." *Morning Advertiser*, May 31, 1847.

Grebe, A., and R. King. *The Vatican: All the Paintings: The Complete Collection of Old Masters, Plus More Than 300 Sculptures, Maps, Tapestries, and Other Artifacts*. Black Dog & Leventhal, 2013.

"Hayti." *Northampton Mercury*, Sept. 2, 1820.

"Hayti." *National Protector*, Apr. 24, 1847.

"Haytian Gazettes." *Commercial Chronicle* (London), Jan. 27, 1816.

Haytian Papers: A Collection of the Very Interesting Proclamations and Other Official Documents: Together with Some Account of the Rise, Progress, and Present State of the Kingdom of Hayti. W. Reed, law bookseller, 1816.

"A Haytian Sermon." *Morning Herald* (London), Feb. 14, 1820.

Heatter, Basil. *A King in Haiti: The Story of Henri Christophe*. Farrar, Straus & Giroux, 1972.

"Henry, Christophe, President and Commander in Chief of the Land and Sea Forces of the State of Hayti." *London Chronicle*, Mar. 27, 1811.

"His Majesty's colonial brig, the Prince Regent." *Royal Gazette of Hayti*, Oct. 10, 1817.

"HRH Monsignor Prince Jean, Duke of Port-Margot." *Royal Gazette of Hayti*, Aug. 14, 1817.

"I have lately conversed with a most respectable merchant." *Morning Chronicle*, Sept. 13, 1820.

Inglis, Robert. "Account of Marie-Louise Christophe in Pisa." *Canterbury Cathedral Journals*, Vol. 5. Oct. 20, 1840.

"It is rumoured that Madame Christophe." *Public Ledger and Daily Advertiser*, Nov. 20, 1821.

James, C. L. R. *The Black Jacobins: Toussaint L'Ouverture and the San Domingo Revolution*. Penguin Books, 1989.

"The King is a bloodthirsty tyrant." *Champion* (London), July 25, 1813.

"Kingdom of Hayti." *Caledonian Mercury*, Nov. 20, 1817.

"Lastly is this dark insidious insinuation leveled at the Prince Regent." *Royal Cornwall Gazette*, July 3, 1813.

"A letter from Port-au-Prince." *Berkshire Chronicle*, Sept. 10, 1825.

"Letters from Prussia." *Berkshire Chronicle*, Mar. 17, 1827.

"Madame Christophe ci-devant Empress Hayti." *Northampton Mercury*, May 4, 1822.

"Map descriptive of London Poverty, 1898–99." https://booth.lse.ac.uk/learn-more/download-maps

Nash, Gary B. "Reverberations of Haiti in the American North: Black Saint

Dominguans in Philadelphia." *Pennsylvania History: A Journal of Mid-Atlantic Studies* 65 (1998): 44–73, www.jstor.org/stable/27774161 (accessed Apr. 25, 2021).

"No. 30, Weymouth-street, Portland Place." *Morning Advertiser*, Sept. 24, 1824.

Peacock, John. *Costume 1066–1990s.* Thames & Hudson, 1994.

"Philadelphia, June 19." *Morning Herald* (London), July 16, 1824.

"The Prince of Wales." *Star* (London), Feb. 7, 1811.

Pückler-Muskau, Hermann von, ed. and trans. Linda B. Parshall. *Letters of a Dead Man.* Dumbarton Oaks, 2016.

"Regency." *Dublin Evening Post*, Jan. 7, 1813.

Riley, Vanessa. *Sister Mother Warrior.* William Morrow, 2023.

Rodriguez, Junius P. *The Historical Encyclopedia of World Slavery.* ABC-CLIO, 1997.

Salmond, C. A. *The Popes of the Nineteenth Century.* Forgotten Books, 2018.

"A singular circumstance took place Saturday evening." *Edinburgh Evening Courant*, June 30, 1828.

"The suite of Madame Christophe, the Ex-Empress of Hayti." *English Chronicle and Whitehall Evening Post*, Dec. 12, 1829.

"Swindler at Paris. The False Prince of Hayti." *New Times* (London), Feb. 17, 1823.

"Taken from Brussels Papers Madame Christophe." *Morning Advertiser*, Oct. 8, 1824.

"Three deputies arrived via England." *Kerry Examiner*, May 18, 1847.

Timyan, Joel. *Bwa Yo: Important Trees of Haiti.* South-East Consortium for International Development, 1996.

Vandercook, John Womack. *Black Majesty: The Life of Christophe, King of Haiti.* Doubleday, 1928.

The Via Casciajuolo at Florence. *Barbadian*, Sept. 5, 1828.

Waterman, Charles Elmer. *Carib Queens.* Bruce Humphries, 1935.

Read More from Vanessa Riley

"This book is not only a one-sitting read, it's a slice of history that needs to be told. Utterly brilliant, powerful, and inspiring."

—Kristan Higgins,
New York Times bestselling author

A sweeping novel of the Haitian Revolution based on the true-life stories of two extraordinary women: the first Empress of Haiti, Marie-Claire Bonheur, and Gran Toya, a West African–born warrior who helped lead the rebellion that drove out the French and freed the enslaved people of Haiti.

"A sweeping look at the political, social, and romantic intrigue surrounding Haiti's first and only queen. Riley's depiction is richly imagined and wholly original."

—Fiona Davis,
New York Times bestselling author of *The Magnolia Palace*

Acclaimed historical novelist Vanessa Riley is back with another novel based on the life of an extraordinary Black woman from history: Haiti's Queen Marie-Louise Coidavid, who escaped a coup in Haiti to set up her own royal court in Italy during the Regency era, where she became a popular member of royal European society.

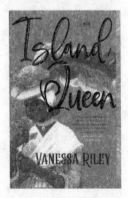

"Riveting and transformative. . . . Evocative and immersive . . . By turns vibrant and bold and wise. . . . Discovering Dorothy's story is a singular pleasure."

—*New York Times* (Editors' Choice)

A remarkable historical novel based on the incredible true-life story of Dorothy Kirwan Thomas, a free woman of color who rose from slavery to become one of the wealthiest and most powerful landowners in the colonial West Indies.